TO HALT ARMAGEDDON

Meg turned to stare up at me with those enormous blue eyes. "It's *important*, Peter," she breathed. "Vitally, desperately important. . . ."

"The most important thing in the galaxy," added the cat soberly.

Meg nodded. "Memphus and I were sent here to try to enlist you to help us. Of all the sapient entities inhabiting all the myriad worlds of the Milky Way, you are the only one with even a semblance of success . . .

"Peter, we are *losing* Armageddon!" she whispered intently. "You *must* aid us." The tears in her eyes were real; no doubt remained. "Only with your help do we have any chance of prevailing. Unless you join us . . ." her breath caught, "perhaps even if you do—*the galaxy is doomed*. . . ."

Bantam Books by David R. Palmer
Ask your bookseller for the titles you have missed

EMERGENCE
THRESHOLD

THRESHOLD

David R. Palmer

BANTAM BOOKS

TORONTO • NEW YORK • LONDON • SYDNEY • AUCKLAND

THRESHOLD

A Bantam Spectra Book / December 1985

ISBN 0-553-24878-2

Published simultaneously in the United States and Canada

Bantam Books are published by Bantam Books, Inc. Its trademark, consisting of
the words "Bantam Books" and the portrayal of a rooster, is Registered in U.S.
Patent and Trademark Office and in other countries. Marca Registrada. Bantam
Books, Inc., 666 Fifth Avenue, New York, New York 10103.

PRINTED IN THE UNITED STATES OF AMERICA

O   0 9 8 7 6 5 4 3 2 1

This book
is dedicated, with love, to
SHERRY,
who makes it all worthwhile.

With special thanks to
Susan Collingwood,
whose acumen and technical knowledge
regularly kept me out of hot water.

CONTENTS

CHAPTER 1

"Peter, we are *losing* Armageddon . . . !" the girl whispered intensely. "You *must* aid us!" Tears sparkled in her eyes. "Only with your help do we have any chance of prevailing. Unless you join us . . ." her breath caught, "perhaps even if you do—*the galaxy is doomed . . . !*"

All right, so Dr. Zarkov, at the peak of his career, couldn't have improved on it; so Tom Corbett, Space Cadet, would have blushed; so Captain Video, rather than live with the stigma of having such a declaration attributed to him, would have fallen on his sword.

But that's what she said.

And I *believed* her. . . .

CHAPTER 2

Of course I believed her—I defy any live, practicing heterosexual male to gaze into those eyes and *not* believe. Least of all one who has been a compulsive Rescuer of Itinerant Distressed Damsels since . . . Well, I guess I knew I had a predisposition toward that sort of thing even before I knew what one saved them *for*. (Learning the answer didn't relieve the condition one bit.)

Anyway, it all started with . . .

Hmm. Certainly I know *how* it started. But, come to think of it, I'm not sure precisely when; nor even what it was, specifically, that alerted me to the fact that my tranquil, solitary vacation—not to mention the entire first chapter of my life—were about to be terminated. Rudely.

The blue-white glare, shining through my eyelids with ever-increasing intensity, would have gotten my attention eventually. Likewise, the nearly subsonic rumble, imperceptible at first but waxing steadily to the point where (despite determined efforts) I no longer could ignore it, undoubtedly would have been enough sooner or later. I suspect, however, that what actually did the job was the audibly hurried departure of the Resident Pelican.

But by then, of course, the question was moot.

My eyes snapped open just a fraction too late to focus on whatever it was that flashed from the sky to impact the beach not ten feet away. Later I was able to reconstruct the visual afterimage of what appeared to be a huge, blazing fireball whose flaming wake seemed to trail out to infinity
. . . and—somehow—beyond.

But at that precise moment, my only conscious impression was of being picked up, cartwheeled, and deposited in disarray upon the sand some fifty feet away.

I kept my head down and covered with my arms until the hail of sundry unidentifiable objects tapered off. Then, cautiously, I looked up to see how much of the island remained.

I goggled, shook my head, blinked sand from my eyes, and stared again. But the vision persisted. . . .

As a child, I always clapped my hands to a rosy blister when Peter Pan implored children everywhere to Believe, to save Tinker Bell's life; and Walt Disney's conception of the tiny fairy's appearance substantially paralleled my own.

Before my eyes, Tinker Bell stood knee deep in the water already seeping in to fill the shallow crater at whose center she stood. . . .

TO: Project Director/Monitor's Log.
FROM: G'lLhytl, Tenth Order.
SUBJECT: Project *Extremis*.

Preliminary readings suggest that the transuniversal shunt functioned properly once again, though study of data recorded during translation will be required to verify this conclusively. Further, no evidence of the shunt's brief existence remains detectable either in this space or any of the others into which it impinged.

Our team is now on Earth; safely, according to the necessarily limited data available to viewer-compatible instrumentation: Their passage through adjacent spaces was without apparent side effects. By visual examination as well, their condition is grossly normal.

With the collapse of the shunt, viewers once again function normally and depict the target area. This temporary interference represents a potentially serious problem. On this occasion, and despite elaborate precautions, our team emerged in close proximity to the subject. Fortunately, for our purposes, he was not injured. A solution is needed, and most urgently.

The subject's initial readings show emotional shock and mental disorientation commensurate to the stimuli; however, I do not expect this to interfere with the progress of the mission. Indeed, his condition probably will work to our advantage.

Automatic recorders were triggered the moment viewer reception cleared, and will operate continuously for the duration of the mission, enabling anyone to watch developments which may be missed due to scheduling conflicts. Likewise, all instruments capable of functioning through the viewer channel are discharging into the Data Field for further analysis.

The mission profile calls for uninterrupted monitoring of our team's progress, as it has been anticipated that remote intervention may prove necessary.

Incidentally, those responsible for its development (Third through Fifth Order practitioners all) are to be commended for their work on the new Project Director/ Monitor's Log mindlike equipment. As specified in the Council's research directive, the mechanics of operation are very nearly instinctive and, unlike the earlier data-entry system, which required both a high degree of manual dexterity and intense concentration upon the keyboard, not at all distracting. Memorialization of personal observations proceeds at the speed of thought, and with no more effort. In my judgment, this system would seem to fulfill all design criteria.

CHAPTER 3

Tinker Bell had almost cobweb-fine, straight blonde hair, evenly cropped to just over an inch in length. Her eyes were enormous, startlingly deep blue, asparkle with a knowing, merry devilment; and something about them, or the shape of her cheekbones, hinted at an exotic slant and imbued her gaze with an almost feline quality. Between a little snub nose, which crinkled when she grinned, and a finely chiseled but firm chin was a small, well-shaped mouth, clearly placed there by Nature for the express purpose of smiling. Her ears were tiny, delicate shells which rose to points.

The girl was not quite five feet taller than the three-quarters of an inch attributed to Tinker Bell, however; and as my scrutiny continued downward the illusion faded: Tink was almost terminally modest—this girl was stark naked and patently unconcerned about it. Indeed, she almost seemed to flaunt it.

She had delicate, almost fragile shoulders, arms, and hands, and a slender, graceful neck. Her breasts were perfect, rose-tipped swellings the size of tangerines. Her waist was very slender; her hips slim; her pubic area devoid of hair. Her legs were astonishingly long, straight, and shapely, ending in remarkably tiny feet.

I recall feeling relieved to note that she did not have lacy wings.

My first startled impression was of a beauty transcending description; this lasted only until she grinned, when it became obvious that actually the girl was just too darned cute for words. And regardless of her expression, or the state of her attire, she radiated an assurance which quite belied her almost childlike appearance.

As I gaped, the girl moved lithely up out of the crater, followed much more slowly by an amazingly obese, yellow-and black-striped, drippingly wet tomcat, in whose baleful golden eyes burned an almost spiritual hatred for all things liquid. The cat heaved himself over the rim of the crater and sat heavily, visibly wheezing from the effort of the three-foot

4

ascent. Aloof to his surroundings, he began to dry himself; while the girl crossed the intervening beach, took my hand in hers, and, with no visible effort, hoisted me bodily to my feet, oblivious to the fact that I outweighed her by at least two-to-one.

"Oh, Peter, I'm *sorry*!" she murmured, brushing sand and fragments of sea shells from my face and hair. A small, still barely coherent portion of my brain noted that her voice complemented her appearance to perfection: low, sweet, somehow musical; with the faintest hint of something which might have been an accent but wasn't. Quite.

"We calculated so *carefully*!" she continued. "I can't imagine what could have gone wrong. It wasn't supposed to *happen* like that; we weren't supposed to emerge so *close*. . . ."

I couldn't imagine what could have gone wrong either, but of course I had an advantage: I had no idea what was supposed to have gone right. I volunteered as much.

The girl ignored my babblings with grace. She retrieved the lounge, righted it, placed it behind my jellylike knees, and gently eased me down onto it. She sat close and took my hands in hers. "We were to have come out at least two hundred yards from your cottage," she explained; "down by the water, the clear beach area south of the piers . . ."

Abruptly she paused. She looked around quickly, then frowned. "*Say* . . . !" she blurted in aggrieved tones. "That's right where we are! What are you *doing* here? You aren't supposed to be *here*; you *always* fish from the end of the piers. Don't you know you might have been killed?"

Perhaps midway through a stumblingly contrite explanation of how and why I had come this day to be fishing from the beach, instead of the pier where I belonged, it occurred to me to wonder . . .

Just what right had this girl to an explanation? What did it matter what she thought? For that matter, who was she? Where had she come from? How had she gotten here? Why was she naked? Where were her clothes? What was that thing that nearly had landed on me? Where was it? What was her connection with it?

Anger and curiosity, each keeping pace with the other, gained momentum rapidly, sweeping the fog from my shock-blunted mental processes. My mind raced, considering varied possibilities, but never straying far from the central issue: *What the hell was going on here . . . ?*

As I paused in my ruminations, the girl opened her eyes, cautiously removed the fingers from her ears, straightened her shoulders, and turned back to gaze at me reproachfully.

The cat, however, merely glanced up briefly from his ablutions. Mildly he said, "You don't have to shout."

CHAPTER 4

The day had begun routinely enough: I woke early to perfect weather; breakfast turned out well; soon I was outside fishing under an unnaturally deep blue, unbelievably clear sky. The sun, looming huge and red, low on the eastern horizon, felt warm and soothing. A gentle hint of sea breeze wafted the scent of the Caribbean across the crystal lagoon to where I sprawled on a lounge at the juncture of glistening white sand and the water's edge. A frost-covered glass of lemonade stood in a slowly spreading puddle of condensate on a small table nearby. A surf rod lay beneath limp fingers across my lap. On a nearby piling, the Resident Pelican drowsed, confident that I would tire of fishing soon and dispose of my remaining bait.

However, RP's confidence was misplaced. Granted, I had a line in the water; but the fish were treating my bait with a respect bordering upon religious taboo. And it didn't take long for the warmth, the hour, and my full belly to exact their toll: Gradually my eyes closed. Soon I drifted in a contented reverie; not asleep, not quite awake.

It had appeared that nothing stood between me and a morning of sloth fully commensurate to the occasion; which was the start of my third day of vacation, and which had given every promise of being an especially fine example of its type.

Until then. . . .

Well, I'd had good reason to relax: I was The Boss; I had to make the most of every opportunity—genuine, all-out vacations didn't come along that often. My schedule called for a minimum of sixteen hours a day, seven days a week; and, in combination with my customary "holidays," would have brought the typical "working man"—those sturdy, independent souls whose unions guaranteed them a day or two of leisure each week, and an eight-hour workday—to profanity, tears, and alcohol. I'd give a resistant subject about two months before he started gazing moodily over the penthouse railing; three to five before he jumped.

Which is not to imply that *I* didn't enjoy life. No, indeed! I cruised, fished, snorkled, partied, raced, rallyed, competed in trials, partied, flew, soared, sky-dived, partied, dabbled in amateur athletics, partied, and so forth—said "so forth" encompassing all the delights predictably available to any indecently wealthy, healthy male whose appearance doesn't actually terrify small children.

However, apart from those rare all-out vacations, I *never* was off duty; I was on seven-day-a-week, 'round-the-clock call. No matter where I was, regardless with whom (and regardless what we might be doing), my staff had instructions to call me if a business crisis arose. To that end, there were phones and computer terminals in all my offices; in every room of my houses, condos, and apartments; in my motorhomes, boats, and each car and plane. My secretaries (six; they worked overlapping five-hour shifts, ensuring that the one on duty at a given moment would be sharp and informed) all carried phones and terminals in their briefcases.

Hell's bells, I had telephones in my *shower stalls* . . . !

(Once, for instance, I negotiated a multimillion-dollar merger from forty thousand feet up in an eighteen-meter sailplane over Minden. Ideal soaring conditions in the lee wave had placed an altitude record within my grasp—I *couldn't* quit—but neither, on the other hand, could I ignore a sudden opportunity to make a couple hundred million dollars.)

But I wasn't complaining. Far from it. I liked what I was doing; I enjoyed working sixteen hours a day, seven days a week. Had it ever ceased to be fun—well, getting by on the income from a multibillion-dollar principal wouldn't have entailed cutting too deeply into my standard of living. . . .

CHAPTER 5

A wisp of a smile played at the girl's features, and her eyes sought mine earnestly; but she began cautiously, as if expecting another explosion. "My name is Megonthalyä—'Meg' for short—and this is Memphus," she said, indicating the cat.

Her eyes were astonishingly wide. And *very* blue. It would have been easy to forget everything but those eyes. Even the shock of—wait, what shock *was* that, anyway? Oh, yes, the cat . . .

"Did . . . did I just hear that . . . that cat . . ." I essayed haltingly; only to be cut off, as Meg brushed the question aside:

"We *are* going to answer all your questions, Peter. At least we're going to try. But there's so much to tell you, and so much of it is going to be very hard for you to understand, to say nothing of believing. . . ."

Actually, I concluded, her eyes were almost sapphire. But it was difficult to give them the attention they deserved, under the circumstances. . . .

"I'm sure I heard that cat . . ." I ventured again—again unsuccessfully.

"That's something we'll have to sort of work up to," the girl continued diffidently. "With your present, uh, knowledge, there isn't any way that I can make you understand how we got here. You simply don't have the background to comprehend it. And I'm equally certain that you're not ready yet to learn where we came from or why we're here."

An unfortunate choice of words: Rapidly mounting blood pressure began sweeping away the mists enshrouding my brain. "Now, see here . . . !" I began hotly.

"That seems to leave the weather and fishing," observed the cat, without looking up; "after which you're going to be in trouble."

"Memphus . . ." the girl began ominously.

"Of course there's always sex," he continued blithely.

Meg sighed. "And you certainly aren't ready for an explanation of Memphus," she stated emphatically, regarding the cat with fond indulgence.

That did it, of course. True, I was still at least partially in shock; not more than a fraction of my brain cells were back in service. But those that were saw red.

Even as a child I had never liked being talked down to; as one of the most powerful capitalists in the world, I simply didn't put up with it. Not ever. Not from anyone.

Least of all from a skinny, naked trespasser who talked not only down but in circles . . . !

"Young lady," I snarled, "I don't *care* who you are. I'm not particularly interested in where you came from. But I do care a great deal about how you got here and what you're here *for*. This is *my* island; I come here for *privacy*! Now you'd better have some good answers, and I'd better start hearing them, or I'm going up to the house and calling security and you can answer *their* questions. The choice is yours. You have ten seconds. . . ."

"I'm tired of this," interjected the cat in bored tones. "All he does is stutter and yell."

"He's just as he should be," returned the girl almost defensively. "He's a leader: a take-charge type; resourceful, authoritative; accustomed to making decisions, accepting responsibility—accustomed to obedience. . . ."

"True enough," replied the cat grudgingly; "else the com-pudicters wouldn't have selected him. They *are* necessary characteristics—but I don't have to like them," he finished grumpily.

Ordinarily I'm not so easily diverted; I still hadn't recovered completely; I responded to what sounded like one of my favorite words like a trout rising to a mayfly: "What are you talking about?" I demanded. "What computers?"

"Not 'computers,'" said the girl, in tones most people reserve to explain how the sum of two plus two is arrived at. "The computers you're familiar with are machines; our com-pu*dicters* are people; a group of adepts back on Isis who were bred for compudiction, which is a *gnää'q*, or talent—partly extra-sensory, partly mathematical, partly the *pwW'r*, which means 'art'—to access and experience the Data Field in its entirety, and then reach conclusions of a very high order of probability concerning future events. Naturally, the more data the Field has, the closer their predictions come to perfection. Here on Earth they would be considered prophets."

The cat nodded. He said, "The compudicters are the ones who selected you for . . ."

"*Memphus!*" The sweet voice throbbed with the sudden lash

of an unquestionable authority, overlaid with a momentary hint of real anger. The cat subsided like a punctured balloon.

"For what?" I couldn't help it; curiosity nibbled at the edges of my wrath.

Meg cast me a long, searching, sidelong gaze over steepled fingers. "I really should start at the very beginning," she said. "Meaning no disrespect to your background, education, and knowledge—yes, I know that's how I set you off before, and I'm sorry—but this is going to be completely foreign to your experience. Unless you absorb it in a reasonably coherent sequence, you'll never keep it straight, which means you won't understand it, which means you won't believe it."

"And that would be very bad," interjected the cat, regarding me for the first time with something approximating interest. "For you, for us, for Mankind . . ."

"For *everyone*," Meg finished emphatically.

"I'm listening." .

The girl eyed me calculatingly. "I hope you are," she muttered. She took a deep breath, hesitated, then the words tumbled out in a rush: "I'm a *wWyh'j* and Memphus is my *fmMl'hr*. . . ."

Even self-made multibillionaires need a break once in a while. Despite all the success (or perhaps because of it?), occasionally I found myself growing a little tired of it all, weary of the chase. The only cure was to get away—completely away: a true vacation; not just a holiday with a phone stuck in my ear. But in the beginning, that wasn't easy.

Not from a purely business standpoint, of course; my executives were well trained and capable. My presence no longer was vital to day-to-day operations; only to continued disproportionately rapid growth. And by that time, money itself had ceased to be the goal; work had become a game, played for its own sake—purely for the challenge: There was little real significance to earning a couple hundred million dollars on any given day when it constituted only a fractional increase in my net worth.

(Goodness knows the staff enjoyed life more with me absent; without weekly or even daily crises as I took aim and let fly— my holding company did not constitute a comfortable environment for conventionally market-wise professionals. Incidence of stress-related illness among my executive ranks was about twice that of any other conglomerate, even though I was known as an easygoing martinet.)

Nor was the problem indecision on my part; I knew precisely what I was looking for: clean water, white sand, warm sunshine, soothing forest, and peace and quiet. A nice little waterfront cottage slightly set back under the trees; nothing fancy, the sort of place available all over the country in one form or another at terms so reasonable that even lower middle-income families could afford them. One merely plunked down a desposit, signed the papers, and relaxed to the tune of "easy monthly payments"—

And the blare of the neighbors' stereo; the metallic scream of outboards tracing high-speed designs all over the water; the relentless banging of the inveterate skeet shooter who owned the place down the shoreline; the staccato "ring-*ding*-ding-ding!" of trail bikers popping wheelies on the beach, gouging ruts into every surface in sight; roaring engines, screeching tires, and honking horns on the road behind the house; barking dogs, squalling and fighting cats and children, and arguing adults; the roar of the game warden's floatplane landing and taking off—not to mention the litter strewn by all those devotees of life in the unspoiled wilderness.

No. By that point in history, if one's needs included water, sand, sunshine, forest—and *privacy*—the problem had become much more complex, and the solution was very much more expensive.

(Particularly if one also happened to be at risk from terrorists the world over, all hoping to fatten their war chests with billion-dollar ransoms.)

Unless one owned the entire shoreline—a whole lake—one couldn't control the activities taking place upon it. And even if one were able to purchase an entire lake—an expensive proposition even for the very rich—problems of trespass and security remained: No one was rich enough to purchase enough surrounding land to prevent hikers, trail bikers, four-wheel-drive hobbyists, all-terrain-vehicle enthusiasts, and indomitable explorers of the wilderness (of whatever stripe) from finding their way in, despite all the "No Trespassing" signs ever posted. Without actual, impenetrable, physical barriers, and/or distance, one's privacy was only as good as others' respect for it.

Buying an entire shoreline was a potentially viable solution, however, if turned inside out: An island, surrounded by a thousand or so miles of salt moat, could be private indeed. True, an occasional yacht or plane might find its way there. But with proper (i.e., cost no object) detection equipment, one never was caught by surprise. And yachts, with few exceptions, were owned and operated by the rich, who, aware (from their own arrangements) of the potential consequences of trespass, tended to approach violation of the privacy of others of their kind with caution.

Besides, the isolated setting allowed dealing summarily and without witnesses with the few exceptions, and the still fewer nonrich trespassers (drug smugglers in stolen yachts or planes, or fishermen hoping to augment their income with a little piracy—and even single-minded, would-be kidnappers): The spray raised by machine-gun fire stitching the water across their bows, or flak bursting in the air around them, generally was sufficient to instill in most unwanted visitors a high regard for others' privacy.

We seldom had to launch the laser-guided homing missiles, and we'd never been forced to use the heavy stuff.

One would have thought that, from a security standpoint, we'd covered every eventuality. . . .

I learned the proper spellings later, of course; but at that moment what I heard were sounds resembling English words with which I had a passing acquaintance: "witch" and "familiar."

Right. . . .

I allowed the ensuing silence to lengthen to the point of gravidity before replying: "Your ten seconds ran out two minutes ago. You're on borrowed time and you have yet to come up with a reason why I shouldn't call security and have you thrown to the fish."

Meg glanced down at the cat. Her smile was almost a grimace. "Memphus," she said slowly, "I was afraid of this. And I'd rather handle it almost *any* other way. . . ."

"I don't think there *is* any other way," replied the cat gently. He turned to glare at me coldly and added, "Not under the circumstances, anyway."

The girl sighed. She looked me squarely in the eye and said, "I'm really sorry; you haven't left me any other choice. We *must* convince you, and you won't even listen. And we have to finish before your security people's next regular patrol."

My expression and tone were grimly scornful. "After that

explosion? Don't be silly. The only reason you're not in custody right now is because security has standing orders never to interrupt me here unless I'm in obvious danger. They're watching from concealment as this very moment, waiting for my sig . . ."

I broke off as my brain replayed Meg's statement: "'Any other choice' but what—*and how do you know about security's regular patrols?*"

"I'm going to put on a limited demonstration of the *pwW'r*," the girl replied, "to establish our credibility."

"She means she's going to show off," explained the cat in a resounding stage whisper. "And don't worry about interruptions," he added comfortably. "Your security people didn't notice our arrival." He paused for effect. "For some reason. . . ." he added smugly.

I looked around. I couldn't see them, of course; but then one never did. Not until they acted—one of the advantages of luring into one's service the very *crème* of Israel's antiterrorist security specialists. I made an inconspicuous signal with my left hand.

Nothing happened.

The tip of Memphus' tail twitched; the cat managed to look even smugger.

"We're empty-handed, of course," Meg continued, ignoring the by-play; "all I have is you. It won't be a very impressive demonstration."

"Peter Cory is the product of a barbarian civilization," replied the cat without malice. "It won't take much, by our standards, to get the point across."

"That's true. Do you feel up to summoning one of the lesser Dää'mn?"

"Of course. That would be ideal for our purposes."

Meg's attention returned to me; she studied me closely. "Peter, if I summon a Dää'mn, will that convince you that I *am* a *wWyh'j*? Then will you stop interrupting? This is *important*."

My mouth was open; I was on the verge of snarling "What's a Dää'mn?" when I hesitated. The girl's tone was impatient; there was an underlying note of tension. However, she didn't sound as if she were making this up—

Not consciously, I hastened to add. Of course! What I had here was a mental case; that was the only logical explanation.

Quickly I changed tacks: "Why, *sure!*" I soothed unctuously—then cringed inside: Talk about obvious; this was not developing into one of my better days for silver-tongued deviltry. I tried again: "Golly, that would convince anybody, all right." My teeth ached—I wouldn't have bought that in my sleep.

I thought fast, desperately groping for inspiration: "You go ahead; give it your best shot, but—oh, I won't do it on purpose—but I've heard that the presence of an unbeliever is supposed to throw magic out of kilter. Why don't I go up to the house and wait while you're doing your stuff?" And hit a security button—*where the hell were they* . . . ! "And when you're done, you call me to come and look. Okay?" Without waiting for an answer, I started toward the house.

I got a step and a half, barely time in which to wonder whether I might have laid it on a little too thick, before stopping midstride. It took a full two seconds to realize that I physically couldn't move—I was paralyzed!

But Meg gave me no time to worry about it, or even to wonder; she was back in front of me before the shock had time to sink in. Her expression, as our eyes met, was something between contempt and pity; but mostly sheerest outrage.

"Memphus," she breathed, "originally I had intended summoning KjJnyrb'n. Now, however, upon due reflection, I think we'll save time in the long run by calling upon The Gğäar´m."

The cat had been reclining on the warm sand. Now he sat up very straight and regarded the girl intently. "Isn't that a little extreme?" he asked, sneaking me an anxious look. "I thought you just wanted to *convince* him. Meg, are your feelings *that* hurt?"

The girl glared at me a moment longer; then she hesitated. Her expression turned sheepish. "You're right," she grudged.

"Peter," she continued, "I'm sorry. I've got a disposition like a *väarz'fing*. It's probably the trip—translation-lag, you know."

I didn't know, of course, but no one seemed to care. Besides, being paralyzed sort of limited my potential responses.

Meg took my hand and pulled. "Come on," she said. "I need flat, damp sand and a stick to draw with." Suddenly I could move again. I followed meekly, my heart racing as delayed shock set in.

I thought fast. I couldn't imagine how she'd done it, but she had my undivided attention: No one who can paralyze a man, even momentarily, is to be taken lightly—

Regardless whether she's hell-bent on continuing a pointless charade involving *wWyh'js* and *fmMl'hrs*—and Däa'mn, whatever they might be—or whether she happens to look like an underaged Pini illustration. . . .

Besides, *security still hadn't arrived*! I began to wonder whether a touch of worry mightn't be appropriate at this juncture.

I debated my options: Obviously the fact that I was bigger and stronger than she didn't hold much water. Still, being paralyzed hadn't hurt. And I was starting to get angry again—I resented the living *hell* out of being pushed around on my own island! If I didn't turn my back, she probably couldn't zap me again without letting me see how she did it. That might lead to an opportunity to disarm her; if not then, perhaps later (if a weapon were involved at all, of course—the current state of her attire made it difficult to envision where she might be hiding it).

Well, it was worth a try.

I planted my heels and dragged us to a stop. Fixing her with a steely glare, I said, "This has gone far enough. I'm not taking another step until you tell me what this is all about."

"I started to tell you," replied Meg coolly. "You didn't believe me."

"Of course not! What do you take me for?"

Memphus smiled privately but said nothing.

Meg's tone was patient: "Your opinion was formed without knowing all the facts. We're going to supply them."

"I don't believe in *wWyh'js*," I said flatly.

"Fulton's neighbors didn't believe in steam engines," Meg retorted. She paused. Her eyes narrowed; then she added thoughtfully, "I'm not sure that *I* believe in steam engines. . . ."

She shook her head impatiently, as if bothered by a gnat; then doggedly plowed ahead: "But if—just *if*, mind you—if I *should* happen to summon a Däa'mn, will you admit that I *am* a *wWyh'j* and listen quietly to my story?"

"Well-l-l . . ."

"No more back talk. Do you agree or not?"

"You don't believe in *wWyh'js* any more than I do," I muttered.

"Not responsive," Meg returned smugly. "That was a yes-or-no question: *Do you agree?*"

"Dammit—*yes*!" I snapped impatiently. I felt like an idiot.

An increasingly scared idiot. "But I still don't believe in
wWyh'js," I added sulkily.

"Do you believe in talking cats?" asked Memphus gently.

"Of course not. Who ever heard—uh . . ."

"Beg your pardon . . . ?"

Over a thousand miles from the mainland, the *in-toto*
purchase of a Caribbean island had seemed the perfect
solution to my vacation home dilemma. Cory Cay was
triangular, about two miles in length and a mile wide, and lush
and green—and lay a good hundred miles from its closest
neighbor. Apart from members of the resident maintenance
crew and my security people (who had orders to remain out of
my sight at all times and never to observe me directly), it
remained totally devoid of humanity.

When I went to Cory Cay, I went to be alone. There were no
executives or secretaries; nor cooks or servants; no television,
no telephones, no market-display terminals or teletypes.
(Okay, security had the very latest, most sophisticated communications equipment in existence—but they knew better
than to bother me with anything less pressing than global
thermonuclear war or the Second Coming).

On Cory Cay I did my own cooking, washed my own dishes,
changed my own bed, did my own laundry, and mowed my
own lawn. I netted my own bait, baited my own hook, and
cleaned and cooked my own fish. The decisions I faced were
limited in complexity to issues such as what color trunks to
wear in the morning, what beach shirt would go with them,
whether to go snorkling in the lagoon, what bait to use if I
fished—and whether to notice the Resident Pelican's elaborately nonchalant, sidling approach to swipe one of the fish I'd
already caught. (Of course I never did; the old gentleman
would have been terribly embarrassed.)

Cory Cay hardly constituted "roughing it," however. Usually I was only a little tired and tense, and a vast difference
exists between comfortable solitude and barren isolation: One
helps rinse the poisons which accumulate from civilization's
pressures out of a man. The other can start him howling at the
moon and other strange habits.

Accommodations, while not sybaritic, were comfortable;
and most of the facilities were the product of my own labors—
therapeutic labors: Sawing lumber and pounding nails is a
refreshing change for someone who makes his living with his

brain and a telephone. During initial visits I ate and slept aboard ship; but after erecting the cottage from prefab sections and making it habitable, I moved in my necessities and lived there during the year and a half of vacation time it took me to finish things off.

The salient feature of the waterfront was, of course, *Capital Venture*, a diesel cruiser whose PT heritage was apparent in her rakish lines, lying in a slip formed by two piers. Several smaller boats (both power and sail) moored to the same complex, nudged restively at their lines in response to the imperceptible surge of the Trade swell, which managed to find its way into the lagoon through the cut in the sheltering reefs.

Caretakers, security people (both resident and those who accompanied me), and their assorted families dwelt at the far end of the island; convenient to the wellheads, power and sewage treatment plants, construction and maintenance shops and stockpiles, and the runway and hangars which housed the various aircraft that served as the island's lifeline.

I understood that accommodations for full-time residents were bigger, better appointed, and more comfortable than my own little cottage. But they weren't visible from the beach, and I'd never seen them—I made a *point* of never seeing them: a small and probably silly ritual, but one which helped preserve the illusion that mine were the only works of Man on the island, and that the only footprints ever to dimple its beaches were my own.

It was a pleasant, satisfying fantasy.

While it lasted. . . .

In days to come I found it curiously difficult to remember what took place in my mind during the next few seconds. The turmoil didn't show from the outside, apparently; but I suspect that I may have lost control completely. I dimly recall realizing that somehow I must have rationalized the cat when he first spoke; protectively blocking from my awareness the fact that there was anything unusual about a cat talking, or perhaps refusing to acknowledge that Memphis *was* a cat. I just found myself conversing with a new acquaintance, an individual, a personality. He ceased to register as a cat.

Obviously.

Cats don't talk . . . !

But now there was no getting around it, consciously or otherwise; the beast had thrown it in my face. I felt like a

computer programmed with a floating decimal and told to find
the true value of *pi*. Had there been an "Overload" sign on my
forehead, it would have been flashing.

The next time I was aware of my surroundings, I still was
being dragged down the beach by Meg—*and that damned
talking cat . . . !*

"I beg your pardon?" he was saying.

I realized I must have been muttering, if not actually raving.
Controlling my voice with some difficulty, I said, "No, I
don't—or haven't until now. However, I can think of any
number of explanations for you which don't violate any natural
laws. You could be anything from a mutation to a—"

"But I'm not," the cat cut me off. "Now be quiet and watch
Meg."

The girl stopped and looked around thoughtfully. "I think
this will do, don't you, Memphus?" she mused, testing the
texture of the sand with a toe.

The cat studied the composition of the surface from his
closer vantage. "Yes," he replied after a moment. "Yes, go
ahead."

Meg picked up a piece of driftwood and began to draw in the
hard-packed wet sand. First came a pentagram some eight feet
on a side. Memphus followed close behind, nose to the
ground, watching to see that no particle of displaced sand fell
back into the groove.

An intricate, quite indescribable pattern was drawn at each
of the five points. Between these appeared strange, distinctly
cabalistic symbols. Three slightly smaller pentagrams duplicated the primary and were placed equidistant around the
outside.

Meg finished; the pair made a final, thorough inspection.
Then she took me by the hand and led me to one of the smaller
pentagrams. She placed me inside, and quite belabored the
point of telling me not to come out until she *physically* came in
and got me; not until I actually could feel her hand in mine.

Then she settled cross-legged in the pentagram on my left
and began to croon a genuinely peculiar little song. I have
perfect pitch, and she had a sweetly musical voice; but it was
awfully modern-sounding and difficult to discern a melody (in
fact, one less charitable might have drawn parallels to the
output of an acoustic modem for computer communications or
pushbutton telephone switching codes). Memphus reclined
sphinx-fashion in the other pentagram, watching closely.

Whatever they were doing, both were completely preoccupied; and by flexing my muscles without moving, I determined that I wasn't paralyzed. It would have been easy to slip quietly into the jungle and not stop running until I reached the security compound.

But I didn't.

For one thing, it would have been humiliating: "Help! I've just been terrorized by a naked twelve-year-old female pixie and her sarcastic talking cat . . . !"

I'd never had occasion to try on a strait jacket, and I wasn't eager to rectify the omission. Besides, I was confident that a rational explanation would emerge once all the facts were in.

However, I knew that whatever was taking place here was outside my experience and I had best be on my toes if I hoped to cope with—with *whatever*. . . .

Plus, I was still all aquiver from being forced to recognize Memphus's reality—and I'd never heard anyone so emphatic about anything as Meg was about remaining inside that pentagram.

Finally, I was also, if I cared to face facts, very close to being scared spitless.

So I remained where I was and watched as Meg, still singing those odd notes, drew a figure in the sand in front of her. For several moments nothing happened and I began to breathe more easily . . .

Until the patterns in the sand began to radiate; a faint bluish luminescence reminiscent of long-wave UV—but perceptibly, if subtly, different. A quick downward glance confirmed that the one in which I stood was glowing as well.

Abruptly a column of smoke boiled up out of the sand inside the big pentagram. It was a particularly unattractive color—somewhere between a greasy yellowish green and a sooty blackish purple. It was also intensely acrid and started my eyes watering and my throat burning. I had to fight back an urge to cough.

But then I forgot my physical discomfort: Something was happening *inside* the smoke; something nebulous and miasmic, upon which I couldn't seem to focus—*something with eyes like Fourth of July sparklers*. . . .

Moments later the eyes had a body to go with them: KjJnyrb'n was perhaps eight feet tall and bore a family resemblance to an acid freak's impressionistic painting of a Tyrannosaurus Rex. There were two small, taloned arms; kangaroolike legs and a forked tail; a bunch of tentacles; two-foot sabre tusks; and a pair of long, curling horns. Flame jetted from the nostrils. A glowing tongue flicked in and out. And as the Däa'mn materialized, it uttered a cry which, though inaudible, somehow resonated every nerve in my body.

KjJnyrb'n stood still for a moment, gazing at Meg. Then it noticed me.

For about ten years.

It seemed amused.

And for perhaps the fiftieth time that morning, I wondered *where the hell was security* . . . ?

Meg stood. She strolled unconcernedly from her pentagram into the Däa'mn's enclosure. She slid an arm about the creature's middle. They held a brief whispered conversation; then both strolled out of the central pentagram to the rim of mine.

Meg grinned and beckoned. KjJnyrb'n did, too—though, on the whole, its beckon was a great deal more convincing than its grin.

On the point of obliging, I felt a sudden chill. I couldn't put a finger on what bothered me; I could see no reason why I shouldn't join them. But Meg had made an awfully big point of waiting until she *physically* came in and got me. The key word seemed to be "physically"; repeated many, many, *many* times.

Now. . . . If a doctor prescribes pills for what ails you and tells you to take one every two hours with milk, and you take three every six hours with water, you don't have much right to complain when they eat a hole in your stomach: You ignored the expert's advice.

I learned a long time ago that, when an expert in a field outside one's own area of expertise goes to the trouble of offering detailed instructions, they are best adhered to, *to the letter*. The longer I considered the matter, the more this seemed to be a textbook example of an adhering situation. I shook my head.

Meg beckoned more emphatically—but she did *not* come in to get me.

I shook my head again—

And blinked: Meg was sitting cross-legged in her pentagram and KjJnyrb'n was back in its enclosure, looking somehow peeved. However, it took practically no effort on my part to resist a momentary impulse to thumb my nose at it.

Meg stood, a single fluidly graceful movement. She performed an eye-baffling series of gestures and exclaimed a final

phrase of gibberish. The column of filthy smoke vanished in a
flash of brilliant blue flame. So did KjJnyrb'n.

Meg's expression of sympathy, as she came over and took my
hand, would have been more convincing had it not consisted
primarily of an ear-to-ear grin. "You look upset," she murmured. "I'm sorry I had to do that. But you'll have to admit,
you didn't leave me a great deal of choice. I had to do
something to get your attention."

I didn't answer immediately; I was catching up on my
breathing. Finally I said, "I understand why you had to do it. I
never would have believed anything like this otherwise—I'm
not sure I totally believe it now. . . ."

Meg's brow elevated; she cast me a sidelong look.

I took a quick step back, hands raised as a shield. "Just a
figure of speech," I hastened to clarify. "I *do* believe—I do, I
do, I *do*!

"But . . ." I added more slowly, "I don't *understand:* If you
didn't want me to come out until you came in and got me, what
was that sign-language routine about?"

Meg's face was a study in puzzlement. "What are you talking
about?"

I told her what I had seen. The sunny expression evaporated.

She took a deep breath and released it slowly. "Memphus,"
she said softly, "please remind me, when we get home, to take
care of this. A treacherous Däa'mn can*not* be tolerated. Do
you have any suggestions? Otherwise I'm going to file a formal
complaint, demand a full hearing, and do my best to see
whether the loss of its license and about thirty *nNäa'ls'* total
sensory overload will get its attention!"

The cat stretched lazily. "I know you suspect my objectivity
where Däa'mn are concerned, because of my own origin. And
probably rightly so. But I do think that's a little stern. I'd ask
for a thirty-*nNäa'l* suspension and maybe three *nNäa'ls* of
sensory-augmented cellular disruption and reassembly."

"That's hardly a slap on the wrist," protested Meg indignantly; "after trying something like *that* . . . !"

"The fault was ours," Memphus pointed out calmly; "and it
did fail. 'Let the summoner beware' has always been the
Däa'mn's motto. We weren't watching closely enough. Treaty
or no treaty, they don't *have* to respond to our summons; nor
are they under any particular obligation to perform the tasks
we set. Their interest in this universe is just that: an interest.

Part of that interest is the fun of trying to catch us with our pants down—think of it as an ethnic weakness. By the standards of KjJnyrb'n's hometown, that was little more than a boyish prank. They don't have quite the same appreciation for the consequences that we do."

"I know," Meg grumbled. "But—well . . ."

"And we learned something important: Considering his utter lack of appreciation for what he faced, I think our prospect here acquitted himself pretty well—perhaps even very well. I'm not all that displeased that it made the attempt."

"I wouldn't go *that* far," Meg replied dryly. "Don't push your luck." Memphus grinned smugly (I know, I know—cat physiology and all—but grin he *did*).

Then he turned to me. "Do you have any idea what would have happened to you if you hadn't followed Meg's instructions?" he asked sternly.

"I can guess," I replied shakily.

Of *course* it could have been hypnosis: Flash something across the sky to rivet your victim's attention; sting him with a fast-acting knockout dart (don't tell *me* they don't work that quickly—I manufactured them for the CIA); load him up with a hypnotic drug (I made that, too); prime him with posthypnotic instructions while showing him a movie calculated to make him remember what you want him to.

Nothing to it. *I* could have done that to a man if I'd wanted to; I had the resources—and so did plenty of others. If I had thought for an instant that I was in the hands of operators capable of working on that level, I might have relaxed and enjoyed the ride: They were *good*.

But I didn't think it. Not for a minute. Not for a second. I knew better: Meg *was* a *wWyh'j*. Memphus *was* her *fmMl'hr*. And *nothing* I had learned in my whole life, right up to that instant, could be relied upon ever again as factual. The entire natural order of things, as I knew it, was at least incomplete, and more probably was utterly false.

And the cat's next words did nothing to help me cushion the adjustment: "No," he replied soberly; "you can't begin to guess. What you're thinking is merely permanent. What it had in mind would have been eternal. . . ."

TO: Project Director/Monitor's Log.
FROM: Sephiloyä, Third Order.
SUBJECT: Project *Extremis*.

Subject Cory has recovered from the physical and emotional side effects attendant to the arrival of our team. He has absorbed and accepted the fact of their alienness without undue disturbance. He even has observed the emergence of an extrauniversal being into this space without lasting trauma.

It should be noted that the lesser Däa'mn, KjJnyrb'n, a native of Häa'l, attempted to entice Subject Cory from the safety of his *wWr'dts* by means of a flawless illusion, but without success. If it had succeeded, much of the time and effort invested to this point would have been lost at a single stroke.

KjJnyrb'n's superior has been notified of this conduct, but has been a problem itself and is unlikely to take appropriate action. The problem would seem to be the mutual-assistance pact. At present, the Häa'l are under no binding obligation to comport themselves in our universe as we do ourselves in theirs. Since they summon one of us more frequently than we do them, it is reasonable to assume that they derive more benefit from the relationship than we do. It is this observer's recommendation that the treaty be renegotiated, and promptly. The present situation is intolerable.

Incidentally, Agent Megonthalyä's performance thus far has exceeded all expectations. This will please those responsible for her selection and conditioning.

The team's next major challenge is expected to arise when Cory is informed of the details of their mission.

CHAPTER 6

There barely was time to return to the cottage, clothe Meg in one of my tee shirts (which was big enough for three of her; and which, gathered in an improvised sash at the waist, covered her modestly to just below the knees but somehow made her look even nakeder), and settle comfortably on the front porch, before security arrived in force.

Security personnel always remained out of sight while making routine rounds; but upon noticing the newcomer, they sent in an alarm and a full complement responded to investigate. I introduced Meg as an acquaintance from Idaho, arrived this morning, and apologized for not notifying them.

Security Chief Rebecca Two-Knives was a sweet, slightly plump, grandmotherly little lady whose kindly expression was a façade behind which lurked undoubtedly the single deadliest, most proficient counterintelligence, antiterrorist, and security specialist ever trained by Israel's secret services for the protection of their government leaders.

Becky regarded Meg with cool professional interest for a long moment; then turned and scanned the area briefly. Unlike some of her male counterparts (not to mention Yours Truly) she did not find a well-turned female ankle (or whatever) distracting—which was only one of the reasons I retained her to oversee my personal and corporate security.

She turned back to me. Her eyes bore into mine without comment. Her aspect was a study in expressionless disapproval—directed toward the tactical situation which we both knew I was forcing upon her; not my young, attractive, scantily clad visitor, nor my presumed plans for same.

Married since age twenty to the same man (but retaining her maiden name for professional purposes), with three children and the better part of a dozen grandchildren to show for it, Becky practiced a conservative, conventional, downright old-fashioned lifestyle. But she was neither a prude nor an evangelist. She liked what she liked; the rest of the world (provided they didn't interfere with her or hers, or harm innocent bystanders) were free to follow the dictates of their own consciences.

Becky had been with me almost six years. This pointed pretty strongly to a conclusion that, while my fondness for motorsport and athletic competition severely complicated her job, she liked me personally and approved of me professionally (with her credentials, she didn't *have* to stay anywhere): She liked how I treated my people (as head of security, she was in an unequaled position to observe my handling of them on a day-to-day basis) and approved of how I ran my business and what I did with my money. She regarded my preoccupation with the fair sex as appropriate for one of my age and physical characteristics, and (without lifting even an occasional editorial eyebrow) did everything necessary to ensure that my trysts were both safe and as private as I wished them.

I was pretty sure she wouldn't resign on the spot over this.

However, this was the very first time that I had sprung a guest on her unannounced. Further, the island's security equipment truly was comprehensive: No air, surface, submersible, or even orbital vehicles could pass within a two-hundred-mile radius without detection. Within the past twenty-four hours, none had. Meg's sudden presence on the island was patently impossible.

Becky studied me briefly; then visibly reached a decision: If the Boss didn't wish to share with her how the girl got here, that was his privilege. Becky's interest in her was limited to a determination of whether she posed a threat or not. Apparently the Boss felt she didn't.

Apparently.

Becky nodded politely; then she and her crew vanished into the underbrush with a speed and silence that would have done both her Comanche and Israeli ancestors proud.

Again apparently: Becky was an instinctive, natural-born cop; I knew her hyperdeveloped bump of caution would cause her to keep us under close observation until she satisfied herself that my *apparent* acceptance of this unexplained visitor wasn't obtained through duress.

I muttered a quick warning: Becky's surveillance was certain to include basic precautions, such as eavesdropping via high-gain parabolic microphones outside and bugs inside the cottage, and observation by means of concealed TV cameras—and the *last* thing we needed was to have her discover that I was entertaining a girl who hobnobbed with Däa'mn. And had a talking cat. . . .

But Meg and Memphus, it developed, had *security* bugged. Or whatever. At least they knew when security was watching and/or listening to us, and the state of their suspicions. And after about half a day of stereotypical visiting—swimming, sunning, sailing, dining, etc.—Memphus reported that Becky had lost interest: "She's concluded that you're following your usual pattern with attractive females," he explained in bored tones. "She approves of your taste, but doesn't intend to watch as events follow what she considers their inevitable course. She is not a voyeur. . . ."

Meg dimpled. "Memphus," she reproved gently, "is that nice?"

"Voyeurism? I don't know. I suppose I could watch and render an opinion. . . ."

Meg eyed the cat with mock annoyance. Then she slid down the sofa and sat close to me. Without thinking, I put an arm protectively about her shoulders. She reached up and took my hand in hers.

"All right," she sighed, with a contented wriggle; "where were we?"

Memphus snickered. "I'm not surprised that you've forgotten, snuggled up against all that whalebone and steel. Peter probably doesn't know what's second-most uppermost in your mind, but *I* do."

"Memphus, please shut up," said Meg absently, tracing the muscle divisions of my chest and abdomen with the fingertips of her other hand. "I haven't forgotten. I had just told Peter that I'm a *wWyh'j* and you're my *fmMl'hr* . . ."

"Meg isn't likely to admit this herself," the cat interjected with conspicuous pride; "but referring to her merely as 'a' *wWyh'j* is akin to describing da Vinci as a tinkerer. She ranks Tenth Order. Tenth is the ultimate achievement of an adept, and she stands high among the Tenths. She's probably the second-most powerful being in this universe, and she *is* the most powerful *wWyh'j*."

"Memphus, how would anybody know that?" Meg teased. "Who keeps score?"

Memphus didn't answer; he just looked superior.

"Never mind; we have more important things to talk about."

"That we do," the cat replied with sudden grimness.

Meg turned to stare up at me with those enormous blue eyes. "And it *is* important, Peter," she breathed; "vitally, *desperately* important. . . ."

"The most important thing in the galaxy," added the cat soberly.

Meg nodded. "Memphus and I were sent here from the planet Isis, my home, located near the galactic core. My people, the Isi, focusing a concentration of *mMj'q* which awes me to contemplate, opened a passageway across the universes and translated us to Earth, to your side, Peter Cory, to try to enlist you—to persuade you, using any inducement within the almost limitless powers of the Isi to grant, fair or foul—to join us, to lead us, to help us in a racial undertaking which has spanned over a hundred centuries and upon whose outcome hangs literally the fate of every being in the galaxy.

"Of all the sapient entities inhabiting all the myriad worlds of the Milky Way, you are the only one to whom the compudicters have assigned odds approaching a semblance of probable success. Even with you we are given only about a fifty-fifty chance. But without you, the probabilities are less than a tenth of one percent; without you the Isi almost certainly must fail. . . ."

And that's when she said it: "Peter, we are *losing* Armageddon . . . !" she whispered intensely. "You *must* aid us!" The tears in her eyes were real; no doubt remained. "Only with your help do we have any chance of prevailing. Unless you join us . . ." her breath caught, "perhaps even if you do—*the galaxy is doomed . . . !*"

CHAPTER 7

For the space of a long breath I sat mute, suffused in a glow of purest admiration: Bar none, that was the corniest pronouncement I had ever heard anyone utter. And in broad daylight, too.

It took another couple seconds, and the stimulus of a tear starting down Meg's cheek, before the content of those corny words sank in, and several moments thereafter to settle on a suitable response.

Having met KjJnyrb'n earlier, "Haw!" and "G'wan!" never even crossed my mind. But "Do tell . . ." and "How 'bout that . . ." seemed inadequate.

Fortunately, before the delay became obvious, my brain shifted into gear: "Why?" I said brilliantly.

Meg was still fighting to control a quivery chin. I looked to Memphus. The cat sat up; he regarded me thoughtfully. "You wouldn't happen to know what the term 'antimatter' means?" he offered dubiously.

"I doubt it. Before this morning I'd have said yes without a second's hesitation. But that's before I met KjJnyrb'n; before learning that the holes in my education are even wider and deeper than I thought.

"I know what what passes for science hereabouts *thinks* it is; and I understand that the folks at Cern and Fermi think they might have detected it. Plus I own several companies which are pooling their efforts, trying to synthesize it. They haven't reported that they're having any luck."

The cat blinked slowly. "If you're uncertain, then they're having bad luck. Which is good luck. There's something quite unmistakable about an explosion which knocks a planet out of orbit."

He turned to Meg. "That's something we'd best look into very soon, and probably take steps to avoid. Grown men, never mind so-called scientists, should know better than to play with such toys on inhabited planetary surfaces. I don't object to their playing, mind you; but they should do it at a respectful distance from breakables—say half a light-year . . ."

"Your motives are exemplary, Memphis," interjected Meg, with a trace of impatience, "but you do wander."

"I do," replied the cat, unperturbed. "This last couple hundred billion trillennia I've been bothered that way. Probably a sign of age. The subject was the end of the galaxy:

"If you know what antimatter is," he continued, "then you probably can form a vague, totally erroneous impression of what I mean by 'antienergy.'"

I pondered briefly; then shook my head. "Not likely," I replied; "but don't let that stop you. There's been a lot I haven't understood this morning. So go ahead; confuse me with the whole story to begin with. Then we can back up, pick out the details I think I understand, clarify them, and expand from there."

The cat stared enigmatically. "I like your attitude," he said abruptly. "You yell too much, but I like your attitude."

He continued: "'Antienergy' is a hopelessly inadequate semantic representation of the concept, but I find that I'm a prisoner of your language; it can't be explained in English— 'You can't get there from here.'"

"Is a detailed understanding necessary at this point?"

"No. Soon you'll be speaking Isi; then we can get as technical as necessary. For the moment, it suffices to state that antienergy exists, and its most salient characteristic is that it consumes what we know as energy, totally—in a fashion which likewise can't be explained in English. . . ."

"And . . . ?"

"And we have discovered the existence of what may be a living entity composed of the stuff, which is distinguished by an insatiable appetite for energy—and I do mean literally insatiable."

"Immaterial monsters of pure energy?"

"*Anti*energy," corrected the cat.

"Which are headed for our galaxy?"

"With a precision that would make your ears lay back."

"My ears don't lay back," I observed absently; "though they've been known to wiggle at parties."

Memphus favored me with a level stare. "I bet you're dynamite with a lampshade," he muttered. He turned to the girl. "Meg, is saving the galaxy really *this* important?"

She managed a wan smile. "Those of us who live here full-time like to think so."

"Which includes me," I conceded. "Okay, I'll try to be good."

"Now, the problem, as I see it, is to head them off somehow, destroy them en route, or make them feel lonely, insecure, and unwanted. Here on Earth, when the UN finds itself facing potential nuclear obliteration and/or the deaths of zillions from whatever cause, they generally send out a Very Stern Letter of Protest. I guess that wouldn't work in this case?"

The cat sighed. "I take back what I said about your attitude. I suspect that you're going to be an aggravating hero."

"I don't," replied Meg with a smile—which faded as she said, "You must believe us, Peter. If we fail—if you won't join us—perhaps even if you do—the galaxy *is* going to be destroyed. Utterly. Along with every living thing in it."

"Relax; I do believe you," I soothed. "Pay no attention to the nonsense. That's just how I deal with stress. And given the events of the last few hours, coupled with what you've just told me, someone less stalwart doubtless would be groveling, gibbering, and foaming at the mouth; which, at the very least, would be pretty gauche. I'd rather make bad jokes.

"Actually, I *have* to believe you; I have no choice. After what I saw you do, I'd probably believe you if you told me that Trans-Pan-Eastern planned to start scheduled flights to the Emerald City, with stops in Nevernever Land and Behind the Looking Glass."

I paused reflectively. "Actually, I think I'd *rather* believe that. . . .

"Now, I don't suppose you people have compiled any useful data on these beasties? You wouldn't know a nice, convenient method of killing them; something simple, economical, and easy to clean up afterward?"

The cat snorted. "We don't even know a nice, convenient method of getting it to *notice* us. And I do mean *it;* I detect that you labor under a misapprehension: There is only a single such entity confronting us. Regrettably, it occupies approximately the same volume of space as the Andromeda Galaxy."

"Oh."

"'Oh,' indeed. And so far as we've been able to determine, it is absolutely unkillable."

"Well, if it were going to be easy, everybody would want to do it; then it probably wouldn't be any fun."

"To be precise," added Meg, "we haven't been able to figure out how to kill R'gGnrök, which means 'final devourer' in Isi, because we haven't been able to learn why it's alive, or even—strictly speaking—*whether*. It doesn't exhibit any of the characteristics one usually associates with life. Except perhaps one . . ."

"Three . . . ?" prodded the cat.

Meg hesitated. "Memphus is reminding me that opinions differ. Some consider it a sign of life that R'gGnrök exhibits judgment in selecting its next victim—its next galaxy. However, during the centuries we have been observing it, only once has it chosen other than the galaxy nearest to the one it had just consumed—and then the target was larger, and radiated *much* more energy. Parallels may be drawn between that aspect of R'gGnrök's behavior and magnetism. Or chemistry.

"Another facet of the enigma is the fact that it apparently consumes energy without changing any of itself in the process, as happens when chemicals interact, for instance. But we don't know enough about this thing to know for certain that it *isn't* being changed. For all we know, it could be nothing more than an energy-damping field, but one of such intensity that any lessening which may be taking place simply isn't measurable by the means we have available.

"But these are side issues, unimportant.

"What convinces *me* that we're dealing with a living, probably self-aware entity is the fact that *the damned thing computes ballistics!* It travels in 'straight' lines: geodesic curves matching the curvature of the universe; plotted to take into account the perturbations caused by other galaxies' gravitational attraction; straight lines terminating *precisely where its target is going to be when it gets there . . . !*"

"We have observed flights of over ten thousand years' duration, involving correction factors of as much as eighteen degrees," added Memphus grimly.

"I'm convinced," I announced. "What's the timetable; how soon does it get here?"

"Too damned soon," grumbled the cat.

"Just under eighteen hundred years from now," said Meg.

I sputtered; I couldn't decide whether to laugh or swear.

"Things are that pressing, are they? My great-to-the-some-thingth grandchildren really are going to hate that."

"You'll know it if they do," responded the girl somewhat heatedly; "they'll tell you personally!"

"My grandparents barely made it into their nineties," I pointed out. "Even granting the advantage of improved child nutrition . . ."

Meg cut me off: "How old do you think *I* am?"

"Entirely too young to be traipsing around the galaxy in your suntan," I retorted. "If you were of Earth, I'd say twelve, if that. But you people obviously look younger at maturity; because if you weren't mature, you wouldn't be entrusted with a mission of this importance.

"Not responsive," came the smug reply.

"Meg is fifty-two years old," interrupted Memphus, rather more loudly than seemed necessary. "She reached physical maturity roughly thirty-five years ago. She will remain unchanged in appearance for the rest of her life; which, unless she meets with an accident, will span a pretty fair portion of forever."

"I see," I replied thoughtfully. "All right, you people do have a problem. But, altruistic considerations aside, what does it have to do with me?"

"I thought you were done bucking in the traces," purred the cat, looking superior. "I thought you were going to believe us from here on out. Meg, are you in the mood for a quick encore?"

The suggestion brought about an abrupt realignment of my attitude. Most earnestly, I did *not* desire another demonstration. Shucks, what was so unusual about a skinny twelve-year-old kid turning out to be a fifty-two-year-old immortal? What was so remarkable about me living to see the end of the galaxy?

(Morosely, I wondered which airline really would get the franchise for Oz.)

"All right—hold it . . . ! I *do* believe you. I just don't see how I'm likely to live long enough to have a personal stake in the outcome. You will, granted; I don't dispute that. But . . ."

Meg grinned. Actually, it was more of a smirk. "You'll live long enough if Memphus and I succeed in our mission. . . ." She paused, eyed me expectantly, then frowned. "Aren't you going to ask what our mission is?"

"No," I replied firmly.

"Won't help," whispered Memphus loudly.

"Our mission," Meg continued doggedly, "is to enlist you and bring you back with us to Isis, where you are to be trained and equipped as befits your position: a *wWyhr läaq* of the Tenth Order."

"*WWyhr läaq* of Earth," added Memphus.

"*WWyhr läaqs* live a long time," said the girl.

"A very long time," agreed the cat.

"Which means that if you fail you'll be cut off in the bloom of your youth, along with all the rest of us."

"Wait a minute," I broke in. "I just figured out what's been bothering me about all this—over and above the obvious, of course: Your species is millions of years older than mine; you even have interstellar travel. We Earthmen, on the other hand, only recently have managed to cross space to our very nearby satellite. And we're still actively in the process of destroying this planet and all it contains with our—what must be to you—primitive technology. What can we possibly—more particularly, what can *I* possibly—offer so advanced a people?"

"Trillions of years older," stated the cat matter-of-factly. "But the Isi know nothing of your mechanistic technology. Moreover, they cannot learn it: Most of the principles upon which your science is founded are more incomprehensible to the Isi than those surrounding the *pwW'r* are to you at this moment; the result of what might be termed a racial mind block—which isn't anything of the kind, of course, but I'll explain after you get the language."

Meg took over: "After grappling with the problem for centuries—*lots* of centuries—and failing to come up with a solution, we took a different tack: We developed an information storage-and-retrieval system called the Data Field, and into it we poured literally *everything* that was known about *everything*.

"Simultaneously, using genetic manipulation, we bred a class of adepts known as compudicters: people capable of accessing and experiencing the totality of the Data Field and collating everything related to a given problem, regardless how peripherally, and somehow putting it all together in the form of predictions of forthcoming events or recommended courses of action. The compudicters were instructed to come up with a solution to the R'gGnrök problem, if possible; or, if not, to recommend approaches which might lead to the development of a solution.

"An immediate, clearcut answer was not forthcoming.

However, the best recommendation suggested that a partnership consisting of the *pwW'r* and material technology probably would come up with one. Since the Isi couldn't handle mechanics, the alternative was obvious: Find a reasonably nearby species—which, as a practical matter, meant someone inside the galaxy—whose society was based on the mechanistic sciences exclusively, select the most promising individual, bring him to Isis, give him the education and training of a *wWyhr läaq* of the Tenth Order; then turn him loose and help him however he thinks he needs it."

"Not a brilliant plan," said Memphus, scowling; "not even offering good odds . . ."

"But immeasurably better than anything else the compudicters, or anybody else for that matter, could devise," Meg continued. "Personally, I consider forty-nine point seven two three six percent quite comforting when compared to the point oh oh three eight percent assigned to the next best idea."

"But surely there must be a more advanced species of mechanics somewhere in the galaxy," I protested. "Memphus said I was the product of a barbarian civilization—I don't think you grasp just how primitive we are:

"We are systematically destroying this world in more ways than you can begin to list. Our unvarying response to a stranger is suspicion and ready hostility—a man with the wrong shade of pigmentation in his skin is as good as dead if set afoot in many sections of our major cities. Hell—the Irish still consider it socially acceptable to blow up school buses full of children, provided they're of the 'wrong' religion—this while professing to worship the same God as their victims but in different words.

"Can you imagine the reaction of Mankind to meeting a planetful of genuine *aliens;* people not just different in physical appearance but apparently supernatural in abilities? And immortal to boot? We can't tolerate the subtle differences that distinguish individuals of our own species—how do you suppose we'll react to you?"

"Badly," acknowledged Meg comfortably. "Adolescents usually are boisterous; adolescent species are no different. One of your first tasks will be to direct the rapid development of your people to a level of maturity where we can meet as equals and work efficiently together.

"Your species was *selected*, Peter—with all its warts. In some fashion known only to the compudicters, your people were determined to possess more of the qualities required for potential success than any other, regardless what superficial advantages others might seem to hold over you.

"And you, alone of your people, were selected as a candidate for the $pwW'r$. It is my understanding that your control eventually will exceed mine; it is probable that you will surpass any Isi when you attain full competence. When we get you back to Isis . . ."

My heart missed a beat. "'When,' you say. How about 'how'? Am I supposed to ride in one of those fireballs you arrived in?"

Meg smiled forlornly. Memphus said, "That was strictly a one-way ticket. It took just about everything the Isi could assemble to get us here. They forced open a shunt across the junctions of various interconnecting universes, and we jumped down through it from the surface of Isis to the surface of Earth. Subjectively, it was about a five-foot drop."

Meg nodded. "Objectively, it's closer to thirty thousand lightyears."

"Now who's being nonresponsive," I chided gently. "Anyone would think you're avoiding the question. I repeat: How do we all *get* to Isis?"

The abruptness with which Meg dissolved into tears took me completely by surprise. She buried her face in the hollow of my shoulder; silent convulsions wracked her tiny frame. Without conscious intent, my arms tightened protectively about her.

Memphus started to say something; then broke off coughing. After a few moments, he cleared his throat elaborately and tried again, speaking with some difficulty: "Actually, Peter," he said diffidently, eyes downcast, toying idly with a leaf which had found its way onto the porch, "that's up to you. The Isi barely got us here, and they aren't here barely to get us back. They reasoned, I suppose, that anyone possessing the brains, determination, and ability required to save the galaxy shouldn't have trouble coping with so trivial a detail as transporting the three of us to Isis."

I stared open-mouthed. This wasn't developing at all in accord with the heroic picture I'd been forming of my role in the expedition. I had anticipated confronting problems which I was even remotely qualified to solve.

Then the secondary implication hit me: "You mean you're marooned here unless I—together with Earth's tinker-toy space travel industry—can come up with something resembling practical interstellar travel . . . ?"

"Do you gut people's illusions for a living?" inquired the cat grimly. "Or does the presence of visitors stimulate you to special efforts? Nonetheless," he finished bleakly, "that *is* a tidy summation of the facts. Depressing thought, isn't it."

It was. "That's practically the same as saying you're expendable!" I protested indignantly.

Meg snuffled once or twice against my shoulder. "Not in so many words, Peter," she sighed. "It's just that if *you* can't get to Isis for training—with or without us—the whole galaxy is lost anyway, so our fate doesn't matter much . . ." her voice caught, ". . . except to us," she added miserably.

She lifted her head; those enormous blue eyes fastened on mine. "Peter," she whispered, "I don't *want* to die way out here—*I want to go home* . . . !" She hid her face in my shoulder again.

Well-l-l. . . . Okay, *nolo contendere:* I never had a chance, did I—shucks, what dyed-in-the-wool, compulsively noble Knight in Shining Armor worthy of his garter could have withstood that appeal? I caught a glimpse of Memphus' triumphantly smug expression from the corner of my eye; but even without it, I knew I was hooked.

I held Meg close, trying to ease her distress—and reflected on the folly that is male. . . .

TO: Project Director/Monitor's Log.
FROM: H'tTirviq, Sixth Order.
SUBJECT: Project *Extremis*.

Our team has accomplished their first objective: Subject Cory has yielded, if not to the reasoned arguments of Agent Megonthalyä and her *fmMl'hr*, then at least to their undisguised pleadings.

It should be noted, perhaps parenthetically, that Cory, while tough-minded, pragmatic, and appreciably more intelligent than his contemporaries, is in fact, as predicted (and to use his own idiom), a "pushover" in the hands of an apparently distressed female.

The Council is to be congratulated on their selection of Agent Megonthalyä as a lure. Despite her well-known tendency to become emotionally involved with subjects (who among us is likely to forget that *däal'fön* puppy?), her selection was well thought of indeed: She is ideally suited to the task by appearance and—once suitably conditioned—by personality as well.

Incidentally, the wisdom of the Council's decision to subject the agent to conditioning prior to this mission has been borne out. Subject Cory's undeniable physical attributes and unconscious personal charm already have had their effect. Almost certainly, absent conditioning, Agent Megonthalyä would refuse to carry out her duties, knowing, as she then would, the truth concerning Cory's probable fate.

As a point of technical interest, the agent has given no sign of recognizing either the falsity of the implanted memories or the blocks surrounding her awareness of the facts of the matter.

Likewise, the Council was well-advised in enlisting her *fmMl'hr's* support in advance. Without Memphus' active cooperation, it is unlikely that the agent could achieve the goal toward which she now unknowingly strives. Notwithstanding its initial misgivings concerning the conditioning aspect of the mission (the result of an adept/ *fmMl'hr* bond as complete as any in my experience), it has performed in an exemplary fashion throughout.

Next Cory is to be given as much "preliminary background" as he is capable of absorbing without benefit of rapport; which will, of course, follow as the Agent judges the moment ripe. . . .

CHAPTER 8

Despite an inner conviction that I had committed myself to a fool's errand (how could I *possibly* singlehandedly invent practical interstellar travel?), the consequences of failure didn't bear thinking about, so I resolved to give it my very best shot. The obvious first step in determining our options was taking inventory of our resources and capabilities. Especially theirs—without moving a muscle, apparently, Meg had *paralyzed* me! Who knew what else they could do. . . .

Wherefore, a physics lesson followed directly—an *Isi* physics lesson: the wondrously expanded, yet oddly crippled, physics known to Isi science.

Appearances notwithstanding, the physical science of the Isi had nothing whatever to do with the "supernatural." Indeed the only connection between the $pwW'r$ and various forms of sorcery, wizardry, necromancy, thaumaturgy, voodoo, monology, demonaltry, diabolism, satanism, or occultism fantasized by the more imaginative denizens of Planet Earth, was entymological:

Meg was a "$wWyh'j$" and Memphus her "$fmMl'hr$." Despite their ominous phonetic resemblance to English words, they translate to "female scientist" and "technical assistant"; just as "$wWyhr\ läaq$," which sounds not unlike "warlock," means "male scientist."

Likewise, the "hardware" of Isi science turned out to be $mMj'q$: monopole particles some twelve magnitudes smaller than tachyons, which leak into our universe from that in which they originate through certain utterly pure crystals of monolithic corundum known as $wWn'dt$. The intrinsic $mMj'q$-transmitting quality of $wWn'dt$ is enhanced enormously by cutting the raw stone into a certain critical shape and "activating" it . . .

"Hold it!" I ordered. "'$MMj'q\ wWn'dt$' . . . ? I like a coincidence as well as the next guy. But this is getting out of hand. . . ."

Meg grinned. "Patience; it gets worse," she promised.

"And none of it coincidental," added the cat. "Now are you going to shut up and listen or must we Take Steps . . . ?"

I shut up and listened.

$MMj'q$ have two unique characteristics: First, their motion through time is lateral. Secondly, upon being forced into twelve-way collision, they generate fusion by-products which affect the bonds that keep native matter, mass, and energy in their respective forms—and may, within certain limits, be used to *determine those forms*. . . .

An adept's manipulation of the $mMj'q$ flowing from his $wWn'dt$, and its by-products, is a function of telekinesis, usually accomplished with help from a $fmMl'hr$ (whose control of certain aspects of the forces involved exceeds that of his Isi partner); and, less frequently, with the further assistance of extrauniversal beings such as the Däa'mn, whose control extends to still other areas of the spectrum.

The Isi learned early in their exploration of the $pwW'r$ that the forces they employed were extrauniversal in origin. Investigation into the source led to the discovery of parallel universes, apparently infinite in number. Virtually at the outset of this extrauniversal mapping, they encountered the Halfworld and the beings who eventually allied with them as symbionts in the Isis' practice of the *pwW'r* . . .

"My people," interjected Memphus helpfully. "We don't have a name, as you understand the concept."

"Nor planets," added Meg.

"Nor bodies," continued the cat with a superior air. "In fact, we don't exist at all, judged by any frame of reference with which you'd be familiar. You might describe us as disembodied patterns of awareness; immortal, immaterial intellects, existing without energy or matter, or need of either. It's a pleasant, introspective sort of existence, but dull. Which is why we— well, 'leaped' doesn't have much meaning when applied to nonphysical beings. But that's why we accepted with alacrity when the Isi invited us to join them as partners in the practice of the *pwW'r* and exploration of the Infinite Universes.

"Mind you, we don't actually leave our own universe to accept a *fmMl'hr* relationship with an Isi. Our manifestation here is accomplished through extension into this universe by means of long-term possession of the bodies of nonsapient life-forms."

"I wondered about that," I interjected; "an apparently terrestrial tomcat hailing from the center of the galaxy. . . ."

"Not 'apparently,'" he replied; "this body *is* from Earth. Since every point of our universe is equidistant from every point in yours, *fmMl'hrs*' hosts tend to be a varied lot."

"In fact, I know of only one adept whose *fmMl'hr's* host is native to Isis," offered Meg.

"Gothyäl," nodded the cat.

"Fafnir was a bit impulsive in selecting his host," explained Meg with a smile. "He chose a *böll'skag*. He's about two hundred yards long, has six legs, and breathes fire. Few denizens of the wilds are as carnivorous as a *böll'skag*, and they *look* it—I've known Fafnir all my life, and I *still* have to fight down an instinctive run-and-hide impulse every time I come on him without warning."

"That sounds like a personal problem," observed Memphus without sympathy; "they're *your* reflexes. Fafnir has always been a perfect gentleman. It's not his fault that your ancestors grew up in a rough neighborhood."

Meg regarded the cat thoughtfully. "You know, sometimes your tendency toward understatement can be positively awe-inspiring."

Memphus beamed.

"Other times," she continued, "it can be a real pain in the—"

"Now . . ." The cat elevated a brow in mock alarm.

Meg glared briefly; then turned back to me. "Of course Memphus would rally to Fafnir's defense: There's room enough on his back to transport a regiment, and he's always willing to carry anyone anywhere within reason—Isis is a *big* planet, and Memphus' aversion to walking is almost as legendary as his appeti—"

The cat started to interrupt, but I cut them off: "Enough! All afternoon both of you have been dropping words and names which, regardless how they're spelled, sound as if they were drawn right out of Earthly mythology, legend, and superstition. First we had '*wWyh'j*,' '*fmMl'hr*,' and 'Isis.' And then '*pwW'r*,' which sounds suspiciously like 'power'; 'Dää'mn,' which is reminiscent of 'demon'; 'Häa'l,' which is awfully close to 'Hell'; and even R'gGnrök, your galaxy-killer, is a virtual homophone for 'Ragnarök'—and I don't want even to *think* about the implications of 'Fafnir.' Practically everything you've talked about thus far—ignoring for the moment the unintentional pun—has struck a familiar chord, and *I want to know why*. The short version, please; never mind the background. And *right now*."

"Leakage," explained Meg, with a mischievous twinkle. I directed a stern look at her. "You said you wanted the short version," she protested; "that's it."

I glared; she grinned, and set about explaining the explanation: "The Isi discovered R'gGnrök some fifteen thousand years ago . . ."

"Hold it! I distinctly heard you say that you've tracked R'gGnrök on flight*s*, plural, spanning better than ten thousand years' duration. How'd you manage that if you've only *known* about it for fifteen thousand?"

"*Damn*, he's a suspicious one," muttered Memphus.

"And alert, too," added Meg, dimpling approvingly.

"There are advantages to being paranoid," I retorted humorlessly. "A paranoid is never lonely; he always knows he's the center of attention—and *this* paranoid still is waiting for an answer. . . ."

"No mystery; we looked backward in time," replied Meg, "just as every astronomer does. The difference is that ours conduct their observations by means of the viewer, one of our more useful inventions, which enables one to place a view-point literally anywhere in the universes.

"To watch an event which happened a million years ago, you place your viewpoint a million lightyears back from it; create a refracting telescope, using gravitational optics of the aperture necessary to achieve the resolution required; incorporate the appropriate level of image enhancement; and start your recorders on the spectra which will produce the information you desire."

"Oh." I shut up. Again.

"Anyway," continued Meg, concealing right manfully the bulk of her smugness, "upon discovering R'gGnrök, we went into an absolute swivet of research, trying to solve the problem. By about 10,000 B.C., we had concluded that we weren't going to be able to solve it by ourselves, had gotten the compudicters' recommendations, and had launched a search for a species of mechanists with whom to ally. And within another millenium we learned that none such existed.

"The compudicters then recommended that we select the most promising of the primitive species catalogued during the first sweep, and concentrate on helping them develop, both genetically and socially, into a mature civilization commanding an advanced, exclusively mechanistic technology, capable of joining with us as equals in our struggle to find a means of saving the galaxy.

"Further research followed; and, by about 7,000 B.C., we had determined that Earth, and *Homo sapiens*, were our best hope. Once the decision was made, we went to work upgrading Man's gene pool.

"We identified six promising bloodlines, one in each of the major continental divisions. A program of controlled breeding was instituted by means of telepathy, augmented by the $pwW'r$ to cover the distance . . ."

"You can read minds . . . ?" I cut in abruptly—then wondered why she hadn't known I was going to.

"Of course; especially if the mind is sleeping. But mental contact with a wide-awake adult subject who has never experienced rapport can be difficult. Your mind, for instance, when awake has very effective natural shielding."

I conducted a quick mental review to ensure that I was indeed wide awake.

"However"—the corners of Meg's mouth twitched but she did *not* smile—"it was easy to slip into the minds of our

sleeping subjects and plant the necessary posthypnotic suggestions. And as the general mental and physical condition of the
members of the lines improved over the centuries, so did the
species as a whole, due to frequent deliberate outcrossing.

"By the time of the Crusades, we had achieved all we could
within individual lines; and we began bringing the choicer
specimens together, merging the six lines into two. That
required more care; the original six wove in and out of the two
primaries like fibers of a thick, frizzy, stranded rope. We
outcrossed, reintroduced, line-bred, and culled."

"And finally," I guessed, "you brought my parents together
and united the two lines in me. Which, I suppose, makes me
an authentic superman . . . ?"

"Yes and no," replied Meg diffidently. "No, you are not the
apex of the pyramid. Yes, you are a superman—you're just not
as super as your children would have been had we not made a
serious mistake, the consequence of which is that we've run
out of time."

"It was a bookkeeping error," explained Memphus. "Somehow we lost track of who was where and when. By the time we
noticed what had happened, you were eleven and your
mother-in-law was about to marry the wrong man."

"I don't *have* a mother-in-law," I pointed out, possibly more
emphatically then necessary.

"On our chart you do," said Meg, smiling. "You have a wife,
too; and she's the cutest little girl you ever saw. Trouble is,
she's only about six—the result of the error.

"We managed to keep your mother-in-law from making her
tragic mistake; but it took time to turn her around and get her
married to the right man. Then, despite our prompting, they
decided to be practical and wait for a while before starting a
baby. One thing led to another; we ended up a long way
behind schedule. She should be just turning twenty-two."

"Do I know her, or her family?"

"No. But if she were the proper age, you certainly would
have heard of her. She'll be even more *terrible* a fiscal *enfant*
than you were."

"She's a lot smarter than you," interjected Memphus.

"Of course she is; she's a girl," added Meg archly. "And, just
incidentally, she also happens to be the ultimate product of a
breeding program concentrated upon developing intellectual
potential. She—

"Stop *looking* at me that way! That doesn't mean *you*— Your line is complementary; your specialty much more versatile. You are the ultimate development of breeding focused on purest, all-out survival: conspicuously affirmative, conquer-your-environment-type survival; not furtive, hide-in-a-hole-between-meals-type survival. Your every characteristic is directed toward that end: You're intelligent, resourceful, utterly determined. Physically, you *are* as close to a superman as anything this planet has produced; your strength, speed, and reflexes are unparalleled—certainly your Omniathelon Gold Medal in last year's Summer Olympics bears witness to that.

"We think those concentrated survival qualities, added to the education we'll give you, will add up to success—in spite of the fact that you're you instead of your children."

"We hope so, anyway," finished Memphis. Then he added: "She's also cuter than you. She's sweet and exquisite and about as harmless as a twenty-foot sphere of solid plutonium."

"And I hate her," said Meg suddenly. "Never mind; you've probably forgotten what the original question was; and if I stop to explain that—which I most certainly will not!—I'll forget, too."

"What question?"

"See? At any rate, it developed that a few of our subjects—enough, anyway—could sense our telepathic presence, even though we implanted suggestions only as they slept, and retained memories of the contact upon waking. Not unreasonably, they concluded that they were having spiritual experiences, divine manifestations, visitations of gods. And from the peripheral thoughts which accompany every direct message, despite our operators' best efforts to narrow down their thoughts to the precise suggestions at issue, they picked up details about our home lives. From these they manufactured an elaborate mythology; and shortly, Earth's Heaven and Hell were littered with Isi nomenclature. You think of 'Mother Earth'; we have a similarly anthropopathic designation for our own planet—and quicker than you could regret it, ancient Egypt had a shining goddess in her night skies.

"You pretty well can tell who had charge of what bloodline just by glancing through the local mythology: Uncle O'dDyn's group initiated the work in Europe. Then, of course, he had those domestic problems and had to turn it over to Cousin Z'hHootz, who got distracted by other work, so Uncle J'pPtar . . ."

"I'm sorry I asked," I interrupted.

Then a thought struck me: "With eighteen hundred years to go, why the sudden rush? Why me? And why now? Why not wait another forty years or so until this girl grows up and we've produced the superchildren you wanted?"

"We can't," replied Meg soberly. "Between the political situation and scientific progress, long-range control no longer suffices. We need to turn over direction of Earth's progress to someone right here on the scene."

"Well, now you're here," I pointed out. "I still don't understand why you need me."

"We are not of Earth. We are Isi; our mental processes and emotional reactions vary significantly from those of Earthmen. And even though the compudicters are astonishingly accurate when predicting the actions of populations, they don't do as well with individuals. In the past, despite having had access to their sleeping minds, we have guessed wrong about how certain leaders would react to specific stimuli, and unscheduled wars have resulted. In the past this was seldom serious or difficult to remedy. . . .

"However, the introduction of thermonuclear weapons has changed the complexion of the problem. Now if we err, all that we have accomplished thus far will be undone. The compudicters say that sooner or later—probably sooner—we're *going* to make another mistake; and when we do, either your civilization will go up in flames, taking our chances of survival with it, or we'll manage to stop the holocaust—but we'll be forced to use methods that will tip our hand. And once Man knows he's being manipulated, the effect on the project will be the same as if we'd allowed the bombs to fall.

"No. We need an *Earth*man; someone who knows how Earthmen think and react . . ."

"Someone with a feel for 'which way the frog is going to jump,'" interjected Memphis. "You're the only one who suspected that the balloon was about to go up in China; you're the only foreign investor who got his capital out in time. Wall Street scoffed at your warning that time; they were even cautiously skeptical about Argentina; but they were right on your heels when you pulled out of Greece and Nigeria in the nick of time. You're the world's leading expert when it comes to prognosticating the actions of fanatical governments."

Well, even though that made a certain amount of sense, I

might have pursued it still further had not an even more pressing question suddenly occurred to me: "What's my 'wife's' name?"

"Jennifer Smith," replied Meg.

"Where does she live?"

"None of your business."

"My wife's address is none of my business . . . ?"

"No. She's only six, remember? But she was bred to find you irresistible, the ultimate male—and vice-versa. It would scramble both your psyches to meet now. The mutual attraction is inborn, instinctive, and will be there regardless of her age. You'd both find the experience extremely frustrating."

"Hmm-m-m. . . ." Given that explanation, Meg probably was right. Still, Jennifer Smith was destined to grow up to be the Perfect Woman. It was hard not to be curious. . . .

But then something else started to bother me. For a moment I couldn't put my finger precisely where the itch lay; then the pieces clicked: "Wait a minute. What about about Memphis? He's been a *fmMl'hr* for only a little over fifty years; only since your birth, I guess . . ."

The cat nodded, already smirking; obviously anticipating the question, waiting to see just how sincere I was about making a fool of myself. (Well, Grandpa always said that if a thing was worth doing at all, it was worth doing properly.) I pressed on resolutely:

". . . so how come he has the same name as the Egyptian cat god? He wasn't even around then."

"Because he has a poisonous sense of humor; that's how come. He adopted that name, I suspect, for the sole reason that the Egyptians dreamed up *their* Memphis independently. Right there is probably as concise a synopsis of Memphis' personality as you're likely to find. . . ."

It occurred to me then that this discussion, while fascinating, wasn't doing much to acquaint me with Meg's and Memphis' capabilities, and how I might combine them with Earth's science to get us to Isis. I suggested as much.

Whereupon, silence fell, growing more pregnant by the moment. . . .

TO: Project Director/Monitor's Log.
FROM: K'nNtïkï, Tenth Order.
SUBJECT: Project *Extremis*.

Subject Cory has received and accepted our team's "explanation" of our plans for him. They concluded theirpresentation by maneuvering Cory into a proper state of mind in which to discover for himself just how immediately his responsibilities are to commence.

It likewise appears that Agent Megonthalyä is nearing the moment when she will take those steps necessary to establish rapport with Cory. One hopes that he will find the experience worth its eventual cost.

CHAPTER 9

I regarded them quizzically. Meg's lower lip was trembling again. Memphus apparently was lost in dissecting a sand flea with his claws. "I said I need to find out what you guys can do so I can start thinking about how your capabilities might dovetail with whatever I can come up with from Earth's science base." The silence deepened. Meg's chin quivered.

Suspicion welled up darkly within me. "You *can* do stuff, can't you?" I prodded. I was rewarded by further silence. "*Can't* you . . . ?"

Meg returned my look with the expression of a three-year-old expecting a reprimand. "N-not exactly," she replied. "At least not right away."

"What's that supposed to mean?"

"Well-l-l . . ." Meg began diffidently, "you know how interuniversal shunts are." I didn't, but it hardly seemed worth mentioning at this point. "Naturally, we couldn't bring any nonliving material—you probably noticed how I was dressed when I arrived. . . ." Indeed I had. "Even my hair—when we left, it was fanny-length; all but this stubble sheared off midtranslation at the point at which the proportion of living cells dropped below the critical level."

I wouldn't have called Meg's hair "stubble"; it was a lovely inch-long golden down which stirred to the bidding of every faint zephyr. . . .

And it was quite as distracting as the rest of her. With an effort, I wrenched my attention back to the question at hand: "*And* . . . ?"

"And"—sniffle—"so we came empty-handed. I had to leave

everything at home—all my equipment. I don't even have my *mMj'q wWn'dt.* . . ."

"A *wWyh'j* without a *mMj'q wWn'dt* is in much the same position as a bare-handed Earthly physician," finished Memphus. "She has the education and training of a *wWyh'j*, with practically no way to use it."

"The ambient *mMj'q* flow here is very low," added Meg apologetically. "There's some; that's how I was able to paralyze you. But there is so little *wWn'dt* on this planet! Only a very few crystals of useful size exist at all, and they're in their natural state; and all are so far away that I barely can sense them, much less draw on them."

"And . . . ?" I swear—it was like pulling teeth!

"So first we have to find a *wWn'dt*, cut it, and activate it," she responded.

"Is *that* all," I sighed. "Why didn't you say so in the first place . . . ?"

Meg's mouth was open to reply but I cut her off before she could get the first word out: "Never mind; let's not waste any more time. Where do we find a raw *wWn'dt*? Just what Earthly substance does 'monolithic corundum' translate into?"

"That *is* English," she responded, looking perplexed. "You mean you never heard of it?"

"'Monolithic' I know, and 'corundum' has a faintly familiar ring; but together they draw a blank. Let's have a look in the *McGraw-Hill Technical Dictionary*." We did so, and . . .

"A *ruby* . . . ?"

"Of course." Meg evinced impatience; after all, it was so *obvious*. "Why? Is that a problem?"

"That depends on what you consider a 'useful' size."

"Oh, about like so." She held her hands about four inches apart.

"That could be a problem."

"Why?"

"The ruby trees here don't bear fruit of that size."

"Sarcasm ill becomes you. There are several *wWn'dts* on Earth of a sufficient size for our purposes."

"Where?"

"Well . . ." Meg paused. "You have a map of the world here, don't you?"

Of course I did. I was born with an insatiable curiosity; one which may waken at any time of any day, pointed in any direction. Even my vacation island cottage contained a reference library measured in tons.

It also boasted a four-foot world globe. Meg stopped before it, wearing a thoughtful expression. She appeared to withdraw into herself momentarily; then she reemerged and pointed out the deeply buried locations of some of the "bigger ones": the summits of certain well-known mountains—Jötenheimen, Olympus, Sinai. . . .

Somehow that failed to surprise me, but I asked anyway. Meg explained: Long-range subconscious manipulation is easier and more effective if the operator can obtain a last-minute, on-site boost, so to speak, from a $wWn'dt$—even a raw $wWn'dt$—in the vicinity of the subject. Naturally the Isi tended to concentrate much of their efforts in those areas.

However, one of the qualities they were breeding for was the ESP potential so vital to the mastery of the $pwW'r$. As the bloodlines developed, certain subjects began to perceive a hint of *something* emanating from the mountaintops in question. And since the Isi operators themselves were conscious of the local source of the $mMj'q$ flow on which they drew, their subjects not unreasonably began to equate that inexplicable radiance with the homes of the godlike beings who visited them in dreams, bringing counsel and wisdom. One thing led to another without detectable lost motion: Legends and myths were born which took on lives of their own; positive feedback set in, with elaboration upon elaboration. The rest is history.

"Unfortunately, most of the $wWn'dts$ on this planet are just about inaccessible," Meg added. "They're buried under thousands of feet of solid rock.

"All but this one," she continued cheerfully. "Right here is a fairly good-sized $wWn'dt$, and it feels as if it's lying under no more than a shallow covering of mud and water. We shouldn't have any trouble getting to it."

"'Trouble,'" I observed, mostly to myself, "is a relative term." Meg's fingertip had dead-centered fifteen-thousand-foot-high Seling Tsho, a thirty-mile-long lake situated in the heart of occupied Tibet.

CHAPTER 10

Getting to Seling Tsho was not as straightforward a project as one might assume. Complications loomed at every step.

First and foremost of which was the fact that, following truly promising beginnings in the '80s and early '90s, China's relations with the rest of the world—and the U.S. in particular—had deteriorated steadily. In fact, during the most recent diplomatic flap, I barely had managed to yank out my invested capital before all foreign businesses and accounts were seized. Most of my fellow investors hadn't heeded my warning and lost everything. Not a few lost lives.

As a consequence, Red China had no diplomatic relations with anyone at the moment; and they were annoyed with me personally over the fact that, not only had I gotten my money out before they could grab it, but I had issued the warning in the first place. So the wide-eyed, smiling tourist gambit was out. It would have to be a covert operation. . . .

And, despite my very best efforts, I still hadn't a hint of how to incorporate Meg's and Memphus' remaining feeble control of the $pwW'r$ into my planning—I had no idea what they could or couldn't do, which struck me as really inefficient tactics. Lounging on the porch, I volunteered as much.

Meg took longer to reply than I expected. I glanced at her more closely. She wore a small, secret smile. I glanced at Memphus. The tip of the cat's tail twitched slightly once and was still.

"There is a solution," Meg began diffidently; "but you've already given indications of not liking it."

"I didn't eith— Uh, how?"

"You reacted like an Old Tyme Movie ingénue to the appearance of a mouse when I mentioned mental contact. But the solution to your problem is the merging of our minds so that each of us can discover and understand the other's capabilities and limitations. We need to go *en rapport*."

A wordless scream of primal protest boiled up from some unsuspected, dark, ugly place deep inside me. I bit it off before it could clear the tip of my tongue and swallowed it with difficulty. Then, astonished by the vehemence of the reaction, I turned my perceptions inward and dug for the cause.

It didn't take long. The answer was obvious, and it was the kind of self-discovery I could have done without.

I took a long breath, held it, and released it slowly before speaking. I didn't *want* to speak.

"That was a knee-jerk reaction," I said uncomfortably. "But it was a *valid* knee jerk; it was an accurate reflection of how strongly I feel about someone poking around in my mind.

"And . . ." I hesitated, then plunged on, ". . . with the best of reasons:

"I've always done my best to follow the Golden Rule; I've never intentionally hurt anyone unnecessarily. But those are my party manners; the thinnest public veneer. They overlie a core of the ugliest, most violently primitive impulses ever to curdle your blood. I think a lot of thoughts that I'm not proud of, but I can't help it: I'm an Earthman—at the center of my soul lives an utterly selfish, totally amoral savage. He has absolutely no self-control; his instant reaction to frustration or opposition of any kind is an urge to drape the offender's guts all over the landscape. His response to seeing something he wants in someone else's possession is a flash of unhesitatingly murderous covetousness.

"And his reaction to the sight of *you*," I finished doggedly, "is a raw, panting, undisguised lust; neither diluted nor distracted by any interest in, or questions of, consent."

"And you were worried that this might be difficult," whispered Memphus.

Meg's eyes were bright and there were spots of color in her cheeks as she gestured for the cat to be quiet. "Peter, *every*one has thoughts like that. They're not something to be ashamed of; the fact that you overcome them in your behavior toward others should be a source of pride."

"Possibly. That doesn't make me want to hang them on the clothesline for the world to admire."

"No one will see them unless you choose to call attention to them. Every Isi knows where those dark corners are located and what they contain; we all have similar faults. But none of us would invade anyone's privacy unnecessarily, ever. Even while manipulating the sleeping minds of your ancestors, we avoided those areas whenever possible.

"In fact, only through achieving rapport can you ensure that that part of you never will come to anyone's attention without your knowledge and consent. Only through rapport can you learn to control your own mind fully; to erect barriers around those portions of your soul into which you don't want anyone to see—indeed, you'll be *expected* to do that, as a matter of elementary courtesy: No one *wants* to see into those corners of your id. We all have them, of course, just as we all have to fart—but we don't have to demonstrate either fact in public!

"And once you've achieved rapport, and learned the basics of managing your mind, I can show you how to identify and unlock your own latent *gnää'qs,* or talents, and teach you to use them. You are the penultimate product of centuries of breeding; you have mental abilities beyond your wildest imaginings, which likewise need to be taken into account in your planning.

"And finally, once we're *en rapport* you'll have a clearer understanding of my *gnää'qs,* and my command of the *pwW'r,* as seen through my eyes."

I had to admit that Meg had assembled a pretty convincing list of arguments (which inward concession brought still another protest boiling out of the primitive depths of my subconscious [my conscious mind wasn't too thrilled either]). She'd covered all the bases; I couldn't think of a legitimate objection. I still didn't like the idea, of course, but . . .

"All right," I sighed. "Let's get it over with. What do I do?"

"That will become apparent directly," said Memphus enigmatically, rising and strolling into the house. "I think I'll take a nap," he called over his shoulder. "For about three hours."

I looked after him in perplexity. "What was that about?"

"This," said Meg matter-of-factly, rising from the couch and pulling me to my feet.

"I beg your pardon . . . ?" I stood open-mouthed as she detrunksed me in a single smooth motion and slipped the improvised tee-shirt dress over her head.

She pushed me back onto the couch and planted herself on top of me. "There are only two ways to achieve initial rapport," she explained cheerfully, "and one works only if undertaken before puberty. This is the *other* approach. . . ."

Becky Two-Knives might have had second thoughts about my "usual pattern with attractive females" had she been watching during the next few minutes. But somehow this was different. . . .

"But we hardly *know* each other," I puffed inanely, trying without measurable success to fend off some of the pettings and nuzzlings. Meg was incredibly strong for her size.

"This will remedy that, too," she breathed huskily. Her

voice came from deep in her throat; it carried overtones of a growl. Then she bit my ear. Hard.

I caught her in my arms. I was given scarcely enough time in which to wonder if that mightn't have been a tactical error before I found myself extraordinarily involved with a small pair of soft, warm, clinging lips and a burning little tongue which seemed to have a life of its own. There was a roaring sound in my head which probably came from the blazing wreckage of my self-control and good intentions: The Savage Within threw off his shackles and, beating his chest, pawed the ground, bellowed his challenge of male dominance, and reached for his woman.

The world shrank and closed in upon itself until there were only me and a small, writhing, warm body which had entirely too many arms and teeth and hands and breasts and lips and legs and tongues and nails. And just as the whole universe was preparing to fly into uncountable little slivers of ecstasy, there soared across the sky of my soul a tiny blazing comet of radiating joy which burst in an irresistible, undeniable explosion of unbearable pleasure. The glowing fragments spread out, settled down over, and soaked into my own happiness and, with it, became One. . . .

Much later we lay in the warm sun, cooled by a gentle breeze, listening to faint echoes from a distant thundershower far out over the Caribbean.

"That was really wonderful," I thought. "That was worth the trip all by itself. Hey, what's this about a trip? I must be cracking up. No, you're not. Yes, I am. No, you're not. Great, now I'm arguing with myself. No, you're not."

Abruptly I sat up. "Hey!" I sputtered aloud, staring down at Meg. "I didn't think that . . . !"

"Of course you didn't, silly," said the little voice in my mind; "I did."

Meg smiled and stretched luxuriously. Then she growled and reached for me again.

TO: Project Director/Monitor's Log.
FROM: L'qQethonl, Fourth Order.
SUBJECT: Project *Extremis*.

Agent Megonthalyä has succeeded in establishing rapport with Subject Cory. She accomplished this through the time-honored method prescribed for opening the mind of nontelepathic adults.

A complete copy of the subject's intellect, together with his total memory to that point, now resides within the agent's brain. Likewise, the germ-plasm trap with which she was fitted operated properly, and Cory's genetic blueprint now resides safely within the stasis container incorporated in it. Should his efforts be terminated prematurely, and if his performance to that point justifies the effort, we now possess everything required to reconstitute him *in toto* for future use. This, of course, will be of no benefit to the present Cory. . . .

Exploration, evaluation, and cataloguing by the agent of the subject's mental qualities will follow, together with instruction regarding their use. It is anticipated that, despite the limitations inherent in his Earthly upbringing, a variety of heretofore unknown, potentially useful *gnää'qs* will be found lurking in the untrained depths of his brain. It will be interesting to learn the degree to which Cory has been able to overcome his environment in this respect. It should be equally interesting to ascertain how readily he employs these *gnää'qs* under the stressful conditions he so soon must face. . . .

Far faster than words, Meg's unsubvocalized thoughts unraveled in my mind: At puberty the mind closes over its unused portions. If telepathy has not been learned by then, mere desire to learn and cooperation no longer are sufficient to achieve initial contact. An invasion is required, an all-out mental thrust against the mind's unconscious shields, delivered when those shields are weakest; at a moment when the soul itself is mourning its isolation: That brief, timeless eternity when lovers strain toward oneness, sharing the ultimate joy in their physical union, is such a moment. For a period measured in fractions, spirits yearn toward one another; at that moment, if one happens to be a skilled therapist, he or she can break through.

"That was you," I thought, "that incredible, wonderful doubling of sensation. That was you, crashing my shields, entering my mind. I felt your sensations reinforcing mine."

Her thoughts were gentle, contented, and—to my astonishment—glowing with unreserved love.

The phenomenon was sufficiently startling that I looked

more closely at it. In the process, I caught a glimpse of my own feelings mirrored there—and they matched . . . !

As Meg watched, amused but radiating happiness, I turned my perceptions inward again and performed a quick self-appraisal. It was true: Meg's happiness was utterly indispensable to, and indistinguishable from, my own. As was mine to hers. And if that wasn't love, it was an entirely satisfactory substitute.

(Damn—talk about whirlwind romances . . . !)

Meg's reply enveloped me like sunlight: "Yes," she purred contentedly; "and I felt yours added to mine. The whole is infinitely greater than the sum of the parts."

I agreed—not that an affirmative expression of my opinion was necessary: At that moment we were a single mind with two bodies.

At first all we shared was love and contentment; it was quite a while before either of us mustered (or was capable of mustering) any interest in anything else. Eventually, however, Meg inserted a tendril of thought down through the labyrinthine reaches of my mind and showed me where the controls for my own mental shields were located. Deftly she showed me how to blank off certain areas of privacy; how to seal my thoughts against intrusion.

Too, she showed me how, with sufficient effort, the minds of the nontelepathic might be read, and even, to some degree, controlled. And when I projected a measure of Dark Suspicion, she all but turned her psyche inside out to prove that she had not attempted to control me. "What you ran into," she added in self-satisfied afterthought, "was pure sex appeal. That was a good, clean, wholesomely sexy seduction. You never had a chance!"

I deliberated briefly; then conceded the point with grace (hardly being in a position to argue. . . .).

Thereafter Meg set about helping me locate and awaken my latent *gnää'qs*. In the process we discovered that I could feel planetary magnetic lines. Not even the Isi could do that!

But one thing I could *not* do was perceive the *mMj'q* flow. . . . Meg tried "literally everything in the book" (whatever that might be); and I did my level best to try to follow her as she performed each step in the process. But in vain; I simply could not perceive whatever it was that she held and manipulated with her mind.

Once we thought I had it: Casting out with my mind, I felt

something stirring within my mental grasp. And whatever it
was, it had many of the characteristics of Meg's description of
the feel of $mMj'q$. So with her guidance, I created an
immaterial channel into which I guided the particle flow. Once
I had that under control, I forced the channel into a curve;
bending it gradually at first, then tighter and tighter; ultimately closing the circle altogether to form a $t'lLiSs'mn$, the
tool which constitutes the very foundation of the practice of
the $pwW'r$.

Thereafter, bracing the walls of the torus ever more firmly
against the mounting internal pressures, I fed in more and
more of the omnipresent background flux which I took to be
$mMj'q$. Meg watched in growing excitement as the velocity of
the trapped particles mounted.

Presently she declared the volume and velocity sufficient for
training purposes. In fact, she informed me proudly, the forces
concentrated inside this $t'lLiSs'mn$ now exceeded anything
she and Memphus *together* had been able to achieve since
their arrival on Earth.

The next step was to teach me to control and manipulate the
energies raging around and around inside the torus. Carefully,
following Meg's step-by-step instructions, I constructed an
immaterial, valved nozzle on the outer rim; the aperture
departed on a tangent from the direction of the flow's rotation.

Preliminarily we pointed the nozzle out to sea. Then, at
Meg's direction, I snapped the valve open. The intangible
mechanism functioned precisely according to plan; it took
probably a nanosecond to open completely. The result,
however, bore no resemblance to Meg's expectations, and
startled both of us just about out of our skins:

With a clap of thunder that would have loosened our fillings
if we'd had any, the total accumulation of energy trapped
inside the $t'lLiSs'mn$ discharged in a single pulse. A painfully
brilliant shaft of something which might have been mistaken
for lightning, had it not been arrow-straight and uniform in
diameter, flared into being at the nozzle's mouth and lanced
across the harbor and out to sea. A huge geyser of steam
erupted where it intersected the surface, becoming visible as
it cooled, mounting into the sky as a vast, fleecy white
mushroom. . . .

Meg and I stared at each other through orange afterimages.
Her reaction was a single wordless burst of incredulity: "*!!!!!?*"
(Which summed up my sentiments exactly.)

Working slowly and very carefully, one step at a time, we reconstructed the experiment, trying to figure out what might have gone wrong (or right; Meg simply *didn't know*).

At length, we determined that I had mistaken the ebb and flow of the ever-present atmospheric electrical convection for $mMj'q$. With that fact to work from, it didn't take long to figure out the rest: Quite by accident, I had employed the $t'lLiSs'mn$ as a particle accelerator, a cyclotron! And despite being fabricated from the intangible substance of the mind and spanning only about two feet, it was a very efficient cyclotron indeed: To produce so glaringly visible an electron beam and so dramatic a disruption of the target over such a distance required astronomical voltages.

This development startled Meg even more than it did me: The Isi routinely worked with electricity; but only by means of the $pwW'r$—I had handled it *raw*. It never would have occurred to an Isi to attempt to control electricity in the same fashion as he did $mMj'q$—it never would have occurred to an Isi that it *could* be manipulated that way. Something akin to awe began to color her attitude toward me.

But she wasted no time trying out the new technique herself. Shortly she was rewarded by a satisfying clap of thunder as her own bolt of lightning blazed out to sea. (Impressing Meg is one thing; intimidating her quite another.)

The lessons concluded, finally, as I learned that, in fact, to this point I did not "know the back of my own hand"—I didn't know *anything* about my body, beyond a few basic functions incorrectly learned in a neglected childhood. But under Meg's tutelage I acquired conscious, precise, cell-by-cell control over every last muscle, nerve, gland, duct, and follicle; a faculty which enabled one to knit bones in an hour; mend torn flesh in minutes, without scarring; and regenerate lost tissue, or even whole limbs.

It wasn't until probably a year later that I realized that practical immortality had been bestowed upon me at that moment; that I had no need to go to Isis for it. But by then it no longer mattered; I would have followed Meg to the end of the universe—any universe.

Or beyond. . . .

TO: Project Director/Monitor's Log.
FROM: Gothyäl, Tenth Order.
SUBJECT: Project *Extremis*.

As predicted, Agent Megonthalyä has discovered within Subject Cory's mind unprecedented *gnäa'qs*. Electricity—who would have anticipated that the man would be capable of direct manipulation of electricity? In the entire recorded history of our species, no Isi ever has accomplished that—nor even considered the possibility, despite the fact that Agent Megonthalyä's example has demonstrated that we possess the capability as well. It is this operator's recommendation that a high priority be given to watching for, observing, and evaluating new-found abilities which Cory may discover for compatibility with our own metabolic limitations.

It should be noted at this point as well that, with the completion of this phase of her duties, Agent Megonthalyä's conditioning has passed a critical test: She was genuinely surprised at being unable to teach Cory to perceive and manipulate the background *mMj'q* flow. But for that conditioning, she would have known that it is fundamentally impossible to teach an adult—indeed, to teach anyone past the age of puberty—to perceive and control the flow of *mMj'q*.

CHAPTER 11

Originally, while contemplating the difficulties of securing the *wWn'dt* from Tibet, I assumed I'd have to enlist a dozen or so well-compensated volunteers from the intelligence and commando-tactics specialists among my security people. But rapport, and an understanding of Meg's and Memphus' abilities (to say nothing of my own) brought a fresh perspective to the problem: As competent, sophisticated, and deadly as Becky's people were, they'd only get in the way in this operation.

Meg, Memphus, and I would go alone. The three of us could move more quickly, attract less attention—and would be free to take advantage of tactics which would require . . . well . . . a lot of explanation if anyone else were involved.

Becky could tell from the outset that Something Was Afoot, of course. She knew how obsessive I was about pretending that I was alone on the island; as well as how downright adamant I'd always been about refusing contact with the outside world while on vacation. So having me show up on her doorstep with Meg and Memphus in tow and demand access to the communications center sent her into such a tizzy that she actually asked, "Boss, is something going on that I should know about?" I reassured her to the extent possible, and placed my calls.

Quite apart from annoying her personally, being left out troubled Becky's finely honed police instincts, and sorely tested her objectivity and vaunted professional disinterest regarding matters outside security. (Actually, she quite properly regarded *everything* I did as bearing on security.) And the prospect of me operating, not only without her there to protect me but actually inside the Bamboo Curtain (which destination she had no trouble deducing from the spy-satellite maps and intelligence reports I had requested), did not make her happy. . . .

My corporate officers received the commando-, camping-, and motorcycling-equipment order with their usual aplomb, and didn't even quibble over the impossibility of locating and delivering it all to the island within the time allotted. On the other hand, the supertanker-full of Number Two diesel and gasoline/oil two-stroke mixture that I wanted standing offshore by week's end, equipped with high-capacity onboard pumping gear and sufficient hose to reach ashore, did create a stir—as did my plans for it. . . .

Now, one learns *not* to ask one's billionaire employer about obviously revolutionary developments before he's ready to talk about them—and learns it promptly or finds oneself otherwise employed. Wherefore, though Becky and the rest of my people wore increasingly strained expressions during the three days it took to pump the *Exxon Patrician's* entire diesel payload into *Capital Venture's* twin four-hundred-gallon tanks (and the eighty-foot-long yacht continued to float at a constant level even as the sixth-of-a-mile-long bulk of the tanker rose higher and ever higher in the water), they contained their curiosity; even managing to hold their tongues while pouring roughly ten thousand gallons of two-stroke mixture into the three-gallon tank of my favorite trials bike. (It would have held more, but a half-million-mile nonstop cruising reserve seemed adequate.)

I was proud of my people.

I was also profoundly relieved. . . .

An explanation would have been awkward, at the very least:

While few mathematicians would have had a problem with a container that was bigger inside than out, it wasn't a concept which translated readily into laymanese—and not even a mathematician (unless he happened to be proficient in Isi math) would have greeted without protest knowledge that those tanks weighed and massed the same full as when empty.

Likewise, I deemed it a kindness not to let Becky know that Meg and Memphus had tightened the molecular bonds of the materials of which the boat's and bike's moving parts and structural components were composed. The result was vastly tougher, harder versions of the same substances, virtually eliminating the possibility of mechanical failure.

Becky's worldwide reputation in forensics was founded on a Ph.D. in chemistry, and her knowledge of weaponry and armor grew out of an equally solid basis in metallurgy. These modifications, involving as they did alterations to the fundamental nature of matter itself, would have disturbed her at least as much as the apparently bottomless and patently gravity- and mass-immune fuel tanks troubled the first-class amateur physicist in her—just as the facts underlying the enhanced reliability of the electronic gear would have bothered her extensive electrical engineering background, had she known about them.

(Rebecca Two-Knives was expensive, but a *bargain*.)

However. . . . One of the problems with employing people whose talents and training render them indispensable is that their responsibilities require them, from time to time, to give *you* orders—particularly in the case of security. Becky was the best counterintelligence/antiterrorist/security operative in the world. Period. She knew it, and knew I knew it. And from the moment that I blocked her inquiry into the question of how Meg got on the island, I had known that it was only a matter of time before she had her revenge. What I did not expect was the manner in which it arrived:

"If you *must* sneak into Tibet," Becky observed in tones of chill neutrality, shortly before we departed, "you need a thorough medical exam, an update on all your immunizations, and some prophylactic medication. Human hookworm, for instance, is rampant in the area."

Of course I didn't need all that: If a hookworm tried to bite me, I'd exercise the control which I now possessed over every cell in my body and absorb the little varmint for his protein content. Unfortunately, that was something else I preferred not to explain to Becky. And without the explanation, the only way out would be to invoke my overriding authority and refuse—

Which I knew better than to try: That would have been the last straw; she'd have quit on me for sure. So I yielded to the inevitable and stopped in to see the island's resident company physician . . .

Who promptly stuck me with the largest needle I've ever had the bad fortune to encounter on a professional basis. There was the usual battery of overseas shots that I'd become accustomed to in my travels, of course. But that last one—it had to be three-sixteenths of an inch thick!

"Damn!" I gasped as the doctor drove it into my thigh. "What's that one for—apart from transfiguring my soul . . . ?"

Becky was there, of course, and answered for him. "It's a special prophylactic targeted at some of the more serious problems you're apt to run into over there," she explained solicitously. "Bet it hurts like the dickens," she added with a feral expression which was supposed to represent a sympathetic smile. (But no one—least of all someone who knew her as well as I did—would have been fooled. She knew it, and she knew I knew she knew it.)

My executive staff, on the other hand, didn't even try to conceal their relief over the news that I planned to extend my vacation. Nothing personal, of course, but the benefits flowing from my vacations were bidirectional: They enjoyed the break from the tensions surrounding my kamikaze investment technique every bit as much as I did. Probably more. Almost certainly more.

CHAPTER 12

I had had *Capital Venture* built during my nautical Sturm und Drang period several years before. The folks at Huckins were ecstatic over the prospect of resurrecting their classic World War II quadraconic PT hull; especially when I made it clear that the superstructure, while embodying the detail changes necessary to provide comfortable accommodations, was to retain as much of the military "look" as possible. With those instructions, the builders outdid themselves; even retaining what, at first glance, one could mistake for torpedo tubes—storage cannisters, actually, which contained ground tackle, inflatable dinghies, scuba and snorkling gear, a folding cargo hoist, deck furniture, lines, docking gear, and the like. Plus it would have taken a naval war buff to detect the slightly lengthened and elevated rdofline of the forward deckhouse which made possible standing headroom inside the spacious main salon. Indeed, the only detail which unmistakably betrayed *Venture* as nonkosher was the massive outdrive units jutting from the stern, making possible the aft engine installation which transformed what had been an engine room in the original PTs into roomy midships sleeping quarters for several guests, with the master stateroom almost all the way aft, where the hull's motion at speed was minimized.

With preparations complete, we took *Capital Venture* out to sea. I advanced the throttles to their stops, circled around the end of the island, and steadied down on course for Gibraltar.

Five days later, with the upper reaches of the Bramuputra River fast becoming too shallow for navigation, even with the outdrives tilted up until only half the propellers' diameter remained submerged, we put in at a Pakistani river village with an unpronounceable name and hired a man to serve as anchor watch in our absence.

During the interview Meg, Memphus, and I managed between us to zap him into a trance state. Once he was under, Meg demonstrated how to implant telepathic posthypnotic suggestions approaching the level of compulsion. By the time she finished, Sajid would have died to protect *Venture*.

"Mind you," Meg cautioned before we wakened him, "this technique is of limited usefulness. He will carry out his programming until I release him. But to anyone who knows him at all would, he'll seem preoccupied with his responsibilities to a degree approaching obsession.

"It would be impossible, for instance, to reshape a government this way. It would be pointless to impose such control on an official who, apart from performing the task you've given him, must continue to perform his everyday duties without attracting attention. His abnormal behavior would render suspect any suggestions or orders he might issue involving sweeping changes in policy or ideology."

I pondered briefly. "I suppose this explains past reports of 'possessions'?"

"No," replied Meg firmly. "It's been thousands of years since we used it on anyone on Earth."

Assembling our supplies for the next phase of the trip, we secured them to the luggage rack now mounted over the rear wheel of the bike. I unlocked the Boston Whaler from the davits and lowered it into the water; then deployed the cargo hoist and gingerly lowered the motorcycle into it. Sajid helped me manhandle the bike over the side once we reached shore (I welcomed his aid: I was still moving a little cautiously; even after a week, that whopping prophylactic injection in my thigh continued to ache). Thereafter he returned to the ship, where he hoisted the Whaler back aboard and stood watching dully as we headed up what passed for a trail thereabouts, bound for what once had been the tiny independent kingdom of Sikkim (swallowed not long ago, together with Nepal, by India), perched on the flanks of the Himalayas.

CHAPTER 13

Bamboo Curtain border security was handled somewhat differently along the Himalayas. While the character of the terrain precluded a conventionally well-defended (by Peking's reckoning) militarized zone, the mountains themselves constituted a most effective natural barrier against invasion. Military installations along this border tended to be small; duties limited to monitoring the few trails leading over the passes. The precipitate slopes in between received little attention beyond an occasional patrol far too busy staying alive to worry about much else.

The military planners of the People's Republic of China had a pretty fair intelligence service; they kept a sharp eye on the U.S.'s military/industrial complex, ever alert for developments which might suggest potential threats to their security.

They might have done better to read the sports pages. . . .

Motorcycling, in those days, was one of my primary passions. I raced Grand Prix (as my executive staff huddled nervously, clicking beads and clutching to their bosoms copies of trust agreements which would come into effect In The Event Of), enduros, motocross, and—my absolute favorite—competed in trials.

Trials riding was a uniquely "British" sport originally, though by then increasingly popular worldwide. It consisted of pitting a man and his motorcycle against the terrain, a stopwatch—and himself. *Precision* riding was the object; speed, while a factor, was a secondary consideration: The rider was required to complete a demanding series of special stages (at patently impossible average speeds, true), all while remaining within a narrow corridor delineated by strings—without removing his feet from the pegs.

Lateness at checkpoints was of course penalized. However, merciless, gimlet-eyed judges scrutinized every inch of each rider's progress through the special stages; and much heavier penalties were assessed each time a rider was forced to touch a foot, or feet, to the ground: typically, five points for a minor steadying "dab," ten for a firm "push," twenty for a "stop-and-brace," fifty for using both feet while stopped, a hundred for violating the course's borders (and a whole bunch for landing on his head).

Naturally the organizers (spawned in Hell, each and every one of them) rivaled one another in their efforts to search out the most "challenging" terrain across which to set up the special stages (and prayed for bad weather—nothing made a trials organizer happier than rain [unless he could arrange for an unseasonable winter storm, with ten-foot visibility in horizontal driving sleet and drifting snow!]).

Routinely, a twenty- to thirty-inch-wide course required a rider to work his way across the fifty-degree incline of a muddy, boulder-strewn hillside; balance across a flood-swollen brook on a foot-thick log (bumping over the broken-off stub of a branch projecting upward at the midpoint); execute a right-angle corner bisected by a two-foot crevasse; claw his way up an icy, sixty-degree slope littered with loose rocks; employ momentum to scale a ten-foot vertical cliff, barely four feet beyond the crest of which lurked back-to-back opposing ninety-degree turns—which exited into a checkpoint manned by personnel wearing the solicitous expressions of wolves inventorying a flock of sheep.

Hosted by a different country each year, the pinnacle of this celebration of self-flagellation, staged by the most diabolical organizers, was the European Six-Day Trials. Grands Prix, motocrosses, and enduros I won regularly; but despite being able to afford the very best equipment and support personnel, endless practice, and the mental and physical attributes the Isi had bred into me, it took two years even to place in the Six-Day, and another to win it.

Our transportation for this expedition was one of my favorite trials motorcycles, which had come into the world as a stock Yamaha factory team bike, inherently competitive right out of the box. However, "stock" is an imprecise term, and it distressed me to see my crew's creative urges frustrated; so after evaulating new bikes in an as-delivered condition, I always turned them over to my boys and girls with instructions to enjoy themselves within the limits of the rules (in other words, no outright cheating). The resultant machines were physically indistinguishable from factory stock, and every part "miked" within specifications—as postcompetition teardowns proved repeatedly. However, they boasted high-speed cornering stability and traction virtually identical to that of my best motocross and enduro bikes—without the usual corresponding loss of low-speed maneuverability—appreciably more powerful, more fade-resistant braking; and smoother, more precisely controllable engine response at very low RPMs, coupled with an increase in both bottom-end torque and peak horsepower.

So mounted, I had beaten the socks off the Yamaha factory team (and everybody else as well) probably three times out of seven for the last several years on a worldwide basis.

Arriving at the Sikkim/China border we concealed ourselves in a cluster of boulders and donned our disguises. These were quite convincing, consisting as they did, of genuine Chinese Army uniforms—and an Oriental appearance which came from within. . . .

"You're not serious!" was Meg's initial reaction when I broached the subject. This was followed, after a moment's reflection, by: "Now, why didn't *I* think of that . . . ?"

I didn't answer; I was thinking much the same thing myself. It seemed so obvious, and the Isi had possessed the technique for . . . well, for a *long* time. I wondered whether the explanation mightn't be that racial mind block Memphus had mentioned previously: the inability of the Isi mind to function in certain areas. If so, maybe saving the galaxy wasn't going to prove as difficult as it first appeared. Heaven only knew what other obvious approaches they might have overlooked. . . .

"Could be," observed a little voice inside my head. "Let's hope so anyway." I glanced up, startled. Meg smiled—then laughed outright, watching my dawning chagrin upon realizing that she had been following my thoughts in all their brutal frankness.

She covered my mouth with her hand and buried my mental apologies under a flood of understanding love. Between the two, I found myself effectively and quite pleasantly silenced. "Don't let it bother you," she soothed verbally. "You found telepathy relatively late in life; it's not easy to remember to keep your shields up all the time unless you're specifically looking for company."

"Actually," she added mentally, moving closer and putting her arms around me, "even your unguarded thoughts are pretty nice." She replaced her hand with her mouth.

Memphus's thought intruded: "And he's got great deltoids, too. Look, I know you two are about ninety-eight percent hormones by weight; but do you suppose we can defer their interaction until we've finished this expedition and have made it back to somewhere offering something approximating safety?"

A single mind glared momentarily with two pairs of eyes; but then we remembered Memphus' position. . . .

(Only recently had I learned the full extent of the risk a member of Memphus' race accepts when it [at home they're androgynous] volunteers for *fmMl'hr* service; knowledge which did much to soften my attitude toward the crusty extrauniversal: Establishing initial possession and control of a host is a complex and difficult process; disengaging from one even more so. It hadn't happened often, but it *had* happened—and certainly it could happen again: The sudden, violent destruction of a *fmMl'hr's* host meant, almost inevitably, the end of the Halfworlder itself—a not-inconsiderable gamble for an otherwise immortal being. . . .)

Meg and I took a collective deep breath, forced our heart rates to slow, and got to work.

TO: Project Director/Monitor's Log.
FROM: T'dDalk, Seventh Degree.
SUBJECT: Project *Extremis*.

A *most* unanticipated development! We have debated the likelihood of Subject Cory possessing useful *gnäa'qs* despite the restrictions of his developmental environment, and certainly the conjecture has been borne out by discovery of his ability to control electricity directly. However, none of this speculation touched upon the possibility that the divergent mental outlook guaranteed by that environment might lead to unanticipated, new applications of age-old techniques possessed and employed by every one of us—as now has proved to be the case.

It is this observer's most urgent recommendation that a priority at least equal to that assigned to Gothyäl's proposal concerning Cory's new-found abilities be given to watching for and evaluating all future uses to which Cory puts those of our age-old techniques which the Agent is able to teach him. It well may be that, standing alone, the unique perspectives from which he views problems may contain or suggest a resolution to our problem—particularly once he becomes aware of the full extent of the challenge facing him and his resourcefulness begins to operate at maximum intensity.

This information is of course being channeled directly into the Data Field, but a brief subjective précis of this observer's impressions may prove useful.

Heretofore we have regarded total, cell-by-cell control of all body components as a discipline useful for no more than physical maintenance and repair. Cory, however, is using it affirmatively; as a tool to change his and Agent Megonthalyä's physical appearance. Cell-by-cell, he and the agent are shifting their facial features and overall skin tones from those with which they were born to those characteristic of the inhabitants of China.

Coupled with their uniforms and forged documents (whose authenticity I have verified personally; this Rebecca Two-Knives is most efficient), their resultant appearance completes an absolutely unassailable disguise. I cannot envision their having any difficulty whatever in convincing even the most suspicious checkpoint sentry of the legitimacy of their errand.

"You look like Ko-Ko," observed Memphus admiringly. "All you need is a snicker-snee to complete the effect."

"Ko-Ko was Japanese," I reminded him. "Besides, he was a good guy basically, if feckless. I'm trying to look *nasty*."

And I did, too: I used Meg's vision as a mirror, as she did

mine, to follow and guide the alterations. I now looked like the sort of Chinese military officer whose presence intimidates, whose glance coagulates blood, whose casual word shatters careers, and whose displeasure ends lives.

Meg, on the other hand, looked like a twelve-year-old Ming Dynasty cheerleader. (I had concluded, by then, that she was intrinsically incapable of unattractiveness.)

Finally, as ready as we were likely to be, we resumed our places on the bike: Meg on the pillion, her arms tight about me; Memphus reclining on a cushion installed for that purpose atop the gas tank in front of me, his claws dug securely into the olefin cover, with a strap snugly across his back.

With Meg scanning ahead for people, we made good progress up the eastern slopes of the Himalayas. Becky had obtained a computer-enhanced, high-resolution military spy-satellite photograph of the area ("'Ask me no questions, I'll tell you no lies,'" she replied primly when I questioned its origin), and had identified a probable alternate route over the mountains. It wasn't a pass per se; indeed, the layperson would have considered it questionable for a well-equipped team of experienced mountain climbers. But Becky was no layperson; she knew the capabilities of a trials bike in the hands of a world-class rider. She allowed as how she was pretty sure we could make it.

As usual, she was right. Barely. It was difficult going, even by trials standards (a Six-Day organizer could have died happy after staging an event there). Grades averaged probably sixty percent; footing was loose, unpredictable, and often icy. Besides, my leg still ached. But the route *was* passable.

An unexpected problem developed about an hour into the climb, in the midst of a long, very steep grade (the narrow, winding bed of a nearly empty thaw-runoff stream, full of large, smoothly rounded boulders): It suddenly occurred to me that I was in a fair way to starve to death—*in all my life I'd never been so hungry!*

Recognition of the condition sank in in a location where we simply couldn't stop: There was no room to turn around, and it would have been impossible to restart uphill on such a grade; indeed, it was all I could do to keep us moving without flipping over backward. Much of the time I stood on the pegs, leaning far over the handlebars, my nose almost touching the front fender, endeavoring to keep our center of gravity somewhere ahead of the rear tire's contact patch, maneuvering around, between, and occasionally over rocks in our path.

Throughout, Meg had remained tightly *en rapport* with me; watching in oft-horrified fascination the techniques involved in working the bike across the outrageous terrain. Memphus, on the other hand, kept his eyes tightly closed, with only a subvocalized-thought-band channel open for conversation as we traveled. He didn't care to have us sending him scenic vistas, he explained with a shudder; the proximity of all those scenic vistas was the reason he'd shut his eyes in the first place.

A needless concern: I had no attention to spare for chitchat, let alone mental imagery; and Meg was so busy, either strangling me with her arms and/or shifting her weight in concert with mine, that she didn't either. All in all, it was a quiet trip at first.

Shortly after the Hunger came upon me, however, Meg spoke up (mentally): "Peter, what's happening? I've never been so hungry in my whole life! And I can feel that you're just as hungry. I don't understand it. We had breakfast only a few hours ago. . . ."

I didn't understand it either. But the hunger pangs grew steadily worse, and soon were so acute that they started to constitute a distraction—something no trials rider can afford when working really rough terrain.

I started looking in earnest for a place to stop. Initially nothing was in sight but the narrow, boulder-filled creek bed winding out of sight ahead and above. But finally I spotted a rock resting against another even larger boulder, forming a shelf contiguous with the bed of the stream; going downhill, it might have served as a takeoff ramp for a jump (if one were given to such patently suicidal impulses as jumping on so steep a slope).

I brought us to a stop some thirty feet uphill of the shelf, partially released the brakes, and allowed the bike to roll gently backward onto the nearly level surface. I killed the engine, leaving the bike in gear. Meg found a pair of rocks of the appropriate size and shape and used them to chock the wheels. Only then did I release the brakes and dismount.

We broke out rations and wolfed them down, still puzzling over the cause of it all. Certainly it wasn't the altitude: We were well above twenty thousand feet, true; but we'd been on oxygen (tiny nose-only masks, fed from two-inch-long, Isimodified ex-CO_2 sparklette containers good for nearly two week's continuous use [*they* had bothered Becky, too]) since about the fifteen-thousand-foot level.

Nor was it the exertion; riding under such conditions is hard work, but I'd gone all day without eating several times during events—organizers thoughtfully had arranged things so one *had* to. . . .

Finally we were full—though, oddly enough, it seemed to take more food than normal to do it. I launched us back into the stream bed from the rock shelf, and we continued uphill.

Barely two hours later the same thing happened again!

Again we found a place to stop. Again we filled up. Again we continued. And again, almost nightfall this time, it happened again.

We pitched camp for the night and ate again. But shortly before dawn we woke—hungry again . . . !

I was utterly baffled, and not a little concerned: At this rate the food wouldn't last us even over the mountains.

And suddenly I knew the answer. "*Stupid!*" I blurted.

"Who . . . ?" asked Meg, round-eyed with startlement.

"Me," I replied in exasperation. "Of *course* we're hungry— do you have any idea how many cells we divided to accomplish these changes to our appearance? And in how short a period of time?"

Then it was Meg's turn: "I *knew* that!" she said slowly, looking puzzled.

Memphus looked at her quickly, but said nothing.

"That's *basic*," she continued, shaking her head. "What's wrong with my memory? Cell division on that scale requires tremendous energy. Usually, during repairs or routine maintenance, we replace it by tapping the *mMj'q* flow. If we can't, we eat almost constantly during the process, and for hours afterward. Now why didn't I remember that? Do you suppose I'm growing senile at a mere fifty-two?" She looked genuinely troubled.

I teased her out of it; then we continued. We crested the summit of the "pass" before lunch, and went more quickly downhill. We camped that night in the river valley which led north to Gyangtse.

TO: Project Director/Monitor's Log.
FROM: Q'vVonykl, Fifth Order.
SUBJECT: Project *Extremis*.

Agent Megonthalyä has detected a break in her memory chain. Obviously we inadvertently trapped a small but elementary fact relating to her command of the $pwW'r$ inside one of the memory blocks comprising her conditioning. She is quite nonplussed at having overlooked so fundamental a detail, and wonders how so basic an omission was possible. It will be necessary to observe her closely to ensure that she does not follow this loose end back to the block itself. Given only slight encouragement, she could do that; and, having found it, little doubt exists that she will be able to break through it. Upon learning what lies inside, she will deduce immediately both that she has been conditioned and our motivation therefor. Given the current state of her feelings for Subject Cory, this must not be allowed to happen.

It would be well to have a Tenth Order team in readiness in case it becomes necessary to reinforce her conditioning by means of long-distance hypnosis, augmented, of course, by the $mMj'q$ flowing from the $wWn'dt$ they seek; to which they are much closer now, its output increasingly available to support such efforts.

CHAPTER 14

Becky's collection of forged documents and our appearance got us through checkpoint after checkpoint with no more than a frequent admiring stare at the bike and Meg—in that order, to her undisguised annoyance.

Another two days' hard riding found us on the shore of Seling Tsho, wondering if it mightn't be a better idea to go home and hire mining crews to dig for the $wWn'dt$ inside Jötenheimen, Olympus, or Sinai. Becky's satellite photographs had indicated construction and activity along much of the shoreline, but we hadn't paid attention to it because the satellite hadn't picked up the underwater stuff.

Meg's scan of the area revealed that much of Seling Tsho was an underwater oil field. Troops of divers prowled the lake bottom, tending drilling rigs, wellheads, and pumps and hoses for transporting crude to shoreside storage facilities. The area where the $wWn'dt$ lay hidden was especially busy.

Cautiously Meg touched the minds of several (much less

difficult now that the $mMj'q$ flow was stronger, so close to even a raw, uncut $wWn'dt$). She learned that most lived down there full-time, in deepwater habitats; eliminating thereby both the risks and time loss associated with decompression at the close of each shift. She also discovered that quartz-iodine lighting eliminated "night" on the lake bottom; operations continued unabated twenty-four hours a day, seven days a week.

For a while we watched, worrying.

Memphus finally broke the silence: "There are just *too many* of them. If you go down there, day or night, you'll be spotted. And they have miniature submarines and personal hydrophones. You'll never get away."

He was right. We pulled back into a stand of trees and put our heads together.

"We have to get in, find the stone, and get out, all without being seen," I observed, mostly to myself. Then reflected that sometimes I have a real flair for the obvious.

"We all do," Memphus chuckled. "You not *much* more than most."

"And . . ." I sighed (I'd just about given up trying to remember to shield my private musings), "we need a means of escaping if we should be seen."

"What do we do now?" Meg asked in unhappy tones. "We *need* it, but this looks awfully dangerous."

She was too preoccupied to notice as my shields slid into place around the germ of an idea. It looked pretty hairbrained on first reading, but seemed to have potential. I kept my own counsel and thought it over as the other two worried independently.

"It is," the cat replied flatly. "I'll grant you, this SCUBA gear is much smaller and lighter, holds a couple weeks' more air, and is less burdensome than theirs"—it was nearly identical to the oxygen equipment we had worn while crossing the Himalayas—"so undoubtedly you can swim faster than they, and go farther before needing to surface. But you can't outswim a minisub, nor can you avoid a search organized by hydrophone . . ."

The cat broke off suddenly to pounce unsuccessfully at a mouse which scurried from under a leaf into a hole under a tree root. He glared down the hole for a moment, then turned back to us, looking embarrassed. "Damned nuisance, these reflexes," he grumbled. "They make you do the most undignified things. What would I have done with the nasty thing if I'd caught it? And where was I?"

"Everything you've said is true," I cut in. "So how about *this* . . . ?" I flipped up my shields.

"You're not serious!" gasped Meg—then broke off, laughing as she realized that she had echoed her reaction to the announcement of my last revolutionary idea. "Oh, dear. You *are* . . . !"

"And it ought to work," approved Memphus.

"Yes, it should," agreed Meg, smiling proudly at me.

"Right, but we'd better accumulate a *bunch* of food in advance," I cautioned. "This is a major project."

"No," replied Meg. "We're close enough to the *wWn'dt* now. I can replenish the energy we use by tapping the *mMj'q* flow."

"Good; that'll save lots of time. Let's get at it. . . ."

TO: Project Director/Monitor's Log.
FROM: Mrayäl, Fourth Order.
SUBJECT: Project *Extremis*.

Subject Cory has done it again! Increasingly, this duty is becoming more a reward than an assignment; an education in eye-opening, fresh perspectives. Cory is a font of unexpected, unprecedented applications for ancient techniques. Currently he and Agent Megonthalyä are in the midst of the most astonishing metamorphosis. Their quest requires them to function efficiently within an underwater environment occupied by throngs of hostile Chinese. Cory's solution boggles the imagination!

What will he come up with when faced with a *real* challenge . . . !

Settling upon our course of action, we had cut cross-country to the southern end of the uppermost of the chain of lakes which drain into Seling Tsho. Kyaring Tsho lay some fifty straightline miles from the *wWn'dt's* resting place, but the distance by water was almost two hundred.

According to the satellite photographs, the shorelines of neither the lakes en route, nor the rivers connecting them, showed construction similar to that which ringed Seling Tsho. I reasoned that, under the circumstances, the water route offered the fastest, most efficient avenue of escape, should we be spotted—should we be reported even if we *were* spotted. . . .

(After all, if you were a hard-working Chinese oil-field engineer whose only interest in life was doing your job while avoiding as much flak as possible, supervised by a fanatic Party member obsessed with seeing to it that his subordinates made him look good to *his* superiors, how eager would you be to report sighting a mermaid . . . ?)

Structural changes were substantial but straightforward. I equipped us with torsos similar from the waist down to those of *Tursiops*, our smiling, bottle-nosed, ocean-dwelling kin. This involved merging the flesh of our legs, but not the bones; lengthening femurs somewhat, and creation of an extra joint midway along the shafts. Feet were everted, flattened, broadened, and lengthened to form flukes. Misplaced pectoral fin equivalants grew from the vicinity of our hips. Dorsals jutted from just below our scapulae.

The question of an air supply gave me pause. Breath-holding at those depths was out: Even if I could duplicate dolphins' lung structure and metabolic efficiency, being forced to surface at fifteen-minute intervals was asking for trouble. (Don't believe me; ask Moby Dick.)

The miniature SCUBA gear would have had no measurable effect on our mobility; however, it, along with practically every other self-contained breathing apparatus on the market, contained an inherent weakness (quite possibly a fatal one, under the circumstances): We would leave a trail of bubbles on the surface that a blind man couldn't miss.

Which left a single solution. . . .

Well, why *not* gills? I knew how they worked; they weren't particularly anatomically complicated. True, they'd have to be pretty large, considering the oxygen/carbon-dioxide exchange area required to support active, warm-blooded animals our size. Likewise, just as those on fish are protected by heavy gill plates, they'd be safer located under our ribs. And since we couldn't admit sufficient water through our mouths, as fish do, I decided to locate forward-opening intake slots just below our pectoral muscles in front, one on each side, and place the exhausts just below the rib cages at the rear.

Then, too, no SCUBA gear meant leaving behind the face masks, of which they were an integral component, which meant impaired underwater vision. This required an adjustment to the shape of the crystalline lenses of our eyes, and creation of nictitating membranes (tough, transparent inner lids) to protect them.

Initially I had planned to try to modify some of the rod receptors in our retinas to register infrared. But then I recalled the efficiency with which water equalizes the temperature of everything in contact with it, and the fact that infrared doesn't penetrate all that well through water in any event.

So first I straightforwardly multiplied our light-gathering powers by several orders of magnitude: A major increase in the numbers and distribution of normal black-and-white-sensitive rod receptors, together with an enlarged maximum pupil aperture, accomplished that simply enough. However, with such a high degree of optical sensitivity, virtually instantaneous light accommodation response was a requirement if we were to avoid being blinded by sudden bright lights. Accordingly, the organic light-meters controlling the irises, and the constrictor/ dilator muscles which operated them, underwent modifications to enhance their efficiency.

(And while I was at it, I rallied a mob of leukocytes to the area of that residual ache in what heretofore had been my thigh muscles. Obviously I had developed a low-grade inclusion-body infection in reaction to that medication. Nothing my immune system couldn't handle with a little coaching.)

Meg was fascinated; both with the theoretical aspects and the results of their application. So fascinated, in fact, that twice I had to remind her to continue tapping the $mMj'q$ flow to keep us from starving as the transformation progressed.

It took about four hours; at the conclusion of which Memphus stood and walked a slow circle around us, staring intently. Then he sat and licked his lips. He snickered evilly. "I hope you both realize the effect this is having on me—upon the reflexes of this body. I'll probably never be able to look at either of you again without salivating. . . ."

The cat had volunteered to remain behind and guard the bike: "If you think for a second that I'm going to set one foot in that *wet* water . . ." he had begun, back arched, tail a bottle brush. Meg and I assured him that the thought never had crossed our minds. (On a tightly focused thought-band we shared the mental image of an obese, lop-eared, yellow- and black-striped, really annoyed catfish.) Memphus regarded us quite sharply as we fought back giggles, but chose to let the matter drop.

Getting from our hiding place in the woods to the water in that condition came next. A gait similar to that which seals employ on land worked pretty well, but it was not a dignified performance.

"This is *fun!*" thought Meg shortly thereafter as, hand in hand, we sliced through the water just above the lake bottom. She was right: Never had I experienced such a sense of power and motion or such freedom of movement.

The physical effort was minimal, the stroke unfamiliar but somehow instinctive—the result dramatic: an exaggerated nodding motion of my head began an anterior/posterior undulation which surged along my body, gaining force, ending in a powerful thrusting motion of my flukes, which drove me through the water faster than I would have believed possible.

"Shouldn't you two be sitting on a rock, combing your hair and singing, luring sailors of whatever sexual persuasion to their dooms?" interjected a smug thought. In Memphus' view, he had good reason for smugness: He was dry.

The only untoward event encountered while covering the two hundred miles from Kyaring Tsho, where Memphus waited with the bike, to Seling Tsho, occurred in a shallow stretch of river between Ngedden Tsho and Seling Tsho, where we disturbed two old men fishing in a reed boat. It hadn't occurred to Meg to scan ahead while traveling just beneath the surface at night; their exclamations caught us by surprise—as our torpedolike wakes, and dorsal fins slicing the moonlight reflected on the water, did them.

(And considering their age, dignity, and probable level of education, it probably wasn't very nice of us to double back and jump over their boat, smiling and waving as we soared overhead, momentarily visible in the glow of their lanterns, but it seemed an awfully good idea at the time.)

We left Memphus sometime around four in the afternoon. We entered Seling Tsho shortly after midnight. With Meg scanning for all she was worth, we scouted the area. She determined that the *wWn'dt* lay under a pile of rock—mere feet from a drilling rig brilliantly illuminated by row upon row of dazzling quartz lights and swarming with workers. We circled the location, remaining beyond reach of the lights, debating strategy.

"Obviously, the first step is to do something about the lights," Meg offered. "Do you have any ideas?"

Of course I had an idea. But it took additional reconnaissance to locate the means of accomplishing it. After further snooping, we located the heavy cables running from shore which powered the entire installation. They led to an under-water habitat which served as a transformer station.

We dropped down and peeked in the windows. I extended my perception into the habitat and studied the control set-up, the switching equipment, and the breakers. I assured myself, with relief, that I could kill the lights without interfering with the habitats' life-support equipment; and that the control room technicians had the equipment and spares necessary to repair relatively quickly the damage I contemplated. A protracted total outage would have proved fatal to everyone concerned—for long-term residents at such depths, decompression amounts to *days*.

I had no desire to kill anyone; innocent bystanders least of all. Militiamen pointing weapons at us, okay, if necessary; but most of these people were hard-working, well-intentioned family men and women. They had no ax to grind against us; I had no right to endanger them.

Meg followed my thoughts. She drifted close; her lips brushed my cheek. "You have *good* instincts," she approved warmly. "But never forget our ultimate goal: If ever you're faced with the necessity of cold-bloodedly sacrificing innocent people to stop R'gGnrök—and I can't *conceive* of a situation in which such a thing might become necessary—sparing them will be an empty kindness. Do you know *anyone* who would insist upon living, knowing that by doing so he doomed his world . . . ?"

I didn't—certainly nobody worthwhile. Still, I was awfully glad it wasn't necessary this time. Meg squeezed my hand without replying, and pressed close.

I felt cautiously for the electricity flowing through the cables. Carefully forming a channel around the main breaker feeding the outside lights, I established a small arc between several metallic components within the breaker mechanism itself, welding it closed. Then I dissolved my bypass channel and shunted the entire current flow to ground just downstream from the breaker, which gave a brief but convincing imitation of an overloaded fuse: The explosion inside the panel startled the technicians half out of their wits.

Suddenly it was very dark at the bottom of Seling Tsho.

Meg eavesdropped on the technicians' thoughts as we turned away and headed for the *wWn'dt's* hiding place. "They anticipate that replacing the breaker should take something on the order of half an hour. We'll have plenty of time."

"Maybe. But watch out for people with flashlights," I cautioned as we slid nervously between clusters of groping divers—it was hard to believe that only we could see; the incredible light-gathering capabilities provided by the combination of our hyperdilated pupils and densely rod-packed retinas transformed the darkness of the lake bottom into a brightly lit, if monochromatic, vista. But already one or two enterprising divers had located portable battery-powered lights; and the painfully brilliant glare seriously compromised our preternaturally acute night vision, alternately dazzling us and causing us to peer uncertainly into the gloom on the other side of flickering after-images.

We braked to a quick stop over the pile of rocks under which the *wWn'dt* lay, our backwash sending a pair of luckless blinded divers tumbling through the water, and began digging our way into the pile. It was hard work; most of the stones would have been pretty heavy even on land—lifting them while swimming was downright laborious.

Adding to the urgency, another string of divers with hand-held lights began trickling in from the direction of the residential habitats. We redoubled our efforts.

A diver lifted from a nearby drilling rig and set off cautiously on a course which would pass close to us; navigating, judging by his body position, by means of the glowing dial of a wrist compass. It wasn't until his outstretched arm contacted the minisub resting on the silt of the lake bottom close by that I realized his destination.

He dropped into the cockpit and reached for the control panel as Meg's exultation surged through my brain.

"I've *got* it . . . !" she thought triumphantly—just as the minisub's battery of quartz lights blazed forth. One beam speared her squarely as she hovered erect just above the bottom, the coconut-sized stone held above her head in both hands. The *wWn'dt* glowed in the beam like a blood-colored sunset.

For perhaps half a second we hung immobile in the glare as our irises strove to protect overloaded retinas, an unlikely tableau confronting the stunned divers all around us. Then, even before our vision cleared, we stroked, hard; to our audience we must have seemed simply to disappear.

With the *wWn'dt* cradled in Meg's arms, we sprinted back up the lake at top speed, snickering to ourselves as we tossed back and forth mental images of the divers huddled together, trying to decide whether to report what they had seen. "By now they've probably talked themselves into believing that what they saw was no more than a pair of big sturgeon," laughed Meg, wheeling through a fluid somersault of sheer exuberance.

But as we raced up Seling Tsho, headed for the river which led to Ngedden Tsho, she quieted. As I followed her thoughts, so did I. Now physically in contact with the $wWn'dt$, Meg was able to tap much more of the modest natural $mMj'q$ flow, substantially augmenting her mind's reach. As we sped upstream, we watched the commotion which ensued in the aftermath of our being spotted.

Things were not going well. The diver who switched on the minisub's lights was not a run-of-the-mill oil-field worker: He was military; his job was security. He was calm, intelligent, efficient—and not at all superstitious. He took in every unlikely detail, coupled what he had seen with the convenient power failure; then quickly, coldly, logically evaluated the situation. His conclusion: that we were, in fact, very ordinary human beings; that our outlandish appearance, speed, and mobility were due to our being encased in sophisticated one-man minisubs—and that we were terrorists bent on sabotaging the oil field. The red-glowing $wWn'dt$, in his opinion, was a bomb. He was pleased indeed that he had caught us before we could arm and place it. The entire installation now was in a state of maximum alert . . .

Which spread rapidly ashore, and *continued* to spread—the military had no idea who these saboteurs might be, but they damned well intended to find out. By the time we entered the river leading to Ngeddon Tsho, the alert encompassed a five-hundred-mile radius centered on the lake. Troops and equipment were pouring into the area.

We swam harder.

CHAPTER 15

"Oh-oh. . . ." Meg braked to an abrupt stop, her mind suddenly a swirl of thoughts so technical in nature that I neither could follow them nor identify the source of her concern.

Physically I tapped her on the shoulder. "What's wrong?"

"'He who lives by the jape shall die by the jape,'" she intoned worriedly in my head. "I'm sorry; I should have known better." With a conscious effort, she invited me back inside her mind and showed me the problem.

Well, it had seemed a harmless enough prank at the time. But not to the two old fishermen, apparently.

Indeed, they were so upset that they had risked the displeasure of the local military-occupation governor by reporting their experience. That worthy was in the midst of angrily dismissing their story as a combination of alcohol and overwrought imaginations when he received word of the incident at the oil field. It took him no time at all to match the details of the "terrorist raid" with the fishermen's story, and less time still to react:

A line of small boats now extended all the way across the river ahead of us. Beneath them hung a net; weights buried the lower edge in the muck of the bottom. A dozen helicopter gunships hovered or bustled about industriously overhead, searchlights burning into the shallow water. Image-enhancing and infrared snooperscopes were the uniform of the day. One boat carried portable mapping sonar; all contained soldiers armed to the teeth.

A minnow couldn't have slipped by. We were cut off. . . .

"I hope the compudicters were right about you." Meg's thought was calm, but I wasn't fooled—the prospect of dying is not something an immortal contemplates lightly.

"How so?" I responded, matching her tone; hoping thereby to keep her from detecting my own concern.

"You're the ultimate development of a bloodline focused on survival qualities, remember? You're intelligent, resourceful. You never give up. This would be a really good time to prove it."

She was right—I hoped the compudicters were, too. There was no possibility of making it by water to Kyaring Tsho where Memphus waited with the bike. Even if we managed, the chances of reaching the border with intact skins dwindled by the moment, as the search intensified and the numbers of troops combing the area grew exponentially.

I linked tightly with Meg as she scanned the area and examined the minds of the ranking officers. The results were not encouraging:

Unbeknownst Free World intelligence agencies, The People's Republic of China had encountered considerable internal opposition to the recent reimposition of the old Cultural Revolution standards of ideological purity regarding freedom of thought, expression, and business practices. (Especially the latter: Once enterprising individuals taste the rewards of capitalism [regardless by what euphemism the State chooses to describe it] they can be equally enterprising in opposing those who would take it from them.) Domestically based terrorism was widespread, characterized by efficient hit-and-run raids and bombings.

The military's response was the development and fielding of massive, specially equipped and trained mobile units who rushed en masse into the area of a terrorist attack, usually arriving before the smoke cleared; employing everything known to the science of criminology—from the most modern gas chromatography and ultrasensitive antipersonnel radar to bloodhounds—to track down and capture the guilty parties.

With much recent practice, these units had acquired a high degree of experience and sophistication. Their apprehension rate was impressive.

We retreated back to the lake and studied the shoreline intently. Seling Tsho was a big lake—but thousands of troops were involved; already they had finished encircling it. Those in charge were pretty sure they had us (the hypothetical terrorists) boxed in.

Which, of course, they did.

And as we continued to observe, we learned that our troubles were compounding rapidly. Additional personnel and equipment were due momentarily: frogmen with high-speed minisubs equipped with the latest portable heat-sensing detection equipment, armed with remotely guided/heat-seeking antipersonnel torpedos. . . .

Obviously the Chinese antiterrorist specialists took their work seriously.

"I don't like this," thought Meg, nervously eyeing the depth-attenuated sunlight leaking in between the structural members that supported and leveled the submerged habitat which served as office and living quarters for the oil field's security officer.

(There is something to be said for being an unbelievably intelligent, incredibly resourceful, utterly determined [if thoroughly frightened], made-to-order superman. It took me remarkably little time to come up with a number of potential means of escape, and even less to discard all but one.)

"This is the last place they'd look," I comforted her. "That is unless we give them time to think of it. Concentrate; we want to be done by dark."

Sneaking back into the oil field proved less difficult than I had feared. Security, while tighter than before, was less stringent than we had any right to expect. Precautions were limited to a few troops stationed underwater, and a couple sonar units in operation. And certainly the make-up and numbers of the depth-trapped resident oil-worker population hadn't changed any in the last few hours.

"The way they've got their forces deployed, there's only one direction open," I concluded. And, as a practical matter, there was only one way to take advantage of it. In Meg's mind I unfolded a picture of what I envisioned (I was getting pretty good at shielding selected thoughts): a mental working drawing, one might call it.

Her eyes went round. "You're not . . ."

I smiled. "Serious? Gee, how do you suppose I know you were going to say that. . . ."

"Smugness does not become you," she replied tensely. "Do you think it's safe?"

"Nothing's safe, the way they're going at it; but it seems to offer the best odds at the moment. It wouldn't surprise me to run into further problems on the way out, which might well require trying something else. But . . ."

I left the word hanging purposely. Meg nodded.

We set to work. We proceeded more quickly this time; shape-changing, like any other skill, benefits from experience. Plus now Meg was physically in contact with the $wWn'dt$; more of the $mMj'q$ flow went to nourish our cells as they absorbed, divided, and redivided in their millions.

First came restoration of our original forms (retaining the gills, of course; it would be the work of moments to seal intake and exhaust slots as we left the water). Then arms and fingers lengthened and were strengthened enormously. Membranes formed and grew to fill in the spaces between widely outstretched fingers; extending from the tips of yards-long "little" fingers to ankles, and bridging the gap between widely spread legs as well. Musculature was enhanced substantially, especially pectorals; and cardiovascular changes boosted oxygen/carbon-dioxide exchange efficiency. A thick covering of warm, downy, water-repellent fur grew to cover our bodies.

The alterations required to transform humans into oversized bats were extensive. They involved considerable intuitive, rule-of-thumb engineering, with important calculations involving wing-loading and center of gravity having to be juggled in my head. It was challenging, and would have been fun but for my constant awareness of the immediate penalties of failure—and the consequences to the galaxy thereafter. . . .

We waited several hours to be sure that night had fallen completely; then slipped from concealment and left the installation with the same care with which we'd entered it. The new shapes weren't nearly as efficient underwater, but a very slow version of the arm motion we expected to use in the air served to propel us through the dark water.

Meg determined that the searchers' use of antipersonnel radar and snooperscopes was limited to sweeping the shoreline, watching for the supposed terrorists' expected attempt to slip from the water and disappear into the forest. Likewise, she made sure that no boats were nearby.

Gingerly we poked our heads through the surface and looked around—which served to remind us that we hadn't readapted our eyes for vision in air: We couldn't see a thing.

We floated on the surface for a while, restoring our eyes' crystalline lenses to their original shapes. We'd almost finished when it occurred to me that the sharper our eyes, the better off we'd be during the next few hours—and there was no reason to limit ourselves to twenty-twenty vision; birds of prey have substantially better distance resolution than humans, despite a smaller eyeball.

We experimented briefly, using the brilliant disc of the nearly full moon to refine the configuration of lens, cornea, and retina; and soon had the satisfaction of being able to discern clearly the larger craters and features within the maria—

The *nearly full moon* . . . ?

Meg picked up the shock that coursed through me a good second before grasping its import, which allowed me to enjoy the thrill of horrified realization twice: first mine, then hers (rapport is not without *dis*advantages). But despite her feelings, she remained silent as I weighed the possibilities.

Finally I reached a decision. "Where are they spread the thinnest?" I inquired grimly.

Meg drew a mental map inside my head; then overlaid it with a pattern of glowing sparks, each registering the presence of one of our pursuers. It just wasn't our day, I reflected; why did they have to be concentrated heaviest in the direction we wanted to go?

Then I brightened. The odds were pretty good that we'd be spotted leaving the lake. With that in mind, maybe heading northeastish wasn't all that bad an idea. It was unlikely that there'd be much surveillance beyond the immediate vicinity of the lake; once in the clear, after laying a false trail, we could loop around to the east, pick up Memphus, and head for the border.

Meg was following my thoughts; she nodded. We closed and sealed our gills. It was time to put my rudimentary aeronautical engineering to the test:

I lifted the fifty-foot span of my wings above the water—and marveled at how light they were; I could hold them above the surface without forcing my head under. I stroked down and back; hard, trying to mimic the motion with which the Resident Pelican lifted himself from the water back at Cory Cay.

It was gratifying (if admittedly unexpected) to feel myself yanked from the water and suspended just above the surface like some outsized kite. Almost immediately, of course, I began to settle, so I repeated the motion and was thrilled to detect instant horizontal acceleration and an increase in height.

I stroked again. And again. And . . .

Damn!—*I was flying . . . !*

Effortlessly . . .

Instinctively . . .

As if I'd been doing it all my life . . .

LIKE A GODDAMN *BIRD* . . . !

"*Quiet!*" Meg's thought burst inside my skull like a gunshot. "All right; it's fun. But do you want *them* to hear you?—do you have any idea how far noise carries across water at night?"

I got a grip on myself—and found that I was probably a hundred feet up and still gaining altitude. With that brightly moonlit sky to serve as a backdrop, that seemed ill-advised. I quit stroking and tilted into a steep glide. I banked into a shallow hundred-eighty-degree turn. As I came to within about ten feet of the surface, I resumed slow wingbeats and cranked into a wide circle centered on Meg.

"Come on," I thought, eager to have her experience

firsthand the ecstatic sensation of flight (and, just incidentally, to be on our way). "What are you waiting for? It's easy . . . !"

I shared her momentary attack of gastrolepidoptrosis; then felt her resolve harden. She took a deep breath and lifted her wings. We remained closely linked as she duplicated my motions, lifting effortlessly from the water.

Meg required little coaching. I felt her thrill to the new skill as she mastered it almost automatically, as quickly as I had.

She stroked again. And again. And . . .

Damn!—*she was flying* . . . !

Effortlessly . . .

Instinctively . . .

As if she'd been doing it all her life . . .

LIKE A GODDAMN B—

"*Quiet!*" I cautioned, suppressing a grin. She subsided sheepishly.

Together we wheeled and headed for the north-northeastern shore, skimming mere feet above the black water, scanning the troop placement ahead, adjusting our course to cross the shoreline at the point where the opposition was the scarcest.

As we approached land, I suggested to Meg that she probe the minds of those ahead of us, to see if she couldn't plant some sort of distraction to keep them from looking up as we passed over. She informed me, a trifle shortly, that that was precisely what she was trying to do—if certain people would quit jostling her elbow.

A bit more diffidently, then, I suggested that she take pains to maintain firm control of the $mMj'q$ flow during the next few moments. (The $wWn'dt$ now traveled in a pseudomarsupial pouch she'd created from her navel; she reported that surrounding it on all sides constituted a most efficient form of contact—she was obtaining virtually one-hundred-percent flow utilization.) If we *were* spotted, I added, the odds were fairly good that one or both of us could expect to draw small-arms fire. With $mMj'q$ fueling our repairs, and if the damage were not too severe (anything short of a major "airframe" bone or the brain; nonvital tissue repairs would take only seconds), between us we probably could manage to stay airborne and keep going.

That hadn't occurred to her. And the more she thought about it, the sorrier she was that it had occurred to me. However, she agreed that I was right; she would do so. We linked even more tightly and swept in toward the shoreline.

TO: Project Director/Monitor's Log.
FROM: H'tTosym, Fifth Order.
SUBJECT: Project *Extremis*.

During the initial days of the project, only this division's operators have monitored the progress of our team and Subject Cory as recorders preserved events for future analysis. In the past several hours, however, the audience has increased. People who don't even know Agent Megonthalyä and her familiar personally are becoming interested; partly, I suspect, as a result of the unprecedented resourcefulness and determination displayed by Subject Cory in overcoming obstacle after obstacle, but mostly because their situation is growing increasingly tense.

So tense, in fact, that I have requested a team of Tenth Order practitioners to stand by during the next few hours, which clearly are pivotal in Cory's and our agents' escape from Tibet with the *wWn'dt*. It would be unworkmanlike, as well as counterproductive, to lose him through sheer bad luck this early in the project; likewise, of course, it is preferable to keep our agents from harm.

Even for the synchronized efforts of Tenth Order adepts, the range is extreme; nonetheless, the difference between a situation from which there is no escape and one offering a fighting chance, however slight, is often minimal, and it is best to be prepared in any event.

Meg did her level best to implant a suggestion in the minds of the wide-awake troops ahead of us that *something* was rustling in the bushes behind them. It was working, too: All eyes (and guns) were trained in that direction as we neared shore. We'd probably have gotten clean away with it if that damned fish hadn't picked that precise moment to jump. . . .

A lot happened during the next few seconds. Two soldiers quickly looked back in the direction of the splash, toward the shoreline. We were maybe a hundred feet away, coming right at them, traveling about fifty miles an hour, ten feet above the beach (we had stayed low to avoid being silhouetted against the sky).

We saw their heads turn and their eyes grow round (within ethnic anatomical limitations, of course). Instantly we shifted our wingbeat rate into high gear and climbed to clear the trees.

The one on the right remained frozen, mouth open, gun obviously forgotten. The other was better trained:

With a wordless shout, he spun, leveling his rifle at Meg. I dived without thinking. He swung the weapon toward me, pulled the trigger, and . . .

Nothing happened—incredibly, the safety was on.

But he was *very* quick; I heard the safety click off only a heartbeat later. Too late; by that time I was on him: I passed bare inches above his helmet, my leg bent; the knee caught him squarely in the forehead. It was a seventy-mile-per-hour impact at least; my leg went numb from the knee down. The unmistakable sound of vertebrae separating was audible over the wind of my passage.

As all eyes converged upon us, and the dead soldier cartwheeled through the air as if he'd been hit by a car, I stroked hard, clawing for altitude sufficient to clear the treetops. Again no one moved for whole seconds, gaining me time and distance. Already Meg was disappearing beyond the treetops.

My victim landed; so did his rifle—against a tree trunk. The burst of fully-automatic fire broke the spell; every soldier in sight reacted as one:

With a sound like ten thousand firecrackers, dozens of scalding-hot needles stitched their way across my wings. I stroked harder . . .

And then it was over: I was accelerating level, just above the treetops, out of sight and out of range.

"Are you all right?" Meg's thoughts were almost panicky, but I could tell that it wasn't herself she was concerned about—and knowing that made the pain almost enjoyable.

I reassured her as we conducted an inspection of my wounds. Two seams embroidered in copiously bleeding bullet holes marched across my left wing; another decorated the right. One of my ears was pierced. And, of course, I had one hell of a bruise on my knee. (Plus, believe it or not, that damned injection site in my thigh still ached.) But no bones, no tendons; nothing vital. Nor were the machine-gun bullet holes spaced closely enough together to cause "tear-on-dotted-line" concerns. A messy business, but nothing serious. We had no trouble keeping me airborne while making repairs.

As Meg fed me energy, I mended my wounds and contemplated the fact that I had just killed a man.

"A man who tried to kill you," she pointed out; "not to

mention me. A man who, had he succeeded, would have accomplished the inevitable destruction of his people, his species, his planet, and our entire galaxy. You're not going to have an attack of guilt or go fugue on me over it, are you?"

No, I wasn't, I realized with some astonishment. And for a time *that* bothered me. I had *killed* a man, after all; emotional trauma is the usual reaction. It took a while, but finally I understood: The campaign to halt Armageddon was a war. People died in wars all the time, usually to no purpose. Even so, if the wrong people died, the war was lost. But for once we were engaged in a war with a worthwhile goal: If we lost this war, we would lose the galaxy. We could not afford to lose. We *must* win. At *any* cost. . . .

No, I felt no guilt over killing that man. I did feel regret, the same sense of regret I always experienced upon hearing of someone's death, coupled with the usual twinge of sympathy for his family. But nothing more.

Had he killed us, the war would have been lost. *Everything* would have been lost.

Flying low and avoiding people, we maintained our north-northeasterly course a good ten miles past the lakeshore; then we swung around to the west.

I continued to tinker with our aerodynamics and musculo-skeletal configuration as we flew, continuously refining our structure. Steadily our speed increased, even as the effort required lessened. By the time I finished, I judged that we were doing close to a hundred miles an hour; quite fast enough to make me thankful that I'd had the foresight to retain the nictitating membranes: Once, as an experiment, I momentarily retracted the left one; and in the fraction of a second it took to blink it shut again, the slipstream so blinded the eye with tears that it took almost a whole minute to clear again.

From the feeble, natural *mMj'q* flow emanating from the raw *wWn'dt* in her pouch, Meg created an immaterial thought-wave-lasing-and-parabolic-dish-receiver apparatus of the type the Isi had used in times past to implant suggestions in my ancestors' subconscious over interstellar distances. Of course those devices were about the size of a respectable solar system; products of the combined *mMj'q* flow of numerous finish-cut, fully activated *wWn'dts*. This unit was *small;* it took Meg three tries to get a response from her *fmMl'hr* from only fifty miles out.

Briefly Memphus affected nonchalance at our tardiness: "Oh, back already? Goodness me—isn't it amazing how time flies when one stays busy. I never even noticed that you were *nineteen hours, thirty-seven minutes, and fifty-six seconds overdue . . . !*"

Tactfully ignoring the momentarily visible chink in the *fmMl'hr's* façade (there was his reputation to consider, after all), we briefed him as we covered the final miles separating us. By turns he was interested, amused, horrified, impressed, horrified, excited, and horrified. He reviewed our plans with trepidation, but concurred that flying out probably offered the best odds.

"I wish you could have reached me sooner though," he grumbled. "It'll take me quite a while to transform myself, using that method."

"No," I cut in. "That'd take too long. Our only chance is to stay ahead of them. I'll carry you."

"You? How? *Where* . . . ?" A full-color, three-dimensional picture flashed through the *fmMl'hr's* mind: him perched between my shoulder blades, eyes tightly closed, front legs locked in a death grip around my neck; me forced to maneuver abruptly; him losing his grip, skidding over the side, falling endlessly. . . .

"Not to worry," I replied soothingly. "I've arranged special accommodations for you. You can't possibly fall."

The cat's thoughts were a swirl of grimness and genuine apprehension. "I certainly hope not," he replied earnestly. "I do not look forward to spending the balance of my years as a grease spot on a lamasery roof."

Moments later we were there. Meg circled, keeping a wary eye out, as I put on the brakes. To my profound relief, landing proved to be no less instinctive than flying. As I slowed, the chord of my wings' airfoil adjusted, without conscious thought, from a high-speed, low-drag profile to one suitable for slow-flight. Barely above stalling speed, I floated down to within feet of the ground. A final forward-sweeping downstroke killed the balance of the forward motion. My body swung down, feet reaching for the ground. With widespread wings cupped and parallel to the ground, I settled the last few inches. I didn't even have to bend my knees to take the impact; there was none.

Memphis stood before me. "Very neat," he approved; "both the solution and your airmanship. I'm beginning to hope that the compudicters might have known what they were talking about after all. Where do I sit?"

Stowing my wings, I squatted with difficulty, then eased down flat on my back. "In the pouch," I ordered, flashing him a quick mental picture of where I'd grown it.

Memphus gingerly stepped up onto my belly, thrust his nose into the opening, and forced the rest of his bulk inside. He turned around with difficulty in the tight quarters and stuck his head out. "This is the most undignified thing I've ever done," he growled. "If you *ever* tell *anyone*, your days are—eeek . . . !"

This last comment probably was occasioned by the fact the only way I could reach my feet (my arms were useless for the purpose, and I couldn't roll over without squashing the cat) was to execute a "kip," a basic tumbling move: Curling up anteriorly as if beginning a backward somersault, I momentarily balanced my entire weight on my shoulders and neck; then lashed out with all my strength, straightening my torso and legs. The momentum jerked me off the ground, rotated me in the air, and deposited me on my feet in a squatting position.

(Being artificially "pregnant" with a twenty-five-pound furry bowling ball lodged just under my wishbone didn't make the trick any easier. . . .)

Drawing snug the muscles surrounding the pouch's opening, I launched. Memphus shut his eyes and discussed my ancestry feelingly in several obscure languages as we mounted skyward.

CHAPTER 16

Now that Memphus was back with us, Meg was able to use the *wWn'dt's* slight natural *mMj'q* flow to better advantage. Together they scanned ahead as we raced toward the border. We kept mostly to the valleys, flying as low as possible; skimming mere feet above the summits of the lower passes when forced by geology to climb.

We made good time, encountering no one. Sunrise found us wearily cresting the Himalayas, slipping through the pseudo-pass we had followed on the way into Tibet, gratefully stilling our aching wings and tilting into a steep, high-speed glide down the southern face of the huge mountain range, headed for the Sikkimese border. With so few miles to go, I anticipated no further trouble.

However, weather conditions worsened as we descended, which posed a problem: So close to the border, I preferred to hug the terrain closely, lest we show up on someone's radar screen. But as the winds increased, the vicinity of the mountainside grew steadily more hazardous. Soon we found ourselves too busy coping with tricky wind shifts and deteriorating visibility to worry about much else. Violent, unpredictable downdrafts repeatedly threatened to dash us against the jagged surface. One close call followed another, encouraging us to keep ever more distance between ourselves and the jagged slopes.

It was fortunate that we heeded the wind's warning: Barely twenty miles from the border, standing well clear of the rocks, we encountered a terrific wind shear: one of those hundred-mile-an-hour-plus downdrafts which so often snatch low-flying jetliners from their glidepaths and dash them the rest of the way to the ground before their crews can react. Both of us came near to having our shoulders dislocated; first from the violence of the vertical acceleration, then from our own efforts to fight free of the downdraft's grip.

So near a thing was it, and so preoccupied were we with avoiding being pile-drivered into the waiting rocks, that we almost failed to notice the six streaks of flame that lanced through the airspace from which the wind shear had just yanked us. But the sonic booms of the missiles' passage, followed moments later by flashes and heavier concussions as they impacted and detonated on the mountainside a quarter mile ahead, could not be overlooked.

A wide-eyed glance behind us proved self-explanatory: ten helicopter gunships; each the latest, most sophisticated thing in mobile violence (I knew *just* how deadly they were; my security forces shopped at the same store); each equipped with missiles and Gatling cannons; all weapons controlled by computerized, integrated radar-, infrared-, and laser-based detection and sighting systems. All were unmarked, an understandable diplomatic precaution, operating so close to the border—especially as they were fully prepared to chase us past it—but there was no doubt who they were.

I broadcast a warning to Meg; without a moment's hesitation she dived for the mountainside with me close behind. We slipped behind a stony ridge just as a hail of cannon fire poured into the slope above us and another salvo of missiles exploded against the rocks shielding us.

We came to the end of the protective ridge and darted for a cluster of boulders; hugging the slope, battling for control as the treacherous winds rocked and tore at us. It was only a matter of time: Turbulence and/or wind shears were bound to trap us, so close to the terrain—and if somehow they didn't, we hadn't a prayer of escaping the speed, maneuverability, and all-seeing, instant-reacting detection and fire-control equipment of those helicopters. Even now they were gaining on us rapidly, swinging out away from the slope, maneuvering for tactical position; shortly they would be directly above us. Once they achieved that vantage, natural cover no longer would protect us. That would be that. . . .

The *hell* it would, I snarled to myself; not if *I* had anything to say about it! We hadn't gotten this close to success only to have it snatched away. There *had* to be some way out of this trap! Furiously I cudgeled my brain, trying to come up with some means of getting us out of this alive.

But even as my thoughts raced, Meg, weaving and dodging among the rocks, rising and falling with the terrain, already was fighting back. Somehow she managed to spare the concentration necessary to link with Memphus (huddled abjectly in my pouch, eyes tightly closed, wondering [not for the first time] what *ever* had prompted him to want to be a *fmMl'hr*). Working with furious haste, they assembled an immaterial thought-wave laser similar to the device she had created to contact him earlier. With no necessity for a receiving dish, sufficient *mMj'q* flow was available to make it larger and somewhat more powerful.

Acting in unison, they drove a mental probe into the mind of the nearest pilot. They wasted no time trying to implant suggestions or compulsions. A vivid full-color, three-dimensional mental picture, accompanied by a shrieked warning, exploded full-blown in the man's mind: A wind shear had him—the mountainside was rushing up! As he reacted instinctively, they got behind his impulse and *pushed*!

The helicopter veered wildly to one side—directly into the path of another. Rotors tangled briefly . . .

Two down, eight to go.

And Meg and Memphus, taking advantage of the momentary shocked lull in the attack, already were exploring for weaknesses in the others. They singled one out and went to work on him.

But this left seven crews unencumbered by distractions, having shaken off the shock of losing two of their number, closing in. And we were fast approaching a really barren stretch of mountainside: no hint of cover for a good half mile. That was followed by a major crevasse whose jagged depths offered some hope of concealment—if we survived long enough to reach them.

But one pilot was almost in position to get a clear shot at us—and with that armament, once would be enough. We were finished unless . . .

Where the inspiration came from I'll never know. But suddenly I remembered Meg's abortive attempt to teach me to recognize the natural $mMj'q$ flow—and the startling result. . . .

Never slackening for one second my frantic dodging, I cast out with my mind, feeling for that same sensation—and *found* it! Quickly I formed a channel and guided that atmospheric electrical flow into it. I closed my circle (bigger this time) and began the build-up, pumping in more and ever more electrons—bracing the torus walls firmly as the voltage mounted and the internal pressures increased.

Finally I let it go: A bar of coherent lightning seared its way across the sky like a real-life Thor's Hammer, catching the helicopter amidships. Judging by the explosion, every scrap of ammunition aboard must have gone off simultaneously.

Three down, seven to go.

"*Good* . . . !" thought Meg grimly. "Why didn't I think of that? Do it again! Do it lots! Do it *quick*!"

I was way ahead of her. I hadn't relaxed my telekinetic control upon discharge; the $t'lLiSs$ $'mn$ still existed. I restored the valve to "charging position" and started pumping in more electrons, building up the voltage, readying another bolt.

"Memphus and I have created own own $t'lLiSs$ $'mns$," continued a tiny, unoccupied fraction of Meg's mind to a tiny, unoccupied fraction of mine. "We're building voltage just as quickly as we can—oh *why* didn't I think of this myself . . . ? The mental attack was getting us nowhere! The concentration required to fly a helicopter in this turbulence is so intense that it constitutes quite effective natural shielding. We were *lucky* the first time. . . ."

It was taking longer to build up the voltage this time—and

one of the remaining seven gunships already was in position, swinging around to bring its weapons to bear . . . !

Voltage was way down from what it should have been but he was hurrying me: I missed the fuselage entirely, zeroing in on the rotor head as accurately as if I'd planned it that way. And weaker or not, the beam sufficed for our modest needs: The rotor hub of a helicopter is a terribly complex mechanism; being welded solid does not enhance its functional efficiency.

Four down, six to go.

"Damn!" crowed Meg, "I like your style—do it *again* . . . !"

On the heels of her words, two brilliantly blue-white shafts of almost palpable light lashed out together: two *t'lLiSs 'mns* at once—Meg and Memphus were showing off.

Six down, four to go.

But as I worked to build a charge for the third time, I began to detect a curious sense of weariness stealing over me. It wasn't physical; fatigue was an old friend from athletic training. No; this was something new. There was no pain, yet I was short of breath, panting. My thought processes seemed to be slowing. And recharging was harder work this time, and it was taking much longer. . . .

Another bar of lightning flashed across the sky from one of Meg's *t'lLiSs 'mns*.

Seven down, three to go.

But my own recharging was taking so very long . . .

Too long—abruptly there was no time left at all: Another gunship was in position and swinging around to fire . . . !

I had nothing resembling a proper charge accumulated yet, but I launched it anyway—and was rewarded by an anemic, bluish flicker which barely reached its target. . . .

Suddenly there were spots in front of my eyes; I felt drained, confused, dizzy. My coordination came unstrung; I staggered through the air like an insect which has just flown through a cloud of DDT.

My *t'lLiSs 'mn* wavered and evaporated.

Meg noticed the feeble shot. "Don't worry about it!" she thought encouragingly. "You wiped his software and he can't hit anything manually; he's out of practice. That'll give you time to recharge prop—"

She cut off abruptly, realizing I was in trouble. *"What's wrong . . . ?"*

Tightening our rapport and investigating personally, she

answered her own question: "It's the *t'lLïSs ´mn*! Apparently using it to manipulate electricity involves a major drain on our own resources. Here, let me help. . . ."

Quickly she funneled a stream of *mMj´q* by-products into my bloodstream. Slowly my vision cleared; some of my strength returned—bringing with it a fresh sense of alarm: Meg had released her own *t'lLïSs ´mn's* to save me from collapse; we were completely unarmed.

As if to emphasize the point, a hail of explosive shells ripped away a portion of the slope beneath us, breaking off the discussion. A volley of missiles followed. Meg was right: That guy was was out of practice.

But the other two had no such problems: Their fire-control systems worked fine and we were totally exposed. They couldn't possibly miss unless somehow we made it to that crevasse in time.

We dived, risking the proximity of the jagged slopes despite the erratic gusts; knowing that dodging wouldn't help once those computer gunsights locked onto us; hoping that a burst of all-out speed might catch them by surprise after all the broken-field running we'd been doing.

We stroked as never before, accelerating downhill, skimming the rocks, feeling the turbulence tear at us—wondering how soon it would be cannon shells.

As we raced down the slope, Meg and Memphus again tightened their linkage. This time their combined efforts were split: They re-created one of their *t'lLïSs ´mns* and started building up its charge; simultaneously they continued restoring the energies I had expended and worked to replace those I used as I labored, with furious haste, to re-create my own particle-beam weapon and build voltage.

Two hundred yards to go. . . .

I risked a peek over my shoulder—and cringed at the sight of our three remaining pursuers lined up abreast, guns and missiles leveled—

But at Meg's horrified, betrayed-sounding gasp, I snapped my eyes forward. . . .

Two more helicopter gunships, identical in every respect to those behind us, were rising in formation from the crevasse in our path to hover side-by-side, blocking our escape.

The shock was too great: My concentration broke; the *t'lLïSs ´mn* flared into nothingness and was gone. A sulfurous burst of thought informed me that Meg's had suffered the same fate—we were unarmed again.

We braked heavily and looked around wildly, but there was nowhere left to go. Not only were we unarmed, we were effectively surrounded . . . !

As if in slow motion, I saw the missile pods of the left-hand helicopter ahead of us belch flame. My muscles twitched, instinctively trying to dodge—uselessly, I knew; but "give up" just isn't part of my make-up.

"I'm sorry . . ." I started to think at Meg—

The apology was interrupted by a concussion, almost heavy enough to tumble us midair—*which struck from behind* . . . !

Then the right-hand copter's pods gushed fire.

Another explosion. I glanced back. . . .

Only a solitary gunship remained; on either side of it, two fireballs faded into ugly black smoke, already being whipped away by the wind. Flaming wreckage cascaded all over the mountainside.

We heard our remaining pursuer's engine note deepen as the pilot spun his craft about and started to accelerate uphill.

Belatedly Meg and I reacted: As one we clawed for lift, climbing desperately to get out of the line of fire—as the Gatling cannons of both hovering ships abruptly vomited destruction.

A third fireball bloomed; more debris clattered and tinkled onto the rocks.

Suddenly we were alone above the windblown slopes with those two enigmatic gunships. . . .

Meg and I eyed each other uncertainly, regarding them warily. But they made no hostile moves; both continued to hover in place, watching us. Cautiously we banked and headed toward the border once more.

The gunships swung around to follow.

They caught up quickly and settled into formation with us, remaining a polite distance, one on each side, as we continued downslope.

The border came and went. Meg and I breathed sighs of relief—which caught in our throats as one helicopter edged closer and a crewman waved for us to follow.

There seemed little choice.

Oh, we did debate a couple alternatives: the wisdom, for instance, of re-creating the *t'lLïSs´mns*, charging them, and keeping them handy, just in case. We decided against it. These ships,   lividually, radiated a no-nonsense air of competent efficiency which managed, somehow, to be more intimidating than all ten of our recent pursuers put together. If we didn't get them both in a single shot, I very much doubted we'd be allowed a second—these guys knew their stuff . . . !

Besides, we were in the Free World now; truly awful consequences were unlikely. Almost surely we'd be allowed a phone call; after that it wouldn't take long before things were back under control.

The helicopters started down. Their destination was an innocuous clearing ringed by unmarked trucks and other vehicles. Two trucks' roofs were a forest of antennas.

The gunships settled to the ground and we heard the turbines' wailing engine note abruptly begin to whine down toward a stop. It occurred to me that if we stalled until they stopped altogether, then bolted, we'd probably get at least a minute's head start.

But on reflection, that didn't seem like a very good idea. There was no telling what what additional resources these people had squirreled away in those trucks. Helicopters aren't the only vehicles capable of launching heat-seekers.

We waited for the rotors to stop; then glided down, braked, and touched down in the middle of the clearing. We stowed our wings behind and above us and turned to meet our rescuers.

Or perhaps captors, depending on their intentions. . . .

The pilot of the nearer gunship exited and turned purpose-fully toward us. This was a short, chunky individual whose features were totally concealed by the visor of a full-coverage helmet which lent a distinctly insectlike aspect to the wearer's appearance. The pilot fumbled with the helmet's chin-strap and started toward us.

I glanced quickly around the clearing. Two other people emerged in the pilot's wake; several others exited the other gunship. Still additional personnel materialized from inside various of the vehicles surrounding the clearing. None but the pilot made a move in our direction; the rest stood quietly a minimum of a hundred yards away—watching, waiting.

Not only was everyone armed, but the location and angle of the holster hanging from the belt of the approaching pilot's flight suit served notice that the wearer knew what it was there for, all of which combined to inhibit rash impulses.

Only then did I remember our physical appearance. . . .

But already it was too late; the pilot was within ten feet, still wrestling with the helmet and muttering. The voice, though muffled and distorted by the full visor, seemed oddly familiar. I barely could make out the words: ". . . can accept bottomless, massless fuel tanks, I guess I can swallow jury-rigged, field-constructed, personal ornithopters capable of knocking down seven out of ten of the best combat helicopters in the world. . . ."

The pilot stopped in front of us and, with a final effort, managed to pull the helmet off. Silver hair spilled onto the shoulders of the flight suit. Dark eyes twinkled merrily through wire-rimmed, circa-1890s "granny" bifocals.

"Boss," Rebecca Two-Knives began earnestly, "would this be a good time to mention how long it's been since I've had a raise . . . ?"

She grinned; her eyes danced; there were spots of color in her cheeks. She looked more like a kid at Christmas than a grandmother who had just emerged from mortal aerial combat. "Good fight, huh, Boss? I haven't had so much fun since the mission where we short-sheeted the Ayatollah."

Then her eyes went round and her jaw dropped.

But all she said was "Oh . . . my . . . *Lord* . . . !"

TO: Project Director/Monitor's Log.
FROM: H'tTosym, Fifth Order.
SUBJECT: Project *Extremis*.

It was indeed well that we had a team of Tenth Order practitioners standing by. Subject Cory, Agent Megonthalyä, and her *fmMl'hr* would not have survived this episode but for that soldier's "incredible oversight" in failing to snap off the safety on his rifle, and especially that "fortuitous" wind shear: They never saw those missiles until they detonated. We were prepared to intervene further, but such proved unnecessary; Cory's endlessly inventive resourcefulness and refusal to give up, together with our team's creditable performance under fire—coupled with prior operation of Cory's unconscious, instinctive infallibility in the hiring of outstandingly competent key personnel—combined at the last second to bring victory out of chaos.

It was, however, a very near thing, and word spread rapidly; I would estimate that probably ten percent of the viewers on this planet were focused on the conflict by the time it ended. I suspect that "Cory-watching" is going to prove quite popular before this project is terminated.

At the risk of repeating myself: Rebecca Two-Knives was expensive—but a *bargain* . . . !

Becky took one look at us; then turned on her heel and ordered everyone into the two big, antenna-studded, windowless trucks and shut the doors. Just as quickly, she bustled us to a motor home mounted on a heavy-duty six-by-six chassis and thrust us inside. Peering through the windows, we watched her yank open the trucks' doors and issue rapid-fire orders. Twenty minutes later, with the camp having metamorphosed into the equivalent of a heavy armored division, we were ready to move out.

Becky returned to the motor home. She looked all directions before opening the door; then slipped inside, closing and locking it after her. She turned and looked us up and down for a long moment, shook her head silently, and slid behind the wheel.

Slipping on a comunit headset, she issued traveling orders, and the procession moved out. Two pseudotank six-by-sixes took the point. These were followed by one of the electronics trucks, three antiaircraft units, two more crew-accommodation motor homes, then us. Three trucks full of spares and tools followed; then the fuel tankers, three more antiaircraft units, and the other electronics truck. The remaining four "tanks" brought up the rear, cannons and missile-launchers traversing alertly back and forth across our trail. The helicopters, refueled and reloaded, hovered protectively overhead, surveillance electronics trained behind us.

Becky had no idea whether the Communists were ready to call it quits or intended to contest the matter further, but she was taking no chances: We were "bugging out" at max— covering our retreat with intensive surveillance and the heaviest firepower.

We drove in strained silence for probably ten minutes before Becky spoke. Without taking her eyes off the path, she said: "Boss, we really *do* have to talk. . . ."

She was right, of course. We should have included Becky in our planning from the beginning; I realized that now. The only reason I hadn't was concern over her probable reaction. Becky was a trained security specialist, after all. The details of her job description, furnished as a medical history, would have produced a clinical diagnosis of acute paranoia.

Obviously I had misjudged her. Meg followed my thoughts and agreed.

Becky listened in silence, occasionally glancing at us in the mirror over the windshield. When I took a breath, Meg took over. When she paused, I resumed the narrative. Between us we pretty well covered everything.

She took it well. She neither argued nor protested during the recital. When we finished, she asked a couple of questions by way of clarification; then drove in silence for a while, digesting the information. Once she turned her head and regarded us quizzically, but turned back to the road without speaking.

Finally she took a long breath, held it, and released it slowly. Briefly she found my eyes in the mirror. "Boss," she began politely, "since the moment I found Meg on your porch, I've been wracking my brains, trying to figure out how she got there without setting off the alarms." She paused reflectively. "I personally tested and reviewed every component. I had all the manufacturers' experts in and *they* tested and reviewed every component. We re-IPL'd the computers, had them test each other; then we had them test the system as a whole. The upshot was that, even with your complicity, she could *not* have gotten through my systems without tripping *something*. Period. Yet there she was. . . ."

Becky shook her head, marveling. "Believe it or not, it's a *relief* to learn the answer. Aliens were about tenth on my list of silly-season speculations once the rational theories fell apart— though that possibility moved up several notches when you sprung those weight- and mass-immune tanks on me! Without something at least that startling to explain it, the only possibility remaining was that I wasn't doing my job; that somehow, somewhere, I had left a hole in the system."

Becky caught my eye in the mirror again. "Now, you're the boss; it's entirely within your prerogative to withhold information from me, or any employee, at your discretion. However, my bottom-line responsibility, stripped of corporatese, is to keep you alive and your assets intact. When you hold back information affecting my performance of that responsibility, you make my job harder. Under the wrong circumstances, you may make it impossible.

Her expression hardened. "Boss, I love you like a son, and

nobody ever accused you of being a cheapskate when it comes to payment for services rendered. I have never enjoyed working for anyone as much as I do you. But if you *ever* do this to me again—*you can start looking for a new security chief* . . . !" For a moment, Becky's eyes almost flashed fire.

I apologized forthwith and assured her that never again would I put her in such a position. She accepted with grace.

Then she regarded Meg intently. Conflicting emotions played over her face. "No kidding," she asked, "are you really an *alien* . . . ?"

"She is," responded Memphus, with a twitch of his tail. The cat lay on the dashboard. He had been grooming nonstop since emerging from my pouch, astonishingly rumpled and profoundly relieved to be alive.

"I'm only half alien, myself," he continued. "This strapping specimen of *Felis domestica* in which I currently reside was made in the U.S. of A. It's only my soul that's alien." He eyed her levelly for a moment, then winked.

These were the first words the *fmMl'hr* had uttered in Becky's presence. The result was unexpected. She stared for whole seconds, then laughed: genuinely, heartily, delightedly.

"Oh, *my* . . . !" she puffed, dabbing at a tear as her merriment tapered off at last. "Boss, I sure hope you never find out how much fun working for you really is—not only won't I get that raise, you'll cut my salary for sure!"

The eyes which regarded me from the mirror twinkled with mischief. "The impending end of the galaxy, half-breed aliens, and now this. . . ." She gestured at our *chiroptera*-based physical structure. "I love it! Compared to working for you, international intrigue was *dull*. . . ."

Up to that point, while I'd been vaguely conscious of a nonspecific disquiet festering somewhere in the depths of my id, I hadn't been able to identify the cause. "International intrigue" triggered the connection.

"Rebecca," I said slowly, "a lot of people would be so grateful to have you pop out of that canyon and save them that it wouldn't occur to them that that was one hell of a coincidence."

"You're welcome," she grinned. Her expression was a study in purest self-satisfaction.

"Okay, you knew from the satellite photographs where we were going to cross *into* Tibet, and you undoubtedly bugged the bike and our equipment. But we abandoned our gear back at Kyaring Tsho; and after we cleared the summit, we departed considerably from our previous course because we were traveling as-the-crow-flies. Yet there you were, armed to the teeth, lying in ambush well inside Tibetan airspace, directly in our path. Now, you couldn't keep those helicopters there on a long-term, just-in-case basis; nor would you have had any reason to.

"So. How did you know where to find us, how did you know we were coming out just then—*and how the hell did you know we were in trouble* . . . ?"

Becky didn't answer immediately, but she looked almost unbearably pleased with herself. "Boss, do you remember that big prophylactic injection the doctor gave you just before you left?"

"I certainly do. Are you trying to change the subject?"

"Would I do that?"

"Is that a rhetorical question?"

"Only if *that* isn't. Does it still ache now and then?"

"Of course. What relevancy . . ." I stopped, open-mouthed. Suddenly I knew the answer: that huge needle; that persistent residual ache—Becky had "bugged" *me*! I was carrying an ultraminiature transmitter inside my thigh muscle.

Realization must have shown on my face. Becky nodded. "It's an amazing piece of microminiaturization, the product of a friend who owes me some favors and knows I'd never get him in trouble. The whole thing's the shape of a multivitamin capsule, and about half the size, and it's powered by your own chemical electricity.

"But the real breakthrough lies in the area of signal generation: Despite its size, the antenna emits far down in the long-wave spectrum. It's an obscure band; unlikely to be monitored by anyone outside the scientific community and, of course, yours truly. Infinitesimal wattage involved, but astounding range; and the signal goes right through mountains, or even the mass of the planet, as if they were so much vacuum. It incorporates the cutest little processing chip, which digitalizes all inputs, making it just as effective at transmitting data as putting out a beacon. To eavesdrop on you, we computer-processed out your heart, lung, and bowel sounds, leaving conversation and background noises. Automatic rifle fire comes through loud and clear.

"We tracked you throughout your travels; but when we

heard you running for the border with the whole Red Army after you, we went in to meet you. Nothing to it."

At the risk of repeating myself—again—Becky was expensive. But a *bargain*!

CHAPTER 17

Returning to civilization was quicker and much more comfortable than the trip out had been. We stayed with the convoy only long enough to change back to our natural forms in the privacy of the motor home. (Becky was fascinated.) Thereafter we transferred to a helicopter and flew directly to Dacca, where we found a jetliner waiting, having been commandeered from one of my airlines. We were back on Cory Cay less than twenty-four hours after crossing the border into Sikkim.

Then we got *busy*. There was so much to do: assembling the mundane components which, once Meg and Memphus finished with them, would serve as our transportation to Isis; gathering supplies and fuel for the trip; arranging interim management during my protracted absence (a couple weeks' or even a month's absence was one thing; disappearing from the face of the Earth for a minimum of a year, and more probably two or three, increased the difficulty factor considerably).

But I delegated enthusiastically, and soon we began to see progress. Choosing a behind-the-screens, overall babysitter for the business took almost no thought. Becky at first protested that she'd be out of her depth in such a position. This was nonsense, of course; her administrative background was at least as solid as mine—and, more importantly, she was a thoroughly professional, eminently qualified *leader*. She lacked the financial sophistication of my market experts, but she was intelligent and seldom had to have anything explained twice. My executive staff all respected her. She was the logical choice.

(Besides, Meg had reported that she was utterly trustworthy [in all her experience she had never encountered a mind so honest—according to the tenets of her own code, of course; she saw nothing wrong with a little corner-cutting in the interests of efficiency] and unswervingly devoted to me. That last came as a shock. I couldn't imagine what I had done to earn such loyalty.)

I left preparations for the trip in her capable hands, which left the three of us free to concentrate on the $wWn'dt$. Under normal circumstances, Meg and Memphus alone would have dealt with it; employing their arcane skills and training to cut the stone into the geometrically perfect dodecahedral shape required to channel useful quantities of $mMj'q$ particles from their home universe into ours. However, when she explained what she had in mind, it occurred to me that we could save a great deal of time by taking advantage of the existing technological base here on Earth. Accordingly, she outlined what had to be done, and I made the arrangements. Experts and equipment arrived the next day by plane.

Analysis of the stone and plotting the cuts took most of the morning. Computerized x-ray, laser, and ultrasonic analysis defined the internal crystalline structure—much more accurately than any Isi could have done it, Meg informed me wistfully—then a powerful industrial-grade laser, guided by the computer, was employed to carve off unwanted material. The actual cutting was over in two hours.

Meg was thrilled almost beyond words with the result, and even I was pretty impressed: Just under six inches in diameter, the stone's twelve equal, smoothly polished, luridly red-glowing, pentangular facets seemed to catch and reflect every chance flicker of light. But, of course, esthetics were the least consideration.

Far more important was the fact that the finish-cut ruby ended up appreciably larger in proportion to the raw stone than would have been possible using traditional methods.

And most critical of all was the stone's conformation: Its facets were aligned with unprecedented precision and constituted virtually unblemished plane surfaces. While smaller than most, this ruby approached the ideal, geometrically flawless dodecahedron which represented the perfect $wWn'dt$ more closely than any in Meg's experience. She expected it to be disproportionately efficient.

"Always assuming activation proceeds without complications," observed Memphus dryly. "That's the *fun* part. . . ."

Meg favored him with a cold stare. "You and I have differing notions of fun."

That night Becky and I watched in horrified (I was; but I don't think Becky had a nerve in her body) fascination as Meg and Memphus activated the $wWn'dt$. Much of my preliminary unease stemmed from the scope of the preparations, which went far beyond those which they had employed to summon KjJnyrb'n, the so'called lesser Dää'mn, for my "benefit."

At Meg's request, a five-foot-high, flat-topped, circular sand mound, thirty feet across, was built up above the surrounding beach, courtesy of a bemused maintenance crew. After everything was wetted down to ensure a firm surface on which to work, the entire mound was enclosed in a sprawling pentagram sketched in the surrounding sand, built up from ten levels of concentric pentagrams, each separated from the next by a complicated pattern sketched in the sand, with the usual indescribable designs at the points.

The ruby lay on a table at the center of the work area. Spaced evenly around it, well within the outer pentagram, were four smaller versions of the primary which, I knew from experience, were intended to accommodate us. Each was about six feet in diameter, and each contained a three-foot hummock of sand upon which, Meg advised us, we were to stand.

My purely academic knowledge of the mechanics of the practice of the $pwW'r$ had progressed to the point where I could begin to appreciate the degree of caution being exercised. Now I understood, for example, that to the particles constituting the $mMj'q$ flow, these patterns in the sand performed a function somehow analogous to that of current-flow paths in solid-state electronics: One outline equated to a transformer, another to an isolation circuit; still others to signal filters, MOP circuits, resistors, amplifiers, antennas, and whatnot.

The Isi word for the enclosures themselves was $wWr'dts$ (pronounced "wards," of course; another mythological word-root uncovered), and the pentagrams themselves corresponded to grounded insulators. The $wWr'dts$ were the very first manifestation of the $pwW'r$ to be discovered by the Isi. In their most fundamental form, $wWr'dts$ bar the passage in either direction of the particular form of energy which, in this universe, constitutes "life." Initially, back in the dawn of history, the Isi had erected them around their primitive enclaves as protection from what Meg referred to as ". . . some of the most inimical wildlife the galaxy has ever seen."

Subsequent research led to development of the $wWr'dts$

Meg and Memphus had established to safeguard us—and apparently the whole rest of the planet—from the forces which would be invoked this evening: immaterial barriers, tunable to exclude virtually any form of life-force and/or matter occurring anywhere in any of the known universes.

"All of which is *necessary*," explained Memphus soberly. "What's required here is an alteration of the sub-sub-sub-, et cetera, -atomic structure of the corundum to enhance the $mMj'q$ flow. In principle, the technique involved is little different from the method we employed to strengthen the vital components of the motorcycle and yacht.

"In practice, the structure of corundum is much more complicated than that of steel, aluminum, or fiberglass. We can't accomplish it ourselves.

"Which means, unfortunately, that we have to call in some really high-powered help. Next to these folks', Däa'mn morality looks like an extension of the Boy Scout motto.

"Under normal circumstances this wouldn't be necessary; we'd draw from one or more other $wWn'dts$ to activate this one. Regrettably, this is the only $wWn'dt$ available. So we have to do it the hard way."

Meg placed us on the sand mounds at the centers of our respective personal $wWr'dts$ with the usual caution about not coming out until she, *personally* and *physically*, came in to get us. I added a personal endorsement to that advice for Becky's benefit—unnecessarily, I'm sure; she was no stranger to the concept of following orders.

Meg began: She slipped off her bikini, tossed it well beyond the area enclosed by the outer $wWr'dts$, and sat, cross-legged and nude, within the confines of her individual $wWr'dts$. Apologetically she severed our rapport: "I'm going to be awfully busy for a little while. I hope you don't mind. . . ."

Once again she began to croon an odd little melody. (Despite appearances, this was not an incantation. Various components of the $wWr'dts$ responded to sound; variations in pitch, duration, and volume were key factors in an adept's control of the apparatus. Needless to say, all $wWyh'js$, $wWyhr$ $läaqs$, and $fmMl'hrs$ had perfect pitch.) Once again she completed the small sketch in the sand before her . . .

And once again the lines in the sand began to glow.

The luminescence was much more visible at night than in bright sunlight; and now I saw the reason for the varying elevations: The mounds placed all four of us physically above the immaterial floors of our individual *wWr'dts*, and them above the floor of the larger *wWr'dts* enclosing the balance of the work area.

The ghostly patterns extended above us as well as below: Each pentagram glowing against the sand formed the floor of an intangible, multilayered, dodecahedral, phosphorescent cage. Each of us was enclosed on all sides—as was the entire work area.

This time there was no acrid, greenish-purple smoke.

But without warning there came a stomach- and soul-wrenching sensation, as if gravity, at least, and more probably the entire universe, had shifted on their mountings. The brightly moonlit beach of Cory Cay no longer was visible beyond the walls of the outermost *wWr'dts;* the full moon and clouds of stars, shining down from what only moments ago had been a brilliant, cloudless tropical night sky, were gone— indeed, the barrier itself apparently had vanished, and *nothing* could be seen beyond it.

The only light remaining was a soft glow from the *wWr'dts'* outlines. And all that could be seen by that feeble illumination were the four of us and the faint red glow of the *wWn'dt* in our midst. Beyond that lay utter darkness. Or perhaps "infinite darkness" might be a better descriptive. . . .

Meg's song dropped into a minor key and the tempo slowed. Flickers of formless luminescence materialized here and there about the interior of the greater enclosure. As their numbers mounted, so did the intensity of their radiation and activity. At first they seemed to concentrate on our personal *wWr'dts*, crawling eagerly over the exteriors as if examining them for weaknesses. Then they withdrew from the *wWr'dts* to swirl around the *wWn'dt*, pressing closer and closer, their shifting luminescence nearly blotting out our view of the stone.

Gradually the interior of the work area took on a disturbing sense of presence: an indefinable feeling that all that remained of our native universe was the sand upon which we stood inside our *wWr'dts*—and a conviction that the Others Who Lived Here were gathered just out of sight, watching, hoping for a single mistake.

Meg no longer sang to the circuitry; now she spoke: loudly, clearly, firmly; addressing the inhabitants of this dark universe into which our work area impinged. The language was unfamiliar but there was no mistaking the authority in her tone.

And suddenly, *out there* in the darkness beyond where the invisible walls of the perimeter *wWr'dts* should have been, something stirred. . . .

Something big. Something huge. Something inconceivably, incomprehensibly vast. Something whose proximity made the hair on the back of my neck stand up but which remained no more than a monstrous, shifting area of still-deeper black out in the darkness.

And suddenly I knew what lay behind Man's instinctive fear of the dark.

I stole a quick glance in Becky's direction, wondering what effect all this was having on her. I should have known: Her face was wreathed in smiles; she was entranced—hell, she was positively delighted!

Meg raised her voice further. She was shouting now: insisting, demanding, badgering, haranguing—almost threatening.

I don't know when it happened; I didn't see it begin. But suddenly my stomach knotted. *Something moved slowly among us . . . !*

Something very dark. Something amorphous and indistinct. Something with neither substance nor texture; yet whose presence absorbed light utterly and occulted whatever lay beyond it.

With great deliberation, advancing like the pseudopod of some incredible, nightmarish amoeba, an extension of *that* which abided in the darkness flowed into the work area. It ignored us in our enclosures and reached directly for the *wWn'dt*. Glowing, flickering nonshapes darted from its path with a single-mindedness suggesting out-and-out panic.

The intangible yet impenetrably dark appendage flowed about the *wWn'dt*, blotting out the blood-colored reflections.

Meg fell silent, watching. Her expression was strained. For long moments the tableau continued.

Then her voice rang out again; not further arcane communications in obscure languages, but a wordless yell of purest exultation. Without being told, I knew that the dweller in the darkness had carried out its part in the transaction.

Now, of course, it expected payment. I wondered what the going rate was for activating a *wWn'dt*.

The dark tentacle moved. No more quickly than it had approached, it drew back from the *wWn'dt* and continued to recede into the infinite blackness beyond.

Confidence and assurance echoed in Meg's voice as she resumed speaking in that unknown tongue, again addressing the darkness.

Then the *wWn'dt* pulsed: an almost palpable burst of . . . of *something* . . .

Something indescribable. Something which should have been perceptible but wasn't. Quite. A radiant emission; but patently not light, for it *felt* dark somehow, and bore no resemblance to any color of the Earthly spectrum.

And simultaneous with the pulse, a dazzling pinpoint appeared far out in the darkness beyond the walls of the *wWr'dts*.

Again the *wWn'dt* pulsed darkly. The pinpoint became a shaft of light, painful to look at in contrast to the blackness around it. The *wWn'dt* pulsed still again, and the shaft became a blinding flood of incredibly hot, fervently blue-white radiation—recognizable at last as sunlight, though obviously not from Sol.

Hungrily the darkness surged toward the light, enveloped it, and then both were gone.

The coin of the transaction had been energy. (Later I learned that, for cooperation in projects of any substance, the dark-dweller demanded that particular form of energy which constitutes "life.")

The *wWn'dt* pulsed again—the perimeter *wWr'dts* reappeared, and through them shown a familiar moon and starry sky; we were back on the beach at Cory Cay. The blue-glowing outlines of the *wWr'dts* wavered and vanished. The night sea breeze stirred my hair. It smelled awfully good.

Meg stood unmoving for long moments, breathing hard. Then she shook herself, almost like an animal. She stepped purposefully over the pentagram sketched in the sand surrounding her, and crossed the intervening beach to the scorched and still-smoking table on which the *wWn'dt* lay. She placed a reverent hand on the stone; then picked it up in both hands and turned to me. She radiated serenity and assurance.

She raised the *wWn'dt* above her head in both hands, standing slim and beautiful in the moonlight. The *wWn'dt* pulsed. For a heartbeat she stood clothed in crackling, blue-glowing, electrical flames, which explored her body like a lover's hands.

Meg smiled. "The *pwW'r* is ours to command now, Peter," she breathed. "We *will* save the galaxy. . . ."

CHAPTER 18

The next day I bought an old DC-9. Not that I didn't have plenty of newer, better, faster, more efficient jetliners of my own—shucks, I had plenty of air*lines*—but the configuration of the DC-9 airframe, with twin engines mounted one on each side, outboard in pods at the extreme rear of the fuselage, lent itself especially well to starship conversion: First, when operating in zero-gee conditions and in a vacuum, it's helpful to have your thrust located precisely behind your center of mass. Then, too, hanging the engines in outboard pods minimized the reengineering required to replace the turbofans with Rockwell liquid-fueled, throttleable rocket engines. Directional control in space would be handled by standard Aerojet thrusters.

The refitters gutted the single long passenger compartment, breaking it into a series of smaller chambers separated by airtight bulkheads. Complete and appropriately luxurious appointments were installed, including such basic amenities as a gourmet galley, stereo throughout, and a Jacuzzi.

The linked central processing and auxiliary memory storage units of the central computer (into which the sum total of Man's centuries of astronomical cataloging had been loaded) dwelt below decks, together with the inertial-guidance navigational system to which it was connected, and life-support equipment. Astronomical optical scanning gear, wired for direct input into the computer, helped crowd the expanded cockpit.

The conversion took several weeks of 'round-the-clock, crash-priority effort by troops of employees (whose silence regarding the particulars of the project was ensured by means of a gentle compulsion planted by Meg [security was only one of the things which were less worrisome now that she had a working *wWn'dt*]). It would have taken much longer had we followed the rules; but FAA inspections of work-in-progress would have raised questions for which we had no satisfactory answers. We'd have ended up controlling minds wholesale. It was less trouble all around to have Meg adjust the FAA's records by remote control, without involving personnel at all.

The end result was *Galactic Venture*: outwardly a sleek,

freshly painted, dark green DC-9; exceptionally luxurious inside, potentially very fast—

And utterly useless, under ordinary circumstances. The rocket engines were substantially more powerful than the turbofans they replaced; they were also spectacularly thirstier: The same fuel capacity which once sufficed for nonstop transcontinental operation now provided barely a four-minute full-throttle burn; hardly long enough to get off the ground.

Of course, these were not ordinary circumstances. The *wWn'dt* pulsed darkly several times: Fuel tanks expanded internally, and the weight and mass of their contents ceased to have relevance in this universe; airframe, operating components, and related materials grew tougher; electronics became more reliable; and a mechanism buried in the bowels of the ship (similar to, but more sophisticated than, those used in high school chemistry classes to demonstrate the principle of electrolytic separation of H_2O into its component parts) underwent a massive boost in operating efficiency. Two other devices, which converted gaseous hydrogen and oxygen into supercooled liquids, suffered a similar fate.

Thereafter we fueled and test-ran the engines. (And several employees' self-control [as well as mind blocks Meg had implanted] were put to their severest test yet: These folks had spent eight days pumping sea water nonstop into those fuel tanks.)

Everything checked out: The main engines performed lustily, exceeding rated thrust by eighteen percent (generating far more noise than one would expect from the modest, almost transparent blue flames, though fortunately little of the racket penetrated the hull's insulation), and throttled up and back smoothly. Likewise, the reaction-control-system thrusters for attitude control were just as happy on a diet of liquid hydrogen and oxygen, following a little attention to mixture, as they had been on monomethyl hydrazine and nitrogen tetroxide.

And suddenly we were done: The last item was crossed off the checklist. Preparations were complete; we were packed. There was nothing left to do but say goodbye . . .

Which proved unexpectedly difficult: The past few weeks had drawn me quite close to several employees—Becky most of all. The prospect of at least a year's separation was surprisingly painful. But there was a galaxy to be saved, and time was wasting. We indulged in a round robin of stiff-upper-lip, manly handshakes—then all fell into each others' arms, hugging and sniffling damply. Afterward, of course, everyone drew back and final goodbyes were exchanged in a dignified, restrained manner, as if nothing had happened.

We boarded, fired up, oriented the inertial-guidance system, and took off. The mach meter settled down quickly to a reading of point ninety-two at twenty percent thrust, which comported with data from earlier flight tests.

We headed southeast across the Atlantic toward a gap in the worldwide radar network with which an acquaintance of Becky's was familiar. There we pointed the nose up in earnest and pushed the throttles to their stops.

At an altitude of about seventy-five miles, despite our ever-increasing velocity, the aerodynamic control surfaces lost the final vestiges of effectiveness, and I switched over to the reaction control system. The accelerometer now read one gee, at which rate we would achieve escape velocity in a little under twenty minutes.

A full gee directed straight aft would have made getting around inside the ship pretty awkward; so Meg blocked the action/reaction effects from reaching us, and locally intensified the intrinsic microgravity possessed by all matter to provide normal weight relative to the decks.

After hand-flying the beast for a while on RCS, just to see if I could, I turned things over to the computer, which had begun to scan our surroundings as soon as the sky turned black enough to distinguish stars, and which already was oriented in space.

Earlier Meg had translated the ephemerides for Isis from Isi mathematics into Euclidean, and I had loaded them into the astronomical data base. Upon assuming control, the computer compared our position with Isis' and requested permission to change course. After reviewing the proposed heading to make sure that it didn't intersect any solid objects (Earth, Luna, the nearer planets—the Sun!), I gave it my blessing.

Then I gave Meg the go-ahead. . . .

Obviously a bastardized DC-9, accelerating at one gee, was not going to cover the thirty thousand lightyears separating Earth from Isis within a useful span of time. Just for amusement, I had the computer calculate how long it would take. It determined that (ignoring Einstein completely) the ship's calendar more usefully could be kept by carbon-14 dating.

But of course that was reckoning without the Isi (Einstein reckoned without them, too). Meg and Memphus huddled

over the $wWn'dt$ briefly, and suddenly the ship was inertialess—and equally suddenly (instantaneously, in fact) our
velocity assumed that value which balanced the engines' thrust
against the resistance of interstellar matter.

In seconds the great blue-and-tan beach ball of Earth,
visible in the CRT tuned to one of the aft-pointing TV cameras,
shrank to a disc, then to a dwindling bright speck. Sol receded
visibly as we watched.

I knew we would pass close to Jupiter on the way out of the
system. I hadn't bothered working out the details; but now, as
it swelled ahead of us, growing quickly from a point of light to a
shining button, then to a striped disc, it started to look as if we
might be on a collision course. I hoped so; that would put the
navigational software to an immediate test. Maybe I wouldn't
have to spend the next couple of days sitting at the helm,
waiting to see if the anticollision program worked.

I wasn't worried about small stuff; inertialess as we were,
collisions per se didn't matter. But the velocity produced by
combining the engines' full-throttle thrust with gravity upon
plunging vertically into a planetary atmosphere would amount
to something in the neighborhood of mach four. And even
though $Venture$'s airframe was immensely stronger now, the
skin still was aluminum—Meg's treatment hadn't affected its
melting point.

Nor was I all that thrilled with the prospect of diving into
the heart of a star at five parsecs an hour . . . !

Accordingly, several optical scanning peripherals "looked"
forward, and the software contained instructions to watch for
and drive around anything in our way big enough to show up
as a disc. And even as Jupiter grew larger in the cockpit
windows and I started thinking seriously about switching to
manual, the computer noticed the obstruction, side-stepped
neatly, and resumed course. I breathed a sigh of relief; I had
not looked forward to splitting watches all the way to Isis.

It was also a relief to find that we still $could$ see our
surroundings at this speed. I'd received conflicting opinions on
the question. Some held that, once above light-speed, photons
wouldn't register at all, either on our instruments or our
retinas. Others opined that, if one's speed through the medium
dopplered the frequency we know as "visible light" too high to
see by, it would correspondingly undoppler longer waves
down to where one could see by $them$. I was glad that the
optimists had carried the day.

Of course the ship's inertia was not "gone" per se; it was merely stored. And that troubled me: How does one "store" inertia? Meg tried really hard to explain. We got as far as the "inertia-storage field" and bogged down in Isi technicalities which I lacked the background to comprehend.

On the other hand, she didn't do much better with my explanation of why *rockets* work.

(And she got downright testy when I asked her how an *inertial*-guidance system worked in an inertia*less* ship. . . .)

CHAPTER 19

Ra is a blue-white supergiant star found near the geometric center of the galaxy. The star's family consists of seventy-six planets, ranging from near-molten Räat'oh, dancing precariously just beyond Roche's limit, to far distant, eternally frozen P'rRmys, half a lightyear out. In addition, due to its location and vast gravitational influence, Ra has, over the ages, captured into irregular orbits countless vagabond asteroids, comets, and assorted drifting debris.

Apart from Ra's size, the numbers of its retinue, and the scale of intrasystemic distances, nothing particularly distinguishes this system from the countless gigagoogles of others to be found throughout the universes.

Except for Isis. Isis *is* unusual. I'm no astrogeophysicist, but even to me, some of the more obvious anomalies leap out of the data:

Though qualifying as captured space drift, Isis occupies an almost geometrically perfect, circular orbit in the temperate zone of Ra's radiant output.

Though two and a half times the size of Jupiter, Isis' surface acceleration exceeds Earth's by barely two percent—and not even the Isi know why. Heavy elements are scarce, of course, but that doesn't explain it: Assuming the validity of the gravitational constant, even a sphere of gasses that size *must* generate a vastly more powerful gravity field.

(But perhaps, if all the facts were known, "gravitational *constant*" overstates the proposition. Or maybe Whoever made Isis hadn't gotten around to thinking about Newton yet. . . .)

Whatever the explanation, the mystery began long, long

ago, and far, far away: Not only is Isis extrasystemic in origin, it is extragalactic—and substantial evidence exists to suggest that the planet may have been left over from a previous Cycle of Creation. The Isis' most distant direct historical projection shows the huge world—dark, unthinkably cold—still a million lightyears above the elliptical plane of the slowly contracting cluster of dust and gasses which one day would condense to form our galaxy.

But certain forms of life—notably those which propagate through sporification—are virtually immune to the ravages of cold or time: Not even the incalculable duration of near-absolute-zero to which the sunless, wandering world had been subject could kill all the life which had existed there before some unknown and unknowable celestial cataclysm tore it from its parent sun and hurled it out between the galaxies.

And so, untold eons ago, when Ra was still young, as these matters are judged, Isis drifted in from the intergalactic void, into the sprawling gravitational attraction of the huge star. An immense comet, itself almost a planet, applied a braking force, and Isis stabilized in orbit—in perfect equilibrium, during a perfect moment of the new star's development.

Isis warmed quickly: The solidified atmosphere resumed its gaseous state; oceans melted; permafrosted soil thawed—already fertile and teeming with life. And at a time when every other planet firm enough to bear the name still was a swamp of lava, boiling seas, and hot rain, Isis had become merely rampantly tropical beneath a still-cooling sun. Shortly, by evolutionary standards, complicated organisms and animals developed from the primitive survivors of the intergalactic passage.

But during the course of that endless voyage, Isis had come too close to other suns on occasion; the resulting tidal effects had left the surface badly wrinkled, a waffle pattern of mountain ranges so massive that many peaks projected beyond the atmosphere. Trapped between them, thousands of pocket ecosystems came into being, in which myriad species competed for local dominance, many achieving high degrees of evolutionary sophistication.

Exoskeletal, insectile developments might flourish in the hothouse, high-pressure environment of great equatorial valleys, their floors depressed fifty to eighty miles below sea level. Perhaps warm-blooded evolution came out on top in other, more moderate areas. Elsewhere, multicellular colonies achieved success. And in still other locations, airborne and even combustion-digestion varieties proliferated.

However, with but a single exception, the dominant species in every area (generally there was more than one) tended to be carnivores of unparalleled efficiency.

The final return of that massive comet at about this time sent Isis into another period of tectonic unease, reshuffling the geologic barriers separating these microcosms one from another, initiating a worldwide battle for supremacy which still continues. Of the most formidable sixty-odd percent of indigenous fauna, no single species proved to be truly dominant—but the question is far from resolved. . . .

One of the then-locally-reigning species hurled into the worldwide competition at that point was the Isi: intelligent and well on the way toward civilization, but physically inferior— weak, slow, soft-skinned; lacking the acute olfactory and auditory faculties possessed by those which now preyed upon them; gentle, inclined toward pacifism; easily killed, emi- nently edible—they were widely regarded as the meal of choice. . . .

Their rudimentary civilization crumbled and vanished in a matter of decades. Whatever technology they had achieved by that stage in their development vanished with it.

Not that it mattered: No technomechanical breakthrough would have had the slightest practical effect on their situation; no physical weapon short of, possibly, nuclear explosives would have sufficed to deal with the quality and intensity of the opposition they faced. Against the speed, strength, size, and single-minded, ravenous ferocity of the incredible varieties and sheer numbers of predators they faced, the primitive weapons of the day probably were less effective than bare hands—a weapon can impart a fatally false sense of security. . . .

Tools, weapons, and their principles were reinvented and lost time and again over generations. Eventually would-be inventors quit bothering: The demands of food-gathering and hiding left no time or energy for useless hobbies.

Simply, the Isi faced extinction. It was only a matter of time and they knew it. With the knowledge that it would take a miracle to save them, they achieved, as a people who didn't believe in miracles, a species-wide level of desperation unrivaled in the history of the universe.

Which *did* produce a miracle. . . .

Out of that desperation sprang the *kï* (pronounced, and loosely translated, as "key") to the *pwW'r;* the first practical application of which was the *wWr'dts*—immaterial barriers proof against even the most inimical of Isi predators.

The Isi were given no choice: They *had* to discover the *kï* to the *pwW'r* to survive. There simply was no alternative. Period.

But they did.

And the rest, as Meg said, is history. . . .

CHAPTER 20

Three months after we lifted away from Earth, Isis detached itself from the brilliantly crowded, magnificently starry firmament which serves as a backdrop at the galactic hub. It swelled in seconds from a pinpoint of light to a disk as we approached. I throttled the main engines back to minimum thrust the moment we discerned the planet; then cut them entirely and proceeded on RCS alone. But still we were inertialess; and even on the tiny maneuvering thrusters, our approach amounted to a respectable fraction of light-speed.

Now, whatever inertia, mass, or momentum (pick a name, pick *any* name) we possessed upon leaving Earth would have been a combination of our own course and speed, Earth's orbital velocity around Sol, and Sol's motion about the galactic center—and it was *suspended*, not canceled. It still existed . . . "somewhere." The moment that that inertia was restored, we would resume our original course and speed— which, originating in a solar system located better than halfway to the galaxy's rim, wouldn't bear much resemblance to that of a planet orbiting a star located virtually at the hub.

Further, as I mentioned earlier, Isis was an *old* planet. Its acquisition of satellites was begun long before the galaxy's coalescence; the process was well along: At this time, Isis possessed something over seven thousand charted satellites. They orbited within a vast spherical volume of space surrounding the planet known as the Zone of Moons, and ranged from Earth-sized and larger to pieces of a moon which had come apart in ages past. Additionally, there were hundreds of thousands—if not millions—of unrecorded itinerant smaller objects, covering the gamut from boulders to grains of sand, captured down through the eons.

Only a few rode in orbits owing allegiance to the plane of the ecliptic. The rest, accumulated at random over the ages, circled Isis like the electrons of an astonishingly complex atom.

The Zone was a grinding cloud of stone extending outward from the planet almost a million miles. Neither Meg nor I cared to be in possession of normal inertia anywhere near it. Likewise, we wanted plenty of maneuvering room around us when she restored our inertia. Accordingly, I stopped us dead in space with about two million miles yet to go.

The $wWn'dt$ pulsed; the computer observed and computed. Shortly it reported that things really weren't too bad: Our residual vector was about a hundred forty miles per second, generally "down" relative to our destination. At that speed we would cover the remaining distance in about four hours. Of course, then we'd arrive with that hundred forty miles per second still intact, still needing to be disposed of. However, a mere six and a half hours of braking would suffice to cancel our motion relative to the planet, leaving around a quarter-million-mile safety margin before crossing that arbitrary plane in space which represented the Zone's border.

Once at "rest," we would go inertialess again, and, in a matter of minutes, maneuver safely past the larger satellites (ignoring the smaller stuff), and enter the atmosphere. It didn't matter how fast we might be going when we encountered it; inertialess as we would be, the first hint of air resistance would slow us instantly to whatever speed balanced our thrust. No dramatic atmospheric braking; no concerns about heat buildup—unless I deliberately applied more than twenty percent power and/or lowered the nose too far. Nothing to it.

I rotated us on RCS, aligned the ship's longitudinal axis stern to our direction of travel, and fired up the main engines.

Then I leaned back in the command seat and, as the engines whittled away at our relative speed, watched the disc of the planet swell in the CRT, and reflected contentedly upon the elaborate technical gymnastics National AeroSpace Transport, Inc., found it necessary to go through to practice space travel. It was difficult to avoid a trace of smugness—life certainly was easier when one had access to a $mMj'q$ $wWn'dt$. . . .

The computer had a field day spotting and plotting the orbits of all those satellites in radar or visual-detection range as we backed toward the planet, slowing steadily. This was a one of the very latest, fastest, most powerful computers on the market; with multiple parallel-acting, four-thousand-ninety-six-byte processors—and even so, a good sixty percent of its capacity was tied up in the effort.

A tightly shielded corner of my mind reflected that here was yet another indication of the wisdom of the compudicters' decision to link the Isi with a mechanistic society: With just over a quarter million miles to go before entering the Zone, and our relative velocity down to barely six miles per second relative to Isis, the computer already had located, thus far, some eighteen thousand satellites; more than twice as many as the Isis' science had identified during their entire history to date.

At the moment the computer was doing its best to display their orbits on one of the larger CRTs. The result was an unrecognizable graphic which bore a distinct resemblance to a big, loose ball of yarn. The outline of the planet was completely obscured.

Meg was intrigued; she had never seen so complete a charting of Isis' moons. As usual, though, her perspective diverged from mine: "I can't wait to get you alone down there," she smiled. "When we talk about romantic, moonlit nights on Isis, we do mean *moon*lit!"

"The Zone probably is the reason we've never had company on Isis," yawned Memphus unromantically. The *fmMl'hr* lay stretched out on top of the instrument panel, his back against the starboard windshield. "This is a pretty densely populated neighborhood, starwise. There are quite a few starfacing species around here, and some are pretty widely traveled. But no one has ever come calling, and I don't blame them. Can you imagine trying to navigate a purely mechanistic ship through the Zone?"

"Peter could do it," Meg said confidently, with only a hint too much wide-eyed earnestness. "Peter can do *any*thing."

The cat snorted inelegantly and rolled over to gaze out the windshield.

I smiled and rested my hand lightly on the throttles. In another fifteen minutes we'd be stationary with respect to Isis. Meg's *wWn'dt* lay in her lap; she was ready to suspend our inertia again the moment we "stopped." Inside of an hour we'd be on the ground at La'ïr, the largest community of the tiny section of the planet the Isi occupied, Meg's home "town."

I turned to look at her (I never tired of looking at her)—and my blood froze. . . .

Materializing in the air above her was a—a *thing*!

Meg glanced up and saw it. Her eyes widened. Her reaction was virtually instantaneous—but still far too slow:

Virtually simultaneously with the mighty pulse which exploded darkly from her *wWn'dt*, the thing moved: With a ghastly wailing scream, and with sheerly incredible speed, it reached/oozed/flowed/shot out in some indescribable manner and enveloped both her and Memphus, who never had even a hint of warning.

And then they were *gone* . . . !

TO: Project Director/Monitor's Log.
FROM: Suvalyä, Eighth Order.
SUBJECT: Project *Extremis*.

At the propitious moment, and without incident, Agent Megonthalyä and her *fmMl'hr* have been retrieved. The agent, while in translation, was placed in deep stasis and remains so; Memphus is not pleased. However, her current emotional state and the status of her conditioning render such measures necessary: Under the circumstances, she would not stand idly by while we proceeded with our plans for Subject Cory—and given the inherent power of her mind and the extent of her control of the *pwW'r*, I, for one, will feel more comfortable with the prospect if she remains in stasis until the matter is brought to a conclusion.

Further, it may prove necessary either to condition the agent further or to wipe her programming entirely, depending on how the work with Subject Cory develops.

And, of course, now that Cory is within convenient operating range, we will bear down in earnest. Teams of Tenth Order practitioners are standing by to inflict ever-increasing increments of grief upon him.

I understand that, at this point, a good quarter of the viewers on the planet are following his progress. I cannot say that I am surprised.

I landed in the empty copilot's seat in a tangle of limbs, cracking my head smartly on the arm of the chair. I hadn't even known I was moving. I had perceived a threat to Meg; I reacted—instantly, without thought, but too late. . . .

Now: As a result of the merging of our minds (and apart from my inexplicable failure to grasp her command of the *pwW'r*), I possessed the same knowledge Meg did. However, *possessing* her knowledge was not at all the same thing as enjoying ready access to it: Her mind was organized very differently from mine; locating specific data without specific stimuli was difficult.

The monster's sudden appearance was specific indeed: My fund of second-hand Isis knowledge promptly identified it as a B'nN´ äs'hï (another myth source uncovered). Which was puzzling: The B'nN´ äs'hï were among the more trustworthy of the Isis´ extrauniversal partners in the practice of the *pwW'r*. What possible reason would one have to kidnap an adept and her *fmMl'hr* . . . ? All it would have had to do, if it needed their skills, was ask; the Isi were quite accustomed to translating into the B'nN´ äs'hïs´ universe to assist in such projects. I wondered whether the B'nN´ äs'hï were familiar with the concept of criminality; what they would make of the news that one of their number had turned renegade.

Well, this was hardly the time to dwell on the thing's inner motivations. If Meg lived—no, strike that.

Meg *lived*! Period.

If she had died, I would have known it—I would have *felt* it. . . .

Wherefore: Meg was a prisoner in an alien universe. I had to rescue her! But it didn't take much thought to realize that I lacked the skills and training necessary to mount a rescue expedition into another universe—

There was nothing I could do to help her . . . !

Barely in time I recognized my rapid descent into mounting despair as impending panic. I managed to put on the brakes, but the effort it took to regain control was almost physical in nature.

Of *course* there was something I could do—I could get to La'ïr, just as fast as humanly possible, and inform the Isi that a rogue B'nN´ äs'hï had invaded our universe—that it had kidnapped Meg and Memphus and drawn them back with it into its universe.

Yes, they would know what to do. All I had to do was get to La'ïr and shortly things would be under control.

Only . . . getting to La'ïr, it suddenly occurred to me, no longer was the straightforward proposition it had been only moments before. Complications abounded. . . .

First: At the moment Meg was taken, *Galactic Venture* possessed full inertia. It possessed it now—and the law of conservation of momentum, as well as the gravitational constant, applied in full measure to all future navigation. Secondly, possession of inertia meant that surviving a passage through the Zone of Moons would require some really hot-dog piloting—coupled with a lot of luck!

I had managed by this time to untangle myself from the copilot's seat and return to my own. I looked around. Almost incidentally I noticed that the engines were shut down. Apparently I had hit the kill switches as I leaped. Good thinking on my subconscious' part; it wouldn't have taken much effort for an entity as intelligent and powerful as a B'nN´ äs'hï to convert operating liquid-fuel rocket engines into bombs.

I turned to the computer keyboard and queried our speed, course, and position relative to Isis. The CPU still was furiously busy locating and plotting satellite orbits; but after nearly a minute's wait (which included thirteen and a fraction seconds' delay while a radar pulse made the round trip to the planet's surface and back) the mission status CRT updated all its figures: just under five miles per second, a little over a million and a quarter miles to go—most of it through the Zone. . . .

Well, we were going the right direction; no point wasting perfectly good momentum. I ran the main engine systems through a power-down sequence, leaving them in five-minute-Hold, standby status, and allowed the ship to continue to coast through space as I turned back to the computer.

I told it to continue locating and plotting satellites, and to retain the data but cancel the display. Then I ordered a projection of our present trajectory relative to Isis. The computer served up two green circles to indicate the planet's vertical and horizontal profiles. Red lines intersecting each represented our course.

Dead center. Or as nearly so as made no difference. That wouldn't do at all.

I keyed in a request to ascertain which direction the planet was rotating; then ordered computation of the course corrections required to achieve an eighty-mile-high graze (Isis' gravity was virtually identical with Earth's; I assumed similar atmospheric depth) on the receding horizon.

Next, for no particular reason beyond the fact that I prefer, when possible, to look in the direction I'm traveling, I commanded the inertial-guidance system to rotate us one hundred eighty degrees on the RCS thrusters.

Nothing happened.

Nonplussed, I sent the command a second time.

And still nothing happened. . . .

That was when I noticed that a certain star cluster (there are *lots* of star clusters in the vicinity of the galactic hub, but this one was distinctive), which had been straight ahead when I commenced braking, had moved. . . .

I called up the view directly aft on an unoccupied CRT. Sure enough, the disc of the planet was off-center. I superimposed cross-hairs and calibration circles over the picture and determined that, somehow, the inertial guidance system had permitted a yaw of precisely twenty-two degrees to starboard and a twelve-degree nose-down pitch.

And the displacement still was in progress: Even as I watched, Isis continued to creep almost imperceptibly across the screen.

I called up the peripherals-status submenu and selected inertial-guidance. The subsubmenu reported the system connected but idle. That was clearly anomalous; it should have been full-time operational. I attempted to call for an inertial-guidance software check.

There was none to check.

Shocked, I asked why. The CPU replied that it had been erased.

For a moment I gaped stupidly at the screen; then it occurred to me to ask when. Three minutes ago, came the response.

Impossible . . . ! How could a program as elaborately safeguarded as this one *possibly* have been erased by mistake—

But then I remembered: At the precise instant that Meg had disappeared—her *wWn'dt* had pulsed. . . .

It was a *really* big pulse.

Obviously the massive burst had been intended to combat the attack of the B'nN ́ äs'hï. Instead, with Meg taken just as it arrived, the *mMj'q* had exploded unguided into our universe; no one was around to direct it to its destination.

So it found one of its own.

I took a deep breath, held it, then released it slowly. Theoretically one's tension is supposed to exhaust with the breath. (At least according to my *New-York-Times*–best-seller-list book on yoga. . . .) Then I got to work:

First I gave the RCS thrusters a bump to start the ship

rotating manually—I still wanted to see where I was going. As I glanced up to check the maneuver's progress, I noticed a fine, almost invisibly transparent, silvery vapor swirling just outside the cockpit windows as the ship slowly pivoted. I leaned forward and looked outside—and my heart just about stopped altogether. . . .

The overpressure fuel-release valves had tripped wide open. Water was boiling into space. It took only a moment's frantic speculation to arrive at the probable explanation; and as understanding sank in, the phrase "in big trouble" acquired new depths.

The mechanism which permitted the existence of fuel tanks larger inside than out had ceased to operate; the excess was fountaining overboard and evaporating into the vacuum. Without a doubt I was witnessing another by-product of the *wWn'dt's* parting discharge.

The only bright note was the fact that the overpressure valves were located symmetrically on the wings: As much water was being ejected above as below them; despite the massive volume involved, the resultant thrust was self-canceling. Otherwise, by that time we'd have acquired a substantial random vector, and probably a wild tumble as well.

Plus, it appeared that the tanks were resuming their normal internal displacement progressively, which definitely was One For Our Side: At the very least, those literally cubic miles of theoretically incompressible sea water instantly reasserting their normal volume would have ripped *Venture's* wings to shreds.

Or more likely, since the inertia intrinsic to such a mass of water would limit the rate at which it could expand, compression *would* have occurred—probably *sufficient* compression . . .

I had quite enough to worry about without finding myself at the heart of a fusion reaction.

I shook my head impatiently, symbolically trying to clear away the welter of irrelevant thoughts churning around in there. Then I thought rapidly: The overpressure valves would reclose the moment the internal pressure fell below their preset release point. That should leave me with "full" tanks—*four whole minutes of full-power operation . . . !*

Okay, potentially that was a problem. But there was no point panicking yet. Early Apollo astronauts returning from the Moon weren't even that well off. First I needed to determine precisely the ship's status. If anything else were haywire as a result of that *mMj'q* burst, the best time to learn about it was now, out in open space, with plenty of room and (I hoped) enough time to deal with it in a logical, methodical fashion.

The first logical, methodical step was to instruct the computer to perform a complete self-examination. It was a major installation; the total self-check would take almost two hours. But I had no choice; I could hardly rely on the output of suspect software. I sent the command.

Long before the procedure was done the overpressure valves snapped shut, trapping the remaining water inside. A glance at the gauges confirmed that my fuel supply was indeed four minutes. Two hundred forty seconds. Or, more pertinent to my problems, a velocity change of just under seventy-seven hundred feet per second. Call it a mile and a half.

The computer finished soul-searching and reported that only the actual inertial-guidance software was gone. ("*Only . . . !*") Everything else was fine.

Okay, I'd have to hand-fly the sucker, but at least I'd know which way to point it.

I glanced at the mission status CRT. It still displayed the trajectory graphics, per my most recent query. I noticed, however, that a new word had been inserted in one line: "Time to Intersect" had been replaced with "Time to Impact." The change was the CPU's choice entirely. Absently I wondered whether it knew something I didn't. . . .

In any event, the read-out was sixty-seven hours, thirty-three minutes, and four seconds—plus three additional digits' worth of blurred fractions as the display updated continuously. Time was wasting. Whether it was an "intersection" or an "impact" which loomed in my future, if I had ambitions of surviving it, I'd better quit woolgathering.

Two hours earlier I'd asked for course corrections for an eighty-mile graze. At the time I'd thought I still had effectively unlimited fuel. Obviously those data no longer were valid.

I commanded the system to retain the planetary rotation it had determined earlier; then I changed the problem: The number one priority was absolute minimum fuel consumption; thereafter I duplicated my earlier specification of an eighty-mile-high graze in the direction of rotation at the equator.

It took almost two minutes for the first of these figures to appear. As I waited for the rest, I wondered what was taking so long; I wouldn't have cared to do it with pencil and paper, but for a system as powerful as this, a straightforward gravitational-constant/multiple-vector equation shouldn't take anywhere near that long.

That's when I remembered the Zone of Moons. . . .

I checked; the computer reported that it still was hard at work locating satellites and computing their orbits. By now it had identified some thirty-two thousand, and was working on objects down in the one- to two-foot size range. Better than ninety percent of its processing capacity was tied up in the project. No wonder answers were slow in coming!

Quickly I called for the system's storage-capacity-versus-load read-out. A fortuitous decision: The system was filling up rapidly (ephemerides for thirty-two-thousand-plus satellites amount to quite a volume of data).

Briefly I debated my options. First I ordered the system to suspend mapping temporarily. This freed most of the processing capacity for work on the approach-trajectory problem, which suddenly had become a very intricate piece of computation. The final figures would have to take into account all recorded satellites which at some point in their orbits approached closely enough to pose a risk of collision (or near-collision in the case of bodies massive enough to produce significant gravitational perturbations in my course). This meant cross-checking all recorded satellite orbits against the proposed course, modifying the course accordingly, then rechecking and modifying again, all the way through the Zone.

In an effort to reduce the load on the system, I instructed it to erase all data pertaining to each satellite as it was proven to be irrelevant for the purposes of the problem.

Then I ordered resumption of satellite mapping; retaining data only on those which met the risk-of-collision and/or -perturbation test. But with the system erasing data faster than it accumulated, it didn't take long for the effect of the housecleaning to make itself felt. Responses grew perceptibly quicker as minutes passed.

And not long after that I had my answer: Though improbable of successful execution, the deed *was* possible. The computer had come up with an approach profile incorporating a series of gravity-well maneuvers involving three of the larger satellites. Thrust vectors and burn timing requirements were critical; but if I managed to pull it off (and assuming no unexpected maneuvering were called for [in the Zone . . . ?]), I'd wind up, as I'd hoped, eighty miles above the equator, traveling in the same direction as the planet's rotation, with better than two minutes' fuel remaining.

That would be more than ample to circularize my orbit immediately prior to contacting the atmospheric interface; which should allow me to ease down into the atmosphere gently enough to control frictional heating—as opposed to NASTI's flaming-plunge technique, which probably wouldn't work out too well in an aluminum-skinned ship whose melting point was only slightly higher than my own.

Of course, there was no way of knowing whether the computer would be intact and serving up data ten minutes into the Zone (any more than I could know whether I'd still be around to read it), so I printed out a hard-copy timetable of course corrections: burn timings and durations, and thrust-axis alignment parameters.

Thereafter I wrote a set of programs which would keep the computer (as long as it survived) scanning in all directions, both optically (processing TV camera output to enhance image resolution) and with radar. Detection of anything on a collision course would trigger subroutines which would plot the intruder's course, speed, and e.t.a., and determine the vector changes required first to avoid it and then to get back on course; all with the least expenditure of fuel. Naturally, the smaller the object, the shorter the warning, and the less time I'd have to react.

And the more fuel I'd use.

Not that dodging the bigger stuff mattered a great deal, practically speaking . . .

Because below a certain meteoroid size, these preparations were moot anyway: The projected five- to ten-mile-per-second relative closing speed of all those pebbles and grains of sand wasn't going to make much impression on radar or optical scanners—but their impact sure as hell was going to make an impression on the structure of the ship. . . .

So, for whatever good it might do, I intended to enclose myself in one of the space suits we'd brought along, just in case. They were the very latest thing in extravehicular mobility units; so "very latest," in fact (courtesy of another of Rebecca Two-Knives' acquaintances), that NASTI's astronauts hadn't even seen them yet. Stronger, lighter weight, substantially better life-support duration (Meg's treatment rendered them stronger still, and extended life-support endurance from a matter of hours to weeks), these EMUs were appreciably less bulky than earlier models. The gloves, in particular, were an improvement: Wearing them while working on a keyboard still wasn't as convenient as typing barehanded, but at least computer operation no longer constituted an exercise in mortal frustration.

With an hour to go before crossing the arbitrary division which constituted the Zone's border, I took a final tour through the ship, looking around and reviewing my preparations. I concluded that that everything that *could* be done in advance was.

Now: Viewed in the light of cold, hard reality, the odds on making it through the next two days were laughable (to an objective observer, of course; at the time, I had little difficulty controlling my mirth): For every satellite the computer had spotted, there were thousands of undetectably tiny projectiles orbiting Isis, each representing kilotons of velocity-conferred kinetic energy. Not even the $mMj'q$-toughened aluminum with which the ship was sheathed could be expected to withstand that kind of abuse.

But one thing racing had taught me was the folly of giving up prematurely:

. . . In terms of winning, of course: I'd won both two- and four-wheeled competitions in vehicles so crippled that they barely could circulate the course (never mind lapping at competitive speeds) by the simple expedient of sticking it out and *finishing*—only to watch everyone ahead of me fall victim to even worse problems and drop out.

. . . But far more importantly, in terms of *survival*: While leading a Formula One race at Spa Francorchamps a couple of years previously, I had crested a hill halfway through a narrow, tree-lined, two-hundred-plus-mile-per-hour curve to discover that someone's engine had swallowed its own entrails and vomited about eight liters of high-viscosity oil all over the road directly in my path. Before I even could begin to react (and I'm *quick*), I found myself spinning like a frisbee.

According to CBC Sports' slow-motion videotapes, which lovingly preserved every detail, my car completed twenty-seven revolutions (five within the first second alone!) before I finally managed to collect things sufficiently to get it pointed frontward and keep it that way. If I had left the road at that speed, the trees would have reduced my car to a handful of tinfoil confetti and me to stringy red goo dripping down the trunks.

But I didn't intend to leave the road. Backward, sideways, frontward, and sideways again—endlessly repeated at over two hundred miles per hour—I kept my head and never gave up: I fought the careening vehicle every inch of the way around the curve and along the ensuing straightaway, using every transitory, second-to-second pretense of control available: momentarily locking the brakes twice per orbit as first one end then the other revolved to the fore but pointed an unfavorable direction; briefly releasing them during those portions of the rotation when the tires' rolling traction could contribute to the hoped-for progress; flicking the steering wheel lock-to-lock twice per revolution to help the car rotate more quickly past the wrong attitude, slowing the spin as it swung to face the desired direction of travel. Before regaining full control, I left over a quarter mile of gracefully intertwining skid marks on the pavement.

Contrast this with the manner in which the "average (i.e., untrained) motorist" copes with an emergency situation—best illustrated by those obligatory winter-storm-coverage film clips so beloved of cliché-ridden TV news directors: shots of feckless motorists losing control of slowly moving vehicles (visibly nowhere near the limits of controllability—but the drivers had given up) and looping gracefully off the road into guardrails or each other. . . .

No one possessing the barest minimum of emergency-driving training (or even presence of mind—let alone competition experience), would have difficulty coping with such minor "moments": A casual tweak of the wheel, possibly coupled with a judicious dab at the gas pedal, and the problem is solved. That people so lacking in basic skills are permitted to drive is inexcusable—that a virtual total absence of public skid-pad training facilities forces the vast majority to do without them, is criminal.

Anyway, preaching aside, the bottom line is that I *never* give up. Period. Ever. And I never intend to. Certainly not while I'm still alive.

The only absolute guarantee of failure is a refusal to try. . . .

So despite the fact that the situation was hopeless on its face, I had no intention of giving up.

Fifteen minutes before we were due to enter the Zone, I paid a final visit to the head and emptied both my bladder and bowels (few injuries involve sequelae as nasty as traumatic rupture of either; and the greater the internal pressure, the less impact is required to produce them).

Then I assembled the EMU around me. I'd be wearing it for at least the next two days, until we dropped into clear space between the Zone's inner border and Isis' atmosphere; and maybe, depending on whether *Venture* was still airtight, until we reached a breathable level in the atmosphere. Accordingly, I made sure that nothing pinched, rubbed, or interferred with my movements in any way. I took particular pains to assemble the sanitary recovery system correctly.

Thereafter, I planted myself in the command seat, secured the five-way harness, brought the engines up to fifteen-second Hold status, rested my hands on the controls, and settled down to wait for the first scheduled course-correction burn.

Or the first emergency evasion.

Or death.

Whichever came first. . . .

Forty-five hours later, *Galactic Venture*, hull riddled like a sieve, coasted silently past the inner margin of the Zone of Moons and fell safely through empty space toward the huge planet below.

Remarkably, considering the almost constant micro-meteoroid machine-gunning she had endured these past two days, no really important systems were disabled. Oh, several radar antennas were junk, as were all but one of the TV cameras which fed optical data to the CPU. Likewise, a few outlying memory storage units here and there, especially in the wings, either were dead or the coaxial cables leading to them had been damaged. But I had anticipated that possibili-ty; any vital data they contained now resided in locations deep inside the ship, close to the CPU itself, protected by several layers of structure. The central processing unit itself had come through intact.

But the truly amazing thing was the survival of the main engines: hanging out there in those vulnerable external pods, nakedly exposed to the bombardment, their function depen-dent upon so many critically interrelated bits and pieces (whose operating tolerances measured in the ten-thousands of a millimeter)—after all that punishment, they still worked!

And so did I, more's the miracle. Earlier while running the gauntlet, air resistance inside the hull had incinerated most of the particles which managed to punch their way through the $mMj'q$-toughened aluminum before they got very far (and a horrendous racket it made, too). But as the number of punctures mounted, more and more occurred in areas I couldn't reach to patch, and eventually all the air leaked out.

As it did so, the odds mounted that some particles would retain sufficient energy after drilling through the hull to penetrate my suit. Astonishingly only two did.

The first resulted in no more than a pinprick leak which I patched without delay or inconvenience. The second forced me to patch two leaks in the suit and one in myself. (It's a good thing that total cellular control includes the ability to regulate sensory nerve transmission: A cauterized puncture through the liver is a rare treat. . . .)

However: Six times during the passage the computer sounded the alarm. Six times it was necessary to perform unscheduled evasions. Four involved only a few seconds' RCS burn and the corresponding counterburn corrections.

But twice significant maneuvering was called for; I was forced to use the main engines. And if the gauges were correct, just ninety-two seconds' full-power operation now remained.

Which was almost enough. . . .

TO: Project Director/Monitor's Log.
FROM: K'dDempbato, Eighth Order.
SUBJECT: Project *Extremis*.

Astonishingly, Subject Cory not only sucessfully negotiated the Zone of Moons, despite mounting difficulties presented by our continuing interference, but emerged from the challenge with his fighting spirit intact.

From a psychological viewpoint, this was an extremely stressful episode, in that it was almost entirely intellectual in character; offering long periods of enforced inactivity between crises during which the subject could not help contemplating the steady erosion of his chances together with the ultimate price of failure. From all available data, this approach should have been productive. The fact that it was not would seem to point to weaknesses either in our data base or our methods of interpreting its contents.

I am reasonably confident, however, that the even

greater stresses attending the upcoming atmospheric entry will have the desired effect.

I understand that a full third of the viewers in La'ïr now are following Cory's progress.

Sometimes maintaining optimism isn't easy: Assuming the overpressure valves had reclosed the instant they could, and assuming further the utter reliability and accuracy of the fuel-flow meters, I lacked thirteen of the final one hundred eleven seconds' thrust duration the computer prescribed for achieving the eighty-mile-high, near-circular orbit from which a gentle, nonpyrotechnic atmospheric entry might be attempted.

Asked how serious that thirteen-second deficit was, the CPU replied that the data fell within the fuzzy area of uncertainty known as the "limits of observable accuracy"; it couldn't be sure, but I might not melt.

Gee, thanks a lot. Glad I asked.

Now, thoroughness is an admirable quality generally, but it is not without disadvantages. One of the worst is the fact that, once you've identified all the risks you face, and taken all the precautions and made all the preparations possible to minimize them, you're left with nothing to do but sit and worry about what you might have overlooked. I had, so I did.

I was well aware, of course, that worry was one of the least productive exercises toward which the human psyche is inclined, and normally I didn't indulge in it. When I recognized the existence of a problem, I analyzed it, took whatever steps I could to solve it, and dealt with the outcome as a fresh challenge.

That attitude was difficult to maintain this time: The stakes simply were too high. In the past, whenever I mounted a bike or climbed into a race car I accepted (academically, at least) the remote possibility that I might be injured or even die. But that was a personal choice; my death under those circumstances would have affected only me and (realistically, though I always chose to ignore the point) those who cared for, and/or depended on, me for a living.

But that kind of selfishness was a luxury I couldn't afford now. If I died, the Isi never would know what happened to Meg and Memphis. Plus, taking Meg's statement at face value, I was single-handedly responsible for the fate of the galaxy. Without me, it would be destroyed ". . . utterly. Along with every living thing in it."

So, despite the fact that I knew I had done everything within my power to improve my chances, and there was absolutely nothing further that I *could* do, beyond following through and hoping for favorable instrument error, I worried.

I worried while *Venture* fell the last few thousand miles to the edge of the atmosphere. I worried as I positioned her for the circularization attempt. I worried as, with about two hundred fifty miles to go, I fired up the main engines on schedule. I worried as I sat there, gritting my teeth and watching the timer count off the seconds.

Then I worried even more: Those "limits of observable accuracy" had indeed led to error—the engines sucked their last drops of usable fuel and flamed out *seventeen full seconds short of the required burn . . . !*

But I didn't worry for long; I didn't have time: Already, even at eighty miles' altitude, the ship was stirring in response to aerodynamic pressures; clearly the Isi atmosphere was deeper than Earth's!

Quickly I leveled the wings and positioned the nose just above the horizon. The remaining fuel pressure was insufficient for main engine operation, but I was pretty sure I could count on another few minutes out of the RCS thrusters; they'd probably last long enough to reach thicker air, where the aerodynamic controls would take over. I hoped so, anyway.

Now, regardless of an object's *absolute* velocity, the degree to which it experiences frictional heating as it passes through the atmosphere is a function of *airspeed.* "Airspeed" is a statement of the relationship between the barometric pressure of a given air mass and the velocity of an object passing through it. The higher the air pressure, the lower the velocity required to produce a given airspeed. Conversely, as air pressure drops toward zero, the absolute velocity required to generate that airspeed increases spectacularly.

The computer's original suggested atmospheric entry profile called for descending only to the point where, even this close to the edge of space, my nearly orbital velocity would generate sufficient airspeed, and thereby aerodynamic lift, to support the ship. There I was to level off and establish a controlled glide, maintaining a safe, constant airspeed while gradually dissipating my frightful absolute velocity against the faint resistance of the tenuous upper atmosphere.

As my speed dwindled, over a course of many hours, the ship would glide progressively lower and lower. Eventually, somewhere near the ground, never having exceeding the thermal limits of the ship's aluminum structure, her absolute velocity would match her airspeed; and it would be time to devote some serious thought to the question of how I was going to land what amounted to a large, heavy, commercial jetliner in one piece—without a proper runway . . .

But there was no point getting exercised over that yet—hell, *the atmospheric entry probably was going to kill me* . . . !

Because things were not going according to schedule: With almost offensive promptness, now that time no longer was of the essence, the computer announced that the main engines' premature shutdown meant I lacked almost four hundred miles per hour of the nearly perfectly circular ballistic curve needed to ease gently into the atmosphere under full aerodynamic control.

By contrast, NASTI precipitated their orbiters' flaming reentries by trimming a mere *two* hundred miles per hour from their orbital velocity. Granted, they usually started their dives considerably higher above the interface than I was—fact is, I was already physically *within* the upper atmosphere and benefitting from the initial (if virtually negligible) frictional retardation.

But no matter how I approached the question, the bottom line remained: I was trapped in a ballistic curve which led downward *much* more steeply than planned.

And the computer, when queried, stuck to its "limits of observable accuracy" disclaimer; however, when pushed harder, allowed as how things didn't look too promising.

Clearly, the "never-give-up" school faced its most challenging test yet. . . .

I took a deep breath; then rested my left hand on the control yoke, feet on the rudder pedals. Already my right hand gripped the RCS controller stick. Experimentally I drew back on the yoke; noted the beginnings of aerodynamic response. Encouraged, I extended full flaps and lowered the landing gear (aerodynamic braking consists of making oneself as "dirty" as possible).

My hopes were twofold: First, I wanted (*needed!*) to pull out of the dive my trajectory rapidly was becoming before it carried me so deeply into the upper atmosphere, while still traveling at astronomical velocities, that catastrophic frictional heating would be unavoidable. Secondly, I wanted to slow as rapidly as possible—to minimize the effects of that same frictional heating in the likely event that my momentum carried me so deeply into the upper atmosphere, while still traveling at astronomical velocities . . .

Et cetera.

The low-range airspeed indicator stirred off the peg; the needle crept across the dial: slowly at first, then more quickly. Within moments the airspeed had mounted above stall; the ship was "flying."

Quickly I overrode the RCS control-stick linkages. I triggered and locked into continuous operation all "downward"-facing thrusters. There were about two dozen such nozzles altogether. Most were twenty-five-pound-thrust units, but a couple were good for eight hundred seventy pounds. Considering the weight of the ship and the speed involved, they wouldn't make much difference. (But it *is* true what they say about beggars. . . .)

The airspeed increased.

I eased the control yoke back almost imperceptibly, edging the nose fractionally higher. The ship began to tremble, indicating that a stall was imminent. I eased the back-pressure a hair; the vibration abated slightly.

The airspeed mounted; lift increased accordingly. I raised the nose further, crowding the stall more closely. The vibration turned into a full-scale, major airframe shudder.

(It's not widely known, but a stall is *not* an exclusively low-speed phenomenon: Anytime your ship's apparent weight [i.e., gee forces from a tight turn or pulling out of a high-speed dive] exceeds available lift, you stall, whatever your speed. Not uncommonly, this is the very last lesson weekend hot-dogs learn, as they wrench a plane into a low-altitude, ninety-degree, hundred-fifty-mile-per-hour bank—and it promptly stalls out from under them and digs a hole in the ground.)

As the airspeed continued to build, it took more and more back-pressure on the yoke to keep the nose high enough to take advantage of the ever-increasing lift. The elevators were located some fifty feet aft of the wings; and as the speed of the slipstream mounted, the leverage against which they attempted to force the tail downward increased.

The vibration got even worse as mach one approached. I retracted the landing gear and reduced the flaps to twenty percent: Despite confidence that the $mMj'q$-reinforced airframe could take the stresses, I was uneasy about the aerodynamics of the situation—even if the structure withstood the strain, a sudden, totally out-of-control tumble would cost altitude that I couldn't afford at this stage.

As the airspeed crept past mach two, I firmed up my grip on the yoke and strained to lever in still more back-pressure. At lower speeds I'd treated the possibility of triggering an actual stall with justifiable caution: Some "T-tailed" jetliners, when provoked, demonstrate a nasty phenomenon known as the "deep stall," where the airflow, as it separates from the upper surface of the stalled wing, blankets the elevators in turbulence and renders them useless.

Such ships are never deep-stalled more than once.

I didn't know whether that caution applied to DC-9s or not; however, *Venture* had a T-tail, and this seemed an inauspicious moment to pander to scientific curiosity.

But at this speed the angle of attack was so close to parallel with the wings' angle of incidence that turbulence from even a full stall wouldn't come close to the elevators' slipstream.

Besides, there was considerable doubt whether I *could* stall it now: I lacked the physical strength required to get the yoke anywhere near its rear limit. And even if I could, it seemed unlikely that even at full deflection the elevator possessed sufficient leverage to force the ship into a stalled angle of attack at that speed.

The airframe's violent trembling, for some time a hellish, vision-blurring massage, had become a physically painful, tooth-rattling nonstop shudder. Unidentifiable objects could be heard tearing loose from their mountings behind me, and bouncing and bashing all over the place.

Meg's treatment had canceled excess internal gee forces, but a glance out the side window showed the port wing deflecting upward probably fifteen feet at the tip. A normal DC-9, made of untreated materials, would have broken up long since.

The mach meter needle edged past mach two-point-five.

Suddenly my blood turned cold—I noticed the beginnings of deformation in the aluminum sheathing the leading edge of the port wing. . . .

The end was approaching; there was no doubt: The combination of heat softening and aerodynamic pressure was beginning to have its effect. It wouldn't be long before the airframe started to break up.

I forced myself to look away. I remember thinking that I'd be *damned* if I was going to give up!—that every single cell of my body still was going to be hauling on that control yoke as the hypersonic slipstream ripped both the ship and me into our component molecules.

I put both feet up on the control panel and used the muscles of my legs to pull still harder. The shuddering became a bone-jarring buffet which made it almost impossible to read the few instruments still functioning.

I vaguely recall hearing an inhuman roaring noise inside my helmet which I'd rather not believe was me.

The last thing I remember was a little voice somewhere inside my head musing absently to itself, "So *this* is what it feels like to go Berserk. . . ."

The next sensation of which I was aware was a leaden ache which seemed to afflict every muscle in my body.

As the scope of my awareness expanded and various sensory groups reattached themselves to my consciousness, I noticed that the ship no longer buffeted or shook. As my vision reconnected and cleared, I realized that I was seeing more-or-less normal daylight shining in the cockpit windows. Through the Lexan of my helmet, my ears now registered a shrill keening sound which a less cautious soul might have recognized as wind noise.

I blinked and shook my head. Somewhere in the package of conditioned reflexes which made up my flying skills, something totaled up the stimuli and concluded that *Galactic Venture* was subsonic once more.

TO: Project Director/Monitor's Log.
FROM: Metehiryä, Tenth Order.
SUBJECT: Project *Extremis*.

Opinion was divided beforehand as to whether the challenge of entering the atmosphere, together with additional obstacles we placed in his path, would reduce Subject Cory to a satisfactory state of despair. I was one who thought it would. I shall be more cautious in the future about such wagers.

I should have known better: Though his chances of living through the maneuver actually were lower than those for the passage through the Zone of Moons, this encounter, once his fuel was exhausted, was fast-moving and almost purely physical, presenting little or no time for introspection. Besides, never has Cory folded up in the face of physical danger. (Actually, never has he folded up. Period.)

And while he still faces the prospect of landing his crippled ship safely, I do not expect that we will make much progress until we get him down on the surface of Isis where, gradually, continuously, in a methodical, step-by-step fashion, we can concentrate the endless terrors of the planet on him until, by degrees, we reduce him to a state of completely and utterly hopeless funk.

It appears that Cory's audience now includes better than half the population of La'ïr, and still is growing.

I looked around the cockpit. The interior was a shambles: CRT screens were empty sockets staring blindly from the instrument panel. Half the gauges were gone altogether, physically ripped from their mounting holes by the violence of the pounding the ship had endured. Several dangled from wires. Of those remaining, not one still worked.

There was an EMU-boot-sized dent in the instrument panel on either side of the control column. I noticed that the $mMj'q$-reinforced spokes of the yoke actually were bent slightly from the back-pressure to which they'd been subjected. I marveled at the strength it must have taken to do that—then realized *whose* strength had done it, and marveled anew. (I was pretty impressed at Spa, too, as I studied CBC's slow-motion tapes afterward.)

I looked out the cockpit windows. Visible below was a great expanse of broken cloud cover. Beneath that lay a darker surface. I hoped that it was dry land and not one of the dozen or so vast, interconnecting seas which break up Isis' land area.

I glanced back at the port wing and physically cringed: Half the sheathing was missing from the upper surface. A portion of the forward spoiler was gone. The heavy leading-edge plating was wilted back against the underlying structural members. Something dangled barely visible below the wing, fluttering in the slipstream. It took several moments' thought to identify it as part of the trailing-edge/flap assembly.

From my vantage in the left seat, the sweep-back made it difficult to get a good look at the starboard wing; but by craning my neck, I could see enough to suggest that it had been shortened by at least fifteen feet.

This led me to notice that we were descending pretty steeply . . . quite steeply—in fact, downright precipitately.

NASTI's oft-maligned orbital shuttles were paragons of aerodynamic buoyancy by comparison. *Venture*'s glide angle invited unfavorable comparisons with flatirons. Or bricks.

Cautiously I essayed raising the nose. Within moments the return of aerodynamic buffeting signaled the proximity of a stall—I abandoned the experiment immediately. Apparently my conditioned reflexes had been through this already: Steep as it was, her present glide angle was very close to optimal for *Venture*'s present battered condition.

In attempting to set up a gentle turn, I noticed that the control responses left a lot to be desired. I looked outside again and waggled the yoke; the discovery that only the port aileron responded did little to fuel my optimism.

I tested the rest of the controls: The elevators responded partially; the rudder not at all. The trim tabs ignored me. Nothing happened when I attempted to extend whatever might have been left of the flaps. Nor did the landing gear deploy.

Yet somehow—incredibly!—*Venture* still flew. . . .

(Discovering, moments later, that the windshield wipers worked brought on an attack of giggles which had to be dealt with quite firmly: Hysteria was nearer than I first realized.)

Focusing my attention back inside the cockpit, and trying to marshall what remained of my wits (I had been at the controls virtually continuously, without sleep, for going on seventy-five hours by now), I noticed smoke rising from various portions of my EMU. A quick review of my physical condition revealed no serious burns but quite a few areas of tenderness here and there. Obviously my portable life-support system had outdone itself during the past few hours.

As I dropped below the cloud deck, I got my first good look at the terrain. This portion of Isis seemed to be divided about evenly between solid forestland and open country. Overall, a breathtakingly beautiful scene. No doubt someone who had time to appreciate it would have found the vista deeply inspiring.

But at the rate *Venture* was losing altitude, time was one thing I lacked: The ground was coming up rapidly; it was time to start setting up for a landing—and thinking about the fact that I lacked landing gear, flaps, instruments, and much in the way of aerodynamic control.

I studied the terrain intently as I spiraled downward, looking for a suitable forced-landing site. The clearing I selected was broad, generally flat, and green; setting down there should pose no particular challenge. True, I'd have to stay alert to avoid being trapped by a premature sinking condition, make sure I didn't dig in a wingtip just prior to touchdown, and, of course, stay clear of a stall until the very last second before contact.

Okay, nothing in that list called for special attention or superhuman skills; those were basics: part and parcel of any landing from which one hopes to walk away—landing gear or no landing gear. (Actually, faced with the necessity of setting down a ship of that size on unprepared, probably soft ground, most experts would *prefer* to make the attempt gear-up).

I intended to work very hard at keeping all that in mind.

Lacking a working airspeed indicator, I "calibrated" the seat of my pants by easing back on the yoke and slowing, feeling for the first tremors of an incipient stall; then, knowing precisely how much back-pressure it would take to trigger one, I lowered the nose again, picked up a cushion of airspeed, and continued my glide.

I rolled into a shallow, sloppy bank to turn onto final. The tops of those big trees ringing the clearing skimmed by just below. To tighten up the control responses I lowered the nose still further and picked up a little more airspeed.

It was a fair distance to the other side of the clearing; there was no rush to get down. I stabilized the sink rate and devoted total concentration to keeping the wings level despite the partial aileron control. Down I floated, lower and lower.

It seemed to take an unusually long time to descend that last few hundred feet from treetop level to the ground, but finally the moment was at hand: With the wings just skimming the tops of the bushes which speckled the clearing, touchdown appeared imminent.

I increased back-pressure, raised the nose, halted the sink rate momentarily, and began to bleed off my remaining airspeed. Trembling on the edge of a stall, *Venture* resumed a gentle mushing descent toward the ground.

And the next time I had any interest in my surroundings, I had such a headache that I would have had to get a little better just to *die*. . . .

TO: Project Director/Monitor's Log.
FROM: Metehiryä, Tenth Order.
SUBJECT: Project *Extremis*.

To the surprise of no one, Subject Cory has executed a survivable crash-landing. No tampering with events was required to ensure that he lived through the experience.

Equally unsurprisingly, the noise attracted the attention of every predator in the vicinity. And since having him prematurely killed while unconscious would accomplish absolutely nothing, I have taken the precaution of establishing a set of *wWr'dts* around his immediate area and have removed from its confines all predators of consequence. I judge it prudent to maintain this protection during his recuperation from the rigors of the past several days. Thereafter, we may allow the local fauna access to him in gradually increasing numbers, escalating the pressures under which he labors until he breaks.

I lay on my back. There was a lump under the point of my left shoulder blade. I could feel grass under one hand and against my neck. A blade of it seemed to be tickling my ear. The inside of my head felt like the floor of the Elephants' Polka Barn. For a time that remained the extent of my knowledge and awareness.

When I finally got around to opening my eyes, I found I was looking up at great, white, rolling summer clouds set against a rich, emerald green sky. Somehow this didn't seem to mesh with my expectations, but I couldn't put a finger on why.

Almost immediately I gave up trying to turn my head to look around. The gravest of errors: All those anvils bouncing around in there made it hard to concentrate. For a while I simply lay there, bemusedly contemplating the sky and wishing my head would go live with somebody else.

I wasn't wondering where I was; I was still working on *who*, and half-heartedly toying with *why*. I had a feeling that I was going to be sorry I bothered.

I was—and then was even sorrier when, after full recollection burst upon me, I sat bolt upright and looked around quickly. . . .

Some time later the red mists again receded to the point where I dared open my eyes. With the utmost caution I rolled over and groggily looked around. My eyes snapped wide. For long moments all I could do was stare about me.

Heretofore I'd always had a pretty secure ego: I was generally satisfied with myself without (I did try) being unduly cocky or offensive about it. But within moments of my first ground-level look at Isis, I was in the grip of a case of humility that would have turned a louse suicidal.

Intellectually, I knew that Isis' diameter was twenty-six times that of Earth. Likewise, I knew that considerable of the planet's flora was in proportion. But this knowledge hardly prepared me for my first glimpse of a forest which jutted upward at least a mile above the ground. Or a "horizon" so distant that atmospheric refraction caused the ground to appear to curve *up* before "greening-out" into infinity.

Now I understood what had gone wrong with the landing: My reflexes were conditioned on a planet eight thousand miles in diameter—and the better a pilot is, the more unthinking his responses. My depth perception and the reflexes linked to it were world-class; they were totally automatic—I had to think to override them. Now they were my enemy. They would have to be watched closely until they got the idea—and then watched even more closely when I got back to Earth: "Landing" two hundred feet too *low* would be a lot more final. . . .

It occurred to me at this point that getting back to Earth had become a somewhat more complicated proposition. As had carrying out my other responsibilities: I had to tell the Isi what had happened to Meg and Memphus, after all, and I had a galaxy to save.

With that in mind, I regarded my surroundings with a new awareness which bordered on growing dislike. The clearing in which I lay was an authentic, fifty-mile-wide *veldt*! Those so-called bushes, whose tops I had been skimming just prior to initiating my "touchdown" stall, were *trees* by my previous standards—damned big ones, too. And surrounding the veldt, the jungle loomed—a mile-high rampart concealing ominously dark and forbidding depths.

And the sun—for the first time I consciously noticed Ra blazing in the sky. Of course I knew that Isis' sun was one of the very biggest and hottest of the blue-white supergiants, a class of stars characterized by extreme size and temperature. But I hadn't thought the implications through; I hadn't realized just how far such a sun must lie from a planet to permit a habitable climate. So distant was Ra from Isis that its apparent diameter was an incredibly tiny spark no bigger than Venus in Earth's night sky; yet its output was perceptibly warmer at this latitude than Sol's.

Yes—quite perceptibly. About a hundred degrees worth,

come to think of it. Inside what remained of my EMU I was fountaining perspiration like an artesian well.

From force of habit, I glanced at my watch; among its many functions was an ambient temperature sensor. But even as conditioned reflex focused my eyes on the dial, the absurdity of the situation registered: What watch could have emerged intact from the events of the past few hours! Then I blinked in surprise (and purest admiration): Not only had my Timex compugraph remained on my wrist after all that—but somehow (metaphorically speaking) it still "kept on ticking."

I pressed a button to switch modes, waited a couple seconds, and checked the reading; then goggled in dismay: No, it wasn't a hundred degrees out—it was a muggy, airless one hundred twenty-three damned degrees and I could hardly breathe . . . !

The discomfort reminded me that my headache still raged. It was time to do something about that. I turned my perception inward and located a hairline crack in the occipital region of my skull; a bruise on the surface of the brain corresponded nicely.

Apprehensively, I looked further; but apart from a few scrapes, cuts, bruises, bumps, and a pulled muscle here and there (none of which were particularly serious) I was in pretty good shape.

(Astonishingly good shape, considering the startling damage to my EMU: Boots and gloves were gone, along with most of the contiguous arm and leg fabric. The back half of the torso/shoulder-joint reinforcing frame had been ripped bodily away, along with the PLSS pack. And how had my head stayed on when all that remained of the helmet was a ragged Lexan collar attached to the neck sealing ring . . . ?)

Fifteen minutes later I was whole again; but in a fair way to roast: The equatorial noonday sun on Isis would have daunted the maddest dog (and maybe even discommoded an Englishman).

Plus I was starving: Even minor repairs involved the accelerated division of millions of cells—and each and every one clamored for nourishment. (Of course, I was pretty hungry before I started; while healing that meteoroid puncture on the way through the Zone, I had gone through every scrap of consumables in the EMU—and there *wasn't enough!*) But hunger would have to wait; a more (op)pressing problem was the heat, and it was becoming more so by the moment. . . .

Well, on the scale of difficulty defined by the list of problems confronting me at this juncture, coping with temperature wasn't particularly complex: First I increased my pigmentation; the resultant skin tone rivaled that of the blackest Negro and cut down on absorbed radiation. Next I transferred all surviving fat deposits (by this time there wasn't much) to locations deep inside my torso to reduce heat retention. Then I improved the heat-dissipation capacity of my skin and lungs by increasing the blood flow to and through them.

The adjustments proved quite effective; by the time I finished, the weather (to my perception anyway) had improved markedly. Indeed, the pleasant warmth of the sunlight helped offset the snap of a refreshingly cool breeze. I felt ready to take on the world.

Unfortunately, it appeared I would have to. From my second-hand knowledge of the major landmarks I spotted on the way down, I knew my approximate location on the planet relative to Meg's homeland, and the news wasn't good: The shortest route to La'ïr was straight down. If I consciously and deliberately had attempted to identify and crash-land on the single point on the planet's surface which lay farthest from the small area inhabited by Meg's people, I couldn't have done much better.

The math was easy: Two hundred ten thousand times pi, divided by two. Roughly three hundred thirty thousand miles—teeming with what Meg had described as the most savagely feral animal life in this universe and several others— lay between me and any hope of notifying the Isi of her fate, let alone getting on with saving the galaxy.

Well, sitting there brooding wasn't going to accomplish anything. I stood, stretched, and looked around purposefully at my immediate resources: It was regrettable that I could think of no pressing need for uniformly small pieces of $mMj'q$-toughened aluminum.

At least, I mused, strolling back along the half-mile trail of wreckage, there hadn't been a fire; using up every drop of liquid hydrogen and oxygen prior to touchdown guaranteed that. Which meant that anything that survived the impact probably still would be usable.

Surprising things turned up intact: I came across my trials bike (the same one we'd left in Tibet; Meg had recovered it as soon as she got the $wWn'dt$ working properly) lying on its side in the grass, apparently undamaged. (This isn't as surprising as it might seem to the layman: Bikes habitually emerge from hundred-mile-an-hour spills with nothing more serious than a dented fuel tank and a dead rider.) Farther on I found a few pieces of more-or-less usable clothing and gratefully replaced the remains of my EMU.

Further searching turned up a rubber life raft (Becky's doing, no doubt; I hadn't known it was aboard) which had self-inflated on impact. I rifled through its compartments eagerly and found a sheath knife, some canned water . . . and C-rations—*food*!

I don't know how many castaways those supplies were supposed to have accommodated, or for how long; but an hour later I had eaten all the food and drunk most of the water, satisfying my hunger to the point where I was merely ravenous instead of actively starving—this after turning my perception inward again and fine-tuning my digestive tract: A gerbil might have contrived to extract more nourishment from that meal; certainly no metabolism less efficient could have generated less waste.

Still, it helped; it felt good to have something in my stomach again. I leaned back, cushioned my head against the inflated lower ring of the raft, and closed my eyes briefly.

Renewed acute hunger woke me thirty hours later. The sun was sinking toward the horizon. I rose stiffly, and spent the remaining hour of daylight prowling the crash site, looking for surviving edibles. I found enough to fill up on, and even managed to locate an undamaged fork. Then I returned to the life raft and died again.

I woke by midmorning, feeling much better. I was hungry again, of course; but at least I was on the way to catching up on my sleep after that marathon stint at *Venture's* controls.

The balance of the morning I spent combing the wreckage for food, clothing, tools, weapons, and other necessities. I found a jar of peanut butter, a mismatched pair of shoes, a piece of blanket, and one more raggedy shirt. Period.

Wrapping my trousseau in a square of waterproof material cut from the life raft, I returned to the motorcycle.

For a moment I stood regarding it dubiously. Meg and Memphus had made no bones about their lack of faith in the ability of mechanisms generally to cope with the variety and intensity of the challenges presented by life on Isis. On the other hand, Memphus had been equally certain that the reason the Isi never had had any star-traveling visitors was because no one could survive a passage through the Zone of Moons in a non$mMj'q$-assisted spaceship.

Well, maybe. True, *Venture* had gotten pretty well used up in the process, and luck had figured strongly in the outcome; but despite the fact that her design had incorporated the assumption that $mMj'q$ would be used to solve many of her problems, she had gotten me through the Zone without it. (The enhanced structural strength hadn't been much of a factor in the Zone itself, though it certainly was critical during atmospheric entry.) On reflection, it didn't seem that it would be all that difficult, given a bare minimum advance notice of anticipated operating conditions, to come up with a design capable of traversing the Zone with impunity—perhaps behind a renewable meteoroid shield constructed of ice or something else equally abundant. Maybe the Isis' lack of faith in mechanisms arose from their failure to run into the right mechanic. . . .

Anyway, the immediate alternative was walking.

I hauled the bike upright and rocked it back on its stand. A quick once-over revealed no damage—but, of course, *physical* damage was the least of my concerns. . . .

Well, there was only one way to find out: I opened the gas tank filler cap, noted the fuel level, then opened the fuel drain tap. Normally, emptying the tank would have required about three minutes, but five minutes later the level was unchanged.

The intensity of the relief that washed over me at that point caught me by surprise—certainly the bike's physically undamaged condition following a crash of such severity demonstrated that Meg's $mMj'q$-based enhancement of the physical structure still was in place and working. Besides (and apart from the fact that, if the extrauniversal-storage mechanism hadn't still been operational, the tank long since would have ruptured) ten thousand gallons of gasoline/oil two-stroke mixture sloshing around *Venture's* interior immediately following Meg's disappearance would have been hard to overlook.)

The absence of visible damage was encouraging from another perspective as well: It seemed unlikely that stresses which failed to exact a toll from the exterior of the machine would have had any effect on those few even more strongly constructed bits and pieces which constituted the internal workings; probably it would run. I strapped my bindle to the toolkit roll at the rear of the saddle and swung aboard.

Switching on the ignition, I tickled the richener a couple times and kicked the starter lever. The engine fired up instantly. I grinned humorlessly, recalling numerous occasions (following exhaustive mechanical preparation) when getting the bike started had involved the frantic efforts of the entire team (and curses in up to eleven languages).

I paused momentarily and cast outward with my mind, feeling for the planetary magnetic lines. Once sure of my directions, I rocked forward off the stand.

I bounced the bike on its suspension a few times with all my strength. The wheels moved freely; there appeared to be no hint of the binding or restricted travel which usually signaled suspension damage.

The clutch disengaged smoothly; first gear meshed without protest.

I cracked the throttle a couple of times to clear the plugs, engaged the clutch, and accelerated across the veldt in the direction of La'ïr. All six gears shifted smoothly and ran quietly, the brakes responded normally when I tested them, and the bike's handling was such that I'd have been satisfied to ride it that way in competition.

Nonetheless, I started out somewhat gingerly, reflexes aquiver, poised for potentially disastrous structural failures, unpredictable steering or braking behavior, or whatever. But nothing untoward happened; and shortly thereafter I was speeding across the plains at between sixty and seventy miles an hour, satisfied that the bike had come through the crash undamaged.

Now, high-speed riding across unfamiliar territory is one of the best ways I know to establish a meaningful relationship with your orthopedist, and usually I don't do it. But this terrain was incredibly smooth; the vegetation carpeting the ground would been suitable for use as a Masters' Tournament putting green. If I had thought for a minute that riding conditions might continue like this throughout, I'd have revised my e.t.a. downward by a couple of years—

Yes, I said *years*. Theoretically, at an average of fifty miles an hour, traveling twenty-four hours a day nonstop, (and ignoring the question of oceans altogether), it would take a little over twenty days to circumnavigate Earth.

To reach La'ïr from where I crashed *Venture*, traveling at the same speed, would require better than nine months. Likewise, theoretically.

Only how long would it *really* take to ride a motorcycle all the way around the Earth?

In a straight line.

Without benefit of roads.

When I won my gold medal in the Six-Day, I averaged barely fourteen miles an hour—and riding ten to twelve hours a day for six days straight almost killed me.

A reasonable estimate was more on the order of five years.

Now, I knew perfectly well that I wasn't going to spend the next five years on that bike. Something would turn up. Something always turns up. I couldn't imagine what form it might take, but I knew it would.

I knew it *had* to.

If I hadn't known it, I might have sat down right then and there and used that knife on my wrists.

CHAPTER 21

Conditions remained smooth all the way across the veldt, and I had no trouble maintaining my cruising speed well above sixty. And though high-speed riding usually implies a fairly intense level of concentration, the terrain over which I traveled wasn't the least bit challenging, so I had ample opportunity to take note of my surroundings.

The alien landscape gave rise to strangely conflicting sensations: It was indeed unearthly, yet I felt curiously "at home." Initially I attributed this to the superficially Earthlike character of much of the plant life: The vegetation beneath my wheels might be mistaken at first glance for grass—but it wasn't; it was too fine, too soft, too thick, too green, and was cropped to a uniform height of about two inches. Likewise, the two- to three-hundred-foot-tall "bushes" resembled various Earthly trees—maples, oaks, palms, banyans, and the like—but upon closer observation, differences were apparent.

Even the shadows on this planet were subtly wrong: The light arriving on Isis from the apparently tiny spark of far-distant Ra was appreciably more intense than that which falls on Earth, and there was virtually no divergence in the photon flow—Isis' sunshine constituted nearly coherent light. The demarcation between sunlight and shade was razor-edged; the only perceptible diffusion was the result of atmospheric refraction. The result was harshly contrasted lighting which lent an aura of surrealism to the scene—yet somehow this, too, felt right and proper.

It took me most of the way across the veldt to figure out the source of this patently impossible sense of déjà vu: Because I couldn't access any of it without direct stimuli, it was easy to forget that as a result of our rapport I had all of Meg's memories and knowledge stored in my head.

But here on Isis, stimuli were indeed direct—and constant: everywhere I looked something new appeared; and almost everything I saw kicked out a memory. I knew, for instance, that the soft, rich, green, grasslike growth which carpeted the ground was *t'gyl'q*, approximately equivalent to lettuce in nutritional value and equally delicious in salad. The smaller trees, which I had mistaken from the air for bushes, belonged to a genus of hardwoods known as *t'gyt'n*.

And as I approached the edge of the veldt, I knew that those incredibly massive, mile-high trees of which the forestlands generally consisted were the lordly and incalculably ancient *t'göllq'gn*.

Ra hung near the zenith as I arrived at the forest's verge; it was only a little after noon. Even so, I found myself in the shade of overhanging branches almost a half mile from the line of hundred- to two-hundred-fifty-yard-in-diameter trunks which marked the forest's effective boundary.

I slowed as I passed the first row of trunks; partly because the light faded rapidly, and I wanted to give my eyes an opportunity to accommodate to the change; but mostly because I had a fresh memory of the consequences of failing to notice a low-hanging branch of the sort common to Earthly forests in time to avoid it: Getting "clotheslined" was not a habit-forming experience.

That proved a needless concern, however: Competition for sunlight among the *t'göllq'gn* was a serious business; the less successful had been crowded out literally ages ago. Survivors were widely spaced; seldom did two of the gargantuan trunks occur closer than a quarter mile apart. And while the intervening ground was moderately grown-up with various species of *t'gyt'n*, even they were spaced far enough apart to preclude interference with my passage; though I was forced to maneuver constantly back and forth between them.

Of course, by the time the sunlight had filtered through the foliage of both the *t'göllq'gn* and the *t'gyt'n*, there wasn't much left to encourage lesser flora to proliferate: There was virtually no undergrowth; only a delicately grayish mosslike growth known as *b'vVet'h*, which ranged in height from a fuzzy blanket covering the soil to patches as much as a foot deep, and which had supplanted the *t'gyl'q* even before I passed the first *t'göllq´gn* trunks. The net result was a continuation of the smooth surface and unimpeded, effortless riding conditions which I was well on my way to taking for granted.

Not far into the forest it occurred to me to switch on the headlight. The dazzling quartz-iodine combination flood/spot beam improved visibility greatly. Soon I was back up to nearly open-country cruising speeds, weaving merrily between the trunks of the *t'gyt'n*, occasionally detouring around the mesalike obstruction of a *t'göllq´gn*, and generally reveling in a combination of esthetic appreciation of the grandeur of my surroundings and the sheer visceral satisfaction of working the bike quickly through the moderately twisty going.

I had camped in the Sequoia National Forest in the past; and except for the element of size, riding among the *t'göllq´gn* generated sensations akin to that experience. But not even the largest Earthly sequoias would have attracted notice in a stand of *t'gyt'n*—and they barely would have qualified as seedlings among the *t'göllq´gn.*

In fact, it was difficult to view the *t'göllq´gn* as trees at all. Nothing in my background prepared me to regard columns an eighth of a mile in diameter, rising through the gloom toward the softly green-lit canopy so far overhead, as "trees." The lowest branches of even the smaller specimens didn't appear until nearly a quarter mile up. One *t'göllq´gn* I passed had sustained major trunk damage—somehow!—and the bark alone was more than fifty feet thick. Among the upper branches, occasional drifting clouds could be detected . . . !

As I progressed deeper into the forest, isolated smaller "bush-sized" bushes began to make their appearance, growing here and there between the *t'gyt'n*, and occasional vines or creepers. Virtually all these smaller plants bore flowers three, five, even ten feet in diameter; and as the quartz/iodine beam of the headlight washed over them, it betrayed a riot of colors which on Earth would have required the application of ultraviolet lighting to achieve. It seemed criminal to waste such radiance in the dimness of the *t'göllq´gn* forest.

However, esthetic considerations didn't trouble me for long: I soon noticed that many of the smaller plants bore what appeared to be fruit and nuts as well. My stomach noticed them, too, and immediately pointed out that it had been a good three hours since I'd eaten last; I had replaced much of

the nutritional deficit incurred while repairing my damages—
but "almost" only counts in horseshoes: I was hungry
again. . . .

My borrowed knowledge of Isi flora failed to recognize any
of the produce, or the plants which bore it, which isn't
surprising: Meg was widely educated but not a botanist; nor
had she spent more than the minimum time required by her
education on field trips beyond the *wWr'dts* which protected
La'ir.

(Of course, to hear Meg and Memphus talk, no one else had,
either—at least no one possessing the least spark of intelligence: It was *rough* out there; that was the consensus of
everything I'd been able to dig out of my second-hand data
bank thus far. Unfortunately, without direct stimuli I was
unable to follow any of these forebodings back to their source;
so I still had only the sketchiest notion of what sort of dangers
lay ahead of me. Or under what circumstances I should be
alert for them.)

I regarded the fruit thoughtfully; then decided against it for
the moment. Now that I possessed total control over my
metabolism, I probably could digest almost anything; but it
might be necessary to adjust my internal secretions according
to the substances involved, and that would involve fairly
intense concentration. I judged it unwise to try to concentrate
intensely on anything besides riding for the moment. A rider
must remain alert.

Just how alert, I discovered shortly before sundown: Five
hundred miles from the crash site I met my first native. It was
light purple and about twenty feet long, including a short tail.
It traveled on a half dozen pairs of short, muscular legs, each of
which terminated in an impressively taloned paw. The animal's
head, apart from a lank, straggly, lavender mane, was reminiscent of archeologists' renderings of Tyrannosaurus Rex: A good
half of it consisted of jaws bristling with long, yellow, sharply
pointed tusks.

My dual-level memory wasted no time in producing a
species identification and thumbnail sketch of my new acquaintance's dietary habits. However, I responded even before
the information surfaced, based on the thing's appearance and
actions alone—fortunately!

As I came into view, the *krRy'fön*'s head came up; already
the beast was casting about for the source of the unfamiliar
sound of the engine. Even before it caught sight of me, I

downshifted from fifth to third and twisted the throttle grip to the stop. By the time the *krRy'fön* managed to focus those balefully glowing orange eyes on me, I was accelerating at full power, all my weight concentrated on the rear wheel to ensure maximum traction. The front wheel lowered gently to the *b'vVet'h* as the engine peaked in fourth; then momentarily lifted again as I popped the shift to fifth.

For an eternity measured in heartbeats I fled through the immense forest, ever conscious of the manic enthusiasm glowing in the eyes reflected in my mirrors as I dodged and weaved between the trunks of the *t'gyt'n*. I fell back into the groove of flat-track, motocross, and enduro racing immediately; and quite outdid myself, tossing the bike from one steeply banked, dirt-throwing power-slide to the next.

But it soon developed that, not only could the purple lion of Isis do a standing quarter mile in ten seconds, it was damnably maneuverable as well. And limited as I was by my surroundings to speeds in the fifty- to seventy-mile-an-hour range, this plain-and-fancy barrel-racing exhibition wasn't gaining me much advantage. The *krRy'fön* held on tenaciously; losing a yard or two here, gaining it back there; and showed no inclination to call it off and seek easier prey. And, of course, the longer the chase continued, the longer the odds grew against my continuing to avoid mistakes.

With a *krRy'fön* on my heels, I'd only make one. . . .

I angled over in the direction of one of the bigger *t'göllq'gn*. The trunk was almost half a mile in circumference, and the ground, within a respectful seventy-five to one-hundred-yard radius, was free of *t'gyt'n* and lesser vegetation.

Now, while a half-mile circle was not, by any stretch of the imagination, a genuine straightaway, it did offer sufficient room to develop some respectable speed. Accelerating hard, I banked into a gentle curve around the monster tree. I wound out fifth, popped it into sixth; then went into a tuck, chin down on the gas tank pad, elbows and knees pulled in tight, and let horsepower and aerodynamics do their job.

At about a hundred, I glanced in the mirrors and smiled: Twelve legs or not, the *krRy'fön* was outclassed; it was dropping back rapidly.

I eased the throttle and slowed a trifle. I didn't want to run off and leave it too quickly while running in a circle—the damned thing might get a notion to stop and wait for me.

So I slowed just enough to maintain a short lead, encouraging it to continue the pursuit. I intended to wear it out thoroughly before resuming course: One such chase was quite enough for an evening's diversion.

It took a while; *krRy'föns* possess an awesome level of endurance. But finally the beast began to stagger; then it slowed in earnest and stopped, puffing and blowing, and glared after me.

I slowed as well, reoriented myself from the planetary magnetic lines, and returned to my original heading—thereafter exercising a level of alertness which some might mistake for paranoia.

Darkness comes quickly on Isis; probably a consequence of the tiny apparent size of their sun: The actual sunset, from Ra's first graze to total disappearance, takes no more than a few seconds. In any event, it sure doesn't take long to get dark in the heart of a *t'göllq'gn* forest, once the sun is gone.

I almost got caught by surprise; but before the light failed entirely, I located a sprawling *t'gyt'n* which had a lot in common with Earthly banyan or fig trees. A little climbing turned up a cranny in which I might sleep without attracting a predator's attention—and without falling out of the tree.

As I made up my bedding and dined on the remains of the peanut butter, I found that my mind kept returning to the encounter with the *krRy'fön*. Now that I had met one, Meg's knowledge of them was available for my perusal—and the content was startling: The *krRy'fön* was one of those highly evolved, major predators responsible for the Isis' pre*pwW'r* decline into barbarism and, ultimately, their endangered-species status. The *krRy'fön*, in Meg's opinion, simply couldn't be dealt with without *mMj'q*.

Only, I *had* dealt with one—and on a purely mechanical basis at that. True, my solution had been to run away; but I was unarmed, and regardless whether one subscribes to the Isis' philosophy concerning such matters, a *krRy'fön* was, unquestionably, a big, fast, powerful, truly hellacious beast. Under such circumstances, running away was the only possible course of action.

However, I had run away *successfully*. And it was Meg's emphatic opinion, based on her knowledge of history, that that just wasn't possible.

I'd have liked to have shown them what was possible, I reflected grimly. Give me a .502 Weatherby magnum double, and I'd have stood my ground and punched its ticket without a moment's hesitation.

Shucks, even a strapping big longbow and a couple of well-placed broadheads would serve in a pinch. (I did pretty well in archery in the Olympics.) Between the knife and the bike's toolkit, I had a fair variety of edged and blunt instruments; fabricating a usable bow and arrows—or even a crossbow— wouldn't be difficult.

On the other hand, coming up with a bowstring could be a problem; nothing I had with me was both sufficiently strong and flexible enough to serve. On Earth I'd have used a length of cured deer or bear gut. In the conspicuous absence of deer or bears (or data on Isi comparative anatomy), gut or the equivalent still tentatively appeared to be the logical first area to investigate. Certainly if conduct were any clue to construction, there ought to be something tough enough somewhere inside a *krRy'fön*—leaving only the question of how to obtain a sample. Politely walking up and asking was out. . . .

Deadfall traps aren't sporting, but they work; and while there didn't appear to be much in the way of the necessary raw materials in the immediate area, some was bound to turn up as I traveled. Okay, I'd make a deadfall, kill a *krRy'fön* (or whatever) and make a bow and arrow.

Briefly I wondered about fletching. I hadn't seen anything wearing feathers since leaving *Venture* (actually, come to think of it, apart from the *krRy'fön*, I hadn't seen any wildlife, period, which seemed odd, considering what Meg and Memphus had led me to believe); but that was a minor detail: Two or three properly trimmed feathers, carefully positioned to impart a stabilizing spin to the shaft without excess drag, are the ideal way to stabilize an arrow; however, just about any lightweight, high-drag substance fastened to the rear of a long, skinny projectile tends to improve its accuracy.

As I drifted off to sleep, I found myself wondering about the Isi: How could a species consisting of intelligent, resourceful, determined, able-bodied human beings, already well along the road to civilization, suddenly find themselves driven to the brink of extinction by mere *animals* . . . ?

A truly intelligent, resourceful, determined, able-bodied person *always* can find a way to cope with his surroundings. Whatever they are.

Somehow.

I mean, escaping from that *krRy'fön* wasn't even *difficult*. . . .

TO: Project Director/Monitor's Log
FROM: T'dDalk, Seventh Order.
SUBJECT: Project *Extremis*.

The Council of Elders has decided that, to restore his spirits preliminarily, Subject Cory shall be allowed to achieve relatively easy victories over the environment in the beginning. It is felt that ultimate defeat, when it comes, will affect him that much more deeply by contrast. Accordingly, the *mMj'q*-enhanced molecular bonding of his motorcycle's components and the extrauniversal storage of its fuel were continued uninterrupted.

While the slight additional speed offered by this mode of transportation means little, in view of the magnitude of the distances facing him, it will have a beneficial effect on his initial outlook; and, as we already have seen, outrunning a *krRy'fön* has indeed operated to bolster his confidence.

Nonetheless, escaping the next major predator we allow near him will prove appreciably more challenging. . . .

I neglected to set the alarm on my watch, but I woke at first light anyway—I was ravenous again. I had finished off what little remained of the peanut butter the previous evening; and the moment my eyes opened, my stomach reminded me that we had some unfinished business to attend to: All those freshly divided cells (not to mention the rest of me) still were hungry and rapidly growing more so.

I sighed and informed them that they'd all just have to wait until I managed to forage us up something; we were out of food.

I stretched carefully, wincing at the stiffness which resulted from sleeping on the heavy bark. Gathering my meager belongings, I climbed from the tree and tied them to the bike.

Plucking assorted fruit and nuts from nearby vines and bushes, I turned my perception inward to supervise the initial phases of digestion. Most of it was delicious; and even that which wasn't caused no problems. However, it did little to offset feelings of impending starvation:

The "trimmings" which accompany an entrée are delicious;

I'd really hate to have to do without them—but to a carnivorous ape, the heart of the matter is *animal protein*. I wanted meat! I *needed* meat! I was accustomed to putting away a twelve-ounce filet or an inch-thick slab of prime rib at least once a day. All my cells (not just the freshly divided ones) were crying out for their daily fix.

Well, they'd have to wait.

I spent probably fifteen minutes grazing on the fruit and nuts, concentrating on how good everything tasted, and how wholesome and satisfying a meatless diet could be. But I guess I wasn't cut out to be a vegetarian: A full stomach eased the actual hunger pangs, but did little for the cravings.

So I ignored them and, assembling a stock of the better-tasting produce, I wrapped it up and strapped it to the rear of the saddle with the rest of my belongings.

The bike started promptly and I resumed my travels. I'd covered a good six hundred miles yesterday; that left only about three hundred twenty-nine thousand four hundred to go. . . .

About an hour later I came to a break in the *t'göllq´gn* forest. The clearing I emerged into was considerably smaller than where I'd crash-landed *Venture*, probably no more than fifteen or twenty miles across at the most, and was speckled with small, startlingly blue plants, remarkably uniform in size, averaging about a foot in height. Each consisted of a number of thickish stems supporting a round, bladderlike central structure. Each was covered by a thick coat of sapphire fuzz.

As usual, the sight of a minor plant produced no information from my second-hand memory storage; and for the first couple of miles I paid little attention to them, apart from weaving carefully back and forth to avoid running over any (it's surprising how solid a small bush can be to a motorcyclist if it catches him just right).

But presently I came to an area where they were packed quite tightly together. To get through, it would be necessary to brush several quite closely and drive right over another. Well, you're less likely to get dumped if you hit something like that squarely and firmly. I slowed, dropped to first gear, and took dead aim.

I was probably two yards from impact when a pair of tiny gold and green eyes blinked into existence amid the blue fuzz coating the bush. They stared in round-eyed horror for a fraction of a second. Then the bush said, "*Yeek!*" and disappeared. Where it had stood was a mound of loose dirt surrounding an eight- or ten-inch hole in the ground.

I stopped abruptly and regarded the immediate area suspiciously. And even as I looked around, between one second and the next, about a third of the remaining "bushes" vanished, all revealing burrows where they had been. Closer inspection of the remaining bushes disclosed honest-to-goodness roots.

Now my borrowed education responded: *nNby'qs* were inoffensive, physically helpless creatures corresponding to Earth's prairie dogs. They lived in great colonies which virtually honeycombed entire clearings. And like prairie dogs, *nNby'qs* faced a major problem: Every predator on the planet knew they were *delicious*, an unparalleled treat. Over time, natural selection had alleviated the threat to a degree by transforming their physical structure and appearance to one virtually indistinguishable (as long as they didn't move) from that of the frightfully toxic *t'göe'tl* plant.

Meg was quite fond of animals, apart from predators (and even those she admired [though preferably from afar]); as a consequence, she possessed an extensive knowledge of Isi wildlife. Piercing the *nNby'qs'* disguise stimulated the grudging release of a little more second-hand information; central to which was an awareness that among the smaller, slower, generally helpless species populating the planet, mimickry was the preferred form of defense, and had been developed to a high degree of sophistication.

Meg knew of avian species which could not be distinguished at rest from certain tumorlike knobs on tree trunks. One variety of *t'gyt'n* reproduced by shedding poison-gas-filled, lighter-than-air seed pods at regular intervals—but if one paid close attention, one might notice that some occasionally drifted upwind. . . .

Later that morning I found myself leaving the *t'göllq'gn* forest again, heading out across a broad plain, as big or bigger than the one in which I had left the wreckage of *Venture*. As I emerged into bright sunlight, I caught a suggestion of movement in one of my mirrors.

My reaction was instantaneous, without thought: I kicked down two gears, cranked the throttle wide, and dropped again into a full tuck. By the time I actually got around to risking a look, I was accelerating at max and tensing for the speedshift into fifth.

A single glimpse was enough.

Memphus had mentioned in passing that his friend, Fafnir, had chosen a *böll'skag* for a host; and Meg had remarked that its presence still bothered her on an instinctive level despite their years of association. But that exchange had been a verbal conversation, prerapport; no mental images had accompanied the description. I was unprepared for the nightmare which came charging out of the jungle behind me:

The *böll'skag* was huge, staggeringly so, at least two hundred fifty yards in length. The monster was similar in form to an Earthly monitor lizard, except for a somewhat longer neck and the fact that the massive body was supported by six long, powerful legs. A layer of thick, glistening scales furnished visibly impervious armor plating. The beast's coloration was an electric, near-fluorescent scarlet; all but the eyes, which were strangly glowing, featureless black slits probably eight feet long and three feet high, which regarded me with disturbing calculation. Finally—so help me—plumes of dense, black smoke gushed from the nostrils at every breath, curling back along soot-discolored flanks to blanket its wake under a ground-hugging pall.

The sight sufficed to trigger Meg's knowledge of *böll'skags;* suddenly I knew far more about the gargantuan carnivores than I ever wanted to—and nowhere near enough. Meg's acquaintance with *böll'skags* was about comparable to the familiarity a well-read New Yorker might have with elephants: She knew they were big, possessed a combustion-digestion metabolism, were perpetually hungry, and ate anything which didn't eat them first. She had the impression, too, that while *böll'skags* were notoriously persistent in pursuit of prey, they were rather slow-moving.

This last was literally accurate but deceptive in practice: The monster moved with the ponderous grace and inevitability of a supertanker—however, even though each step took two full seconds to complete, those six long, powerful legs covered something over a hundred yards per stride. Their combined efforts produced an awesome, if lumbering, rate of progress.

I had probably a half-mile head start when the chase began. Five minutes later, though my speed had peaked in excess of a hundred twenty, my lead was dwindling steadily toward an unplanned luncheon engagement: The *böll'skag* was overhauling me with the ease of a greyhound running down a rabbit—

Oho! There was a thought: No rabbit worthy of his cottontail would maintain a straight course while fleeing a faster pursuer.

I slowed to forty and watched my mirrors as the smoke-streaming colossus bore down on me. I waited until it was only a couple hundred yards back; then I pitched the bike sideways, poured on the coal, and shot off at a ninety-degree angle.

After a couple hundred feet I pulled up to watch the results. I smiled: There simply was no way that that economy-size garter snake could stop in much less than two miles. The momentum it had developed by now was downright appalling.

Justifiable smugness is a delicious sensation—

But first one should make sure that it's really justified! My smirk faded abruptly. There was indeed a great deal of momentum—but there were six enormously powerful legs, each ending in massive talons. . . .

The *böll'skag* glared and muttered something in Profane Thunder as it pounded by. Then it braced its legs, splayed out its toes, dug those talons into the ground, and, fountaining dirt like a high-speed plow (and in the process leaving a set of ruts that would have bogged a bulldozer), skidded to a stop in something under a hundred yards.

Deliberately the *böll'skag* extracted its talons from the ground, yanking one foot free at a time and shaking it to dislodge the twenty or thirty cubic yards of soil which still adhered.

It turned slowly and regarded me with palpable annoyance.

It "chuffed" a great mushroom cloud of smoke from each nostril and surged forward.

So did I. But quickly it became apparent that, despite the fact that the bike accelerated much more quickly than the huge reptile, and was vastly more nimble, I couldn't dodge forever; and I'd already learned that I couldn't match it in sheer straightaway speed. I'd have to come up with something clever—

I'd *better* come up with something clever, I realized with alarm, as an unexpected roundhouse swing of the *böll'skag's* football-field-long tail very nearly smashed me like a mosquito at the conclusion of what should have been an effortless *paso de muerte*. Next I narrowly escaped being incinerated as the monster demonstrated that "where there's smoke," et cetera; and that it was capable of jetting an impressive stream of "et cetera." Moments thereafter, I lost my eyebrows and some

hair as I learned that the damned thing had sandbagged me!—
that it could project fire *much* farther than it had led me
originally to believe.

I began to regard the gigantic, furnace-bellied carnivore
with something approaching respect: *Böll'skags* were smart;
they learned fast. This could get serious!

And ten minutes later things were getting serious indeed:
Each time the monster lurched into motion, or strained every
muscle and tendon to change the direction of that tremendous,
onrushing mass midcharge, or skidded ponderously to a halt as
I narrowly eluded rush after rush, those huge talons sliced
whole yards down into the billiard-table-smooth ground. The
surface was becoming fraught, if not downright suicidal, for
high-speed motorcycling; and I couldn't seem to find the
maneuvering room necessary to lead the beast toward fresh
turf. Sooner or later, the way things were going, I was going to
get dumped, and that would be that.

Inspiration, when it finally arrived, came as such a relief that
I didn't even waste time berating myself for failing to think of it
sooner. (Priorities are important: First you keep the *böll'skag*
from eating you—*then* you indulge in self-flagellation. . . .)

I set to work immediately: casting out with my mind,
locating the flow of atmospheric static electricity, setting up a
telekinetic channel, and warping it into a circle to establish a
t'lLïSs 'mn; then pumping in electrons, and building voltage
just as hard and fast as I could—all while starting, stopping,
dodging, weaving, and bobbing like a mad thing, around and
over talon-generated furrows which would have given an
armored-column commander pause; trying to keep out of the
böll'skag's clutches long enough to accumulate an adequate
charge.

With a resounding crash of thunder, the electron beam
struck the titanic fire-breather in the chest. I blinked furiously
to see past the pink afterimages. The result was gratifying:

Despite the fact that the charge wasn't nearly what it should
have been (I was rushed), the huge body convulsed from one
end to the other (an impressive phenomenon in its own right)
and went to its front two pair of knees with an explosion of
flame and a sulphur-scented bellow reminiscent of Mount St.
Helens clearing her throat.

I braked to a stop the instant the *böll'skag* went down,
freeing most of my attention to concentrate on accumulating a
fresh charge. Simultaneously I began eating furiously from my
collection of fruit and nuts, and tried to spare a little attention

to increasing the efficiency of my digestive processes—I remembered all too well the aftereffects of flinging electrons around wholesale; and Meg and her *wWn'dt* weren't there to bail me out if I ran up a deficit again.

The *böll'skag* gathered all its legs beneath it and rose laboriously. There was an ugly, blackened discoloration in one of the scales on its chest and its movements visibly lacked coordination. Nevertheless, the monster fixed me with a rage-filled, coal-black glare, and a huge, spreading fireball exploded outward and upward as its challenge echoed and reechoed from the distant trunks of the *t'göllq'gn* surrounding the plain.

Then it started toward me again.

But this time I wasn't hurried; there was ample time to develop a full charge, select my target carefully, aim deliberately—and remember to put my fingers in my still-ringing ears before releasing the bolt: The resultant shaft of coherent lightning was almost a foot in diameter and struck the *böll'skag* squarely between the eyes. A yard-wide circle of scales exploded outward, leaving a blackened hemispherical pit at the bottom of which isolated scraps of reddish meat showed here and there through the charred surface. The mammoth beast crashed onto its belly with a literally ground-shaking impact and went into an awesome series of convulsions: writhing, lashing the ground with all six limbs, head, and tail, and filling the air with flame and smoke.

Simultaneously I felt the first hint of that well-remembered nonphysical weariness which had presaged my near-collapse above the slopes of the Himalayas. If that experience were any guide, I had one more shot left; then I was in trouble.

I regarded the *böll'skag* anxiously. The convulsions had ended; the monster lay unmoving across more than an eighth of a mile of Isi real estate. I hoped the engagement was over—

Damn! The beast stirred. It lifted its head slowly and those huge, black-glowing eyes focused unsteadily on me. Moments later, it was attempting to stagger upright . . . !

I turned most of my attention inward. Already the process of digestion and distribution of nourishment was pretty efficient. I wasn't bothering to chew; I just ripped off bite after bite of the fruit and gulped them whole. My stomach greeted each mouthful as it arrived, mashed it to a liquid much more quickly and thoroughly than my teeth and tongue could have, and immediately bustled the remains into my small intestine where chemical breakdown and distribution of nutrient products proceeded at an incredible rate.

I returned full attention to my surroundings. The *böll'skag* was standing now; a bit unsteadily to be sure, but standing. The cauterized wound between its eyes had begun to bleed. It rocked forward . . .

And I fired again. The discharge, my third within only minutes, probably would have discommoded a *nNby'q*; not seriously, of course, but he'd have noticed. Surprisingly, the *böll'skag* noticed, too:

It stopped short, swayed for a moment; then toppled with a sound like a railway collision.

So did I, but more quietly. I managed to push clear of the bike as I fell so it didn't land on me. I also managed to hit the kill switch. There were spots in front of my eyes (distinct from the afterimages of the lightning). I felt sick and dizzy. The *t'lLiSs'mn* had vanished.

I lay where I landed and continued shoveling in the food— watching the *böll'skag* to see whether it was going to stay down.

The status remained quo for perhaps half an hour, during which time I recovered enough to sit up cautiously, then stand. As I did so, the *böll'skag* stirred again as well. . . .

I ignored it. I had to; I had no choice: If that *böll'skag* had jumped to its feet, made a rude gesture with a forefoot, and done a tap dance before resuming its charge, I couldn't have responded. But I was pretty sure it wasn't going to. At least not right away; clearly the exchange had taken more out of the *böll'skag* than it had me. It seemed a fair bet that, even if the monster managed to regain its feet in the immediate future, it wouldn't have nearly the speed it displayed at first. It was time for our apprentice *wWyhr läaq* to make himself scarce.

By exerting every ounce of strength remaining in me, I stood the bike up. Taking careful aim and mentally rehearsing the necessary muscle sequences in advance, I swung a five-hundred-pound leg over the saddle and sat heavily, resting briefly before unfolding the starter pedal. The engine started on the first kick, feeble as it was.

Engaging first gear, I twisted the throttle grip, and released the clutch with a bang. I traveled the first fifty feet on my rear wheel—not intentionally; my coordination reserves were as depleted as everything else.

I glanced in my mirrors as I hit sixth. The *böll'skag* was attempting to stand again. After a couple of tries it succeeded; then staggered off in the wrong direction. Attempting to turn, it tripped over its own feet (considering the number of which was hardly surprising). Then, tiredly, it started over again.

It was about eighty miles across that clearing. It took me fifty minutes to cover the distance. I'd have gone even faster if I could have used both hands, but I still was a long way from recovering from the nutritional deficit—I was eating!

I looked back from the shade of the towering *t'göllq´gn* forest to see the distant, smoke-trailing silhouette of the *böll'skag* slowly moving off in another direction. Apparently it had concluded, finally, that the expenditure of yet another four or five million calories to run down a mere couple hundred pounds of protein and roughage could not be justified.

I could have told it that in the beginning.

It was with a cautiously heartfelt sigh that I swung back into the cool, dimly lit beauty of the *t'göllq´gn* forest, on course once again. Quickly I settled back into the rhythm of working the bike rapidly through the labyrinth, weaving smoothly and continuously between the boles of the *t'gyt'n* and detouring around the *t'göllq´gn* when one blocked my way.

As I rode, I found myself reviewing the experience in light of the Isis' history: *Böll'skags* were one of the most dreaded, utterly irresistible predators on the planet, according to my second-hand data. Before the discovery of the *pwW´r*, it was believed, no Isi ever had escaped a *böll'skag* which had chosen him as prey. No mere human (Earthly or Isi) possessed any fraction of the speed, agility, and endurance required to elude one; no barrier was proof against their strength and determination—*böll'skags* had been known to claw their way into the trunk of a *t'göllq´gn* after someone who had sought shelter in a vacant *lsS'b* hole.

And if no Isi ever escaped from a *böll'skag* bent on eating him, certainly none ever bested one in personal combat. (Though, actually, "draw" probably was a fairer description of the outcome of my encounter.)

All of which I found extremely puzzling: *There was no reason they couldn't have. . . .*

Even back before the comet's final passage freed the predators to overrun the planet, the Isi possessed most of their present *gnää´qs;* in particular, telekinesis was a well-developed parapsychological faculty. Meg's experience demonstrated that the Isi could have done just what I did at any point during their history—if only they had thought of it. And if a group had banded together to wield electron beams en masse, history might have followed a very different course.

I shook my head in perplexity: If it was difficult to envision an intelligent, imaginative, resourceful people who, on discovering that they possessed such wondrous powers, failed to explore their every aspect and possible application to everyday problems—it was downright impossible to understand their failure to exhaust every possibility in determining whether their *gnää'qs* (or anything else within reach) could head off impending racial extinction!

Maybe there was more to the differences between Earthmen and the Isi than that "racial mind block" which prevented them from grasping certain concepts of physics. . . .

CHAPTER 22

I was still eating virtually nonstop, so I paused briefly at a cluster of vines and bushes to restock my larder. I had begun to recover from the aftereffects of overusing the *t'lLiSs 'mn,* but I was beginning to wonder if I'd ever be free of hunger again—I wanted *meat!*

In fact, by early afternoon, a *krRy'fön* possessing full knowledge of the situation would have thought twice before venturing anywhere near me. It was time I did something about that.

I stopped under a smallish *t'gyt'n* set in the middle of a clearing well-dotted with *t'göe'tl* plants and/or *nNby'qs.* The nearer *nNby'qs,* of course, all dived for cover the instant they realized I wasn't just passing through.

Gratefully I slid from the saddle and parked the bike on its stand; then sat on the ground at the base of the *t'gyt'n,* leaned back comfortably against the trunk, and relaxed.

It felt good to rest; plus, the physical inactivity allowed me to concentrate on restoring my physical condition. I was pretty sure that I'd eaten enough to replace what I'd used; the problem was distribution.

Assuming direct control of my metabolism, I overrode the automatics and searched for excess fatigue-toxin concentrations. Intriguingly, most of it was clustered in certain of my brain cells and along portions of my nervous system; only normal amounts showed up anywhere else. But wherever I found it, I flushed it thoroughly; then shifted my nutritional transport system into high and got everything fed.

An hour later I was fully recovered, though still in the throes of that psychological craving—*I wanted MEAT . . . !*

But even now, several pairs of tiny, suspicious, green-and-gold eyes belonging to potential solutions to that craving peered from burrows not fifty feet away. I hadn't moved so much as a hair since settling myself against the *t'gyt'n* trunk; and it is a Universal Truth that the shyer the beastie, the bigger its bump of curiosity. *NNby'qs* are very shy. Correspondingly, they are very curious. I knew it was only a matter of time before one or more couldn't stand it any longer; before they simply *had* to emerge and investigate this new and extremely odd addition to their neighborhood.

Remaining absolutely still, I felt for the atmospheric electrical currents and began to construct and charge another *t'lLïSs 'mn*.

As I continued to remain motionless, the *nNby'qs'* curiosity mounted. First one, then another, then still another of the fuzzy blue heads popped above the rims of their burrows to get a better look—ducking back almost immediately. But as I failed to react, the periods of surveillance lengthened; soon a number of the little beasts were staring fixedly at me with no effort at concealment.

Inevitably the time came when they began to lose interest; by ones and twos they emerged from their burrows and returned to their normal, everyday activities (whatever those might be). That was my cue.

I trained the *t'lLïSs 'mn* on the biggest, plumpest *nNby'q* in sight. I was all set to fire when it occurred to me that my previous targets all had been considerably larger. If I zapped a *nNby'q* with the same beam I'd used on the gunships or that *böll'skag*, I'd undoubtedly vaporize the little critter. Clearly a degree of care was in order: Vapor is not filling.

I squeezed down the discharge aperture of my nozzle, then let fly.

At the crash of thunder which accompanied the bolt, all the other *nNby'qs* vanished.

Blinking through pink afterimages, I discovered that a still smaller aperture was called for; I very nearly had disintegrated the little varmint. The scraps which remained were distinctly well-done—but they bore out the opinion held by predators the length and breadth of Isis: *NNby'qs* were delicious! The flavor combined the better qualities of both top-grade prime rib and southern-fried chicken.

I stuffed myself until I simply couldn't hold any more; then turned my perception inward to review my condition. I had to determine whether telekinesis, used sparingly, was going to be a practical means of obtaining fresh meat, or whether the cost in energy output would exceed that brought in. I checked the areas where excess fatigue toxins had built up during previous overuse, and found little or none following the meal. Okay, so much for hunting with bow and arrow. . . .

I wondered how long it was going to take before I started to remember my newly discovered *gnää'qs* without mortal prompting. I doubted that it would have taken more than a single well-placed zap to discourage that *krRy'fön*.

I paused reflectively. It was beginning to appear that the reported difficulties of non*pwW'r*-assisted life on Isis might have been exaggerated—things just *weren't* that tough. My opinion of the Isi as a species was starting to wane.

No, it was too early to form such an opinion; insufficient data.

I wrapped up the four or five leftover drumsticks for supper, and resumed my travels.

TO: Project Director/Monitor's Log.
FROM: Sephiloyä, Third Order.
SUBJECT: Project *Extremis*.

Subject Cory has been allowed to triumph over both a *krRy'fön* and a *böll'skag* (though his method of dealing with the latter came as a surprise to us), and has killed his own food. His confidence in his ability ultimately to win through to La'ïr is high and on the rise. If he emerges intact from this next encounter, his self-confidence will be firmly entrenched—he will be ripe to meet the real Isis in all its fury.

As the day wore on, the terrain changed. The riding surface remained smooth, but my surroundings grew steadily more rugged, and the *t'göllq'gn* forest thinned. Occasional rocky outcropping thrust up through the soil.

I continued to make good time generally, but I had to work harder at it. Twice I was forced to slow and pick my way across patches of boulders.

Shortly thereafter I took advantage of a slight rise in the

ground to jump a small stream. And as I closed the throttle momentarily to keep from overrevving the engine while the bike was airborne, during that instant of near-silence I *heard something*. . . .

It was like nothing I'd ever heard before; yet my hackles bristled instantly. It was a keening, wailing sound; faintly akin to the cry of an Earthly coyote, but with more hollowness, more loneliness; a deeper, heavier-sounding voice—a *hungrier*-sounding voice. My second-hand racial memories had no difficulty making the connection. . . .

You might achieve something resembling a *däal'fön* by crossing a German shepherd with a Kodiak bear. Massive, heavily furred canine analogs averaging six feet at the shoulder, weighing between a thousand and fifteen hundred pounds each, they have "only" four legs (each terminating in a paw armed with six retractable, inches-long talons) but move with the effortless speed of a cheetah, and possess virtually limitless endurance. Heads are massive; muzzles short, blunt; jaws brutal; eyes are clear and intelligent.

(As a footnote: Among Meg's childhood memories was an encounter with a four-week-old *däal'fön* puppy. It stood not quite eighteen inches at the shoulder; it was very round and furry, and tended to be somewhat unsteady on its feet. Nevertheless, it took itself extremely seriously and was utterly fearless, displaying a self-assurance more appropriate for something five times its size. Particularly about the face, it resembled an oversized, black-faced, Earthly chow chow puppy of similar age. Meg had to be restrained almost physically: "But *Daddy*, it *likes* me—can't I keep it? Oh, *puhleez* . . . !")

No such emotions are generated by the adults, however: Very few Isi predators inspire the widespread, sheer panic evoked by a *däal'fön* pack on the move. *Däal'föns* are single-minded carnivores, living and hunting in packs numbering around ten thousand. They're a nomadic species; they have to be: No geographic area can support a population of such carnivores for long—little remains alive in the wake of a *däal'fön* pack but tree-, burrow-, and air-dwellers. According to Meg's information, *krRy'föns* and even isolated *böll'skags* defer to *däal'föns* in numbers when their paths happen to cross.

Hunting is the pack's major industry, centering on game-sweeps organized and executed with unrivaled efficiency and

thoroughness, involving virtually the entire adult population:
The majority forms a miles-long, semicircular line across the
wilderness, driving everything edible before it; usually toward
some natural barrier ahead, but just as often into the clutches
of a smaller group of their number lying in wait ahead. The fate
befalling a *däal'fön* pack's victims invites comparisons with the
consequences to those who blunder into the path of Earthly
army ants—only here the hordes of killers weigh between half
and three-quarters of a ton, and operate with an unhurried
teamwork suggesting a high order of intelligence.

I stopped immediately, shut off the engine, strained my ears
for further clues—and received them without delay: The cry
was repeated in front of me, to the rear, to the right; only to
the left was the way apparently open.

I glanced wistfully at the trees around me. But this was the
heart of a *t'göllq´gn* forest—and *t'göllq´gn* are patently
unclimbable without special equipment; the lowest limbs were
thousands of feet above the ground. Even the *t'gyt'n* were
effectively unassailable; might as well try to shinny up a
sequoia. Climbing to safety was out.

Well, retreat offered at least a temporary solution while I
mulled my options. I restarted the engine and headed off in
the only direction still open, even if only temporarily.

Initially I proceeded at a deliberate pace, keeping a watchful
eye to the rear and sides; I wanted to know where I was in
relation to the boundaries of the game-sweep. It took only a
few minutes of riding slowly before dark shapes became
visible, coursing easily through the forest behind me in a line
which extended as far as I could see in both directions—no
doubt remained: I was being invited to dinner. Again. . . .

I speeded up to put some distance between us, and juggled
the possibilities. Presently I concluded that they were limited,
as a practical matter, to two: One, I could turn back and charge
the *däal'föns'* line, trying to break out through the ranks
forming the perimeter of the drive; or two, I could turn up the
wick and outrun the pack, arriving at the site where the trap
was scheduled to be sprung before the *däal'föns* manning it
were ready, catching them by surprise, and slipping through in
the confusion (aided by a well-placed bolt of lightning, if
necessary). I'd only get off a single shot, of course; but the
unexpected blinding flash and accompanying groundshaking
blast of thunder reasonably could be counted on to freeze the

rest in their tracks for the critical fractions of a second it would take me to squeak through.

I happened to be passing through a small clearing at this point in my deliberations; and a glance to the rear allowed me a clear view of my pursuers for the first time. One look ruled out any idea of trying to break out in that direction: There were *lots* of *däal'föns* beating the bushes behind me; and every one looked as if it would welcome the diversion.

I cranked on more speed and cast out with my mind for the atmospheric electrical currents.

Fortunately, manipulation of intangible forces was becoming almost second nature by now. "Fortunately," because shortly I found myself too busy trying to stay upright and out from underfoot to spare much attention to the complexities of reestablishing a *t'lLïSs´mn* and bringing it up to working voltage—I was trapped in the midst of an all-out stampede!

It was an amazing sight: There were ruminants, herbivores, lesser predators, reptilian-looking things, and unclassifiable monstrosities; they ranged from substantially larger than an elephant to smaller than a breadbox. All the colors of the Isi spectrum were represented; there were dozens of opinions as to how many legs constituted a quorum.

There was, in fact, only a single common factor: The *däal'föns* were *this* way; wherefore, emphatically and without delay, everybody else was going *that* way—each at its absolute maximum speed. All personal differences were forgotten in the common panic: *KrRy'föns* bounded uncaring in the midst of herds of delicate, defenseless, equally disinterested, *t'gyl'q*-eating *p'rRöf*. A small *böll'skag* lumbered blindly through the forest shoulder-to-shoulder with a *b'vVec'h*-munching *t'jJ's*.

All of which made for entertaining riding—if one could ignore the penalty for spilling. Outrunning a hungry *krRy'fön* through the winding maze of the *t'göllq´gn* forest was a pretty spooky business under the best of conditions—overtaking and *passing* one on a twisting game trail was downright hairy! But apart from rolling a scared eye (white showed all the way around the orange, black-slitted iris) sideways at me as I pulled alongside on a short straightaway, the big, many-legged carnivore paid me no attention.

On the other hand, it didn't offer to make room as I outbraked it into the next corner. I had to scramble as best I could with the traction available in the loose stuff on the verges.

By dint of riding which would have won me any dirt-track race I'd ever entered, I worked my way to the forefront of the stampede. Once in the clear, I had no difficulty pulling out a lead. But I eased my pace slightly then; I didn't care to build up too much advantage over my fellow fugitives: I only wanted to ensure enough room to maneuver when we arrived in the trap—I wasn't looking for the undivided attention of several thousand hungry *däal'föns*.

This gave me time to reflect further on my plans (if one could call them that) for the forthcoming encounter. And the longer I dwelled on the matter, the less comfortable I became with the notion of relying on the hypothetical lightning-flash-and-thunder-induced momentary startlement, achieved by zapping a single *däal'fön*, to stun the rest long enough to do any good.

What I knew about *däal'föns* was limited to what Meg knew. None of which—together with the fleeting first-hand glimpses I'd gotten of them thus far—suggested that they startled easily.

I started wishing my *t'lLïSs´mn* were a repeating model. Single-shot weapons place an awful lot of emphasis on accuracy and timing. Not to mention luck.

Absently I reviewed the valve's design. It wasn't difficult to envision a theoretical valving mechanism which, if one ignored the more untidy aspects of engineering reality (electronic- and mechanical-component response-lag time, friction, inertia, and tiresome stuff along those lines), ought to permit firing off several bolts before the entire charge was spent. Of course they'd all discharge within a fairly small fraction of a nanosecond, which would make it difficult to shift the aiming point; and all those practical considerations pretty well ruled out—wait. . . .

An immaterial mechanism *shouldn't* be affected by crass engineering practicalities; it ought to react at the speed of thought—effectively instantaneously. I *could* devise a valve which would permit repetitive firing—for as long as the charge held out, of course.

Only that still didn't solve the problem of retargeting between shots. Okay, forget multiple discharges. Instead, how about squeezing the aperture down to about a thousandth of an inch. Damming the flow would extend the beam's duration. Then, by mounting the nozzle on an off-center pivot, the action/reaction pressure of the electron discharge would act to traverse the beam as long as it existed, or until the nozzle reached the end of its designed travel, whichever came first. One swing of the resultant immaterial but unimaginably penetrant sword ought to take the starch out of a dozen or so *däal'föns* and distract the rest long enough to allow me to duck past.

And that, of course, was the extent of my ambitions toward them; I just wanted to be on my way with a minimum of trouble—I had no desire to "punish" the *däal'föns* for their natural and, in their view, entirely appropriate interest in me.

Gleefully, if somewhat preoccupiedly as I continued to maneuver through the *t'göllq'gn* forest, I reengineered the valve. Soon it was ready, and the voltage was about as high as I was capable of achieving—now, just bring on those *däal'föns* . . . !

It occurred to me that I was grinning like an idiot. Once again I was facing a mortal challenge, relying on an untested solution. This was getting to be a habit—in fact, I suddenly realized, I'd been doing it practically since Meg dropped into my life.

Well, she never promised the work would be easy or safe; just interesting and *necessary*. . . .

It suddenly occurred to me that I'd been building voltage in the *t'lLïSs'mn* steadily for several minutes now. I'd already learned what it was like to be on the wrong side of the energy curve, and I didn't like it. If I wanted to avoid doing it again, I'd better start doing something about it.

Quickly I dug out the remaining *nNby'q* drumsticks and started eating furiously. At the same time I diverted a fraction of my attention inward, shifted my metabolism into high gear again, and began accumulating surplus nutrients in the brain and nervous system cells which previously had been affected.

In the process I noticed that, despite the fact that the *t'lLïSs'mn* had been in existence for several minutes now, its maintenance had drawn little energy thus far. This seemed to suggest that perhaps the nearly lethal drain I'd experienced in the past might be limited to the actual discharge. That was a tempting notion; it would be quite comforting if, in times of uncertainty, I could create a *t'lLïSs'mn* and maintain it charged and ready for extended periods without rendering myself prostrate in the process.

I rounded the monumental trunk of a final *t'göllq'gn*, shot between the boles of a pair of *t'gyt'n*, and burst out into another clearing, the size of which I couldn't ascertain due to a slight rise immediately ahead—

And there it was: the *däal'fön* trap.

I slowed quickly, taking in the scene at a glance. . . .

The big, black hunters waited quietly, arrayed in an almost militarily precise semicircle probably two miles long, which began and ended in the forest behind me. No more than a yard separated the massive, furred shoulders one from another. Their eyes were alert, watchful, calculating—hungry.

So much for catching them by surprise.

The thundering horde came pounding out of the jungle moments later. The vanguard was probably a hundred yards behind me; I had just about the lead I wanted.

But unbidden came the thought that Custer probably had wanted maneuvering room, too. Briefly I hesitated, pondering the wisdom of reversing my strategy and allowing most of the panicked animals to blunder into the waiting *däal'föns* first; then dealing with those still unoccupied as necessary.

It was a short debate: Even as I watched, the *böll'skag* mashed two lesser animals under its feet and leveled another half a score with a distracted swing of its tail. Thank you, no; I didn't need that kind of help. I picked a point in the *däal'fön* barricade and cranked the throttle wide open.

Fifty yards from the line—close enough to see the intelligent, calmly appraising eyes; the drool running from the big carnivores' jaws as they contemplated my approach—I shifted into fourth gear and aimed the *t'lLïSs´mn's* nozzle slightly to the right of center.

The thread of dazzlingly brilliant violet fire that lashed out existed for the briefest fraction of a second; but in that fraction it fanned across a ten-degree arc, slicing probably twenty of the shaggy throats directly in my path. The *däal'föns* convulsed; most bounded into the air, fountaining blood, landing in tangled heaps, writhing and snapping blindly at themselves and each other.

I didn't notice whether the crash of thunder accompanying the discharge had had any effect on the others in the area; closing rapidly and still accelerating at max, I was looking for an opening through the minefield of lashing bodies, flailing limbs, and gnashing teeth which suddenly had materialized before me . . .

And there it was . . . !

Barely in time, a slot of daylight opened between the flank of one thrashing, inverted *däal'fön* and the back of another—a narrow opening, canted almost forty-five degrees from vertical. I wrenched the bike into a matching bank, tucked my knees and elbows in close, and dived!

A random, undirected talon brushed my hip as I shot through, razoring through pants and shorts; touching, but miraculously not quite breaking, the skin. And then I was in the clear, racing madly up the rise on the far side of the *däal'fön* trap, flat out in fifth.

Shifting into sixth, I glanced at my mirrors—only to discover that both had been knocked hopelessly askew in my dive through the opening in the *däal'föns'* line (the gap had been even tighter than I thought!).

Briefly I peeked over my shoulder. The breach I'd punched through the line had been noticed; the stampede pounded along in my wake. The *däal'föns* would have meager rations from this day's hunt.

I grinned. For the second time that day I had escaped the clutches of one of those legendary, utterly irresistible predators which had all but driven the Isi off the face of their own planet. And once again I had done so without the aid of the *pwW'r*—by means of a combination of my own resourcefulness; an inborn, absolute refusal to admit defeat; a *gnäa'q* available to the Isi from the very beginnings of their prehistory; and a rude, crude, brute-force mechanism.

It was difficult to avoid a trace of smugness: The intelligent, determined, able-bodied human *copes*—always, somehow. Period.

That's what enabled relatively puny Mankind to rise to ascendance on Earth, despite the presence of dozens of species whose sharper senses and greater strength and speed should have given them the advantage; that's why I was well on my way, despite what should have been a fatal lack of knowledge of the environment, to triumphing over the still more formidable competition here on Isis. More and more I was coming to the conclusion that there simply was no excuse for the Isis' failure to do likewise.

Again I glanced over my shoulder to check for pursuers (I doubted that anything in the vicinity could match me for all-out speed, but Isis had surprised me before)—only to note, to my bemusement, that I no longer was being followed: Despite the fact that doing so reduced their chances of evading the *däal'föns* sprinting from the far end of the line to intercept them, my fellow fugitives were bearing off almost ninety degrees to my left.

Sudden doubt assailed me—what could be more frightening than *däal'föns* in quantity? Quickly I turned eyes front again— just in time to enjoy a really good view as I rode off the edge of the world and plummeted downward, turning slowly end-over-end. . . .

TO: Project Director/Monitor's Log.
FROM: Sephiloyä, Third Order.
SUBJECT: Project *Extremis*.

A completely unexpected crisis—and why did it have to happen on *my* watch! Why couldn't he have done this when Suvalyä or G'lLhaltn or one of the properly qualified Tenths were on duty! Or why couldn't one of the Tenths be watching privately, as probably three-quarters of the population seems to be?

But then, who possibly could have anticipated that the idiot would crest a rise at over one hundred miles per hour—*looking over his shoulder* . . . !

What to do? Cory is within operating range of even my limited control; I could intervene. Yet I cannot envision a means of doing so under these circumstances without disclosing to a mind of that caliber the fact that an outside agency is at work.

To complicate the question further, this incident may accomplish through inadvertence that toward which we have worked so long and hard: It is possible that Cory's recognition of his utter helplessness in the face of certain death, particularly experienced over what must be perceived by him as a span approaching eternity itself rather than the several minutes which it will take events actually to run their course, will suffice to reduce him to the requisite state of ultimately hopeless despair (it certainly would me!).

However, it is at least as possible that it will not. And, of course, if it fails to do so, Cory's premature death is inevitable and will be totally without profit . . . !

If only there were time to assemble a team of Tenths— but of course there isn't. I placed an emergency call immediately, but . . .

Well, some few minutes remain still within which to observe and try to think of a solution before I am forced to decide whether to allow him to die, here and now, or to intervene regardless of consequences. . . .

CHAPTER 23

Driving off a cliff of significant height is tantamount to a death sentence—everyone knows that. On the other hand, most would agree that the prospects of someone who "loses" a Grand Prix race car in a two-hundred-mile-per-hour, downhill, tree-lined, oil-slick curve, as I did at Spa, or traverses Isis' Zone of Moons in a converted DC-9, with only four minutes of fuel reserves and without benefit of the $pwW'r$, are equally slim.

And, in fact, if the victim under such circumstances is inclined to give up as soon as the going gets tough (never mind waiting for "downright impossible"), generally the outcome bears out the prediction.

But I don't, I didn't—I *can't*. . . .

For probably half a second, my motorcycling reflexes did their world-class level-best to bring order out of chaos: My arms and shoulders hauled "up" on the handlebars in an effort to cancel the tumbling motion, and I "steered" violently in an attempt to regain a semblance of balance; while, simultaneously, my left foot and right hand applied absolute maximum braking—all as the bike continued its downward plunge.

Moments later, without a conscious awareness of having made the decision, I found myself spread-eagled midair in the skydiver's classic maximum-drag posture—face-down and stable, watching the bike dwindle below me as the retarding effect of my outstretched arms and legs made itself felt— enjoying an unimpaired view of the scenery below.

Of which there *wasn't* any. . . .

Directly behind me, and as far to each side as I could see, the cliff flowed swiftly upward. And, so very far beneath me that I couldn't even estimate the distance, the dark, craggy wall faded into a formless gray nothingness which comprised the entire remainder of my field of view.

I shook my head and blinked to settle those protective inner nictitating membranes more firmly in place over my eyes; then looked more closely. But the scene remained unchanged.

As a practical matter, this seemed to leave two possibilities: Either the ground down there was totally obscured by a cloud layer so even in coloration and texture that I couldn't discern sufficient detail to make it out—

Or maybe I really *had* gone off the edge of the world.

My second-hand memories, faced with perhaps the most pressingly direct stimulus to date, wasted no time disgorging the answer: At various times during Isis' timeless voyage through infinity, tidal effects from close approaches to various stars had caused entire sections of the planet's crust to settle en masse, leaving the planet pockmarked with enormous, roughly circular valleys tens of thousands of miles across, ranging from fifty to eighty miles in depth, surrounded by sheerly perpendicular cliffs. Obviously I was falling into one of those great geological depressions—which knowledge offered a better-than-average excuse for a wallow in the psychological kind as well.

Granted, after the first fifty feet, it doesn't matter a great deal how far you fall—dead is dead. However, the initially helpless realization that, at minimum, a fifty-mile drop lay ahead of me, coupled with the sudden, enforced inactivity of prolonged free-fall, triggered for the first time a genuinely nasty thrill of purest terror. To this point, events had kept me too busy for fear.

Only now I had even less time to be scared. Assuming a sea-level atmospheric density similar to Earth's, my velocity was somewhere in the neighborhood of a hundred twenty miles an hour—about twenty-five minutes remained for my vaunted, genetically enhanced resourcefulness and survival instincts to come up with something brilliant, or they needn't bother.

Accordingly, I thought fast. During the next couple of heartbeats I came up with and discarded probably thirty different impractical (and/or silly) strategies for living through the next half hour.

Shortly, however, I found myself backed into a metaphoric corner, contemplating with dismay (not unmixed with growing panic) the realization that my sole chance (if one could stretch the term that far) of survival again hinged upon combining garden-variety Earthly physics with one of my recently learned Isi *gnäa'qs*.

Most people know that air density decreases with increasing

altitude, eventually turning into the hard vacuum of outer space. But few have had occasion to note that the corollary is equally true; that density increases as one descends; that, for instance, barometric pressure at a depth of fifty miles below ground level amounts to roughly ten times the sea-level value.

Now, for a given shape, air resistance (or "drag," as the engineers refer to it) is a function of velocity and air pressure. And even though I couldn't remember the equation (it's not a linear relationship) while hurtling downward at a hundred twenty miles an hour, increased pressure yields increased drag: As I fell ever deeper into the monstrous sinkhole, I would encounter a substantial increase in drag, and that drag would slow me appreciably . . .

Though nowhere near enough.

Unless I managed to shed quite a bit more speed before impact, the phrase "terminal velocity" shortly would acquire a deeply personal meaning for me.

Obviously the solution was to increase my drag. A lot. A quick review (and I do mean *quick*) of my resources disclosed but a single means of accomplishing it: my bastard misapplication of the Isis' total cellular control. Somehow, in the time remaining, despite the patently distracting environment of unplanned free-fall, and with access to neither food nor any other form of energy supplementation, I had to change my shape again.

Not that there was time enough to perform a complete metamorphosis. Even now, as familiar as I was with the technique, it would take a good two hours to change into the batform Meg and I had used to escape from Tibet. Besides, without her there to replace the energy I used, I'd undoubtedly find myself slipping into a starvation-induced coma before the transformation was complete.

However, soft-tissue changes consumed less energy than skeletal modifications, and proceeded much more quickly. It shouldn't take all that long, and wouldn't require nearly as much energy, to generate a skin-based membrane spanning the area between my arms and legs, and between the legs themselves.

Of course, without lengthened arms and fingers, I'd be an awfully short-winged bat. But the resultant wing area, given the physics of the situation, probably would suffice to permit a controllable, if high-speed, glide and, while probably not an enjoyable landing, at least a survivable one. (I wasted no time dwelling on the potential character and severity of the injuries which might fall within the definition of "survivable". . . .)

Disrobing in free-fall was not the easiest gymnastic exercise I'd ever attempted; the pants were particularly difficult. In the process, I started to tumble again; and as my field of vision swung upward, I was astounded to see the edge of the cliff still in sight—I had fallen less than a quarter mile.

(Ever notice how time drags when you worry . . . ?)

Once free of clothing, I stabilized myself again and concentrated on growing membrane as rapidly as possible. Simultaneously I turned my perception inward. My stomach and G.I. tract were full of $nNyb'q$ meat at that point, which would furnish at least part of the requisite nourishment. Quickly I shifted my metabolism back into the nearly total-conversion mode, and pumped energy to the cells of my flight membranes as they began to form.

Midway through the metamorphosis I began to wonder why I was going to so much trouble: All Peter Pan needed to fly was a sprinkling of fairy dust. Shoot, wasn't I as clever as Peter Pan? Damn right; at least! And wasn't Meg basically a slightly oversize fairy? Of course she was. And didn't I know everything Meg did? *Sure* I did—except for that nonsense about the $mMj'q$ particle flow. All I had to do was remember where I'd put my fairy dust. I giggled; then noticed that I was crying—somebody had hidden my fairy dust. . . .

Fortunately a glimmering of lucidity surfaced then; briefly, but long enough to allow me to recognize the symptoms: nitrogen narcosis . . . ! Rapture of the deep—the insidious intoxication which results from absorption into the blood of excess amounts of nitrogen while breathing compressed air. Frequently unrecognized until too late, nitrogen narcosis is responsible for the deaths of hundreds of scuba divers each year. The condition usually first manifests in an increasingly "happy-jag" drunken sensation; then progresses with depth and/or time to unconsciousness and, finally, death; usually as a result of running out of air while comatose.

I was well into the first stages before I realized what was happening. Then, grimly, I held on to what little rationality remained to me, and diverted the whole of my attention to modifying my metabolism: placing a cap on my nitrogen absorption regardless of ambient pressure. Happily, a nitrogen "binge" is not followed by a hangover; no headache or related phenomena afflicted me once my nitrogen blood level returned to normal.

As that threat abated, it occurred to me that the next problem to emerge as I continued deeper into the sinkhole probably would be oxygen poisoning: O_2, dissolved in the bloodstream in concentrations equal to that achieved by breathing pure oxygen under two atmospheres of pressure, is every bit as toxic as nitrogen, saturating red cells to the point where they're no longer capable of absorbing carbon dioxide from exhausted cells. The unconsciousness which results is total and unheralded by any warning. And as with nitrogen narcosis, if continued long enough, death results here, too.

This was a somewhat more complicated piece of chemistry than the nitrogen-level cap, but shortly I had a blood-oxygen-level control matrix installed in my metabolism.

I returned my full attention and efforts to growing wing membrane. The project wasn't far along before I ran out of food and found it necessary to look elsewhere for nourishment. I started by cannibalizing muscle tissue in regions where weight-room work had produced hypertrophied mass and power exceeding any reasonable demand.

By the time I finished, a good bit of vertical motion had been converted to horizontal, and I was maneuvering with a fair degree of precision. However, despite the increasing density of the air, my angle of descent was quite steep.

By now I was approaching the cloud deck. I hoped fervently that the ground lay well below it. If so, I still would have several minutes during which I could continue to work on augmenting my rudimentary aerodynamic qualities before my glidepath intersected the terrain.

True, any further extension of wingspan would involve bone growth; which, necessarily, would take longer and require a lot more energy. On the other hand (as it were), the bones of the fingers were considerably smaller in cross section than those of the arms; limiting my efforts to the phalanges would net quicker results and impose less drain on my metabolism.

I switched my attention to lengthening my fingers as soon as the membranes were complete, and redoubled my efforts. I added probably a foot of span to each side before plunging into the cloud deck. Thereafter progress slowed as I was forced to divide my attention between continuing to oversee the nuts-and-bolts management of forced mitosis and maintaining a hair-trigger level of vigilance in case the clouds continued all the way down to the ground.

This latter concern proved needless: After augering blindly through the mist for some minutes, and quite without preamble, I broke out of the overcast and found myself gliding through relatively clear air toward the ground.

Over the years, and through countless miles of high-speed competition, I'd acquired a fairly reliable eye for speed; given stationary visual referents, I could estimate my speed with a high degree of accuracy. And my first glimpse of the ground informed me that, due to a downright precipitous angle of descent, my airspeed was close to a hundred thirty.

I essayed a half-hearted flap, which confirmed, as I suspected, that though my aerodynamics were marginally adequate for high-speed gliding, as yet I was incapable of anything resembling level flight—let alone a proper, put-on-the-brakes, hover-momentarily-and-put-your-feet-down, avian-style landing. I'd be forced to employ conventional, fixed-wing-aircraft touchdown technique: slowing to nearly stalling speed while sweeping down to within a couple feet of the ground, stalling out just as the landing gear contacted; then killing the balance of the speed with the brakes. Nothing to it. Except . . .

I didn't have landing gear. And I had a *very* high stalling speed.

All of which forcefully recalled to mind one of the side effects of making mistakes in motorcycle Grands Prix: Recovering from "pavement rash" never was one of my favorite pastimes—but at least while racing I had enjoyed the protection of an approved helmet, boots, gloves, and full-body leathers—not to mention an armored jockstrap! The prospect of touching down on my unclothed frontal aspect at that velocity—of performing, in essence, a hundred-plus-mile-per-hour, naked bellywhopper (initial contact involving whatever hung lowest)—filled me with the deepest personal misgivings . . . !

Anxiously I scanned the terrain below, hunting for a suitable landing site. At first glance, conditions didn't look promising. A dense haze hung in the air beneath the clouds, limiting visibility to maybe half a mile. Within that radius the ground was paved with curiously uniform, generally dome-shaped, whitish-gray boulders, most of which were around thirty feet in diameter.

Of more pressing interest, however, was their equally uniform, very close spacing: Nowhere was there anything resembling the ten-foot-wide, couple-hundred-yard-long stretch of flat, bare ground where a thin-skinned, high-speed glider (with a low pain threshold) might stand a chance of surviving an attempted belly landing.

Fact is, even two hundred yards was cutting it close. Shucks, I'd probably use half that distance bleeding off the last of my surplus airspeed still inches above the ground before easing into a stall and touching down. And while, in my experience, you do tend to slow pretty quickly when sliding along on your belly (or any other part of your anatomy), there wasn't much likelihood of getting stopped in any lesser distance: I'd still be "going like a bat" as I slid past the end of the "runway"; thereafter either thudding solidly into the first boulder I met, and using up the rest of my kinetic energy right there; or ricocheting squishily off stone after stone until what was left of me finally bounced and rolled to a stop.

Awareness of these factors served to intensify my study of the landscape. I held to a straight course as I descended, maximizing glide efficiency (turns increase drag; increased drag steepens the glide angle), which continuously brought new terrain into view out at the limits of visibility.

I found myself a lot closer to the ground than I liked, and was getting pretty darned nervous about it, before a opening among the boulders materialized out of the murk. It was a small, roughly circular clearing, perhaps three hundred yards in diameter, but adequate for my modest needs. Better still, the surface was a solid carpet of grayish, fuzzy vegetation resembling *b'vVet'h*, but thicker. My second-hand memories drew a blank on its name and characteristics; but its appearance at a distance suggested that it ought to be less abrasive than bare ground. Cautiously I allowed my spirits to rise a notch; maybe this wasn't going to be so bad after all. . . .

Arriving over the clearing with surplus altitude in hand, I used some of it to circle several times, scrutinizing the ground, trying to determine where it was smoothest.

Then it was time to set up a landing approach; altitude was running out in earnest. I headed out a short distance; then cranked into a gentle two-seventy from which I emerged on final, slightly high, with barely a quarter mile to go before the perimeter of the clearing.

Briefly I experimented, cupping my wings into a high-drag, low-lift airfoil, hoping to shed the excess altitude quickly, without building up airspeed. The tactic proved almost too effective: Moments later I found myself skimming the reaching tops of the boulders, conscious that the tickling sensation I felt on the skin of the upper surface of my wings was turbulence created as the boundary layer airflow separated and reattached as I flirted with an impending stall. Suddenly I found myself devoting every effort to *conserving* altitude.

It was a bad moment, but fleeting: Quickly it became obvious that I still had enough height to make it, and my heart rate started to slow toward normal.

I even had time, at that point, to wonder whether it would be worthwhile trying to locate the bike again. There was no doubt in my mind that it had survived the fall intact; it would take more than a fifty-mile fall to damage $mMj'q$-reinforced chrome-moly, nylon, rubber, and the other materials of which it consisted.

I had no intention of resuming my travels on two wheels, of course, now that the incident had jogged my memory: Flying was faster, safer, and easier in every respect. But I did hate to give up my knife, fork, and the contents of the toolkit roll.

The wind shear caught me utterly by surprise.

So did the impact, as I clipped the top of the first boulder with a crunching, splattering noise; rebounding violently, to the accompaniment of genuinely horrific sound effects, from one stone to the next for what felt like a major segment of forever. . . .

CHAPTER 24

I held very still when I finally came to rest. There was no pain; but when I opened my eyes, I couldn't see anything, I was conscious of a warm, wet, trickling sensation over most of my body, and I couldn't breathe.

Very cautiously I turned my perception inward to see how bad the damage was . . .

And stopped, confused—*there wasn't any . . . !*

All bones were intact, there were no bruises or sprains anywhere, and my hide was undamaged.

Further exploration revealed that I was lying on my face on or in some sort of resilient, almost jellylike substance. When I attempted to move, I encountered a gently yielding resistance. Then my head and upper body pulled free with a juicy, sucking noise, and I was able to roll over, partially sit up, and take a breath.

A thick, gooey coating of whatever it was still adhered to my face. I cleared it away as best I could with the backs of my hands (next to useless now, with eighteen-inch-long fingers), and opened my eyes.

I found myself sitting (or, more accurately, reclining) in a semiliquid crater located nearly at the summit of one of those odd, rounded boulders over which I had been flying. In front of me, and as far to the sides as I could see through the haze, the rounded shapes continued into the distance.

The very top of the boulder immediately adjacent to mine, and directly in front of me, was missing. In its place was a craterlike notch which closely resembled the one that held me. Beyond that was a hundred-yard-long trail of similarly notched boulders.

I looked more closely at the structure which supported me. The texture was almost reminiscent of flesh: soft, jiggling at the touch; firm, but yielding to deeper pressure; tending to liquify when torn or crushed.

I held a gob to my nose and sniffed. Instantly my mouth began to water: The stuff smelled positively delicious.

As I started to drag myself from the crater, the shift in perspective allowed me to see farther down the side of the "boulder" nearest me. The rounded surface curved down to vertical and past, curling under and ending a good twenty feet above the ground, revealing the fifteen-foot-thick stem which supported the entire structure. . . .

A mushroom—a thirty-foot wide, forty-foot high, honest-to-goodness *mushroom*!

And *now* my secondhand memories vouchsafed their contents on the subject: B'vVec'h was indeed an Isi mushroom-analog; and every bit as delicious and nutritious as it smelled.

I sampled a bite—then lay back, closed my eyes, and sighed: The combination of flavor and texture of *b'vVec'h* produced a level of satisfaction almost spiritual in nature. It was the most intensely delicious substance I'd ever had the good fortune to allow past my lips: better than the best prime rib, better than filet, better than Grandma's chicken and dumplings, better even than one of Filthy McNasty's open-pit-charcoal-broiled Interim Malthusian Solutions (a monumental triple-decker cheeseburger of unrivaled greasiness with *all* the trimmings; positively guaranteed to contain no beneficial ingredients)—on a par with the *very* best extra-bitter Swiss chocolate, except that it didn't fill you up so quickly, nor leave a queasy-making aftertaste if you overindulged.

Now, I recognized, even then, that much of the nearly sensual satisfaction contained in the combination of flavors and texture of *b'vVec'h* grew out of my once-again depleted physical condition; at that point dried soybeans probably would have tasted pretty good. But even after allowing for craving-founded bias, that stuff was *great*. . . .

So for a while I just lay there, resting, eating, and reflecting on the events of the past couple of hours; marveling that I still lived: It had been tough sledding even for me; an Isi would have been dog meat (analogically speaking). Or even if, somehow, he'd managed to become the first of his people in history to escape a *däal'fön* gamesweep, he'd have ended up a grease spot at the base of the cliffs; because even if he'd managed the conceptual quantum leap, from using total cellular control for maintenance and repair to shape-changing, he'd never have recognized the symptoms of nitrogen narcosis, nor anticipated the need thereafter to deal with the threat of oxygen hypersaturation.

No; I understood now why the Isi had been forced to find and develop a fundamentally mechanistic, inherently problem-solving species to serve as their ally: They couldn't even cope with the conditions of their own planet without resorting to unnatural (to this universe) solutions—how could they possibly be expected to deal with the threat posed by the approach of R'gGnrök, which thus far had proved immune to their best *mMj'q*-based efforts? They couldn't. Of course.

It distressed me to view Meg as intrinsically helpless. But despite her quick wits and an all-out fighting spirit as sheerly gutsy as any in my experience, the fact was that she was an Isi; and, looking back, I was forced to admit that each time we'd faced catastrophe together, it was either my actions or her implementation of one of my ideas that ultimately had saved our bacon.

Not to minimize their good qualities—the Isi were an intelligent, altruistic, warmly compassionate, wondrously gifted, and altogether fine people—they just weren't equipped to handle crises. They lacked that spark of utter determination which leads to meeting and overcoming challenges, whatever the odds; whether by bending, twisting, hammering, and/or abusing unrelated mechanisms or principles into performing functions for which they weren't designed and never were intended, finding solutions where none had existed before, or simply discovering, through necessity, heretofore unsuspected depths in themselves. Baldly put: The Isi had feet of clay.

I shook my head sadly upon reaching this conclusion; then regarded the warm, form-fitting, gelatinlike couch which supported me. After a moment's thought, I decided that there wasn't much point in moving just then: Apart from an eventual need to wash off the semiliquid crushed matter of the *b'vVec'h*'s, crown with which I was coated, I was relatively safe, as well as comfortable, plus literally surrounded by food. Awkwardly, with my distorted fingers, I stuffed another handful in my mouth, and shortly fell asleep.

TO: Project Director/Monitor's Log.
FROM: G'lLhytl, Tenth Order.
SUBJECT: Project *Extremis*.

Myrayä was correct: Monitor duty on this project is less an assignment than a reward; it is no wonder that so many of our people are following Subject Cory's progress.

I arrived just as Sephiloyä was despairing over whether to save Subject Cory, and thereby risk not only jeopardizing the project but attracting the undivided attention of a disappointed T'fFelteshezr and the rest of the Elders. However, before I could contribute even advice, Cory metamorphosed into the aerial form which he had developed for his and Meg's escape from Tibet—and which Sephiloyä (and, I must confess, I as well) had forgotten—and saved himself.

I suspect that it would be difficult to ascertain at this point which of the two was more relieved by the outcome, Sephiloyä or Cory.

On the occasion of the subject's initial crash-landing on Isis, I took the precaution of erecting a set of *wWr'dts* around him, lest something eat him while he recovered from the ordeal of passaging the Zone of Moons, atmospheric entry, and the crash itself. The same logic applies in this situation, and I have taken the same precaution while he recovers from his metabolic and electronic excesses and this most recent crash-landing.

Likewise, and for the same reasons, I brought him down short of the clearing for which he was trying.

The episode has bolstered Cory's self-confidence further—in fact, I judge that he is getting downright cocky, and I think it is time that we begin to do something about it. Once he recovers, we will begin (English is such an expressive tongue) to "tighten the screws" in earnest. . . .

As usual, following metabolic tampering, hunger woke me before I was anywhere near rested. I ate and slept again, finally waking refreshed and only a little hungrier than normal.

I had breakfast while reviewing my plans. Obviously the next step was to complete the metamorphosis I'd started while hurtling downward a day or two earlier (I wasn't sure about the date after all that sleep; I'd had to discard my watch as well as my clothing to grow the wing membranes).

Well, I could hardly imagine a better setting to engage in a major shape-changing project than the crown of a *b'vVec'h*, considering that the key prerequisite was food—lots of food. Accordingly, I lay back again, turned my attention inward, and, concentrating hard, began to eat.

It was difficult to judge how long it took. The sun remained hidden by the clouds, and *b'vVec'h* is particularly rich in nutrient value so I never got behind the energy curve. Finally, however, the job was done.

I sat up; then looked around in amazement: I hadn't eaten the *b'vVec'h's* entire forty-foot crown; but the crater in which I sat had grown considerably, both in depth and width, since my arrival.

I extended my wings for balance, got a foot under me, and, despite the jiggly surface, managed to stand, shuddering slightly as my two- or three-day-old accumulation of crushed *b'vVec'h* relinquished its sticky grip (I *really* needed a bath).

I worked my muscles to get the kinks out, stretched my wings to their full fifty-foot span, and launched out over the clearing which I'd been trying so hard to reach just before the wind shear caught me.

I was probably thirty-five feet up and just passing over the middle of the clearing in a shallow, climbing turn, when my peripheral vision picked up a flicker of movement.

My response astonished me: Instantly, instinctively, I stroked hard, catapulting myself skyward; this, even before my eyes focused on whatever it was that was doing the moving. I blinked in surprise, remembering Meg's comment about her automatic reaction to the sight of Fafnir, Gothyäl's *böll'skag*-housed *fmMl'hr*. Maybe there was something after all to Memphus' dig about growing up in a rough neighborhood. . . .

My first impression, upon catching a clear look at the source of the alarm, was that somehow a Panzer division had gotten loose on Isis. This was dispelled when I noticed that, instead of treads, the apparition traveled upon six armored legs, and boasted a set of jaws which extended fully a third the length of its body. In fact, apart from its size (comparable to a long-wheelbase Ford van), the intruder bore a striking resemblance to an Earthly stag beetle. As it charged into the clearing, it somehow radiated an air of bustling, short-tempered preoccupation which reminded me of a rhinoceros I once met on a photo safari ("'Evenest-tempered animals in Africa,'" misquoth my guide: "'Mad all the time.'").

My dual-level memory pondered for a moment; then kicked out an identification: *Böll'fings,* encountered under the wrong circumstances, were as dangerous as any other predator on the planet. But despite considerable physical strength and a fair turn of speed, they were extremely stupid, which limited their attention span, and too clumsy for efficient close-quarters combat. They seldom posed much of a threat to humans who kept their wits about them.

I was about to file the experience and continue about my business when it happened. . . .

At the geometric center of the clearing a ten-foot trapdoor burst open, revealing a silver-lined tunnel leading down into darkness—and out of those depths swarmed a creature which no self-respecting nightmare would have claimed: More than any single Earthly species, the *väarz'fing* resembled a coarsely hair-covered scorpion—*a twenty-foot-long scorpion!*—whose shaggy, ten-foot-long legs propelled it as if they were fashioned from spring steel.

The monster launched into the air, landing on the unsuspecting *böll'fing's* back from better than fifty feet away. A pair of four-foot-long chela sheared off several of the huge beetle's legs, a twelve-inch sting lanced down over the *väarz'fing's* back, punching through the armor covering the thorax like so much balsa; a set of six-inch fangs drove into the abdomen.

The *böll'fing* thrashed wildly . . . for all of five seconds. Then it toppled over with a boiler-plate crash, wiggled feebly for a moment, and was still. The *väarz'fing* remained on top; it had begun to suck the still-pumping juices from its victim even before the final shudder shook the massive frame.

Round-eyed (and at a respectful altitude; that thing's leaping ability was awesome), I circled the clearing to get a better look. The monster broke off eating. It crouched lower on the carcass and pivoted, following my motion with glitteringly alert, mad little eyes. That deadly tail curled forward over its back, swaying imperceptibly, almost hypnotically; chela opened and and closed in mindless anticipation; fangs twitched eagerly.

A belated chill of purest horror flooded through my bowels: Only the intervention of that wind shear had prevented me from touching down in the *väarz'fing*'s clearing. On foot, even in the best of health, I couldn't possibly have kept out of the monster's clutches—and following a hundred-mile-an-hour slide on my bare belly (et al.!), I doubted very much whether anyone would have mistaken me for healthy. . . .

I shuddered, and had to fight to hold onto my breakfast: It was difficult to imagine a nastier way to die!

CHAPTER 25

Twenty wingbeats a minute produced an airspeed which I estimated at something over a hundred miles per hour. At that speed, which I could keep up for hours on end, I coursed steadily over the depressing panorama of the vast sinkhole's floor. Perpetual cloud cover obscured the sun; virtually nothing was apparent but fungus and decay—especially decay: At ten atmospheres, even at the reduced oxygen percentage assured by the fact that only the most stubborn and photosynthetically efficient green plants could survive in the dim lighting, housekeeping bacteria and fungi were plentiful and energetic: Decomposition was rapid.

In short, it was an ugly, uninspiring place. As well as breathtakingly dangerous. . . .

Logically so, of course: All larger, more efficient, exoskeleton-based predators originally had evolved down there in the lowlands, where the extremely dense air enabled them to attain incredible size despite the initial limitation of inefficient, spiracle-based respiratory systems. Likewise, the high ambient pressure permitted winged species to retain their powers of flight as they developed, despite aerodynamic and musculoskeletal characteristics otherwise inadequate to lift weights ultimately measuring in the tons.

When seismic activity accompanying the comet's final passage caused sections of the heretofore sheer escarpments which constituted the lowlands' boundaries to collapse, rugged, boulder-strewn but passable ramps were created between the great sinkholes' floors and sea level. Thereafter, generation by generation, various species worked their way up the grades, eventually adapting to sea-level conditions; in the process evolving increased intelligence, true lungs, ever larger wings and more powerful flight muscles and skeletal attachments on which to mount them—and losing none of their voracious, single-minded enthusiasm for the hunt.

Sea-level beasties inhabiting the territories surrounding the lowlands likewise wasted no time responding to the challenge: migrating *down* the ramps; some evolving tolerance for the high-pressure, low-light living conditions; most failing to notice the difference.

The result was the present-day lowlands' environment: an endless expanse crawling with every form of predator possible of imagination—and quite a few which weren't. . . .

As I flew over the dead and decaying surface, I observed many of my prior acquaintances from sea level engaged in nonstop natural competition with the "locals": a pack of *däal'föns* locked in pitched battle with a migration of *sqQr'fings* (a species resembling Earthly army ants to the degree *väarz'fings* remind one of scorpions); a *böll'skag*, affecting the air of a man slurping a strand of spaghetti, contentedly munching its way along the still-wiggling hundred-foot-long corpse of something reminiscent of a millipede; a blissfully immobile *väarz'fing* feeding from the carcass of a *krRy'fön* . . .

Et multiply cetera. All within about the first ten miles.

Without impossibly good luck, an unforewarned, unarmed man wouldn't last a day in the lowlands. No wonder the Isi fell on hard times. Even indomitable ole Yours Truly would have had a rough time, I concluded grudgingly—notwithstanding all that alleged inborn intelligence, resourcefulness, and determination (not to mention the speed, strength, and lightning reflexes). None of those sterling qualities would have done me much good if a fifty-foot-long *b'jnNöllq'fing* had stumbled across me mindlessly asleep, exposed and vulnerable, atop that *b'vVec'h*. Once those huge, mantislike talons closed about a victim, the time for imaginative solutions was past.

Horsefeathers . . . ! Angrily I chopped short the impending bout of self-pity. The Isi knew their environment, I reflected stubbornly; they had no excuse. Certainly, given the barest minimum advance notice of conditions, and barring just plain bad luck, *I'd* manage to survive. Of course, I wouldn't *remain* unarmed; I'd skulk from concealment to concealment, gathering materials, and remain hidden until I'd manufactured weapons. Once properly armed, and exercising the least degree of common sense, exoskeletal beasties should be even less trouble to deal with than warm- and cold-blooded sea-level predators.

Because from everything I'd seen thus far, bugs were bugs: Regardless of size, and whether here or on Earth, rudimentary intellects simply aren't capable of responding to more than a single major stimulus at a given moment. A well-placed broadhead arrow should distract even the biggest, baddest, hungriest of bugs. And a blast of tightly focused, high-voltage electrons would be more effective still.

Not, I noted with sudden awe, that a guy couldn't run into impossible odds if his luck ran out: Just ahead, a pair of *böll'fings* were engaged in mortal combat. Repeatedly they charged each other, coming together with a crash audible for miles.

Already a circle of spectators had gathered: fifty or so *däal'föns;* scouts, not a pack. Like spectators at a sporting event, they sat or lounged at ease around the perimeter of the field of honor, tongues lolling, tails wagging, luxuriously scratching itches here and there; patiently, confidently watching the great insect fortresses tear at one another. They knew from experience that one surely would kill the other pretty soon, and that the survivor would be fatigue-slowed and probably would have sustained crippling injuries. That added up to a lot of easy meat.

However (though they should have anticipated it), the *däal'föns* were ignorant of the fact that the sound of combat was attracting additional attention: From the north and east came a pair of *krRy'föns;* bounding along like toothy caterpillars, their twelve-legged strides churning up rooster tails of mud and fragments of decaying vegetable matter. From the west, a smallish (less than a hundred yards long) *böll'skag* approached. And a short distance south of the immediate conflict—visible to me at altitude by virtue of the telescopic properties of the avian eyeball construction I had adopted—a ten-foot circle of ground was propped up a few inches on one side. Through the resulting crack, a pair of glittering, malevolent eyes observed the proceedings in a steadily mounting excitement of killing fury.

I altered course momentarily to overfly the scene. Banking into a three-hundred-sixty-degree turn directly overhead, I smiled grimly as things below grew even more hectic:

The first of the *krRy'föns* arrived and joyously began wreaking havoc among the startled *däal'föns*. *KrRy'föns* aren't afraid of just any old gathering of *däal'föns*; it takes a proper, formally announced game-sweep with all the trimmings to command that kind of respect.

Simultaneously with the arrival of the second *krRy'fön*, the *väarz'fing* burst from its lair, hitting the already-busy *däal'föns* from the rear, killing and dismembering a full half dozen before they could react to its presence.

But *däal'föns* are smart: Inconspicuously they led the monster in the direction of the *krRy'föns*; then faded to the sidelines, leaving the three battling nightmares to do unto one another as they chose.

Moments later, enormous, smoking jaws descended and closed about the body of one of the *krRy'föns*. The *böll'skag* lifted the squalling, clawing, purple carnivore into the air, and shook it like a rat.

The other *krRy'fön* could have escaped at this point; instead, it launched skyward, sunk its tusks into the *böll'skag's* throat, and hung there, ignoring the efforts of a huge, taloned foreleg to scrape it off piece-by-piece.

The *väarz'fing* could have escaped as well—so it swarmed up the nearest leg of the flame-belching giant and began roaming around the broad back, stinging and biting for all it was worth.

While this was transpiring, the remaining *däal'föns* circled unhurriedly into a position from which they could hamstring the thrashing behemoth, should a convenient opportunity present.

I shuddered: Blundering onto this scene of chaos on the bike would have presented more challenge than I cared to contemplate.

With a deeply heartfelt sigh of relief, I flipped up on wingtip and pulled a couple or three gees in a ninety-degree bank, swinging back around toward my original course—

And several tons of TNT detonated about three feet away; the concussion impacted virtually every cell in my body simultaneously, leaving me barely conscious. In the same instant, a line of fire seared its way across my right-hand wing as the sudden pressure split the membrane from edge to armpit.

A gigantic shape—long, broad, and flat; moving at patently impossible velocity—registered vaguely on my shock-blunted awareness as it pulled out of a dive below me and swung into a climbing turn. It took my intellect whole seconds of fumbling through second-hand memories to make the identification. When I finally succeeded, my heart missed a beat, and the shock momentarily sufficed to shake off even the concussion-induced wooziness that gripped me—a *voor'flön* . . . !

The accompanying précis of the monster's characteristics and capabilities seemed positively Paul Bunyanish; but already I could confirm at least one outlandish claim personally: *Voor'flöns* did indeed achieve supersonic velocity when stooping for the kill; and even if they missed with teeth and claws, the benefit to their quarry was arguable: The sonic-boom shock wave involved in a near-miss was little short of lethal in its own right!

Not that that was my most pressing concern by then; it was obvious, as the red mists closed in again, that by the time the flying juggernaut managed to complete its turn and get headed back in my direction, I wouldn't be where it could get at me: I was in a board-flat spin, hopelessly out of control, descending directly into the middle of the riot below. . . .

TO: Project Director/Monitor's Log.
FROM: Kyärin, Seventh Order.
SUBJECT: Project *Extremis*.

When G'lLhytl loses his patience with someone, he does indeed "begin to do something about it." I judge that, in amassing this concentration of environmental fury, he has skipped at least two levels in our tentatively scheduled, progressive build-up of stress, and possibly more. If I were the sort of practitioner who allows sympathy to affect my attitude toward a subject, I think I would be quite sorry for Cory.

Of course, allowing him actually to be killed at this point would accomplish nothing: Only now is the reality of his situation likely to begin to sink in. However, I do not intend to intervene short of the very point of brain damage and/or death. Cory should be able to repair any lesser injuries, and can be expected to emerge from the experience with a clearer appreciation of the odds confronting him.

Down I drifted, spinning like a maple seed, growing dizzier by the moment, and, despite the obviously dire situation, less able to concentrate on how I proposed to stay alive down there (always assuming I lived through the landing). Grimly I clung to consciousness; retaining barely sufficient awareness of my surroundings to note that one *däal'fön*, less pressingly occupied than others, was gazing upward with disturbing interest. It nudged a couple neighbors, which glanced skyward in response; then the threesome headed purposefully in the direction of the spot toward which I was descending.

All my life I've had this tendency to get the giggles at clearly inappropriate moments. It suddenly occurred to a tiny, unoccupied fraction of my mind that I was developing an unhealthy relationship with gravity; that most of my more serious problems recently seemed to revolve around falling!

It is impossible to pass out while laughing; at least I found it so. Concussion and blood-loss notwithstanding, my head began to clear. I was still awfully dizzy, and the endless spinning wasn't much help. But at least my eyes focused, and once again I could comprehend and evaluate my surroundings.

I found myself about three hundred feet up, descending in a straight line terminating at a point equidistant from the three waiting *däal'föns*, who looked quite pleased.

A *very* quick review of the situation showed but a single potential out: About thirty feet to one side of my trajectory, the canopy of a large *b'vVec'h* beckoned. I gave a convulsive flop, gritting my teeth against the pain that flared as the tear in my wing membrane lengthened further.

A moment later I thumped lightly onto the resilient surface. Dizzily (I'd stopped spinning; the world had not), I fought down nausea, turned my perception inward, and stilled the swirling of my semicircular canals.

Then I took a quick look around—and marveled: Fate had contrived to bring me down almost two hundred yards from the mêlée. I was out of the *däal'föns'* reach and the *krRy'föns* and *väarz'fing* were otherwise occupied. Nor had the *böll'skag* noticed; seriously beset by now, it surged back and forth and around and around, attempting to bring teeth, claws, tail, and/or flames to bear upon the *däal'föns* (whose numbers continued to swell as time passed and the noise level mounted).

All I needed to worry about was the very real possibility that the theater of operations might shift in my direction: Every swing of that tail leveled *b'vVec'hs* by the acre.

For a guy who occasionally has had trouble walking and chewing gum at the same time, the next quarter hour was busy. My attention was split four ways, and each aspect required total concentration if I hoped to get out of there in one piece: Hardly pausing to breathe between swallows, I began wolfing down *b'vVec'h* nonstop; simultaneously I worked feverishly to repair my wing and create and bring a *t'lLiSs 'mn* up to full charge; all while keeping an eye on the progress of the battle, lest it show signs of heading my way.

I had the wing nearly finished when suddenly I felt something jostle my *b'vVec'h*. I spun—and there, only yards away, was the ghastly grin of yet a third *krRy'fön*; this one in the very process of clawing its way up the curve of the crown of the *b'vVec'h* with its last three pairs of legs.

Seldom has time been so of the essence; there wasn't even time to aim the *t'lLiSs 'mn*. All I could do was hurl myself painfully into the air, feeling wind from a taloned forepaw which swiped through the spot I had just vacated.

With labored, uneven wingbeats, I managed to cover several hundred yards, landing on another, slightly taller *b'vVec'h*, and turned quickly to see where the *krRy'fön* was.

This purple kitty apparently had chosen me for its very own. It ignored the general commotion. Descending to the ground in a single, effortless bound, it trotted after me. It wasn't even hurrying. For a *krRy'fön*.

I glanced at the wing. As I suspected from the way it felt in the air, I had partially reopened the tear. Another few minutes' work would be required before I'd be airworthy again—even for emergency hops as short as that one.

I glanced in the direction of the Main Event, jittering in momentary indecision. Between the flash and the thunder, there was every likelihood that firing off a bolt would attract further attention. . . .

For perhaps two seconds more I blithered, wondering morbidly at the lack of overall quality displayed by the galactic labor pool, as reflected by the fact that the Isi had picked *me*— surely they could have done better. . . .

Then it occurred to me that there was no decision to make: Granted, it might become necessary to worry about the crowd over in the center ring if I attracted their attention. However, that, as a practical matter, was no more than a mere possibility—and, in any event, would become a problem only if I lived that long: That mutilegged, lavender pussycat with the hypertrophied dentures was an absolute certainty. (Priorities *are* important!)

Well, at least I hadn't lost control of the *t'lLiSs´mn* during all the excitement (maintaining it was becoming a conditioned reflex). And while I couldn't be sure how much charge it still retained at this point, from the mental pressure required to brace the torus' walls, it probably was fairly substantial; plus, during the final seconds of the *krRy´fön's* approach, I worked hard at funneling in additional atmospheric static flow and boosting the voltage even higher.

I held my fire until the last possible instant; until the *krRy´fön's* balefully glowing orange eyes leered up at me from the base of the *b'vVec'h*. Without conscious election, I had equipped this *t'lLiSs´mn* with a large-diameter, nontraversing nozzle; and, with a literally ground-shaking roar, the inconceivably hot plasma shaft raved out. The *krRy´fön's* head, neck, and front three pairs of shoulders exploded messily. What remained toppled over and lay twitching.

Instantly, as the thunder echoed and reechoed, I flattened against the *b'vVec'h's* crown and rolled to the far side, placing the curve of the giant fungus between me and the balance of the combatants. But I might as well have saved my energy; nobody cared.

I indulged in a few seconds' restful collapse; then, keeping a weather eye out in case the festivities should show signs of moving my direction, got back to work, shoveling down the *b'vVec'h* to replace the energy I'd just used, and repairing my wing.

As I worked, I digested Meg's knowledge of *voor´flöns*, and the implications regarding my travels, and (not for the first time) wished that I could access her memories without specific stimuli—Heaven only knew what further surprises this world was saving for me!

The news wasn't good, but neither was it totally bad: Despite their immense size (adults ranged upward of two hundred yards in length), *voor´flöns* were not prisoners of the dense air down in the lowlands; you could encounter them virtually anywhere on the planet, flying at altitudes up to tens of thousands of feet above sea level. Fortunately, however, there weren't many of them; the calories required to fuel protein engines on that scale guaranteed a distribution of no more than about one per hundred million square miles. The chances of running into one were close to zero.

However, their eyesight was extremely acute, particularly long-distance resolution, and included perception well down into the infrared; a *voor'flön* could see as well at night or in clouds as it could during daylight hours in clear air—the mere fact that you couldn't see one at any given moment was no guarantee that one couldn't see you. And with a level-flight maximum of better than twelve miles a minute, it didn't take long for a *voor'flön* to cover any distance within the radius of its vision.

I finished repairing my wing and prepared to take off—then hesitated. The battle was no closer now than when I landed, and no other threat seemed imminent. I had consumed a lot of energy in repairs, and using the *t'lLïSs'mn* had taken still more; plus that sonic boom had left me sore in every muscle and nursing a terminal headache.

Further, according to Meg's information, *voor'flöns* had one of the longest attention spans of any predator on the planet; chances were excellent that my recent acquaintance still would be hanging around, hoping for a rematch.

Besides, if that one were representative of the species, *voor'flöns*, as a class, were just too big, too fast, and too powerful to take chances with. Heading back upstairs before I was completely recovered—before I'd built up a solid energy reserve and gotten the *t'lLïSs'mn* recharged and ready for action—struck me as poor tactics.

Not that I had any intention of going looking for trouble (that would be counter-survival); I merely was determined to be supremely ready for it next time.

The fact that I had a score to settle was irrelevant. . . .

CHAPTER 26

And the next time a *voor'flön* dived from the clouds at me, I was ready indeed. The shaft of lightning which struck it between the eyes was calculated to take most of the ginger out of even a *böll'skag*. The titanic flier convulsed violently, momentarily losing flight rhythm and stability.

Side-stepping the huge jaws and reaching talons proved no

trouble at all; but as the disoriented leviathan hurtled past mere feet away, the shock wave from its supersonic velocity again inflicted a body-blow of literally tooth-rattling intensity. Ears ringing, vision obscured by the galaxy of stars exploding inside my head, and painfully aware of the tear which had opened in the flight membrane between the third and fourth phalanges of my right-hand wing, I tumbled and spun like a leaf in the vortex of the monster's wake.

Righting myself with difficulty, I blinked my vision clear, and located my attacker: The *voor'flön* was well below me, gradually pulling out of its dive.

This was my first opportunity actually to observe one closely (the previous encounter was over too quickly for detailed study). If the Armed Forces Committee of the United States ever had to design a flying squirrel, the result probably would look a lot like the apparition which confronted me: a hundred-thirty-yard-long body (this was a small one), nineteen of whose twenty pairs of legs supported a flight membrane spanning thirty yards; and a ten-yard-long head which vaguely resembled that of a pterodactyl. A *voor'flön* propels itself through the air by combining a graceful vertical undulation (reminiscent of the horizontal motion with which an Earthly water moccasin swims) with a rhythmic, front-to-back rippling of the edges of its flight membranes.

It was well-equipped for its role as a predator: Each leg ended in a foot boasting talons five feet long, and fully half the length of the head was devoted to jaws bristling with yard-long teeth. However, as I'd already learned, a *voor'flön*'s most formidable aspect was its speed; that sonic boom was no joke.

Two more times the beast took a run at me; two more times I zapped it between the eyes and managed to dodge out of reach. But, though the third try proved to be the charm, rewarding me with the sight of more than a thirteenth of a mile of airborne appetite fluttering ribbonlike and limp toward the ground below, dead or unconscious, it was a textbook Pyrrhic victory: I, too, was spinning downward again, my own consciousness fading, my wings tattered like hurricane-shredded sails. . . .

Through the intervention of far more luck than I deserved, my plunge terminated in a small stream, whose shallow, blood-temperature waters absorbed most of the impact. The splash, followed instantly by water up my nose, restored me to full alertness, choking, sputtering, and struggling to get my feet under me—

Only to discover that Isi quicksand differs from the Terran variety in no important characteristic. Twenty-five-foot-long, blown-out wings in place of arms weren't much help. Before I realized what was happening, I was buried to the waist in the stuff. Only the tip of my nose still cleared the surface of the stream whose slowly moving waters camouflaged the trap.

Few of nature's legendary booby-traps are as widely feared and little understood as quicksand. Folklore has it that quicksand "sucks you down." It doesn't; it's ordinary sand beneath which there happens to be located a *slow* spring. The gently upward-welling water renders individual particles of sand almost weightless, robbing them of substance, preventing them from packing underfoot, which allows the victim to sink immediately to the point of normal, water-borne, floating equilibrium.

Whereupon, Mother Nature drops her other shoe: Once those individual sand particles reach quiet water above an object (in this case me), full weight is restored. They sink, packing down on top of any approximately horizontal surface (the remnants of my flight membranes were a big help), the accumulation growing heavier and ever heavier, until . . .

My head was entirely under water, with the quicksand up to my neck, almost before I could react. I probably wouldn't have survived the next few minutes without all those years of skin-diving experience. Even so, it was difficult to control an impulse to panic; to explode in a burst of mindless, totally unproductive struggles whose only effect would be to force me deeper still. I forced myself to relax, and concentrated on conserving oxygen—and then I thought *fast*!

Generally my breath-holding reserve under skin-diving conditions ran between three and four minutes. It took less than half that time for the quicksand to close over my head.

Only then did I remember that the gills I'd used in Tibet were still right there under my ribs where I'd left them. I'd never bothered to absorb them, reasoning that they might come in handy someday.

(Seldom has my foresight been so profoundly and gratifyingly vindicated . . . !)

Of course, before I could use them, I had to create a series of fine screens to keep the sand out, which took time; and by the time I got the intake and exhaust slots open and could

begin pumping water over the oxygen/carbon-dioxide-ex-
change tissues, my heart was pounding, blood thundered in
my head, and patches of blackness were flickering about inside
my eyelids.

For quite a while thereafter I lay unmoving beneath the
quicksand, allowing the strength slowly to seep back into my
muscles. Beyond closing off a few still-oozing bleeders in the
ragged tissue scraps which were all that remained of my wings,
I didn't bother undertaking repairs. It seemed pointless to
restore a shape which mounting evidence suggested was
totally inadequate for conditions. A major strategy review was
indicated.

For it had begun to dawn on me that my growing contempt
for the Isi might be somewhat premature. Sure, I'd escaped
krRy'föns, *böll'skags*, *däal'föns*, and a couple *voor'flöns*;
managed to avoid getting overly involved in that free-for-all
back there; I'd even killed a *krRy'fön* and very possibly one of
the *voor'flöns*. Indeed, in every tangle with Isis' minions, I'd
not only come out on top but in the process gained knowledge
critical to avoiding such risks in the future. On the surface, and
to the uninitiated, it might appear as if I were ahead on points.

But suddenly, with cold conviction, I knew better. The
primary factor in most of those "victories" was luck, pure and
simple. Fate's books *always* balance; it was only a matter of
time before the pendulum reversed its swing. Objectively
speaking, I'd won all the battles, but sooner or later, if I kept
on like this, I'd lose the war. I'd end up part of the Isi food
chain, Meg wouldn't be rescued, and the galaxy would come to
a bad end.

All in all, not a very impressive performance from one of the
penultimate products of a breeding program spanning nine
thousand years. Mournfully I reflected that Jennifer Smith
(even at six) probably would have done better; her bloodline,
after all, concentrated upon intelligence, a quality notably
absent in my recent conduct.

Briefly I found myself distracted, wondering what my
"ultimate woman" would look like at maturity. The way things
were going, it didn't look as if I had much chance of finding
out. . . .

Self-pity is an emotion rooted in positive feedback: The
sorrier you feel for yourself, the easier it becomes to dredge up
justification for feeling sorry for yourself. Et cetera. Before I
recognized the symptoms, the loop was solidly established and
humming merrily:

How *was* a person supposed to achieve a respectable rate of progress, traveling on this nightmare-infested mudball . . . ? I'd lost the bike long since—

(Not that *that* mattered: Motorcycle travel was barely faster than walking, given the scale of distances on Isis; and, in view of the "wildlife problem," continuing in that mode constituted little better than suicide in the long run. Besides, there were substantial areas of the planet where a bike simply couldn't go; I'd never be able to enter or leave one of these colossal sinkholes on two wheels, unless I happened to stumble over an area where the cliffs rimming them had collapsed—and detouring around them involved distances comparable to circumnavigating most *planets*! Plus, now that the subject had come up, it occurred to me that while traveling on two wheels I had carefully avoided thinking about how I proposed to cross those incredible mountain ranges, towering to [and, not infrequently, beyond] the very edge of space: Internal-combustion engines functioned poorly in vacuum [come to think of it, so did I]).

—and now the *skies* were barred to me . . . !

What was left? Bitterly I wondered whether Isi *moles* were carnivorous—only to discover that the conjecture contained sufficient detail to release yet another of my second-hand memories: Indeed they were.

"*Here's* a pretty state of things . . ." observed Ko-Ko when things looked bleakest, and I couldn't have agreed more. Regrettably, however, my problem couldn't be solved by launching into a song-and-dance number (though the mental picture my subconscious served up at that point, of my participation in a Gilbert and Sullivan patter-song-and-dance trio, with a *böll'skag* taking the basso profundo and a *krRy'fön* handling the soprano end, triggered a rueful smile despite my mood).

In fact, the longer I thought about it, the more it started to look as if my problems couldn't be solved at all. Maybe the Isi were right. . . .

TO: Project Director/Monitor's Log.
FROM: H'tTirvig, Fifth Order.
SUBJECT: Project *Extremis*.

Much better! Subject Cory is sinking at least as quickly into depression as he did into the quicksand.

At first I wondered if it might prove necessary to act to

keep him from drowning, but he solved that problem for himself. And thereafter, the instruments monitoring his emotional state began a steady swing toward the critical level. Clearly his present physical helplessness, the close brush with death the first time he encountered a *voor'-flön*, this most recent experience, and his overall lack of progress toward La'ïr, considering the distance involved, have combined to precipitate him into a most satisfactory plunge toward emotional collapse.

I suspect that the time is rapidly approaching when termination of this project will be appropriate.

Dammittall . . . ! Suddenly I was hugely, furiously angry; at the planet, at the animals, at my situation, at the Isi—but mostly at myself: By God, was I or was I not Peter Cory—*the* Peter Cory—a closet millionaire by age ten, the youngest self-made multibillionaire in history by eighteen; at twenty-six, world-class race driver, pilot, and master mariner; overall male Olympic champion; black-belt-holder in three different forms of unarmed combat; undersea explorer; mapper of some of the most remote territories on Earth (plus a list of varied lesser accomplishments which would have constituted a full life for most people) . . . ?

Of *course* I was!—and I didn't get to be who and what I was by rolling belly-up at the first sign of an obstacle. To the contrary: If there was one single personality trait which exemplified my accomplishments, it was an utter determination—virtually a compulsion—to overcome whatever problems came my way. In fact, it would not be totally inaccurate to suggest that the number of problems I'd solved, their degree of difficulty, and the speed with which I'd solved them, pretty well defined and underlay my level of success; in business as well as nearly every other area of life.

So! It was *necessary* to travel upon the face of Isis; in reasonable safety, but with reasonable speed: That was the problem.

And without exaggeration, it was a humdinger. A lot of people would regard it as insuperable. But it wasn't; it merely hadn't been solved.

Yet.

Hell, it hadn't been *addressed* . . . !

Not since recovering consciousness amid the wreckage of *Galactic Venture* had I taken a long, thoughtful look at the problem of traveling from Point A to Point B on this planet. I had responded from moment to moment to whatever stimuli were most pressing; exhibiting all the shrewdness, foresight, and planning ability of an amoeba: Hello, there was the bike; I got on and rode. Mercy, there was fiendish thingie; I fled or fought, whichever was handiest. Gracious, I was falling; I shape-changed into my already-familiar bat-form. Wow, I was a bat; I spread my wings and headed for La'ïr.

Yes, it was time to take a businesslike look at the problem—*past* time, in fact. (I shuddered to contemplate the grade I'd have received if Rebecca Two-Knives were to review my performance since arriving on Isis.)

Generally, in solving problems, I used what was known as the "top-down" approach: First define the objective; second, identify foreseeable obstacles; third, inventory available resources; fourth, create the solution itself, and test it; and finally, put it into operation, initially watching it like a hawk, alert for bugs which might not have surfaced during testing.

The objective here was to get to La'ïr—preferably alive—sometime within the useful future. Foreseeable obstacles were the wildlife, terrain, and scale of distances. Resources were limited to natural raw materials and my own physical prowess; the latter augmented by my ability to manipulate static electricity, change my shape, and heal virtually any injury not instantly fatal.

It was apparent from that that the solution necessarily hinged upon designing a new body for myself: one capable of maintaining useful speeds regardless of environment; sufficiently formidable to outfight anything it couldn't outrun; fast enough to outrun anything it couldn't outfight.

Foreseeable operating conditions included dry (desert, veldt, jungle, and mountains), wet (anything from water to [as I knew now] quicksand), and air.

With the notable exception of *däal'föns*, known and foreseeable opposition wasn't terribly bright, by and large, but usually was very fast, could be extremely large and powerful, and often showed up in large numbers; and everything I'd met thus far had displayed astonishing endurance and a perseverance seldom encountered outside a full-blown, formally declared *jihad*. Weaponry included blunt as well as sharp instruments (with and without toxins) and, occasionally, fire.

Now: However professional that analysis might sound, my real-world approach to stress evaluation, material selection, design, and execution was (and probably always will be) straight out of the Yankee Mechanic's Handbook; and the First Law of the true back-alley engineer is: "There's no limit to how gently you can apply a big hammer, but there definitely is to how hard you can hit with a small one." Accordingly, if the SAE specs said a sixteenth of an inch of mild steel would take the load, and weight wasn't critical, I invariably used three-eighths of an inch of chrome-moly. (Unless I was feeling especially paranoid, in which case I probably used titanium.) Engineering preventive overkill was as deeply ingrained into my make-up as refusal to give up.

Meticulously, then, facet by facet, I dissected the problem. Each individual facet demanded its own solution. Each individual solution had to be compatible with every other individual solution, as well as dovetailing into the overall matrix of which it was part. It was a long, tedious, complex process, but I forced myself to take it a step at a time, without hurrying—I knew that impatience, leading to impulsive, short-sighted actions, lay at the heart of my previous reverses. I was determined not to repeat that mistake.

Only after assuring myself that every threat was completely defended against or avoided, every weakness shored up, and every objective covered, was I satisfied with the basic design—at which point I went through one last time and strengthened everything by a factor of three.

Only then did I give thought to the mechanics of the shape-changing process itself: I was, after all, buried in quicksand; I had discharged three major electron beams in swift succession; I had no access to food or any other source of energy, and what I had in mind would require *lots*.

Cannibalizing excess bone, muscle, and flight membrane for energy, I reabsorbed my wings, shrinking my arms and hands back down to normal from their nearly fifty-foot span. Then I experimented briefly with various motions and swimming strokes until I found one that worked: the reliable old dolphin kick. I drew my arms down to my sides and went at it.

Shortly thereafter, my head popped through the quicksand/water interface. After a quick look around to assure myself that no carnivores lurked, I began stroking with my arms as well. Moments later I was entirely free of the clinging muck.

Cautiously I stuck my head above the water and scanned the vicinity. Still nobody around. I sealed my gills and took a breath with my lungs.

Quietly I swam to shore and pulled myself onto land. With equal care, I crept through the underbrush, headed for a stand of *b'vVec'hs* which I'd seen from the air just prior to my most recent *voor'flön* encounter.

Locating it without incident, I scouted the area for predators, happily coming up empty; then found a small cave, which I stocked with a couple dozen small *b'vVec'hs* (maybe a ton altogether), which I uprooted and dragged inside. I concealed the cave mouth by leaning the largest *b'vVec'h* against it.

Thereupon, I leaned back against the resilient crown of one of the giant fungi, ripped off a ten-pound chunk, and, turning my attention inward, started eating, and got down to work.

And by the time I finished, two days later, I was the most ghastly looking being in this universe—and probably a good many others. . . .

TO: Project Director/Monitor's Log.
FROM: Q'tTzekötl, Tenth Order.
SUBJECT: Project *Extremis*.

H'tTirvig's enthusiastic prediction of impending success would seem to have been premature. In fact, upon review, the Council of Elders (who should have been notified long since of our repeated failures to break Subject Cory), has concluded that what we face at this point is the distinct possibility of failure. For this reason, and distinct from the increasing numbers of our people who now watch Cory's exploits at every opportunity, only Tenth Order practitioners will monitor Cory's progress henceforth; and when even the slightest doubt arises as to the correct course of action, the Council will be called in to make the decision.

Cory must *not* be allowed to reach La'ïr unbroken.

CHAPTER 27

It was a massive undertaking and no hint of my original form remained when I finished. In its place was a frightful concentration of potential violence whose inspiration lay in Earth's most dreaded legend: a dragon. . . .

A small dragon to be sure: A length of about twenty-five

feet, counting the tail, together with a weight of probably nine hundred pounds, seemed a reasonable compromise between sheer physical power and aerodynamic necessity. But small or not, if Saint George had had the bad fortune to run up against me, the legend would have ended abruptly.

I had six limbs, not counting the wings. Exaggeratedly oversized hindquarters (similar to those favored by the jack-rabbit school of biological engineering) permitted an erect posture when desired; but the configuration was selected primarily for the enormously powerful spring they put into my four-legged gait. The middle pair of limbs were slightly less massive, and were articulated and muscled to serve mainly as forelegs, but could double as arms. The front pair were mounted just ahead, and though twice life size, were standard-design, full-time human arms and hands. A retractable claw five inches long lurked within each toe; those in the ends of the fingers were a little less than half that long.

I enlarged my skull considerably, and surrounded my brain with literally inches of solid bone. The eyes were placed well to the sides, providing over three hundred degrees of vision. Heavy brow ridges and cheekbones sheltered them without interfering unduly with visibility above and below. Ears were large, almost batlike, and mobile. Jaws were as long and heavy as those of an adult *däal'fön*, opened a full hundred eighty degrees, and sported eight-inch canines, top and bottom.

My tegument was a thick-but-flexible layer of scales which combined the strength of bone, the toughness of cartilage, and the exterior case-hardening of tooth enamel. Added to which, a row of razor-edged, triangular plates protected my spine from nape to tail-tip, and a ruff of needle-pointed spikes guarded my throat.

My tail ended with a mace, a spike-studded morning star a foot in diameter; the longest tine was hollow, a sting which I intended to arm with *väarz'fing* venom. The yard-long, razor-edged, upward-curving horn projecting from between my brows was to be similarly toxic.

My wings were still batlike in form, but smaller in proportion to my mass than before, intended for a more rapid flapping rate. I expected much better speed out of them; plus (theoretically) I should be able to hover and back up like a hummingbird.

After due deliberation, I decided to pass on breathing fire. However, as I surveyed the final result—the massive muscles rippling under glistening, virtually invulnerable, jet-black scales; talons extending and retracting almost reflexively in response to half-heard sounds from beyond the cave mouth; the powerful, supple, fifteen-foot-long, sting-equipped tail stirring restively, almost as if it possessed a life of its own—my confidence grew that once I obtained a sample of *väarz'fing* venom and duplicated the formula, I'd be able to handle whatever Isis might throw at me. Anything I couldn't outrun or outmaneuver, I'd *eat!*

Actually, I'd probably have to: The food required to fuel the organic juggernaut into which I had transformed myself seemed likely to qualify me as one of the single most ravenously dangerous predators ever to prowl the face of Isis: sixty thousand calories a day—*minimum . . . !*

First, however, it was shakedown time. Counting that prehensile tail, I now had nine extremities to keep track of. I'd created entire systems of muscles, tendons, and ligaments to operate the new limbs, together with the vascular, lymphatic, and nervous systems required to supply, drain, and innervate them; and I'd upgraded my pneumocardiovascular system to power everything.

Initially the multiple inputs proved to be just too much to keep track of—never mind managing the outputs. For a while I tended to push the wrong button for almost any given situation. Such as the time I launched off a low cliff, furiously pumping my forelegs. By the time I landed I had just about everything I owned flapping. Even my ears. Everything but the wings. . . .

But thirty-foot falls are educational, even for structurally overdesigned and -built pseudodragons, and I learned quickly. It took only about three days to establish the basic matrix of interrelated, semiautomatic, coordinated responses necessary to walk, run, and jump normally, using two legs or four, according to the dictates of the situation. And once I mastered that, and could count on the correct number of legs under me when I landed, flying proved no more difficult in this form than the previous. Even four-handed manipulation wasn't all that complicated, once I got over the initial strangeness.

On the other hand, it took some doing to master the numberless muscles and nerves required to control the virtually limitless flexibility of that prehensile tail but I managed eventually—then rather got to like it: It's a real convenience, once you run out of hands (even with duplicate equipment), to be able to swing your tail to the fore and take a loop around something. And it didn't take me any time at all to acquire the habit of using my tail as a tripod prop when standing erect, leaning back against it as I would a wall or tree trunk.

However, it took two full weeks of intensive drilling, using a complicated special *kata* I'd devised (six taloned limbs, the tail, plus teeth and horn), before I acquired what I considered sufficient competence to risk exposing my new body to fraught situations.

And before I could continue on my way, I would have to do just that: To complete my armament I needed a sample of *väarz'fing* venom. . . .

Preparations for the *väarz'fing* hunt were minimal: I bit off a three-inch-thick sapling and stripped it of branches with the razor edge of the claw on my index finger. I bit off the smaller end; then whittled it to a point, producing a crude-but-serviceable, heavy lance probably twenty feet long. I returned to the quicksand-bottomed stream and, after a little searching, found a bed of grape-sized, water-rounded pebbles. I gathered up a handful; then lifted into the air.

A brief, cautious aerial reconnaisance turned up a suspicious-looking clearing. I buzzed it several times from different angles until I discerned the circular hairline crack in the middle which outlined a *väarz'fing*'s trapdoor. I hovered to a stop directly overhead, a good hundred feet up, and dropped one of my pebbles. It landed on the trapdoor with an audible "thud."

The *väarz'fing* burst forth, swapping ends probably three times in the first second alone, looking for the intruder who had had the audacity to trespass upon its very roof.

This accomplished two objectives: First, I verified (with blood-curdling thoroughness) that this was in fact an inhabited *väarz'fing* lair; I didn't want to waste time stalking a vacant burrow. Second, now I knew which way the trapdoor hinged; I had no desire at all to approach from the side that opened—no point in making it easy for the damned thing to swarm out and leap at me without even having to aim.

I lifted higher, retired a short distance from the clearing, and landed among the *b'vVec'hs*. I gave the *väarz'fing* some time to settle down; then lifted back into the air, high enough to verify that the trapdoor was closed again, and returned to the clearing.

After circling a couple times to make sure the *väarz'fing* wasn't peeking through the crack, I focused my attention on the ground about thirty feet from the burrow's mouth and, turning up the optical magnification level of my new eyeball construction, identified a small hollow in the ground which appeared suitable for my purposes.

Grasping the spear firmly in both hands, I swept downward. Landing rather heavily behind the trapdoor, forelegs braced on either side of the hollow, I jammed the butt end of the spear into it and leveled the point in the direction of the trapdoor.

The *väarz'fing* exploded from its den. It landed ten feet from the opening, facing the wrong direction, swapped ends, caught sight of me, and launched into the air again, all virtually in a single continuous motion.

But I was ready: The point of the firmly braced spear passed just below the hurtling monster's compound jaws, almost grazing the tip of one fang. It entered the thorax from the underside in front and tore all the way through, driven by the weight and momentum of that prodigious bound.

And the very instant the point penetrated the anterior thoracic armor, I moved pretty briskly myself—straight up, out of range of those shearing chela and venom-filled fangs and sting. Then, safely out of harm's way, I hovered overhead, waiting to see what effect the spear would have.

The *väarz'fing* landed. There was a moment's stunned, quivering immobility; then it hissed, convulsed, and went utterly berserk: It spun, leaped, and flip-flopped; sometimes right side up, sometimes upside down. Chela lashed about and chopped at random; once, by purest accident, snipping off the butt end of the spear where it protruded from the underside of the thorax—once severing one of its own antennae. The legs thrashed and jerked spasmodically. The fangs tore furrows in the ground. The tail slashed, repeatedly stinging at the nearly three feet of spear point jutting from the armored back, but just as often scoring on air or the ground.

There wasn't much doubt that I'd dealt the *väarz'fing* a mortal wound; but in common with most large, exoskeletal Isi predators, it possessed a very simple, almost rudimentary nervous system—it could take hours for the idiot killing machine to realize that it had itself been killed! And it was only a matter of time before some other predator heard the commotion and offered to wrestle me for my prize. (The noise factor was the reason I had ruled out using the *t'lLïSs´mn*.) I knew that if I wanted that venom sample, I'd better bring things to a speedy conclusion.

I took a deep breath, mentally rehearsed my strategy, and dived headlong into the buzz saw. The first few seconds were busy: The *väarz'fing*, while mortally distracted, still responded instinctively to attack. I used my own tail to parry the stinger's overhead thrust; then took a quick loop around it and held on. Simultaneously I grabbed one chela with a forefoot and kept it out of mischief; but it took both hands to deal with the other. The remaining forefoot and both rear legs I used to deflect the fangs, and to twist the monster's head around to where I could reach the slender neck with the razor edge of my horn.

That should have ended the matter but didn't; if anything, the violence of the creature's struggles actually increased, although now they were completely random.

I debated my options in spurts, with difficulty; my thought train frequently derailed by the recurring need to renew one grip or another as the *väarz'fing* plunged and thrashed like a bucking bronco on angel dust. The solution, when it finally occurred to me, was so obvious that I wasted whole seconds wondering what had taken me so long.

Tightening my grip on everything, I tensed my tail and forced the *väarz'fing*'s foot-long stinger downward, driving it into the chink between segments, deep into the monster's own thorax.

Incredibly, the struggles underwent still another quantam increase—but only briefly: seconds later the *väarz'fing* went limp. I held on for another minute, just in case; then let go and leaped clear. But it was a needless precaution; the *väarz'fing* stayed dead.

Quickly I checked myself for damage. There was none; plus, despite the undeniably aerobic quality of the exercise, my heart rate was only slightly elevated and my respiration was virtually normal: Clearly my new industrial-grade pneumo-cardiovascular system was a success.

I dissected the *väarz'fing*'s stinger mechanism and extracted the venom sac. The initial moments of analysis, after swallowing the venom sample, were not the stuff from which lifelong habits are formed: The substance burned like fire going down, and lay in my stomach like a pool of molten metal; for a while I wasn't sure I could handle it long enough to break it down. But by isolating the sample in an inert, insensitive compartment (which I manufactured in a big hurry) while subjecting portions of it to varied enzymes, I managed to figure it out. It proved to be an absolutely dynamite neurotoxin, but the product of a rather simple chemical processs. I had no difficulty evolving a ducted gland with a contractile sac at the base of my stinger and horn.

And then, satisfied at last that I was on equal terms with the planet—utterly confident that I could handle anything I couldn't outrun, and outrun everything else—I resumed my oft-interrupted trek.

TO: Project Director/Monitor's Log.
FROM: Gothyäl, Tenth Order.
SUBJECT: Project *Extremis*.

Things are going from bad to worse: Subject Cory has adapted his body into one embodying perhaps the most formidable combination of natural weapons ever seen on this planet. The sheer physical power and speed of this new form, together with his *gnNäa'q* for manipulating electricity, both combined with his brains and determination, pose a challenge which may in fact prove insuperable.

Given a subject possessing an intellect of the power of Cory's, there is a limit to how much intervention we dare attempt; beyond a certain point, he must begin to suspect that these endless tribulations are too much even for a planet as fraught with hazards as Isis. And once he begins to suspect that he is being manipulated, failure is upon us; we never will succeed in breaking him—and in his present form, there is little doubt that he will succeed in reaching La'ir sooner or later.

That must not be allowed to happen.

CHAPTER 28

My confidence proved justified: My new physique was everything I'd anticipated. . . .

In terms of speed, the design worked better than I'd dared hope: Traveling on the ground, those four powerful legs produced an effortless, fifty-yard, bounding stride, generating speeds which I estimated at around ninety miles an hour; which pace I could maintain all day long. And by coordinating wings with legs, I found that I could improve considerably on that: Half-running, half-flying, my progress over the ground was faster than any land-bound species Isis ever spawned.

Pure flight, however, was where the real speed lay: Anytime it was safe to leave the ground for good, I was capable of nearly three hundred, flat out, with probably two hundred available for sustained cruising. Plus my low-speed engineering had worked out as well: I could hover, dart, and back up like a hummingbird.

In terms of violence . . .   Well, suffice it to state that the next five or six months proved that I was a match for Isis— *finally* . . . !

But it was an "interesting time," to borrow from the ancient Chinese curse. It stands to reason, of course: As you travel, you're bound to encounter a certain percentage of the predators inhabitating any given territory. That percentage, while random, will tend to stabilize over time. Accordingly, the faster you travel, the more territory you cover—and the more predators you meet on a daily basis.

I traveled *very* fast; I met *lots* of predators. In fact, I seldom got through two consecutive hours without a brawl of some sort.

From one perspective this was a plus: At the rate at which I burned calories at speed, I needed to eat roughly every two to three hours; more often still following combat, even on the occasions when I managed to avoid firing the *t'lLïSs´mn;* and even more often than that when I had to play really rough (I now maintained the immaterial cyclotron, charged and ready, on a continuous basis). With the almost constant interruptions, it rarely was necessary to hunt.

And while a diet rich in predator flesh generally involved more exercise than one based on ruminant flesh or slabs of *b'vVec'h* (the giant fungi generally were available only in the lowlands areas anyway), it was every bit as nourishing and usually there was plenty of it.

(Besides, if you've got to fight the damned things anyway, you may as well eat them afterward.)

Routinely I met, fought, and killed *krRy'föns, däal'föns, väarz'fings, sqQr'fings, b'jnNöllq'fings,* and *pfFäap'fings.* . . .

(Have I mentioned *pfFäap'fings*? No? Picture an Earthly dragonfly—thirty feet long—whose legs ended in grappling hooks tipped with armor-piercing points, and whose compound jaws appeared capable of swallowing subcompact cars whole. They occurred in swarms numbering in the hundreds, and normally fed on lesser avian species. They classed me as a lesser avian species at our first meeting. The aerial dogfight which ensued covered probably three hundred miles of sky, and left me painfully aware of deficiencies in certain areas of my armor, as well as in need of a thorough *t'lLïSs´mn* recharge. Thereafter I remained as alert for *pfFäap'fing* squadrons as for *voor'flöns*.)

Conditions varied enormously, but my dragonform physique, with detail modifications now and then, was able to handle them all.

For instance, the first time one of those awesome mountain ranges stretched across across my path, I found it temporarily necessary to quintuple my wingspan to find lift in the rarified atmosphere of the upper passes (fifteen to twenty miles above sea level). Likewise, at that altitude it took serious measures to prevent body-fluid boil-off: Reinforcing my tegument was one step; pressure-sealing the edges of the tough, transparent nictatans already covering my eyeballs was another. Plus I had to strengthen my eardrums to cope with inner-ear pressures. The final step was modification of my respiratory system: To maintain air quantity and pressure in my lungs sufficient to keep my blood-oxygen level above minimums, I was forced to implement separate airways for inhalation and expiration, with one-way valves regulating the flow through each; the whole system operated by a muscle-powered, high-volume, double-bellows air compressor located on the inlet side. (And, incredibly, even under those conditions it was necessary to remain every bit as alert for predators as at sea level.)

To cross one of Isis' sprawling inland seas, I readied my gills for quick reopening, webbed my feet, and temporarily added a pair of flukes to the tip of my tail, in case I should need to take refuge underwater. (But it's a good thing the need didn't arise often; the evolution of Isi marine predators paralleled that of those dwelling on land to about the degree that an Earthly forty-foot–long great white shark resembles a weasel.)

I crossed only one desert during that interval (and a lesser desert at that)—an endless expanse of incredibly fine, gently but insistently resistant black powder into which my feet sank to the knees at every bound; and which soaked up Ra's heat so efficiently that to avoid burns I had to insulate my legs and the soles of my feet by inserting inches of inert, spongy callus under the scales. The area was crawling with specially evolved Isi wildlife; weird and wonderful nightmares whose bodies and metabolisms were adapted to the horrendous conditions even as Earthly tarantulas, centipedes, scorpions, sidewinders, and the like are adapted to the more moderately arid conditions obtaining in Earth's deserts.

So it went—and went and went and went, day after day after day. . . .

CHAPTER 29

Until one early morning I emerged from hiding (already thinking about breakfast), stretched my limbs, flapped my wings, and lashed my tail to work the kinks out—and suddenly it struck me: I'd been *six months* on this trek; yet, based on my knowledge of Isi geography, and my magnetic-lines-of-force navigation, I'd covered barely *fifty thousand miles* . . . !

It wasn't difficult to understand how I could have failed to notice the passage of so much time, or my lack of progress: Exigencies of survival and travel had kept me *busy*—and as I thought back upon it, it seemed that every day found me even busier—I simply hadn't had time to spare for abstractions.

But now I had noticed. At this rate (and always assuming I survived that long) it was going to take another six *years* to reach La'ïr. By which time I'd probably have forgotten the purpose of my journey—along with my name, the English language, and what little remained of my refined upbringing . . . !

No. Impossible. Totally, completely, inarguably out of the question. There had to be a better way—there simply *had* to be!

And, of course, there *was*. . . .

All I had to do was find it.

Grumbling under my breath (far, far under; subsonics were useful for that, as well as for intimidating would-be challengers when my belly was full), I glanced around the horizon for *voor'flöns* and *pfFäap'fings*, then lifted into the air. A brief aerial reconnaisance turned up a small herd of delicate *p'rRö'f* grazing in a *t'gyl'q*-carpeted clearing. They bolted instantly as

I dived for them, but I zapped one of the larger males through the head before they'd gotten a hundred yards.

Swooping down and scooping up the body on the fly with my talons, I returned to my hidey-hole. Dragging my kill inside, I settled down to some serious thinking over breakfast.

Now: The fact that I was still alive and fifty thousand miles of wilderness lay behind me presented a fairly compelling argument for the proposition that an intelligent, resourceful, resolute human being was in fact a match for the challenge posed by non*mMj'q*al survival on Isis. Without access to the *pwW'r*, using only those *gnNäa'qs* possessed by the Isi from their earliest recorded history; existing not as a hunted fugitive, furtively skulking from concealment to concealment, but setting forth in affirmative exploration and travel, I had met the environment head-on—as an equal.

Unfortunately, it was becoming obvious that equality wasn't enough. The problem confronting me was similar in type (but only faintly comparable in scale) to that facing a member of *H. sapiens* (lacking *gnNäa'qs*) given the task of circling the Earth fifty thousand years before the dawn of civilization: His rate of travel was limited to whatever he could generate with his own muscles. The armament which lay within his crude manufacturing capabilities, coupled with his human intellect, provided a shakily equal footing with most of the predators he'd be likely to meet. Given the distances and hazards involved, he'd be lucky to complete the journey at all, much less in anything under a span of years.

I pondered my dragonform physique, speculating whether there might be room left for further developments; whether I might be able to come up with additional improvements which might enable my muscles to propel me still faster, while holding risks to an acceptable level.

But after considerable thought, all I could come up with was the possibility of substantially increasing my size and, thereby, sheer physical power. That might help some; but the flaw lay in the necessarily protracted interval during which I'd be too big to hide and too small to cope with just anything that might happen by. And Isis was not an environment forgiving of awkward stages.

Repressing a shudder, I tore off a seventy-pound drumstick, bit off a ten-pound mouthful, and chewed absently as I reflected further.

Nor was the problem really a lack of speed relative to the

scale of the distances involved. If only I could figure out some means of *maintaining* that speed, my two-hundred-mile-per-hour airborne cruise was more or less adequate: At that rate (positing a mere eight hours' travel a day [in reality, I seldom put in less than sixteen or twenty]) I'd have covered the entire distance from where I crashed *Galactic Venture* to La'ïr in only two–hundred-odd days—I'd almost be there by now.

No; the problem was that during so much of that time I wasn't traveling; I was fighting: In fact, thinking back, I couldn't remember the last time I'd actually gotten through an entire morning or afternoon without mortal interruption. Something always seemed to crop up; something which demanded my undivided attention—often as not, of late, several somethings at once. And heroic feats are death on the average speed.

Actually, so was a minimum intake of sixty thousand calories a day: My nutritional requirements were close to the point of diminishing returns. It took me nearly an hour to fill up after a physically tiring encounter; longer still if I had to singe something's whiskers with a beam of tightly focused electrons. Between engagements, to avoid delay, I generally tried to snack en route: I'd kill something on the order of a large, fat *nNby'q* every half hour and nibble on the fly.

Yes, clearly the interruptions were the main obstacle standing in the way of making decent time; and how to cut down on them was the central question. By now I felt reasonably safe in concluding that my present physical characteristics constituted just about the most practical overall solution to the problem of travel on Isis. And while further tinkering might squeeze out another few miles of airspeed and/or surface-travel velocity, I was pretty sure that the improvement, if any, would be limited to no more than a few percent—and what I needed was a gain of several whole magnitudes: I had to get to La'ïr tomorrow, or next week— soon . . . !

Dammit!—what I really needed was *Venture*, back in one piece, with all its *mMj'q*-enhanced goodies intact. Above the atmosphere, riding a ballistic curve, it wouldn't take more than a few hours to cover the remaining distance. Shucks, even at sea level it shouldn't take much more than a couple weeks.

Hmmph, talk about pointless speculation! *Venture* was a half-mile trail of useless scrap fifty thousand miles behind me, and there certainly wasn't anything else on this essentially

primitive, utterly nonmechanical planet capable of that kind of
sp—

WHOA . . . !

The hell there *wasn't*. . . .

Of course, how I expected to get it to fly in the direction I
wanted to go (as well as how I proposed to keep it from eating
me in the process) were questions for which I hadn't the hint of
an answer.

But I *did* know that a *voor'flön's* level-flight cruising speed
was on the order of *mach point seven* . . . !

So. How did one go about riding (much less controlling) an
eighth of a mile of ravenously single-minded, carnivorous
appetite? The question brought to mind the ancient homily
concerning the recipe for tiger-tail soup, which begins, "First
catch a tiger . . ." On first impression, this seemed an ample
challenge in its own right.

But, to my considerable astonishment, several possibilities
came to mind immediately (some appreciably better thought-
out than others [though none struck me as particularly well-
advised if longevity were the major criterion]). In fact, one
method, I was forced grudgingly to conclude, was downright
practical. Maybe catching a *voor'flön* wouldn't be so difficult
after all. . . .

On the other hand, *controlling* a *voor'flön*—probably an
extremely annoyed *voor'flön* at that point—aye, there indeed
was the rub. I had a feeling that it would take more than
waving a piece of raw meat under its nose and murmuring
"Nice doggie." And since I lacked a kitchen chair, whip, and
the rest of the implements customarily employed by wild
animal trainers, that pretty well narrowed it down again to a
single possibility—a possibility which failed to suffuse me with
enthusiasm.

However, apart from substituting the fourth word, the
beginning of the recipe remained unchanged: "First catch a
voor'flön. . . ."

From ten miles up, visibility through the crystal air was
probably on the order of two hundred fifty miles; nowhere
near the distance to the huge planet's actual horizon, which
was completely greened-out by the sheer volume of intervening atmosphere despite its clarity, but an awesome vista
nonetheless. At that range, with my eyeballs cranked up to

their maximum telescopic magnification, objects the size of *voor'flöns* were easy to resolve.

The only one in view at the moment was just fading into the greenish haze at the extreme limits of my range of vision. I had begun my climb the moment the monster passed overhead, reasoning that it probably would have learned that it was more likely to spot its next meal by scrutinizing the ground ahead than by looking where it had been (it worked that way for me). Nevertheless, I kept a close watch on it as it dwindled rapidly in the distance; and between frequent, suspicious glances after it, performed virtually nonstop, three-hundred-sixty-degree sweeps of the "horizon" for others of its kind.

I felt reasonably safe up there despite the complete lack of concealment: *Voor'flöns* were capable of attaining great heights, but they seldom went to the trouble. Since most of their prey was on the ground, or within a couple hundred feet of it, diving from two or three thousand feet furnished sufficient added momentum to boost them ahead of the noise of their passage; and since that supersonic dive formed the basis of their hunting technique, that was all the altitude they needed.

Besides, even if a *voor'flön* happened to spot me up there against the glare of the midday sun, it would take quite a while for it to get above me and/or approach closely enough to pose a threat. Almost surely I'd have time to power-dive out of harm's way and conceal myself on the ground.

With any luck at all, that is. . . .

Fortunately, another *voor'flön* materialized in the distance before my calorie-consumption rate caused me either to call a halt to the stakeout or dip into the nearly hundred pounds of fat I'd accumulated for the occasion. The sight of the monstrous ribbon of appetite rippling out of the haze completely banished thoughts of food, along with all other extraneous considerations.

Miles below me lay a broad clearing in which herds of *t'gyl'q*-eaters fed, some grazing recklessly far from shelter. No *voor'flön* passing near enough to serve my purposes could fail to notice the opportunity. And it seemed unlikely that, while concentrating on the feast spread below, it would notice a tiny, bat-winged shape plummeting out of the sun above and behind it.

That was the strategy anyway.

It took the *voor'flön* about half an hour to meander from the point at which it first appeared in the far distance to within a few miles of that game-filled clearing beneath me. Several times it darted to one side or the other and dived; whether successfully or not, I couldn't tell.

In either case, the moment when the *voor'flön* first spotted the game below me was unmistakable: The alteration of its course and speed was abrupt and pronounced. It was too far away to begin a lethal dive at that point, but it closed in rapidly.

I maintained my position for several more seconds, observing its approach and calculating its speed. I took a deep breath and held it for a long moment. Then, releasing it slowly, trying to slow my racing heart, I peeled off, stood on my nose, and accelerated at maximum—straight down.

I didn't attain supersonic velocity as I plunged out of the sky, but I came pretty close to it. In the half minute it took the giant predator to attain a position from which it could commence the dive which would sweep across the clearing on a line calculated to scoop up as many *prRö'fs* as possible, I descended six miles, already maneuvering to set up my own line to intersect the *voor'flön's* as it rose from the clearing, burdened with its kills and slowing to a reasonable velocity.

The *voor'flön* began its dive. As it accelerated downward, I was a mile and a half above it and maybe half a mile ahead, already beginning my flare-out.

At the base of a *voor'flön's* neck, between the very forwardmost points of the bony plates which serve it as scapulae, there's a spot which, according to Meg's information and my own observation, it simply can't reach. If everything went as planned, I would match course, speed, and angle of climb with the great carnivore at the conclusion of its climb-out, and be in position to lock onto that spot and, quite literally, hold on for dear life.

And everything did go as planned—at least up to that point. . . .

The *voor'flön*, rising from the clearing with prey clutched in the basketlike talons of about half of its forty feet, never saw me until I thudded onto its back, planted my claws in its hide, embedded those eight-inch tusks in its scruff, and buried, set and locked in place the four ice-tonglike sets of bony grappling hooks which I'd created on my underside just for the occasion.

Thereafter, however, events developed at their own pace. . . .

TO: Project Director/Monitor's Log.
FROM: G'lLhaltn, Tenth Order.
SUBJECT: Project *Extremis*.

A totally unanticipated development. I cannot imagine what would impell Subject Cory to attack so formidable a predator as a *voor'flön*. I hope this does not signal the collapse of his intellect. Insanity always has been a possible consequence of the endless stresses which we have been heaping upon him over these past months, but I never believed it probable. Now, however, I am not so sure. I can only watch and wait and see what develops.

On the other hand, if his mind has *not* come unstrung, what could he be up to . . . ?

I understand that non-Cory-related projects have come to a virtual standstill at this point; it is difficult to find anyone doing anything but remaining glued to his viewer as events unfold.

The year I won the U.S. and world aerobatics championships, I did a number of things with my plane that the experts said couldn't be done. Now I understood their amazement: The moment the *voor'flön* felt the sting of my teeth, claws, and grapples, its talons released their grip, showering the countryside with dead animals; simultaneously it launched into the most outrageous series of nonstop acrobatics imaginable—immelmans and crack-the-whips; inside and outside vertical loops combined with snap rolls and endos; sunfishing, windmilling, corkscrewing, and myriad elaborate gyrations for which there are no names—the *voor'flön* used them all.

But after learning in the first few minutes that the monster couldn't dislodge me regardless what it did, I paid no further attention. Phase Two was in progress.

Previous experiments on *nNby'qs* had verified that the theory was sound and that the mechanics were possible—at least on *nNyb'qs*. . . . Whether those same principles could be transferred to *voor'flöns* was a question yet undetermined.

From a newly created sphincter on the underside of my upper thorax, a tough, flexible, bone-tipped, two-inch-diameter tube of well-vascularized and -innervated cartilage emerged. With the fat reservoir furnishing the requisite energy, the tube steadily lengthened, biting into and through the foot-thick tegument to which I clung; boring inexorably through yards of underlying tissue toward the spinal cord within.

My total perception and concentration were focused on the end of that drill; the moment it penetrated the myelin sheath and entered the intrathecal space, but before it contacted the actual tissues of the spinal cord itself, I halted its progress. Anchoring the end of the tube to the surrounding bony structure with ligaments ensured that minor changes in my position relative to the *voor'flön's* (the beast certainly was doing its best!) wouldn't result in unexpected movement within the intrathecal space and possible damage to the delicate spinal cord.

Down the tube I extended a branch of my own nervous system: a nerve-fiber bundle duplicating in most respects my own spinal cord, but including additional neurons linked directly to my higher function centers which allowed me to monitor directly the progress of the invasion.

Once inside the myelin sheath, I turned the direction of growth upstream and headed along the intrathecal space toward the brain. Arriving eventually inside the *voor'flön's* skull, I created an intricate network of nerve tendrils and filaments which surrounded and enveloped the entire brain; then paused briefly to survey my prize.

So far, so good: Though much larger, the *voor'flön's* brain appeared virtually identical to those of the hapless *nNby'qs* upon whom I had experimented in preparation for this undertaking (and whom I ungratefully devoured at the conclusion of the research). In fact, to my limited knowledge of anatomy, Isi brains appeared identical to those of Earthly species as well.

Thereafter, working carefully, I infiltrated the brain itself, delicately expanding my nerve-fiber network down into the frontal lobes of the huge carnivore's cerebrum and into the cerebral cortex, seeking the motor and sensory centers which I had located during my practice on the *nNby'qs*. . . .

Ostensibly to further my grade-school academic studies, I had prevailed upon my parents to allow me to buy a modest, floppy-based personal computer as soon as the income from my "public" portfolio made it possible. Thereafter, ostensibly to keep closer tabs on the stock market, I prevailed upon them to let me install communications capabilities.

They never knew about the ten-megabyte mother board and ultrahigh-speed modem which the serviceman installed during a routine maintenance visit, nor about the four-hundred-megabyte hard-disk central processing unit which resided in a locked, temperature- and humidity-controlled room in my attorney's suite, which I accessed and controlled by phone, all of which were paid for by the income from my *real* portfolio.

Now, I want this clearly understood: Despite the formidable potential of my equipment, and the level of proficiency which I attained, I was *not* a hacker. True, I never met a security system I couldn't penetrate (without triggering alarms or leaving a record of my presence in the system) regardless what precautions and/or traps might have been installed. Equally true, I never met a program I couldn't peel like an onion, analyzing it right down to its machine language.

But that didn't make me a hacker—not a *real* hacker anyway: I was neither spiritually obsessed nor emotionally driven. My motive was intellectual curiosity; my interest scientific; my methods illegal only when absolutely necessary. . . .

In one way, breaking into the *voor'flön's* nervous system was easier than gaining access to any computer in my experience: Being physically present eliminated the normally touchy business of having to enter the system surreptitiously to conduct the preliminary analysis.

Of course I didn't tap into the *voor'flön's* nervous system directly, at least not at first; instead I spiral-wrapped individual nerve fibers around my host's neurons upstream of the spinal cord bundle, establishing induction "bugs" which permitted monitoring of nervous activity without affecting its operation. And as the number of contacts increased, I studied the signals, matching them with the monster's observed actions and outside stimuli.

The "machine language" on which the *voor'flön's* nervous system was based proved uncomplicated. Soon I was receiving, translating, and reading signals as clearly and automatically as if they had been generated by my own brain or sensory nerve endings. And shortly thereafter, as I completed and activated more and more induction taps, the information flow mounted in volume and complexity until I found myself experiencing a hint of what it must be like to feel my own huge, multiplex muscle groups contracting rhythmically, driving the enormously powerful length of my massive body through the air at high speed, desperately trying to dislodge a midge clinging to my lower cervical spine—*a midge whose bite itched until I thought I'd go mad . . .* !

It took an effort to wrench myself all the way back inside my own skull; the *voor'flön's* sensory output was vivid stuff indeed. If I hadn't had the experience of sharing rapport with Meg, I might have had trouble keeping straight whose senses were whose.

For a while, then, I merely observed: learning the complex musculoskeletal rhythms which propelled the huge beast through the air; committing them to my own cerebellum's collection of conditioned reflexes.

But finally it was time for the tricky part: Working rapidly yet carefully, and in a very specific order, I physically interposed my own neurons' axons and dendrites into certain of the *voor'flön's* synaptic gaps, diverting the sensory input which would have reached my host's brain to mine, substituting my motor-center output, and assuming control of the monster's entire voluntary musculoskeletal system.

The abrupt surge in sensory input volume and intensity, as I switched from induction pickup to direct reception, was briefly disorienting. Likewise, suddenly to find myself (according to every shouted evidence of my reeling senses) a one-hundred-fifty-yard-long *voor'flön* was an experience which brought with it a heady, almost giddy-making sense of freedom—of speed, of maneuverability, of sheer, irresistible *power . . .* !

In the time it took the alleged higher functions of my so-called intellect to wrest control back from my mindlessly reveling emotions, I learned how it felt to use "my" muscles to power-zoom three miles straight up, exceed the sound barrier straight down, and execute a silly bunch of fast- and slow-flight antics possible only to the unique combination of physical strength and aerodynamic qualities embodied in a *voor'flön.* I even managed to get it to hover, rippling the edges of the flight membranes in a complicated pattern to generate lift.

In the process of this joy ride (which constituted a thorough [if unplanned] test flight), I inadvertently verified that my patchwork neuromuscular control network functioned properly, which suggested that I probably hadn't scrambled my host's functions to the point where I need worry about losing coordination and crashing (or whatever spastic *voor'flöns* do), or perhaps short-circuiting something among the involuntary systems and triggering cardiac arrest or something equally fatal.

Eventually regaining a measure of composure, however, I reoriented myself from the magnetic lines of force, swung the *voor'flön* around on course for La'ïr, brought it up to cruise— something over six hundred miles an hour!—and, despite my very best intentions, found myself starting to "count my chickens."

It was at about about this time that I realized that I was starting to get that *watched* feeling. . . .

Quickly I scanned my surroundings to the limits of the *voor'flön's* vision—dramatically better than my own: Those six-inch pupils admitted a lot of light, and the retinal area comprising the backs of five-foot eyeballs contained a huge number of rod and cone receptors; the resultant brilliance, clarity, and detail of resolution filled me with envy. Those eyes could distinguish a *nNby'q* from a *t'göe'tl* bush at probably two hundred miles.

But not even looking through those eyes could I detect anything which might have had the slightest practical interest in a *voor'flön* (apart from keeping out of its way, of course): No other *voor'flöns* were in view, nor *fäap'fing* squadrons of sufficient numerical strength to pose a threat; no potentially dangerous weather conditions (even a *voor'flön* is well-advised to avoid an all-out Isi squall line or thunderstorm). In short, I could see nothing to account for my unease—which was no comfort at all; if anything, the negative visual results intensified my concern.

At this point the *voor'flön* took a deep breath, opened those fifteen-foot-long jaws, and, at a volume level guaranteed to cause cracks in structural steel, said, "*GRR-RONK-K . . . !*" This was followed by a series of further pronouncements in more moderate tones, possibly under two hundred decibels. I hadn't tapped into my host's speech centers yet (and hadn't particularly intended to), so it was apparent that the source of the uproar was my landlord.

Now, I certainly held no ruth for *voor'flöns* specifically, and in general had no compunctions about killing for food or defense—in fact, in retrospect, I'm really not sure what motivated me at that point. But I've never been able to stomach needless cruelty, especially involving animals; and the sure knowledge that a dumb (however feral) animal was trapped inside that nightmarish skull, cut off from most of its body, unable to comprehend what was happening to it, and utterly terrified, disturbed me profoundly.

So I expanded my network of connections more deeply into the *voor'flön's* cerebral cortex, looking for a suggestion of the dim matrix of awareness which, together with a basic set of reflexes and conditioned responses, doubtless served as the huge predator's intellect. Looking back, I know I had no idea what I expected to accomplish once I found it—*if* I found it. I suppose I'd have attempted to calm its fears by sending nonverbal emotional patterns of reassurance, security, and comfort (sort of nonphysical hugs and head-pats), while murmuring, "There, there; everything's going to be all right; daddy's here."

But that's not what happened. I dug, probed, and hunted, and eventually found—

Sapience . . . !

CHAPTER 30

The *voor'flön* was a barely adult female whose mind registered the presence of mine within hers at virtually the same moment the implications of what I'd found dawned on me (nothing in Meg's knowledge of the species had suggested any such possibility). It was a toss-up as to which of us was the most astonished.

Recovering promptly, however, the *voor'flön* got right to the point: "STOP THAT!" her mind thundered in mine.

Momentarily I froze, shaken to the core—how could a *voor'flön* communicate in English . . . ? But then, suddenly if somewhat belatedly, I understood: Though unvocalized, the huge predator's thought images were sharp and unambiguous; my mind, already attuned to the code employed by her nervous system's "machine language," had responded automatically by translating the images into words drawn from my own vocabulary. My blood pressure subsided a fraction.

But even then I failed to respond immediately. The impact of absorbing the entirety of the *voor'flön's* personality and intellect in a single glance quite took my breath away—never, in my wildest dreams, could I have imagined such starkly defined, utterly implacable ferocity.

The world was an uncomplicated place to a *voor'flön:* Right and wrong were as clearly delineated as black and white. Justice was absolute; all rewards were immediate, all crimes capital.

Everything that moved fell, automatically and without exception, into one of three possible categories: kin, enemy, or food. Kin required a direct blood link (siblings or her own mother or young; fathers didn't count) and were worth dying for at any time of the day or night. An enemy was anything capable of, and which displayed any inclination toward, eating her (that seemed reasonable; I tended toward a similar view myself). Everything else mobile was food. *Every*thing. . . .

Of necessity, the *voor'flön* was completely uneducated and lacking in sophistication; however, her intelligence was apparent, and it was obvious that she learned quickly: In the instant of registering my presence, she had grasped the fact that she faced another mind not unlike her own. This was an absolutely stunning development; one for which nothing in her past had prepared her.

Yet unhesitatingly, without fuss or lost motion, wasting no time in startlement, fear, or skepticism, she had expanded her universe to accommodate the new facts. And despite having had no previous inkling—not only of the concept of interpersonal communication (apart from a few rudimentary vocal and/or body language threats and warnings-off)—but even of any purpose to which such a mechanism might be put, she hit upon the idea of assembling, in coherent form, her disapproval of my actions, together with a demand that I cease, and transmitting them back up the link through which I controlled her.

Suddenly my plans were in disarray again. . . .

"STOP THAT!" the *voor'flön* repeated angrily, with more emphasis. "Who are you; what are you doing to me? *Stop it*, I said—STOP IT *THIS INSTANT* . . . !"

I thought fast. True, there was nothing the *voor'flön* could do to regain control of her body; I was securely in charge at this point, and anticipated no difficulty maintaining the status quo all the way to La'ïr.

On the other hand (it occurred to me then), I faced nearly the same predicament as the typical lifelong city-dweller set down in the middle of nowhere with only a horse for transportation: How would he know that the easiest way to kill a horse is to let it eat all the grain it wants. Or that the second-easiest way is to let it drink its fill when it's hot and tired. Or that a horse will keep going, regardless of exhaustion, until its heart bursts.

He wouldn't, of course; nor would he know about any of the numberless other mistaken "kindnesses" which unfailingly result in a dead horse.

I knew almost as little about *Voor'flöns,* Care & Feeding Of. Maybe I could dig the necessary information out of her mind—or maybe not. At best, I faced the same problem I'd been having with the second-hand memories I'd received from Meg practically since arriving on Isis: Unless something specific triggered a connection, I couldn't get at them. Especially in advance.

Almost certainly, if I tried to rely on "common sense" and dug-out information in the management of my *voor'flön* host, I'd kill her. If not through ignorance of metabolic requirements, then through tactical errors while hunting and/or defending my/ourselves from attack.

Capturing this *voor'flön* had been a chancy business; I wasn't thrilled with the prospect of having to do it all over again. Possibly several times. Besides, now that I'd looked into her mind, I couldn't be nearly as casual about being responsible for her death as when I thought her just one more mindless Isi organic killing machine. (She was still an Isi organic killing machine, but she wasn't mindless. That made a difference.)

Yes, there had to be a better way. And quite probably, if I'd had time to think the matter through, I would have come up with several. But as things stood, I could think of only one.

The chances of making friends with the *voor'flön,* after what I'd done to her thus far, looked pretty slender. For one thing she was . . .

Well, just how angry *was* she? Miffed? Piqued? Nettled? Sorely vexed? Really ticked? Positively steamed? Absolutely furious? In a blind, killing rage . . . ?

I probed more deeply. "Blind, killing rage" appeared to sum things up nicely. And with perfect justification: Granted, my teeth, claws, and grapples hadn't done any real damage to that foot-thick hide; but the remote-control umbilicus connecting my nervous system to hers itched infernally—not to mention the added detail that I had deprived her (by force!) of her ability to control her own body, and then used it myself without her consent (treatment which, with or without sexual overtones, most women of my experience would tend to equate with rape).

On the other hand, her anger, murderous though it was, reflected no more than the intensity of her desire to end my takeover. Revenge was not a factor; indeed, the concept appeared nowhere in her mind. She was neither willfully cruel nor actively vindictive; she was merely a trapped predator who wanted free in the very worst way.

Now. . . . Never in the *voor'flön's* entire life had she encountered the concept, per se, of a promise ("friend" either, for that matter); but there was no doubt in my mind, assuming we got that far, that her word could be trusted. Honor is something which either you possess the basic instinct for or you don't. One glance into the depths of that proudly savage intellect was enough to assure me that, despite the rage which flamed there, she had it.

Which was not to suggest that I had any misapprehension that what I contemplated was likely to prove easy, particularly given the manner in which our relationship had begun. The *voor'flön* had grown up under the influence of, and lived strictly according to, a set of rules which only could be described as unyielding (damn well carved in stone is what they were!) as well as limited in outlook: They contained no provision for *friendship*.

Success or failure hinged upon her willingness to forgive and forget, as well as to compromise. On first impression, she didn't strike me as the forgiving kind. However, already she had demonstrated a capacity to adapt intelligently and constructively in the face of circumstances utterly without precedent in her experience; and adaptability, as a concept, is at least partially rooted in compromise. That was a start.

So ignoring the complaints of a tiny portion of my mind (which wanted to know [in the shrillest possible terms] why I never conducted these experiments except when my own life was at stake), I took a deep breath, assembled my thoughts into something approximating coherent form, and opened relations: "You're probably wondering why I've arranged this meeting. . . ."

To this day I don't know how I managed to calm the raging leviathan and talk her into giving me a chance to demonstrate the benefits of friendship. But somehow, considerably later, I found myself assigned the role of probationary hunting partner and navigator as the *voor'flön* tore through the Isi skies, on course for La'ïr.

My umbilicus remained in place. My axons and dendrites were withdrawn from the synaptic gaps of the *voor'flön's* neuromuscular system, but I remained hooked into her higher functions for purposes of communication as well as to access her far more capable sensory faculties. And, of course, I had blocked the nerves responsible for transmitting to her brain the horrendous itch my neurological probe caused.

Likewise, I had tapped into her metabolism long enough to have her grow a snug cockpit between her shoulder blades for me to ride in. Now only the top of my head (down to the eyes) projected above the surface of her skin, protected from the wind blast by the aerodynamic shelter of her head and neck. In addition, I adjusted her immune system (which had been raging at my own defenses virtually from the outset) to disregard my presence.

Once we got past the (metaphoric) shouting stage, it occurred to me to ask the *voor'flön* her name; only to learn that she didn't have one (unless you counted a recurring appellation awarded in the distant past by her nestmates, which [in addition to being unpronounceable] amounted to possibly the most repugnant, concentratedly obscene condemnation of gluttony and not waiting in line I'd ever had the bad fortune to encounter).

Of course the primary function of a name is to identify, from among many, the specific individual with whom one wishes to communicate, as well as to record property rights. It made sense that a "society" lacking both communication and property would have little reason to bother with them.

Nonetheless, *I* was accustomed to bothering with them; and the longer our relationship continued, the more I found that conversation with a genuinely nameless individual left me feeling strangely off balance. Obviously, under the circumstances, I had no choice in the matter: I had to name her myself. Only . . .

What does one name a ravenous behemoth half again the length of a football field, whose propensity for casually direct action would make Attila the Hun blanch?

(I mean, if it's only a pet you're talking about, it's not that difficult: "Eureka" for a stray cat who finds you; "Trip O'Neal" for a well-intentioned, bumbling Old English Sheepdog who's always in the way when you try to turn right; "Krakatoa" for a Clydesdale with a propensity for stepping on feet; "Heraldo" for a ferret who's always poking his nose where it doesn't belong; and so forth.)

However, within moments of applying my imagination to the problem, I knew I had the answer: German mythology supplied the name of a couragous, strong-willed warrior-aviatrix made even more famous by generations of grand opera performers, many of whom themselves exhibited qualities reminiscent of the *voor'flön*. These legendary ladies (almost to a man!) were forthright (petty detractors were wont to use the word "overbearing"), physically imposing, and possessed sheerly awesome vocal power and range.

In support of the suggestion, I offered the *voor'flön* a carefully edited version of her would-be namesake's history, pointing out that she was a fine, brave warrior (omitting the fact that, like all Wagnerian characters, she was also very stupid); and that it was a name which only someone of equal courage and stature rightfully could wear.

The *voor'flön* cocked her head and regarded me thoughtfully with a five-foot, red-and-yellow eye. Then she nodded slowly. "Very well, Brünhilde I shall be. . . ."

"How*ever* . . ." she continued briskly, practically in the same breath (mind-to-mind communication isn't dependent upon breathing, though in practice there's a tendency to forget), "now you must demonstrate the benefits of this friendship stuff, and quickly."

"What do you have in mind?" I replied cautiously. Already I had explained what I expected my contributions to be, and I knew she wasn't planning mutiny. Still—

"I am in distress," Brünhilde announced calmly. . . .

TO: Project Director/Monitor's Log.
FROM: G'lLhytl, Tenth Order.
SUBJECT: Project *Extremis*.

The man is nothing less than a juggernaut! Who could have anticipated that Cory would attempt to domesticate a *voor'flön*—let alone that such an effort would be rewarded by success . . . ! On his own he was virtually unstoppable. Now that he controls a *voor'flön*, he surely will reach La'ïr—and in a matter of weeks—unless we are able to develop a solution more effective than any we have attempted thus far.

Part of the problem (which, of course, we have realized somewhat belatedly) is that success breeds success. In our attempt to break him, we have challenged Cory with

apparently insuperable obstacle after obstacle. In overcoming them, he has acquired what must be regarded as a
fully justifiable confidence in his abilities; he has developed a sheerly awesome psychological momentum—and
by now the magnitude and complexity of the intervention
required to challenge him, let alone maintain a steadily
mounting level of mortal pressure on him without
prematurely killing him outright, is such that it is
becoming increasingly difficult to conceal the presence of
our hand in his problems.

Months ago the day-to-day level of danger to which we
were subjecting him exceeded that which drove our
ancestors to the brink of extinction, and still he shows no
sign of weakening.

Perhaps the Council of Elders can suggest a solution;
certainly we who are involved in the project on a daily
basis have failed to thus far. However, what we need now
is a tactic to separate him from that *voor'flön;* any
recommendation emerging from the Council will be long-
term and strategic in nature.

If the events which I have set in motion do not produce
the desired result, I think it may be said without fear of
contradiction that we may *not* be able to break him before
he wins through to La'ïr—at least not without resorting to
methods which almost certainly will kill him outright.

"I am in distress," Brünhilde had announced.

(I had to keep reminding myself that the *voor'flön's* vocabulary and sentence structure were my own, as my mind
translated her nonvocalized thoughts into English.)

"Whether through disinterest or ignorance, you failed to
monitor my physical condition during your temporary occu-
pancy of my control centers. As a result both of my prolonged
efforts to dislodge you, and your subsequent excesses in the
operation of my body, I find that I am more fatigued than ever I
have been before. I must have food, at least, immediately; the
question of rest must await a determination of whether I live
out the next hour."

"'Live out the . . . '?" For a moment I failed to grasp her
meaning. Then, abruptly, comprehension burst upon me—
accompanied by the deepest personal chagrin: Of course! I had
totally worn her out with all that foolishness: I had ridden her
almost to death—a performance to shame the rankest novice
equestrian. Poor monster—I hadn't realized . . . !

I was well into the throes of self-flagellation, with my guilt feelings rapidly gaining the upper hand, before it occurred to me to wonder—if the *voor'flön* were all that exhausted, *how come she still was traveling at better than mach point seven*?

"I have no choice," she responded, still in the same unruffled manner. "Yes, it is difficult to maintain such speed; very difficult, tired as I am. But I must—we flee a pursuer. He has been after us since shortly after you returned control to me."

"A pursuer? Who? Or should I say what? —And why didn't you *say* something . . . ?"

"I thought you knew," came the somewhat tart reply. "You have access to my vision and thoughts. How could you fail to notice something as obtrusive as a large male of my species?"

Briefly I wondered that myself—obviously I hadn't been paying close enough attention to the *voor'flön's* sensory input. I was on the point of resolving to do better in the future—

When suddenly I realized precisely what Brünhilde had meant when she expressed doubts about living out the hour; my treatment of her had nothing to do with it: "A *male*, you said . . . ?"

"Yes."

"In rut?"

"I don't believe I have ever encountered anyone more so."

"Are you feeling receptive?" Horrors! What if she were—with me installed precisely where a male initially locks on with his teeth to facilitate mounting and coupling.

(*Now* I understood why nature had arranged things so *voor'flöns* couldn't reach that spot on their own bodies [my hindsight has always been above reproach].)

"Not in the least." Good, that was a relief—

Or was it? Was that an undertone I detected in Brünhilde's reply . . . ?

"Uh . . . what happens if he is and you aren't?"

"Males do not respond favorably to frustration. They become quite angry. Angry males are violent. Exhausted as I am, I possess neither the strength required to drive him off nor the speed necessary to elude him. Failing both, he surely will kill me—and you in the bargain if you're still here. I do not know how we will get out of this. Do you have any suggestions?"

I wished I did! "Where is this Lothario?" I demanded, as much by way of stalling as from a desire to size up the opposition.

In reply, Brünhilde focused her eyes astern. There, possibly a hundred fifty miles behind us, was another *voor'flön*. Even at this distance it was obvious that he was easily half again Brünhilde's size.

Equally apparent, he was putting his whole heart and soul into the effort (ain't love grand!): His neck was outstretched, his head perfectly aligned with his body; his undulation rate exceeded Brünhilde's by easily thirty percent. And even as I watched, he gained perceptibly.

I thought fast. "Brünhilde," I began, "how much food will it take to restore your strength?"

"I do not know that food alone will suffice," came the grim reply; "at least not in the time remaining before he catches us. I have never been this tired before. But food is a beginning; without it I have no chance at all of recovering enough strength to cope with him once he closes with us."

With the *voor'flön's* attention focused on her physical deficits, I was able to follow her thoughts and take a quick inventory of her condition. No, food alone wasn't the solution; that much was obvious. (At the finish of my last record-setting Hawaiian Iron Man Triathlon I'd been almost as tired myself; and if anybody had offered me food right then I'd have thrown up on him.) First the *voor'flön* needed to restore her fluid and electrolytic balance. Only after her metabolism was back on an even keel would she benefit from a solid meal and a prolonged period of rest. However, the male was gaining by (figurative) leaps and bounds; there simply wasn't time to solve Brünhilde's problems through R & R. Clearly it would be necessary to explore other avenues.

Briefly I pondered the advisability of suggesting to her that she "fake it"; that she accept the big male's attentions even though she wasn't in the mood. (The premise of a Fate Worse Than Death tends to enjoy better standing among those who haven't faced Him personally.) But the *voor'flön* picked up the thought and explained that romance among her kind was a seasonal thing—strictly physical.

Under normal circumstances, a nonestrus female would have no difficulty outdistancing a male whose interest was, from her perspective, untimely. In fact, Brünhilde added conversationally, if she were in season she would have no objections whatsoever to a dalliance with the approaching male. Even at this distance she could tell that he had many sterling qualities; and Under Different Circumstances she'd

very much have been inclined to succumb to his blandish-
ments. But, of course, as things stood, she simply *couldn't*.

Which was fascinating, but not very helpful. What we
needed at that point was an answer to the question of how to
deal with the rejected suitor once he caught up with us. I
cudgeled my brain, trying to come up with some means of
saving our bacon.

Brünhilde couldn't escape through sheer speed and/or
maneuverability, and she was too small (quite apart from her
exhaustion) even to think about direct confrontation—even
with my help: Our pursuer was twice the size of the *voor'flön*
I'd managed to knock out of the sky earlier; all I'd accomplish
by zapping him with the *t'lLiSs'mn* would be to make him
madder still.

Well, what was left?—craftiness, that's what . . . !

"Brünhilde," I called tentatively up the nervelink, "what do
you think of the idea of letting down into the *t'göllq'gn* forest,
landing on a good-sized limb, and remaining out of sight until
Lothario gives up and goes about his business?"

"Not much," came the immediate reply. "I'd rather be killed
by one of my own kind than get tangled in a (sudden
untranslated image of a shockingly fast-moving, frightfully
violent, blurred something resembling an oversize *väarz'-
fing*)'s web." The *voor'flön* actually shuddered.

Moments later I matched the picture she'd shown me with
an arboreal, web-dwelling variation on the *väarz'fing* theme
with which Meg was familiar: A mature *gäajh'fing* could reach
over fifty feet in length and lived in silken traps fashioned of
incredibly sticky, inch-thick strands which bridged spans
measured in miles among the mid and upper reaches of the
t'göllq'gn. Boasting unrivaled predatory enthusiasm, astonishing speed and physical power, coupled with venom of un-
matched toxicity, the *gäajh'fing* qualified as one of the
deadliest beasties on the planet, regardless of size. A full-
grown *voor'flön*, entangled in that tenaciously clinging, virtually unbreakable web, would be hard-pressed indeed to
emerge from the experience alive.

Brünhilde had a point; there were deaths and there were
deaths. On the other hand, she wasn't exactly bombarding me
with alternative suggestions, and our lead was dwindling by
the moment.

I hesitated, juggling the possibilities; then continued in
what I hoped would pass for a confident, forthright manner:

"Suppose you slowed almost to a hover before descending into the *t'göllq´gn*; with your incredible eyesight, wouldn't you be able to detect any *gäajh'fings* and their webs in time to avoid getting caught?"

The *voor'flön* reflected at length. "Probably," she grudged eventually, distaste for the idea reflected in her thoughts; "but I sure would hate to try it."

"Not even to evade Lothario?"

"No. There's no point to it; it wouldn't do any good. If he were that close, he'd smell me. Once he was on my scent, he wouldn't leave the area until he'd caught me. He'd be waiting when we came back up, even if it took all week."

"Oh." Curses, foiled again. That was something I hadn't had occasion to discover yet; who would have suspected that *voor'flöns* might possess bloodhound-quality olfactory sensitivity.

Damn, this was getting serious! If it kept up, we were going to end up lunch for sure. . . .

No!—those were Brünhilde's thoughts and feelings, I suddenly realized; not mine. But their effects were insidious: Almost before I was aware of it, I was well on the way to being infected with the *voor'flön's* wild-born fatalism—an outlook difficult to distinguish from the rankest defeatism.

But not me: I couldn't give up—even if the fate of the galaxy hadn't depended upon me, I was constitutionally incapable of giving up . . . !

Granted, the odds were starting to mount again; the outlook was growing less favorable by the second: Brünhilde was exhausted; Lothario was bigger, faster, stronger, and more maneuverable than we were, and gaining rapidly. Remaining up where he could get at us was tantamount to suicide. And, of course, the threat of *gäajh'fings* rendered operation down in the depths of the *t'göllq´gn* an exceedingly risky business.

Clearly it was time for the Isis' prize survivor/galactic-savior-genotype to dip into his vaunted reserves of resourcefulness and pull out a rabbit. After all, I was supposed to be a professional problem-solver, wasn't I . . . ?

I took a deep breath, tried with mixed success to clear my mind of distractions, and settled down to some intensive, industrial-grade strategy planning (not unmixed with frantic scheming).

Vaguely I recalled a self-considered pundit who once observed brightly that "A problem is nothing more than an opportunity in disguise." For a brief, mean-spirited moment, I wished I had him there with me to share in the opportunity. The disguise in this case was dauntingly effective.

On the other hand, it suddenly occurred to me, juxtaposition of the two elements of the problem did suggest a possible solution. The operative word, of course, was "possible": It was a long shot at best, and required Brünhilde's fullest cooperation. It also relied heavily on her strength and agility; I wondered whether she had enough left of either to pull it off—to say nothing of how she would react to the news that it was time to upgrade mere craftiness to unabashed, full-blown treachery . . . !

(Naturally Brünhilde never had had occasion to encounter *aikido*, the ancient, so-called passive self-defense system developed in Japan, nor its almost tongue-in-cheek philosophy of "gently educational" *semi*nonviolence: It is impossible to attack someone using *aikido;* the system contains no offensive moves—however, for every gambit an attacker might employ, there is an absolute counter. Inevitably every such attack concludes with the offending party's limb or limbs enmeshed in a gently unyielding cat's cradle formed by the intended victim's arms and/or legs, unable to move further without onset of severe pain and dislocation of the involved joints. In every case it is the aggressor's own strength and hostile actions alone which lay the foundation for his undoing. In fact, true masters of the art who might find themselves at odds would be limited to verbal sparring; both because of the lack of aggressive techniques and because the first affirmative move by either opens the door for the other to end the discussion with painful finality. [Of course, such masters never find themselves at odds with one another; the accompanying spiritual discipline renders such discord unthinkable.])

These deliberations took place during the briefest fraction of a second behind mental shields through which Meg herself couldn't have discerned activity; and my next communication with the *voor'flön* followed on the heels of her reply without a perceptible break: "I don't blame you for not wanting to get involved with a *gäajh'fing* personally—but I can't help thinking that it sure would be convenient if your admirer should happen to blunder into one of those webs. . . ."

Brünhilde regarded me dubiously. "Why would he do something like that?" she responded in perplexity. "What reason would he have even to be down there? No *voor'flön* ventures down there. Ever. We *know* better."

"Of course you do," I assured her. "But you said that a frustrated male is an angry male. How frustrated and angry do you think he'd have to be to forget caution and common sense and chase you down into the *t'göllq'gn* forest?"

"He'd have to be awfully angry," she observed patronizingly. "That would be a very stupid thing to do."

"Do you think you could *make* him that angry?"

Abruptly I was conscious of one of the *voor'flön's* huge red-and-yellow eyes focused on me. From the disturbance roiling the surface of that feral mind it was evident, even without digging deeper, that Brünhilde's perception of the Universe was undergoing another profound adjustment. . . .

She barely had finished absorbing the impact of learning that she was not alone as a reasoning entity, together with the simultaneous discovery of interpersonal communication. Now she was realizing that that communication could be used to transmit false information and impressions. And even as I watched, Brünhilde's grasp of the mechanics of deception expanded from that point, in a single intuitive leap, to include the possibility of doing so for the specific purpose of taking advantage of the erroneous behavior which that false information could induce in another.

(Briefly, and behind tightly braced shields, I pondered the long-range wisdom of teaching a single-minded carnivore [stretching nearly the length of the Washington Monument and massing almost as much as an intercontinental jet] to lie. . . .)

As she digested the concept, and the various implications and possibilities began to sink in, the faintest tinge of something, which in someone more worldly might have been interpreted as smugness, edged into her thoughts. "Yes," she replied with unexpected assurance, "I *can*. . . ."

Brünhilde wasted no time acting upon the suggestion: Even as I explained more fully what I had in mind, she pointed her nose downward and dropped from the sky like a stone.

From cruising altitude the roof of the *t'göllq'gn* forest appeared impenetrable. The greenery stretched unbroken in every direction as far as the eye could see. But as we descended, openings between individual branches materialized; and it was toward one of the largest of these that Brünhilde's dive was aimed. Her drag brakes and spoilers were fully deployed; and even as we plunged earthward, our velocity melted rapidly until, a mere body length above the treetops, the *voor'flön* shifted her musculoskeletal system into hover mode and eased in among the branches at barely thirty miles per hour.

The prospect of getting snagged in a web didn't trouble me as much as it did Brünhilde. A full-grown *gäajh'fing* was quite a bit larger than a *väarz'fing*, but there was no doubt in my mind that a well-placed zap of coherent lightning would stop its clock; and it shouldn't be too difficult to cut our way loose thereafter.

(On the other hand, there seemed little point in complicating Brünhilde's life with unnecessary details. If she wanted to be ultraconservative, I wasn't going to argue with her. In fact, despite knowing that my eyes were inferior to hers in every respect, I judged that two pair were bound to be more useful than one, and remained tapped into the *voor'flön*'s optic circuits only to the extent of keeping track of where she was looking so I could be watching everywhere else.)

It didn't take long to find a *gäajh'fing* (for which I was acutely grateful; hovering is awfully hard work, and Brünhilde's respiratory and cardiac rates were approaching the critical level). "There's one," she announced, abruptly shying off to one side, ripples of dread running the length of her body, somehow without interfering with her lift-generating rhythms.

Suddenly I understood why so formidable a being as Brünhilde would prefer being eaten by her own kind. Once I watched a fifteen-foot-long *väarz'fing* kill a seventy-foot-long *böll'skag*—this *gäajh'fing* stretched at least sixty feet. Its legs and tail were much longer, in proportion, than those of a *väarz'fing*, and more supple. The legs, tail, and fangs twitched constantly. The monster's movements, as it pivoted to follow our flight, were unbelievably quick; they conveyed, somehow, a malign awareness and an impression of almost personal vendetta.

Poor Lothario. . . .

A shrug of revulsion traveled the hundred-fifty-yard length of Brünhilde's body, briefly causing her to flutter like wind-blown ribbon. With a shudder that would have registered high on the Richter scale, she accelerated to minimum lift-producing speed, and circled the miles-wide web twice, fixing in her mind (and mine) its shape and location with relation to the surrounding limbs.

Then she shot skyward, emerging above the trees just as her

date, even more imposing at close range, soared gracefully down from the clouds.

"Gronk!" he rumbled seductively. "*Gronk! GRONK!*" Coyly he banked away, displaying persuasive evidence of his interest. Freud would have been impressed—I've seen smaller semi-trailer tankers.

Brünhilde was pretty impressed, too, and regretted that she was in no condition to take him up on the offer. However, she was fully aware of what her refusal would lead to once she convinced him that she meant it.

Lothario completed his three-sixty and swung back in our direction. Brünhilde side-stepped the rush easily: The male really hadn't meant it that time; in terms of *voor'flön* foreplay, he was still at the wolf-whistling stage.

Brünhilde cranked into a gentle climbing turn. This was a signal indicating acceptance; and quickly Lothario maneuvered to pace us, maintaining tight formation slightly below and just outside the radius of our turn.

Brünhilde predicted that he would make no move toward us as long as she continued to spiral upward: The mechanics of *voor'flön* coupling required a receptive female to glide in a straight line while the male closed in from behind and above; this necessitated considerable altitude, and normally he would be justified in assuming that she was gaining height for that purpose.

She wasn't. About five thousand feet up, and completely without warning, she stood on edge and ripped into a heavy-gee, vertical turn toward the male. She passed close behind his head, just above his back. As the length of his body continued forward, passing under hers, she reached down with the talons edging her flight membranes on that side and opened up probably a half-dozen slices across his back before he could hurl himself clear. A bellow of purest outrage dislodged loose objects for a ten-mile radius.

But as Lothario rounded to follow, blood in his eye and revenge in his heart, he beheld Brünhilde, already obligingly stabilized in an unmistakably receptive glide, tail held invitingly to one side, glancing coquettishly over her shoulder. Briefly he balanced pain and anger against lust. . . .

The outcome never was in doubt—quickly Lothario tucked in behind and above us, slowing as he maneuvered for position. His jaws reached for that all-important spot behind her neck, his talons felt for hers; his probe groped for her socket . . .

But abruptly, an instant before contact, Brünhilde flipped over onto her back and, in the fractions of a second it took her to begin falling away, did her level best to disembowel him (and worse!). Lothario's response probably triggered slippage in any geological fault lines in the terrain below.

This time Brünhilde didn't stick around to see if he still retained an interest in continuing their *tête-à-tête*—she knew better. She righted herself as she fell, nosed down, and accelerated for the foliage below. Lothario was less than a quarter mile astern as we shot through the opening into the gloom below, and there was no doubt at all about his intentions.

Brünhilde hurtled past the edge of the web and banked steeply behind it as if trying to elude the raging male, who cut sharply to the inside in an effort to head her off. He came very close to tearing all the way through the web by virtue of his momentum.

But, of course, this wasn't horseshoes. Poor Lothario. . . .

TO: Project Director/Monitor's Log.
FROM: Metehiryä, Tenth Order.
SUBJECT: Project *Extremis*.

G'lLhytl's attempt to separate Subject Cory from the *voor'flön* has failed. Neither I, nor any other Tenth on the project, have been able to think of any means of accomplishing it either.

And, incredible as it may seem, as I came to work I passed groups of people following the subject's progress on wide-screen viewers—and cheering his success! Perhaps, in their enthusiasm, they have forgotten the objective of this project, and our ultimate intentions for Cory.

In any event, I have recommended calling a convocation of all compudicters. Possibly a massed rapport will prove equal to the crisis. If not, then I am very much afraid that we may be facing failure; that nothing short of actual death will break Cory. And if that does prove to be the case, then we had best begin making plans for a suitable reception for him here.

I recommend that, as he approaches La'ïr aboard his incredible steed, we continue to apply as much pressure as we can on him. There continues to be, of course, a slim possibility that we may achieve our goal, through mischance, if nothing else. But more importantly, an abrupt reduction in the level of stress might be all too revealing to a mind of that caliber; it would be doubly frustrating if he were to deduce our activities over these past months because of the fact that we had ceased them. . . .

Brünhilde mounted back into the sky, rumbling under her breath like a restless volcano; she was insufferably pleased with herself. "That worked pretty well," she admitted grudgingly, swinging back onto course for La'ïr. "But *now*"—she continued sternly—"What about getting me *fed*? I *must* have food and rest soon or perish . . . !"

"You've certainly earned it," I enthused; I was pretty darned pleased with us myself. "Let's go hunt us up a couple gross of *p'rRö'f* and pig out!"

The silence which ensued was both unexpected and (since I knew for a fact that little was so dear to her heart as food) downright ominous. "What's wrong . . . ?" I asked finally, as the delay stretched to the point of awkwardness.

A massive sigh disturbed the *voor'flön*'s flight rhythm. A huge red-and-yellow eye swiveled back to gaze at me. "To eat I must catch something," she pointed out in disconcertingly mild tones.

"Well, of course," I replied, nonplussed.

"To catch something I must quietdive."

"What's the point?" I prodded. The *voor'flön* rapidly was acquiring the annoyingly human habit of responding to an inquiry about the time with a detailed description of how to build a clock.

"I don't believe I have enough strength left to achieve quietdive velocity," Brünhilde confessed wearily. "And I've yet to meet food that would stand still while I approached slowly."

Oh. Oh! *Oh!* Now I understood! That definitely constituted a problem—

Or did it . . . ?

Hmm. . . . Maybe not.

Brünhilde's initial misgivings over the prospect of eating *b'vVec'h* proved short-lived. Even though her eyes squinted in revolted anticipation, and her tongue recoiled shudderingly to the very rear of her oral cavity as her jaws closed reluctantly about the first sample, once the flavor exploded upon her palate the *voor'flön's* hesitation evaporated. In fact, by the time she began to show the first signs of slowing down (possibly twenty minutes later), several tons of the huge fungus had disappeared into her maw, and I was beginning to wonder whether introducing Brünhilde to *b'vVec'h* mightn't have been potentially an ecological mistake. (Not from a dietary standpoint, of course; I had adjusted her metabolism [heretofore exclusively carniverous] to produce an enzyme capable of processing the protein-rich vegetable matter.)

But eventually the *voor'flön* lifted her head and emitted a belch (echoes of which still rumbled in the distance thirty seconds later). She swallowed a last mouthful and lowered her chin to the ground. A contented sigh uprooted a forty-foot-tall *t'gyt'n* growing nearly a hundred feet from her nose.

"You know, there might be something to this friendship business after all," she observed thoughtfully, her lids sagging ever lower across those huge, now-rapidly-glazing eyes (seriously compromising the normal ferocity of her glare). "I don't know when I've had such a good meal."

"That's what friends are for," I replied diplomatically. "Now, why don't you catch up on your rest. I'll stand guard so nothing can sneak up on you while you're asleep."

The suggestion met not even token resistance. Gratefully Brünhilde allowed her eyelids to close the rest of the way. Another enormous sigh wreaked further havor for a hundred yards out in front of her. As her consciousness receded, she sent a final, almost apologetic thought:

"I never sleep more than a couple of hours at a time," she assured me dreamily. "I won't be long. . . ."

Some fourteen hours later Brünhilde woke with a start and looked around a bit blearily. She was mortified to discover how long she had been asleep—she *never* slept for more than an hour or two in the past, she'd declared defensively. She couldn't imagine how it had happened. . . .

I knew, but I had no intention of telling her. It had occurred to me that if for any reason I found it necessary to dismount, it was unlikely that I'd be allowed back aboard. In fact, the longer I considered the matter, the more positive I became that I wouldn't—certainly if our positions were reversed I wouldn't have let her regain control of me once she'd lost it. I resolved, therefore, to arrange things so that, if necessary, I could remain aboard and linked to her nervous system all the way to La'ïr. So, keeping her sound asleep (with a metaphoric thumb pressed on her sleep center), I implemented further modifications to the umbilicus which joined us:

First I branched off extensions of my aorta and superior vena cava and extended the pair down the tube into Brünhilde's upper thorax where I plugged them, respectively, into her internal carotid artery and internal jugular vein. I'd already made peace with her immune system, but considerable work was required to iron out the differences between our blood types. However, the potential benefits were well worth the effort: Now I could tap the *voor'flön's* bloodstream for my own nourishment.

Thereafter I had reengineered the probe's physical structure, turning it over to Brünhilde's metabolism for blood supply and routine maintenance, and created a quick-release attachment for my own vascular and nervous system extensions at a point just within the *voor'flön's* tegument. If the need arose (and it required little imagination to envision situations in which it could—suppose we hadn't managed to distract Lothario, for instance), I'd be able to disengage from (or, assuming I was allowed to, reconnect to) my host on a moment's notice. Prior to this, it would have taken over half an hour to withdraw all my various connections—the alternative being to shear off the entire umbilicus at the level of my chest wall, and cope with the resulting trauma if and when I found the time.

Finally I had equipped Brünhilde's end of the quick-release fitting with a sphincter to enable her to close it off for protection of the tender umbilicus terminal components anytime I wasn't tied in.

I soothed the *voor'flön* by suggesting that maybe she had been unusually tired as a result of the previous day's excitement; that perhaps her subconscious had taken advantage of knowing that with me on watch nothing could slip up on her while she slept. The explanation mollified her sufficiently to allow me to get her onto another subject—

Which turned out, of course, to be *food*. After all, the poor baby hadn't eaten a thing in fourteen hours—and how long could the nutritional content of a mere eight or ten tons of *b'vVec'h* be expected to last a growing girl . . . ?

So, after putting away another three or four tons of the stuff to tide her over until she could find a real meal, Brünhilde lifted from the ground, climbed back to cruising altitude, pointed her nose in the direction of La'ïr once more, and accelerated to cruising speed. And as she rippled through the green skies of Isis at mach point seven, the *voor'flön* scanned the ground below through force of habit, ever alert for her next meal. (Mind you, she wasn't averse to the occasional wallow in alien perversion—that *b'vVec'h* really was good stuff!—but she was a *voor'flön* and *voor'flöns* eat *meat.* . . .)

And as the miles unraveled beneath us, I kept to myself and watched, almost forgotten, as Brünhilde mulled developments: In the past twenty-four hours she had been captured and enslaved by a creature hardly bigger than one of her claws. Control of her body had been restored to her only after she promised to carry him wherever he wanted to go. In the process of being captured she had been worn to a nub, which rendered her incapable of eluding a rut-maddened male without resorting to . . . to one of the *neatest* tricks she'd ever seen, she mused admiringly. She wondered why something like that had never occurred to her—certainly the principle was obvious once it had been explained. Clearly this tiny creature's mind worked differently from hers. Therefore, she resolved thoughtfully, as long as she was stuck with him, she would pay close attention; she might as well pick up some useful ideas in the interim. . . .

Voor'flön-style hunting, it soon developed, bore little resemblance to the casual swoop-and-grab which I, in my ignorance, had envisioned. The physics inherent in mach-one-plus stunt work imposed severe limitations upon what Brünhilde could or couldn't do. At those speeds her momentum was sheerly appalling; to pull out of a quietdive required *lots* of room. However, that velocity was absolutely necessary to a productive hunt; below mach one, the bulk of a *voor'flön* tearing through the air was audible over distances measured in miles.

Potential prey which grazed in small clearings, or stuck to the edges of larger ones, close to the mile-high *t'göllq'gn*, were safe from her and her fellows; it simply wasn't possible to operate at supersonic speeds in such close quarters without serious risk of collision either with the ground or the trees themselves. And at those velocities even the slightest graze almost certainly would prove fatal.

Correspondingly, eons of natural selection had produced a crop of ruminants with particularly acute hearing, hair-triggered reflexes, and eyes spaced for maximum peripheral vision; most of which beasties scrupulously avoided wide-open spaces. (Those which hadn't, in times past, had tended to get eaten at an early age, which limited their opportunity to pass on to future generations genes permitting such foolishness.)

Brünhilde's appetite reappeared within an hour of our departure, and intensified rapidly. But the ruminant population was playing it cagey this morning; nothing grazed out where she could get at it. And by noon it was becoming evident that the *voor'flön's* reserves of patience were inversely related to the level of her hunger. When I caught her casting calculating glances at an adolescent *böol'skag* almost half her own length, I concluded that it was time to lend a hand.

"Brünhilde," I called up the nervelink, "you don't seem to be having much luck. Would you like me to help?"

The *voor'flön* learned fast: No longer did she scoff at suggestions merely because they were new to her experience. I could see her mentally comparing my size, strength, speed, and patently inferior vision with hers, and wondering what my participation possibly could contribute to the outcome; but she merely nodded almost imperceptibly and replied, "What do you have in mind?"

I persuaded her to descend to within a couple hundred yards of the roof of the *t'göllq'gn* forest and slow to just above her minimum lift-producing airspeed, which reduced the sound of her passage to little more than a deep, muted rushing noise, not unlike that created by wind in the trees.

Thereafter I had her swing out barely past the edge of a small clearing, where I eyed the distribution of the game below, and, cautioning her that there would be a loud noise, aimed my *t'lLïSs'mn* carefully, and let go a burst of electrons, using the traversing nozzle. The electron beam scythed across the clearing, killing four lumbering *t'jJ's*.

Brünhilde, after an involuntary twitch at the flash and concussion, was duly impressed: "That was a pretty good trick," she volunteered as, slightly round-eyed, she gently spiraled down into the clearing, scooped up the still-twitching corpses in her talons, and headed back for the clouds.

"Just one of the fringe benefits of friendship," I observed obliquely. "Stick with me, Brünhilde, and I guarantee you'll never have to go hungry."

Briefly the *voor'flön* fell silent, ostensibly concentrating on her meal. But even the most cursory glance beneath her surface thoughts disclosed that I had just scored heavily: The ancient homily, "The quickest way to a man's heart . . ." et cetera, just as well could have been written with *voor'flöns* in mind. As I said, very little was as dear to Brünhilde's feral little heart as food; and the discovery that I could provide it virtually any time she wanted it, without risk or effort, was a telling point. In fact, as I continued to eavesdrop on her thoughts, it became apparent that the campaign was in my pocket; the *voor'flön* had become a "believer" (however pragmatic her motives) in friendship—I was as good as in La'ïr right now . . . !

And despite my very best intentions, my emotional barriers wavered momentarily, lowering far enough for an unguarded portion of my soul to wonder plaintively how Meg was faring in the hands (or whatever!) of that B'nN´ äs'hï. That she still lived after all this time was unlikely; the "rescue" expedition might well be limited to exacting vengeance. Well, at least the question soon would be answered. . . .

And even if the answer proved as unpalatable as logic would suggest, *I* still had a job to do. Regardless of Meg's fate, R'gGnrök was coming. . . .

CHAPTER 31

Then followed a grand month! A *great* month! A month overflowing with bold exploration, skirmishes, brawls, battles, hazards, challenges, exploits, and Glorious Adventure . . . !

Brünhilde and I were fated to be partners: Our strengths and eccentricities complemented one another to form an absolutely invincible team, an organic killing machine which nothing could oppose—together we were *more* than a match for the planet. . . .

Joyously, with boundless enthusiasm—without malice but without mercy—we blazed a bloody, ever-lengthening trail across the endlessly resistant vastness of the mighty planet. Together we wallowed in the awesome splendor of Isis; a grandeur whose living feral savagery was such that separately we'd have been unable to spare the time from the demands of remaining alive to appreciate it.

Yes, it was a *fine* month. . . .

One of our first discoveries was that the time we had spent

physically mindlinked had resulted in our sharing a partial rapport even when I wasn't occupying the snug little cockpit between the *voor'flön's* scapulae with my nervous system plugged into hers. This enhanced our hunting efficiency appreciably: I was able to glide down silently and inconspicuously and peek through the *t'göllq'gn* ringing a clearing; and then either relay the make-up and distribution of the game grazing there up to Brünhilde, or zap something myself for her to come down and pick up. Either course was satisfactory to the *voor'flön*; she didn't hunt to satisfy the compulsions of an artistic temperament—she wanted the *food*!

Endlessly we flew over jungles and lowland areas, out of which swarmed every indigenous airborne predator, flocking up to greet us as we entered their territories. Under constant attack by voracious (and delicious) swarms of lightning-fast flying fish, we traversed vast seas; in the process discovering a particularly grim form of jellyfish, which was capable of lashing out, even above the water, with lethal stinging tentacles literally miles in length.

Each of us saved the other's bacon repeatedly; often under circumstances where rigorous adherence to self-interest would have dictated running for it, and "devil take the hindmost!" This tended to suggest that Brünhilde's stoutly defended claim of "pragmatic" acceptance of the concept of friendship might have acquired additional, hitherto unsuspected depths.

One of the more memorable episodes of the journey was associated with our "shortcut" under the Shï'olt Mountains, the largest, most imposing range on the planet; extending from pole to pole, the highest peaks stood well clear of the atmosphere. The Shï'olts were a much more formidable range than any I had encountered thus far; but even so, there was no doubt in my mind that, by resurrecting the ultrahigh-altitude modifications I had devised previously, I could have made the crossing myself.

Unfortunately, even the very lowest passes lay above Brünhilde's flight ceiling; and though I could have guided her through the necessary modifications to her tegument and respiratory system, the aerodynamic changes required to permit her to operate at those altitudes would have taken much too long—and walking was not one of her strongest suits. I'd have had to leave her behind, and the possibility never crossed my mind until later: Brünhilde was my friend.

The sight of the ramparts looming up ruggedly before us

promptly triggered my borrowed memories; and I "remembered" Bäa'ynpt, the great cavern-world which honeycombed virtually the entire Shi'olt range. However, one detail Meg's knowledge failed to include was the fact that many of Bäa'ynpt's entrances were guarded by the legendary *voor'-skags:* immense, winged evolutionary cousins of the *böll'skags.* The omission was significant. . . .

Streaming a thick contrail of black digestive smoke, the *voor'skag* rose to meet us as we descended toward the cavern mouth, an opening almost a mile high and at least three across.

Brünhilde spotted it first, as usual. Her initial reaction was a burst of thought so intense as to be all but untranslatable; but "*Cripes!*" summed up the emotional content nicely, and "Is this trip *really* necessary . . . ?" did much same for the substantive portion.

The monster was simply colossal! While the dictates of aerodynamic necessity meant that the beast was much more slender and lightly constructed (a good seventy percent was neck and tail), the *voor'skag* was easily three times the length of any *böll'skag* I'd ever seen. The forelimbs had evolved into batlike wings spanning better than a quarter mile. Intermediate and rear legs were atrophied to the point of near uselessness; obviously the thing did little walking. But of course it didn't have to; it soared through the air with an effortless grace which seemed out of place in something so huge.

For the first time since Brünhilde and I had joined forces, a trace of doubt crossed my mind as to the outcome of an encounter. However, it was evident from the moment the great flying snake hove into view that it was faster than we were. There was no point trying to outrun it; it would have to be dealt with. . . .

Asking "What do you suggest?" had become second nature for Brünhilde during our weeks together; so I was surprised when she took the initiative: "Bail out!" she thought, studying the onrushing behemoth intently. "I'll hold its attention; you burn it wherever it looks most vulnerable. Then I'll hit it while it's looking for you. We've got to keep it off balance. . . ."

I didn't argue. I had no idea where she might have gotten her information on how to fight *voor'skags*, but this struck me as an inopportune moment to inquire. Without hesitation, I disengaged the quick-release attachment, reeled the stub of the umbilicus into my chest, pulled myself out of the cockpit, and pushed off into Brünhilde's slipstream.

Once I was clear, the *voor'flön* wrenched into a climbing turn to the left; just as quickly, I headed off to the right. The *voor'skag's* challenge dislodged numerous boulders on the slopes behind it; then its wing-beat rate shifted into high and it bore down upon me—totally ignoring the much larger caloric content still climbing off to the right.

I blinked in surprise: This was hardly according to plan! But as the hundred-foot-long jaws gaped wide, I peeled off and power-dived at maximum out of harm's way; continuing well beyond the *voor'skag's* apparent immediate reach on the off chance that it shared with its surface–not—prowling cousins the ability to hurl flame. A toasty glow in the vicinity of my nether regions as I plunged downward confirmed the suspicion, but by then I was safely out of range.

Pulling out of the dive, I looked back to see where the monster was, and what Brünhilde might be up to. The *voor'skag* had given up on me now and was banking grandly to follow the *voor'flön's* turn. I heard her derisive "Gronk!" as it overshot by a full mile.

Of course—Brünhilde had known at first glimpse that nothing that size possibly could function effectively in close-quarters aerial combat. It was merely a question of staying out of its clutches—and avoiding getting roasted in the meantime—until we figured out how to bring the engagement to a close.

Brünhilde was in a steeply banked turn, her radius just inside that possible to the huge flame-breather at such speed. For the moment she was safe: The *voor'skag* was unable to close the gap, and she was out of range of its breath, though just barely. If it slowed, attempting to turn tighter, she would pull ahead; if it accelerated, trying to overtake her, she would tighten her turn.

I headed in their direction, climbing to get above them. Brünhilde saw me coming and broadcast a greeting. Her thoughts were somewhat hyper but unafraid. "It can't catch me as long as my strength holds out, Peter. But this is hard work; I don't know how long I can keep it up. I'll lead it past you. Try to damage it enough to slow it down. Then we can get away."

I eyeballed the curve they were following and stationed myself ahead of them and slightly above; and despite the fact that maintaining a *t'lLïSs 'mn* fully charged and combat-ready had become almost as automatic as breathing, gave it a precautionary once-over. (Wyatt Earp would have understood: He undoubtedly checked the chambers and worked the action of his six-shooter immediately prior to a confrontation no matter how many times he'd already done so that day.) I was using a fixed nozzle with a relatively large aperture, and it was evident from the torus' internal pressure that the charge was at peak.

As the *voor'flön* and her shadow headed back in my direction, I cranked up the magnification of my own eyeballs and studied our opponent, searching for weak points. I would have preferred to scan with Brünhilde's infinitely superior optical equipment, but she was too preoccupied to let me in without a physical connection. However, both were within four or five miles; I got a pretty good look at the *voor'skag's* construction as they closed on me—and found what I was looking for. . . .

While larger than my own to an almost preposterous degree, the *voor'skag's* wings were virtually identical (i.e., batlike): Enormously long, but essentially delicate, "fingers" supported a broad expanse of tough, flexible, lightweight flight membrane. Each finger was jointed in three places; the knuckles were visible as relatively tiny, barely perceptible swellings against the acres-broad membranous lifting surfaces.

Aligning my internal crosshairs on the first true phalangeal knuckle of the forward "finger" on the starboard side, I followed the wing's motion through several strokes to synchronize with the rhythm; then fired as an upstroke reached its zenith. The beam lanced out, a slender, dazzlingly blue-white shaft of incandescence which struck the knuckle edge-on, instantaneously punching through the thin, scaley hide covering the leading edge of the *voor'skag's* wing, and searing deeply into the cartilage which separated the articular surfaces of the enormous joint.

The *voor'skag* vomited a quarter-mile-long tongue of flame, and thundered in rage and pain, as the leading edge of its starboard wing, hinging at a point about midway out along the span, slowly folded upward and back over the top of the remaining structure. With death in its eyes, the *voor'skag* attempted to divert from Brünhilde toward me—but already it was losing altitude; it passed so far below me that not even its proverbial (not to mention literal) hot breath reached me.

I watched the *voor'skag's* descent. The landing was rough: The monster bounced and slid for a good half mile before stopping. However, it scrambled to its feet promptly, if ponderously, and issued a glowing condemnation of our ancestors and all their ancestors' ancestors. Then it fell silent, smoke rising from its nostrils, and regarded its damaged wing.

I didn't mention it to Brünhilde, but I decided at that point to make sure, once we got to La'ïr, that the Isi either healed the *voor'skag*'s wing or ended its suffering—I had the feeling that, despite the necessarily accelerated metabolism required to fuel the energy needs of an aerial species, it would take a long time for something that size to starve.

After so dramatic an overture, the actual passage through Bäa'ynpt under the Shï'olts Mountains proved downright anticlimactic: A day, and a mere seventeen aerial dogfights later (second-stringers, these, of no consequence), we exited through an unguarded portal and mounted back into the sky. . . .

Early one afternoon, no more than a week after besting the *voor'skag*, I began to detect a change in Brünhilde's behavior. The clues weren't obvious; reading *voor'flön* facial expressions is something of an acquired art, and I no longer had unlimited access to her thoughts.

(It had occurred to me, after she'd saved my skin for probably the tenth time, that maybe it was time to demonstrate some faith in our newfound friendship myself. The first step, of course, was restoring her privacy; with a little coaching, she learned to enclose those areas of her mind which she regarded as private with a set of mental shields as impervious as my own.)

Nonetheless, her customary damn-the-torpedoes, let's-do-it-and-deal-with-the-fallout-as-necessary attitude was conspicuously absent; replaced by an indefinable but almost palpable tension, which intensified by the hour.

Clearly something was amiss. However, it wasn't until Brünhilde flew past a small herd of *p'rRöf*, loping across a miles-wide veldt, completely exposed to "quitedive" attack, that I began to worry in earnest.

"Brünhilde," I began diffidently, "is something eating you?"

"What! *Where? GET IT OFF . . . !*"

Even after a month and a half of near-symbiotic partnership, I still committed occasional blunders along those lines. By now the *voor'flön* was thinking in English and/or Isi virtually one hundred percent of the time, but her interpretation of slang tended toward the strictly literal.

"No, no," I hastened to clarify. "I mean, I get the feeling that something is bothering you."

Brünhilde turned her head slightly and transfixed me with an unconvincingly belligerent, five-foot-in-diameter, red-and-yellow glare. With visibly forced nonchalance she responded, "Nonsense! What possibly could bother me . . . ?"

"At the moment I don't know," I retorted dryly. "But when I think back to a few of the things which seemed to at the time, my mouth gets dry, my palms get wet, and my blood clots *in situ*. Now, what's up? You don't seem to be yourself."

"How can your blood clot inside me?" the *voor'flön* snapped impatiently. "And who else would I be? I'm Brünhilde, the fearless, far-ranging—"

"*Voor'flön* who hasn't had a bite to eat in four hours, and who just failed to notice a herd of *p'rRö'f* out in the open," I finished helpfully.

"I just don't happen to be hungry," she replied, with the suggestion of a pout.

"Brünhilde, if I thought for one second that that might be true, the theological implications alone would trigger ventricular fibrillation. Now quit it, before you really scare me. Out with it—what's got you so worked up . . . ?"

The *voor'flön* blinked thoughtfully; the process occupied nearly fifteen seconds. "Well . . ." she began truculently, "if you must know, I've just recognized where we are. . . ."

"Don't stop now."

"You'll think me a coward. . . ."

"Brünhilde, if there is one single quality which I never have suspected you of lacking, and never will, it's courage. I, on the other hand, scare very easily—I would remind you of our relative sizes, strengths, speeds, and respective edibility. Now *what's the matter* . . . ?"

The *voor'flön* scanned the horizon uneasily, then sighed. "It's where we are," she thought confidentially. "It's this area. Things *happen* here. Bad things."

"What do you mean?" I asked, taken aback; a locale which a *voor'flön* regarded as hazardous—the concept positively boggled the imagination. "What's unsafe about it?"

"I don't know," Brünhilde continued uncomfortably. "All I know is that I've lost kin hereabouts."

"Who?"

"A brother, several hatches senior to me." The *voor'flön* paused to sweep the horizon again. "He disappeared right before my eyes."

"How?"

"I don't know how," she repeated uneasily. "All I know is that he'd just gotten up to quietdive speed, going after something on the ground, when *boom!*—there was a bright flash and a terribly loud noise, and he was gone. And no one has seen him since."

For long moments thereafter I was forced to devote all my energies to keeping my shields tight as, behind them, I celebrated a brief but satisfying bout of total hysteria: The phenomenon Brünhilde had just described matched perfectly the visible manifestations of the workings of the gigantic *wWr'dts* surrounding La'ïr—it couldn't have been anything else! Obviously her brother had rammed the barrier head-on at something in excess of mach one point five. And as rapidly as it absorbed it, the *wWr'dts* field had returned the multimegajoules of energy comprising his momentum as heat; the *voor'flön* had been vaporized instantly. Which meant that . . .

That I'd *made* it!—that, massed opinion of the flower of the Isi to the contrary, a brute-force-oriented, non*pwW'r*-using mechanist had crossed the wilds of Isis and lived to tell the tale!

I'd reached La'ïr . . . !

(Not that I was entitled to credit for the achievement; whatever qualities I possessed which made it possible were the result of the Isis' breeding program—they might not be much in a crisis, personally, but they sure knew their stuff when it came to breeding supermen.)

Oh, the hell with that—I *was there!* All that remained now was to inform the Isi of Meg's plight and, to the extent my limited talents might prove useful, assist in their efforts to rescue her—

Assuming, of course, against all logic, that I was in time for such efforts to have any meaning. . . .

If not, there still remained the matter of saving the galaxy from the approaching R'gGnrök. Intellectually—viewing the question in the cold, hard light of dispassionate logic—I knew this was the more important of my two objectives. As the only entity with any chance at all of saving the galaxy, and the countless myriad species populating it, from the "final devourer," the responsibility fell to me: I had no choice but to get on with the *wWyhr läaq* training which was to equip me with the knowledge and skills needed to accomplish that task. Meg

would want me to, regardless of her own fate; she'd made that
abundantly clear. And regardless of my feelings at that point, I
intended to do my damndest to see that her final wishes were
carried out

. . . But not *before making sure that the B'nN´äs'hï
responsible paid a penalty that would haunt its fellows for the
balance of this Cycle of Creation . . . !*

At about this point I became dimly aware of my surroundings once again. The sight of Brünhilde's worried expression
restored much of what I foist upon the universe as a rational
state of mind. At first I feared that my shields had been
leaking; that the *voor'flön* had been a witness to the entire
episode. Then it occurred to me that a more probable
explanation was that she expected a response and hadn't gotten
one.

On the point of replying, it suddenly occurred to me that
Brünhilde was in imminent danger of meeting a fate similar to
that which befell her brother: *WWr'dts* discriminate by *intent*,
screening out anyone or anything whose intentions are inimical to its occupants. Something would have to be done about
Brünhilde's tendency toward indiscriminate nibbling, and
promptly.

But first things first: The *wWr'dts* were not visible to the
unaided eye—if we encountered them at this speed . . .

"Brünhilde, slow down, *quick!*" I transmitted urgently. The
voor'flön's faith in my intentions and judgment had firmed over
the weeks until now she wasted no time demanding an
explanation; instantly the brakes went on at maximum. Ten
seconds later we had slowed to barely a hundred miles an
hour, and the *voor'flön* was regarding me with an expression in
which the concern was even more pronounced.

"What for?" she inquired cautiously, casting yet another
glance around the horizon.

In the past few weeks I had gotten considerable practice at
arguing *voor'flön* logic; indications were that I was getting
fairly good at it. Now, however, the acid test was upon me.

I took a deep breath, formed a mental image of Meg in
Brünhilde's mind, and asked, "Have you seen anything like
this before?"

"No, I haven't," the *voor'flön* replied, examining the picture
attentively. "Looks tasty, though."

Ignoring the faint red mist which floated briefly before my

eyes, I responded grimly: "That's probably what your brother was thinking just before he disappeared!"

Brünhilde's eyes snapped wide. Suspicion course darkly across the texture of her thoughts. "What do *you* know about my brother's disappearance . . . ?" she demanded.

"I know a lot of things you don't," I retorted. "Knowing things is my chief contribution to this partnership, remember? And uppermost in my knowledge at this moment is the certainty that, if you continue to regard creatures like this"—I flashed the picture of Meg again—"as food, you're going to disappear in a flash yourself, sooner or later. It's only a matter of time. . . ."

Brünhilde regarded me in silence. "You've been keeping secrets, Peter," she thought presently.

"I have *not* been keeping secrets," I protested indignantly. "The subject hasn't come up until now because it wasn't necessary until now. Have I ever held back anything you needed to know . . . ?"

There was another contemplative silence. "How would I know?" replied the *voor'flön* at length. "Except for when and where you choose to open them, I can't see into your thoughts. And in the time we've been together, I've been given no hint that such creatures even existed. What are they and where do they come from?"

No. . . . Was it possible? Could I have spent almost two months with the giant carnivore without ever having thought about Meg and the Isi while *en rapport* with her? Quickly I thought back over our relationship, and was forced to conclude that probably it was. We'd been so busy dealing with the present that I hadn't had time or energy to brief her about my past.

"In fact," Brünhilde continued reflectively, "I don't know anything about your background before we met—and, come to think of it, I've ever seen anything like *you* before, either. Exactly what are you and where do you come from?"

"That's not important now," I began—only to be cut off:

"Says who?" the *voor'flön* interrupted tartly. "I thought you weren't keeping secrets. . . ."

"I'm not!" I snapped impatiently. "And it's *not* important now!" It wasn't; the critical thing was to reorient Brünhilde's thinking before she encountered the *wWr'dts*. "Just as soon as we clear up the question of the status of these"—I gave her another look at Meg—"'human beings,' as they're called, I'll tell you my entire life story, down to the tiniest, most boring detail, if you like, I swear.

"But first," I continued urgently, "it's absolutely vital that you accept as fact the premise that human beings are not food. They're . . ." I groped frantically for a moment. "They're my *kin*," I finished with an inspired rush.

"All of them . . . ?"

"*All* of them."

"Not food . . . ?"

"Not food," I reemphasized. "They're not even to be *thought* of as food. They're my kin. And since you and I are friends, my kin are your friends, too.

"But, Brünhilde," I added grimly, "unless you agree, and mean it, and *show* me that you mean it, our partnership ends right here and now. I'll go on without you, and you can head back toward your own territory. I am *not* going to risk having you strike that barrier in your present state of mind."

A slight glazing of the eyes was the only outward sign of the struggle taking place within the *voor'flön's* feral little soul; but as instincts rooted in the origin of her species warred with newly discovered capacities for abstract reasoning, her thoughts and emotions churned.

Actually, after nearly eight months in the Isi bush, I could empathize: Humans were indeed smooth and warm and visibly tender, and in general quite tasty-loo—

Oops, that was no way to set an example. I think that's what they call "going native." (Much more of it, and I probably wouldn't make it through the *wWr'dts* myself.)

Fortunately Brünhilde was too wrapped up in her own dilemma to have noticed. I wondered how she would resolve the conflict—in fact, as the minutes ticked by, I began to question whether she could, and started polishing additional arguments calculated to help her over the conceptual hump.

I was just on the point of jumping back into the discussion with both feet when the *voor'flön* abruptly surfaced from the depths of her introspection, shields down, her every thought visible and aglow with an uncharacteristic tenderness. "Peter, you are my partner," she stated unequivocally. "I don't want to lose you. Your kin are my friends. I will not harm them. . . ."

The relief which cascaded through me at that point caught me by surprise. I knew that I was quite fond of the giant predator, but I hadn't realized the depth of my feelings for her. Of course, if she'd forced me to, I would have proceeded on

to La'ïr without her (I'd have had no choice; I had responsibilities), but I had found the prospect unexpectedly wrench-
ing—dammit, Brünhilde was my *partner* . . . !

TO: Project Director/Monitor's Log.
FROM: T'fFelteshezr, Tenth Order;
        First among the Council of Elders.
SUBJECT: Project *Extremis* Termination.
    He comes. All is in readiness to the degree possible.
    In accordance with the recommendations of the fused minds
of the compudicters, Megonthalyä has been removed from
stasis and conditioned further. Memphus, her *fmMl'hr*, has
agreed to cooperate.
    We of the Council will be on hand personally and, so it
would seem, will the entire population of this planet, whether
off-duty or not. I wonder who will be minding the store.
    Now we wait. . . .

CHAPTER 32

The stir generated by Brünhilde's appearance over La'ïr might
have been approximated on Earth by the spontaneous appearance at a Joint Session of Congress of a large, radioactive,
loudly ticking box, labeled in Libian script, "Fragile, do not
drop." The presence of a *voor'flön* within the *wWr'dts* was
without precedent. Everyone had turned out to watch—and
perhaps to help cope, if coping should prove indicated.
    I judged it prudent to descend alone initially, leaving
Brünhilde orbiting high above the village which constituted
the *de facto* capital of the small Isi-inhabited region. While the
good-hearted earnestness which characterized the *voor'flön*
was readily apparent to me by now, it seemed a lot to ask that
strangers, inculcated over the ages in conventional Isi environmental wisdom, be equally perceptive on such short notice. A
prior explanation might avert a potentially cataclysmic mis-
understanding.
    Slipping from my cockpit between her scapulae, I crawled
forward to peer down over her left-side leading edge. With my
own eyesight I could just make out the multitudes of dots
scurrying to congregate in the middle of a large, centrally
located clearing.

"This is my stop, driver," I thought, unfurling my wings and preparing to step off into space. Brünhilde angled a lugubrious eye back at me, winked, and rolled neatly out from under me. With a chuckle, I extended my wings and trimmed into a spiral glide—

And suddenly found it necessary to devote serious attention to the task of composing myself. Because, despite my very best efforts, and firm intentions to the contrary, I found that I was getting into quite a state. It was growing more difficult by the second to maintain the barriers which I'd erected around my memories of the emotions I'd shared with Meg. They were beginning to leak through: memories of Meg happy, Meg pensive; Meg laughing, grinning, smiling, in repose—and her expression as the B'nN´äs'hï snatched her from our universe. . . .

Likewise, I was having difficulty keeping a lid on my panic over her probable fate. All the standard Damsel-In-Distress tableaux kept flashing through my mind: dozens of different forms of torture, rape, and death—none of which made the least bit of sense—what *possible* use could a B'nN´äs'hï have for a fundamentally human woman . . . ?

In an effort to derail what rapidly was becoming mounting hysteria, I focused my attention toward the ground coming up, on the people below. These were the Isi, Meg's people. I'd probably have guessed that even in another setting; the resemblance they bore to my own little *wWyh'j* was unmistakable: All were small, close to tiny by Earthly standards; and slender, almost slight. All were physically youthful, though the bearing and manner of many belied their appearances. And, of course, all possessed those distinctive, faintly "elflike" facial characteristics: the high cheekbones; the huge, slightly slanted eyes; the delicately pointed ears.

Like the proverbial moth to the flame, my attention was drawn to the women. It had been quite a while since I'd seen a woman; my attention quickly turned into an intensive study (the word "leer" would not be completely inappropriate). All were slender by my pre-Meg standards; but, without exception, each and every one was absolutely beautiful. All the shades of the feminine spectrum were present: Skin tones ranged from a rich, lustrous brown (almost ebony) to the purest, most translucent Nordic cream; hair colors encompassed every variation from glossy jet through redhead to blonde.

Blonde . . . ?

My eyes snapped wide. There, in the midst of the gathering, was a breathtakingly lovely little blonde who, but for a fanny-length, glowing golden mane, looked a lot like . . .

"*Meg* . . . !" I bellowed. She'd escaped!—*she was alive!*

Any pretense of dignified descent vanished. I folded my wings and plummeted from the sky like a stone, my heart hammering, the blood pounding in my head, my breath coming in sobs, calling at the top of my lungs, "Meg! I'm here, Meg . . . !"

I suppose if I hadn't been so utterly, deliriously happy, I might have noticed at that point that nobody responded to my call; that no one—not even Meg—so much as waved back. If I'd thought about that, I might have started wondering then. However, I was too far gone to pick up on extraneous details— hell's bells, after all this time *I was looking at Meg!*

In any event, a moment later I was braking hard for landing. Thudding recklessly to the ground with enough residual momentum to drive me momentarily to all fours, I sprang erect immediately and enveloped her in both pairs of arms. And as I crushed Meg's tiny form ecstatically to me, my happiness was nearly complete.

Her sudden screams and struggle to escape took me completely by surprise. And then, mere fractions of a second later, even before I could investigate, I was downright flabbergasted to find myself sailing end-over-end through the air, and then bouncing and rolling along the ground, my ears ringing from the concussion which accompanied the burst of $mMj'q$-based force responsible.

I skidded to a stop probably a hundred feet away and climbed unsteadily to my feet; all four of them, to provide a secure base from which to combat the sudden touch of vertigo I'd acquired en route.

Quite nonplussed, I turned back to Meg—gasped: She had gone pale; she had practically collapsed into the arms of those around her! *Something was wrong with my Meg . . . !*

With a worried exclamation I bounded forward—only to be blasted back again. . . .

This time I remained where I landed—considerably dizzier now, and conscious of a few new sore places here and there beneath my armor. I studied the scene before me and absently scratched an itch in the vicinity of the base of one ear with the longest point of the mace at the tip of my tail.

Meg wrenched free of her fellows. Drawing herself erect, she glared at me with an expression in which revulsion and offended outrage contended for dominance.

I couldn't believe my eyes. Assembling what remained of my wits, I launched them at her: "Meg," I transmitted, "what's the matter? What's going on?"

Ten feet from her my thought probe struck a set of shields which made mine feel like so much gauze. There was no response and her expression never wavered. Even calling her name aloud evoked no hint of recognition; though, oddly enough, it did elicit a generalized wince from those assembled.

At about this point it occurred to me that none of this was on the schedule; that the ecstatic greeting which I had expected from the Isi (never mind the fantasies I'd concocted based on how glad Meg would be to see me again) was noticeably absent; that, in fact, to someone less well acquainted with the facts, it could appear that Meg was rejecting me.

Obviously something was amiss. Perhaps even seriously so. I wracked my brain, trying to come up with an explanation.

And suddenly, with a clearly perceptible click, a number of heretofore unrelated facts, details, and events fell into place. The pattern they formed was a very nasty one indeed!

First: the $mMj'q$-based viewing devices which Meg had mentioned, which enabled the Isi to observe anything, anywhere. . . .

Second: Meg's inexplicable "kidnapping" by an extrauniversal being—a member of a species known to be one of the very most trustworthy of the Isis' allies—with the ship restored to full inertia, vulnerable to collision, and committed to entry into the Zone of Moons. . . .

Third: The "accidental" side effects of the massive flare of $mMj'q$ which Meg had evoked just as she disappeared, which had erased my inertial-guidance software, forcing me to hand-fly though the Zone. . . .

Fourth: Said side effects' simultaneous elimination of the extrauniversal storage capacity of my fuel tanks, leaving me four whole minutes of fuel with which to navigate through the planet's grindingly complex satellite system and attempt atmospheric entry. . . .

And now—fifth—undisguised rejection after I fought my way across the length and breadth of her hellish planet to save her—by the very same Megonthalyä who, according to my most recent information, should have been at least a prisoner in another universe, if not actually dead. . . .

For a moment I had difficulty fitting into the matrix the fact that the bike had retained its various $mMj'q$-based enhancements, and had come through the crash of *Galactic Venture* intact. But the bafflement was fleeting—after a moment's thought, the final piece fell into place.

Of course. How subtle. . . .

By preserving the bike, the Isi had made it possible for me to expose myself to the horrors of the planet's incredibly feral environment at a brisker pace than I could have managed on foot. After all, it wouldn't do to let the floor show drag, now would it . . . !

At last I understood: I'd been *had*! And on a scale unrivaled in all my experience—yes, on a truly galactic scale.

No galactic doom impended! It was all a *lie* . . . !

All, that is, except for the fact that the Isi were an immensely old race. . . .

They were, indeed—an immensely old and enormously *bored* race.

The arena always has been popular with bored peoples— witness the entertainments favored by the ancient Greeks and Romans, and the sadism widely practiced by present-day dog-, bull-, and cockpit proprietors the world over for the amusement of degenerates, even in so-called civilized countries. The Isi employed the entire galaxy as an arena—and especially their frightful planet!

Which conclusion brought me inevitably to the final crushing realization: Whether she was a coldly calculating, thoroughly professional "talent scout," regularly dispatched to round up fresh blood, ready and willing to do anything necessary to achieve her goal, or perhaps merely a thrill-seeking, decadent amateur, hoping to find temporary relief from terminal ennui in danger and/or primitive alien sexual perversions, mattered little in the end; the bottom line was obvious—*Meg never loved me . . . !*

Her role in the scheme was equally apparent; as was the probability that she was only one of a host of "recruiters" comprising the Isis' press gang.

The mechanics of the operation were self-evident: The Isi used their viewers first to scan the humanoid-inhabited worlds within range, looking for physically sound, usefully intelligent specimens, whose demonstrated spirit and resourcefulness suggested that they'd be likely to give a good account of themselves.

It was even possible that a grain of truth lay behind Meg's claim that they'd indulged in a long-distance breeding program involving Mankind—though however many planets might be involved, the purpose obviously would have been to breed gladiators, not galactic saviors.

Once a promising candidate was selected, and with the audience following by means of their viewers, one of Meg's cohorts was dispatched to stalk, hook, and reel him in, using whatever bait he (or she, for that matter) seemed most responsive to. In my case, of course, it was an appeal targeted at my overdeveloped do-gooder instincts, combined with (figuratively speaking) blowing in my ear.

At the proper moment (no doubt earlier, if genuine physical danger materialized—after all, I had only Meg's word to support the proposition that they couldn't return to Isis without my help!), one of those good ole reliable B'nN' äs'hï could be counted upon to retrieve the recruiter; who, in the final seconds, would take whatever steps might prove necessary to ensure that the victim wound up stranded in the wilds on the wrong side of Isis, surrounded by every opportunity to wind up dead.

In their efforts to combat what must have become a monumental problem with boredom, the Isi had achieved the ultimate "live" entertainment: The life-and-death struggles of real people against an endless variety of insurmountable odds must have been diverting fare for the jaded immortals.

Briefly, inanely, I wondered how I'd done in the ratings—it would be humiliating to learn that I'd gone to all that trouble only to be a flop. But as I thought back to the events which had led me to this point, I felt confident that I'd provided an adequate level of amusement just in getting us to Isis, let alone thereafter, as I carved a bloody trail across the planet.

Then, for still another moment, I found myself grudgingly admiring Meg's workmanship: Never, even during our most intimate moments, had I picked up so much as a hint that our rapport was anything less than the wide-open, totally unreserved merging of souls which it was purported to be.

I couldn't have begun to do that: Not even during those first hours of my relationship with Brünhilde, as unsophisticated as she was at that point, could I have withheld facts without locking them behind readily apparent shields. And as for outright *lying*, mind-to-mind—I couldn't conceive of an intellect capable of deception *en rapport* without betraying the truth in a thousand stray peripheral thoughts, let alone spinning so elaborate a complex of falsehoods as Meg's "Save-the-Galaxy" scenario required. . . .

In fact, from what I knew by now of the mechanics of telepathy, I'd have sworn it was impossible. . . .

Dammit, it *was* impossible!

So what did that leave . . . ?

Of *course*! Call it hypnotism, brainwashing, conditioning—whatever! No wonder nothing showed! Obviously the Isi programmed their agents before sending them out: They would have equipped them with a set of shields, unbeknownst to the operator's own consciousness and therefore indetectable even to the mindlinked observer, behind which lurked the truth; and installed a bogus matrix of "facts" for the victim's benefit. At the time, Meg herself undoubtedly believed what she was telling me—

Wait. That no more excused her participation in this affair than intoxication excuses the reckless and/or negligent conduct of a drunken driver. I judged it highly unlikely that programming in such depth could have been established without cooperation. Almost surely she was a willing volunteer; she knew what they intended for her—and for me—before she submitted to the programming.

Further, the fact that, even today, here and now, face-to-face, she was making no attempt to deny her involvement in the scheme, or to condemn it for the patently barbarous cruelty that it was, surely amounted to an unspoken endorsement both of her people's goals and their methods.

Suddenly, if belatedly, it occurred to me that, having made it finally to La'ïr, having played out my rôle in their little drama, my continuing existence probably equated to obsolete inventory: I constituted a loose end; my usefulness was over. (And it seemed highly unlikely that a people accustomed to practicing this sort of "morality" had heard of, or would have any use for, the time-honored tradition [at least among the Warhoons of Barsoom] of granting freedom to the final victor of the Great Games.)

I was as good as dead. . . .

It was approximately at this point that I noticed the ground beginning to tremble underfoot. Absently casting about for the source, I detected a heavy subsonic rumble, whose volume continued to mount even as I wondered where it might be coming from.

The discovery that the sound emitted from my own throat came as a shock. But then I noticed that my body had begun to work and ripple, with creaking, snapping, popping, crackling noises. My tail lashed. My claws emerged of their own volition. Venom beaded at the tip of both the horn jutting from between my brows and the sting affixed to the mace at the end of my tail.

From the vantage of the remote corner of my mind which seemed to constitute my crisis command center, "I" observed these escalating developments with a curiously icy detachment, as if they were happening to someone else. After dispassionately noting the signs and deliberating briefly, I concluded that the only reason someone would manifest such phenomena would be if he were in the grip of a great, consuming anger; perhaps even an uncontrollable rage. Was I really that angry . . . ?

Well, for the love of a woman and in the spirit of altruism I'd left a life of success and luxury to travel thirty thousand lightyears across the galaxy, and had no way to get back. For her, and to save the galaxy, I'd fought my way halfway around the most hostile planet in the universe—

Only to learn that, not only was the galaxy *not* in jeopardy, and not only did Meg *not* love me—but that she'd personally snookered me into this mess with malice aforethought, doubtless was laughing at me over it, and, just incidentally, death at her hands, or those of her fellows, was surely only minutes away, and it appeared that I was powerless to do a thing about it.

Yeah. I *was* that angry.

On the other hand, it dawned on me, maybe I wasn't *completely* powerless to do anything about it. Death was almost a certainty in any event, of course: There was no point in even speculating about escape; with their power, the Isi could track me down and blot me out anywhere on the planet. In fact, I mused, it was amazing that they'd allowed me get this far. . . .

No; on second thought, I understood: The temptation to gloat is one of the more addictive vices. It's much more satisfying to let your victim discover for himself the extent to which he's been hung out to dry before pulling the plug. And the most delicious satisfaction of all, of course, is to be there, watching, when he does so.

However, the most successful (i.e., least frequently apprehended) con artists understand that trap, and avoid it like the plague. The Isi, whether through failure to understand the inherent risk, or a deliberate, arrogant decision to ignore it, hadn't. And maybe—just *maybe*—I might be able to take advantage of that carelessness; I might be able to make my closing performance on Isis long-remembered indeed, not only due to my success in winning through to La'ïr, despite the odds—but because of the cost. . . .

Yeah. I was *that* angry.

But now it was a conscious, focused anger. I knew that the outcome was a foregone conclusion: It was most unlikely that I'd be allowed to account for many (if any) Isi before they finished me; and certainly I wouldn't have a chance to get at any of the ringleaders. However, my interest was very specific and implacably Old-Testimentarianish: Meg . . .

She represented all that the Isi had done to me. I could die happy if only I could reach her first. In particular, I wanted to crack her shields; to get into her mind; to let her know precisely what I thought of her and her kind. It was distinctly possible that so concentrated a burst of rage/contempt/loathing could prove lethal all by itself.

However, even if she survived, no matter how long she managed to live thereafter, neither Meg nor all the Isis therapists who ever lived, regardless how skilled, would be able to cleanse such a scourging from her soul. I'd have the satisfaction of knowing that, regardless of her fundamental lack of morality and compassion, my opinion of her, from the perspective of my own values, would be burned forever into her psyche: For the rest of her life she would have not only a conscience—but a very, very troublesome one.

Of course I also wanted to get my hands on her. And teeth. And claws. . . .

With luck, the Isi might find it more difficult in the future to find volunteers for their recruiting squads.

For the briefest moment I regretted having dragged Brünhilde into this mess; once the Isi turned their attention to her, she wouldn't have a chance. But there wasn't anything I could do about that now; the best I could hope for was to avenge her in advance. I put her out of my mind, more fully to devote my attention to the matters at hand.

The violence of my explosion startled even me: A shaft of dazzlingly blue-glowing electrons blazed out (I wasn't even conscious of aiming); three feet above the ground, it traversed horizontally probably twenty degrees, and should have cut half the populace off at the waist.

Simultaneously, putting every ounce of strength I possessed into the bound, and adding the thrust of my wings to that of my legs, I catapulted forward. Squinting against the fiercely actinic glare in the fractions of a second it took me to cross the intervening distance, I saw the bolt strike—and then watched it rave blindingly along the immaterial surface of *something* (not the *wWr'dts*; they wouldn't have affected raw electricity) which suddenly had come into being ten feet in front of the nearest Isi. Almost unanimously the adepts flinched back before realizing that their defenses were holding; that the beam was splashing harmlessly, if dramatically, off their barrier.

But even before the Isi could react to the energy lance which constituted the first blow of my attack, I arrived personally. Feet first, claws deployed, I struck the unexpected obstacle.

I felt nothing; the barrier was as impalpable as it was invisible. Nonetheless, I slowed quickly, if progressively, to a stop; then slid down the face of the shield, dropping to the ground barely eight feet from Meg, glaring into her round, frightened eyes.

Quickly digging the talons of all four legs into the turf for purchase, I put my head down, leaned into the gently insistent resistance, and drove ahead, step by step.

But likewise step by step, the resistance increased by logarithmic increments until, with my reaching fingertips only inches from Meg's shrinking form, with faintly orange-glowing auras surrounding the point of each claw as the energy comprising the Isis' field intensified in response to the near-Berserker-level strength which I possessed at that moment, I found myself unable to progress further.

Roaring in frustrated rage, I strained to advance: The turf beneath my feet shredded as my talons sought traction. A cloud of torn-up grass, sand, and dust particles raised by my furiously driving wings billowed a hundred yards behind me.

All in vain: Try as I might, I could not gain so much as another fraction of an inch in Meg's direction. My wrath mounted—I *had* to reach her. . . .

Furiously I assembled, aimed, and launched a mental probe the likes of which I'd never thought myself capable—only to watch it flatten impotently against shields so unyielding and solidly braced that I scarcely could believe that one small *wWyh'j* could be the source of them.

Then it no longer was possible to avoid facing the truth: I couldn't reach her; not physically, not mentally—Meg would emerge from this encounter as doubtless · she had from countless others: untouched.

Worse, I could tell that she knew it. Her initially strained expression smoothed. She smiled, assurance returning.

Then her eyes hardened. She lifted a hand; she made a complicated gesture. *Something*—roughly spherical, glowing with a cold, greenish inner light—materialized in the air above her palm. She drew back her arm. . . .

Motivated now by an anger beyond endurance or control, I cast about, straining mentally, physically, and even spiritually, for a solution—*any* solution!—some means of scoring at least one telling blow against these damnable ghouls; some way to give them something to remember me by, before they loosed their powers . . . !

And as I strained ragingly, somehow in every direction at once, I felt, deep in my soul, a sudden indescribably poignant sensation, almost as if something had *torn*—

Abruptly the air around me was filled with surging, incredibly fast-moving, ever-shifting currents—currents of *something* so intensely concentrated that I wondered how I could have failed to notice them before; currents which resembled, to a very slight degree, the flow of atmospheric static which I was accustomed to manipulating. Equally suddenly, I found that now I could perceive the structure of the barrier which had frustrated me: an impervious yet flexible immaterial bubble which enclosed the Isi on all sides.

Effortlessly I reached out with my mind and embraced the flow. Its feel was both soothing and exhilarating; somehow imparting confidence and conveying a suggestion of virtually limitless power.

With a thrill of grim satisfaction, I realized that at least part of Meg's cover story had been true (which made sense; the fewer the falsehoods, the more reliable the programmed memories—simplicity *is* the mother of reliability): The Isi's discovery of the *pwW'r* really had grown out of desperation.

But I was an Earthman; my most fundamental reactions were different from those of an Isi: Ultimately I don't despair— *I get mad!*

They should have killed me out in the wilds, without warning, while they had the chance. Because now, by allowing me progressively to discover how easily I had been manipulated, and ultimately how hopeless my position was, they had succeeded in driving me to a level of rage which served to trigger my own discovery—I had found the $k\ddot{\imath}$ to the $pwW'r$ . . . !

Cataloging the implications of this development, and juggling its various possible applications to the problem on hand, occupied mere fractions of a second. I couldn't see much likelihood that the bottom line had changed: There was a whole planet-full of Isi and only one of me; they possessed milleniums of experience in manipulating the $mMj'q$ flow, while I had only just stumbled over the $k\ddot{\imath}$. Eventually, inevitably, they had to triumph. But now it was going to be a *lot* more costly. . . .

The mechanics of the operation, of course, were mental; but I always have had this weakness for cheap theatrics: I stood erect and reached out with the index finger of my right hand. Meg, arm drawn back to throw, hesitated, watching, as curiosity got the better of her.

Extending the talon, I punctured the screen at a point about eight feet up. Then, with a single swift movement, I slit the barrier to the ground, stepped through, and seized Meg with both forelegs. With one hand I grabbed the miniature energy-implosion field which she had planned to use on me and flipped it back into the crowd, where it detonated, causing a gratifying commotion.

With the other hand I took Meg by the neck. Needle-pointed talons extended and dimpling the soft skin of her throat, ready to tear it out of the first hostile move, I whirled to face the balance of the Isi, who stood rooted to the spot, watching in dumbfounded silence. Only now were some apparently beginning to comprehend the fact that their erstwhile victim now possessed a measure of control over the $pwW'r$—and no longer was on the defensive. . . .

I'd already learned that I couldn't pierce Meg's mental shields—but telepathy wasn't the only way to reach her mind. She was a lot smaller than Brünhilde; physical invasion shouldn't take more than a couple of minutes. I judged that I ought to be able to hold them off that long.

Meg's face went gray as the umbilicus emerged from my chest and extended toward her. Immediately I perceived a massive flux of $mMj'q$ particles converging toward us. Instinctively I blanketed her shields with my own mind, probing and digging for the slightest opening. She was forced to abandon the effort to control the $mMj'q$ flow; she knew that if she opened even the tiniest crack in her defenses to reach it, I'd have been inside in a flash and running amok.

Turning Meg around, I tightened my forelegs' grip about her tiny body, pressing her back rigidly against my front; then used my arms to twist her head face-forward, exposing the back of her neck. Inclining her head forward, driving her chin down almost to her chest, I forced her cervical spine into full forward flexion, which opened the intervertebral spaces more widely at the rear. Meg shuddered and stiffened as the tip of my umbilicus touched the back of her neck. . . .

"*STOP . . . !*"

The thought resonated inside my head like thunder; freighted with such unquestionable authority and self-assurance that, inadvertently, I actually did stop.

I looked around quickly for the source. A small group of Isi detached themselves from the mob and strode forward. They stopped a couple paces back and regarded me with a warm approval which seemed distinctly at odds with the situation.

"Truly, youth," began the leader verbally, without preamble—*and in English!*—"in fashioning your qualities, we enjoyed almost too much success. For a time we feared that you never would achieve your own discovery of the $k\ddot{i}$. The harder we worked to bring you to the appropriate level of despair, the more determined you became not to give up. It never occurred to us to seek your threshold in rage."

He glanced around at his companions; then said, "Now."

The sensation, while entirely mental, bore a cousinly resemblance to the feeling attendant having someone yank a chair from under you as you sit down: Completely without warning, those incredibly resistant shields, at which I had been boring nonstop, vanished. Suddenly I found myself inside Meg's mind, staring in complete amazement at the contents. . . .

Nowhere was there a hint of malice directed toward me—nowhere, in fact, was there the slightest awareness of me. Meg's mind contained no sign that she'd ever met or known of me, or even that I was present then. Occupying most of her attention at that moment was a concern for her own safety and that of her people: Apparently some hitherto-unknown mon-

strosity from beyond the *wWr'dts* had gained a degree of
control over the *pwW'r*, found its way past them into Laïr, and
posed a real threat.

I glanced at the picture in her mind and had to agree: So
frightful-looking a beastie certainly would have gotten my
attention; the winged, horned monster positively bristled with
teeth and claws and spines and scales and . . .

I was given barely time to register a momentary doubt, a
feeling that something about the creature's appearance stirred
vague memories, when the foremost Isi again said, "Now."

Meg blinked. I suspect that I did, too. Memories cascaded
in on us from all sides as Meg's internal mental blocks, which I
hadn't perceived until that moment, dissolved—

Abruptly she *knew* me . . . !

Within the double circle of my suddenly limp arms and
forelegs she spun to face me. "Peter!" she breathed, incredul-
ously looking me up and down, "is that *you* . . . ?"

"Of course it's me," I snarled. "Who else would it . . ."

For a moment she stared up at me, round-eyed, and open-
mouthed. Then, abruptly, inexplicably, a giggle was born in
the depths of her soul; it ballooned upward and outward until
it exploded as a burst of almost hysterical laughter.

"Oh, Peter . . ." she gasped, streaming tears, "you actually
don't know—you've *forgotten what you look like* . . ."

Oh. Yeah. So I had.

EPILOGUE

It was an awfully nice party. It took place out in the clearing
under the myriad stars and multiple moons so Brünhilde could
attend, too. Everyone assocated with Project *Extremis* was
there, as well as their families. I was made to feel very much at
home; and, despite the fact that her presence triggered an
instinctive response in every Isi similar to that produced by
Fafnir (and for the same reasons), so was Brünhilde.

I got to meet Meg's family and Meg got to meet Brünhilde
(the *voor'flön* had accepted my new appearance with equanim-
ity [nothing I did surprised her anymore] after T'fFelteshezr
and the rest of the Council, in the space of barely ten minutes,
helped me to restore my natural form).

There was lots to eat and drink (Isi drinks don't rely upon

alcohol to make you feel good; they gently stimulate the "mellow center" directly), and several brief speeches expressing welcome, congratulations, and amazement were offered. (Apart from everything else, my discovery that *voor'flöns*, as a species, might be sapient [so far the only evidence we had was Brünhilde] had opened still another unprecedented area of exploration: What about *böll'skags* and the other major predators?)

Apologies, explanations, and technical talk gradually deteriorated into a round of contentedly silly that-reminds-me's, which eventually wound down as the Isi, their society unencumbered by restrictions on how many of each constituted a relationship, drifted off to bed by twos, threes, sevens, or whatever.

Finally Meg and I found ourselves alone (effectively so anyway: Brünhilde had fallen asleep, and Memphus was curled up on her shoulder [the two had hit it off immediately]). With Meg's head on my shoulder and my arms tight around her, we snuggled close, and I reveled in the joy of having her back again.

To Meg, of course, virtually no time had elapsed since she had seen me last: The B'nN´äs'hï had placed her in stasis instantly, and her intact memories had not surfaced until my tantrum. However, she evinced no reluctance when I proposed making up for lost time.

And she was absolutely correct: A sky full of moons is romantic indeed.

Much later we lay, arms about each other, staring dreamily into the sky, musing about the future. Meg could hardly wait to get me into *wWyhr läaq* training. . . .

"You'll be an absolutely terrific *wWyhr läaq*, Peter," she breathed warmly in my ear. "And with your brains, determination, and Earthman's way of looking at things, I just know that you'll find some way to save us from R'gGnrök!"

In all modesty, I had to agree. Things were coming into focus now: I was a problem-solver by trade; the question of how to halt Armageddon, albeit challenging, was just one more problem awaiting my attention.

I've always been a quick study; no doubt I'd be an "A" student in *wWyhr läaq* training as well, achieving Tenth Order in record time. And at that point, of course, my Earth-born and -raised mechanist's perspective unquestionably could be counted upon to shed new light upon the problem. Added to which, the awesome capabilities of the massed Isis' control of the *pwW'r* were mine to command, together with the technological might of Earth.

And if all that weren't enough, the woman I loved lay warm in my arms—

Shucks, with all that going for me, what could *possibly* go wrong . . . ?

GLOSSARY OF TERMS

Bäa'ynpt —a vast system of interconnecting caverns underlying the Shï'olt Mountains, through which the intrepid may shortcut from one side of the range to the other.

b'jnNöllq'fing —Isis' equivalent of Earth's preying mantis—adults ranging up to fifty feet in length.

B'nN´äs'hï —one of the more reliable and trustworthy of the Isis' extrauniversal allies in their practice of the *pwW'r;* given to (and notable for) ghastly, haunting, wailing screams.

böll'fing —a van-sized exoskeletal predator resembling an Earthly stag beetle.

böll'skag —a six-legged, combustion-digestion, Isi predator growing up to two hundred yards in length.

b'vVec'h —extremely large, mushroomlike fungi occurring in the lowlands.

b'vVet'h —a mosslike ground cover occurring in *t'göllq´gn* forests.

däal'fön —an Isi predator resembling the results of crossing a German shepherd with a Kodiak bear; black, with heavy fur; about six feet at the shoulder; nomads, living in packs numbering in the thousands; methodical, efficient hunters.

Däa'mn —an inhabitant of Häa'l.

fäap'fing —Isis' equivalent to Earth's dragonfly— twenty feet long, occurring in huge, ravenous swarms.

fmMl'hr   —an extrauniversal Isi technical assistant.

gäajh'fing   —a web-dwelling, arboreal variation of the *väarz'fing;* substantially larger and more voracious.

The Gḡäar´m   —an extrauniversal *really* Bad Thing.

gnNäa'q   —a talent, or knack; often ESP-based, usually relating to an adept's practice of the *pwW'r*.

Häa'l   —the home universe of the Däa'mn.

Isis   —home world of the Isi, a pixyish-looking race of humanoids whose science is the *pwW'r*, and who find the workings of much of what Earthmen regard as physics completely incomprehensible.

ki   —the key to the manipulation of the *mMj'q* flow.

krRy'fön   —a warm-blooded predator whose twelve short legs provide a speed and endurance capable of outrunning almost anything on the planet.

La'ïr   —the largest community in the tiny section of their planet which the Isi inhabit.

lsS'b   —a wood-boring, grublike species living within the trunks of *t'göllq´gn* and *t'gyt'n*.

mMj'q   —an extrauniversal particle, twelve magnitudes smaller than a tachyon, manipulation of which forms the basis of the *pwW'r*.

nNäa'l   —an Isi time measure.

nNby'q   —a small, multilegged, blue-pelted, delicious Isi rodent analogous to Earth's prairie dog, which, through evolution, has come to resemble closely *t'göe'tl*, a highly toxic plant.

p'rRö'f   —a smaller, multilegged, antelopelike Isi ruminant; intensively hunted by most predators; generally considered to have the keenest senses of hearing and scent of any species on the planet, and *very* fast.

pwW'r   —the Isis' science, based on manipulation of the *mMj'q* flow.

R'gGnrök   —a nonmaterial, energy-consuming entity occupying a volume of space roughly equal to that of the Andromeda Galaxy, discovered by the Isi to have consumed numerous galaxies in the past, and now approaching the Milky Way.

Shï'olt Mountains   —the largest range on Isis; running from pole to pole; the highest peaks of which project above the atmosphere.

sqQr'fing   —a species of predatory exoskeletal omnivores reminiscent of Earthly army ants: migratory, traveling in columns numbering in the millions; made up of various physical types, each according to genetic assignment; warriors average four feet in length, half of which is jaw.

t'gyl'q   —Isi grass.

t'gyt'n   —smaller treelike hardwoods.

t'göllq´gn   —massive, mile-high trees of which the Isi forestlands primarily consist.

t'göe'tl   —a bluish, fuzz-covered, multistemmed, highly toxic plant which serves as the basis for the protective mimicry of the *nNby'q*.

t'jJ's   —a large, clumsy, multilegged Isi ruminant.

t'lLïSs´mn   —a telekinetically generated, immaterial cyclotron; originally employed by the Isi to concentrate and intensify the *mMj'q* particle flow emerging from a *wWn'dt*, subsequently discovered by Cory to be equally useful in the assembly and hurling of electron beams so concentrated as to be virtually coherent in phase.

väarz'fing   —an Isi arachnid, twenty feet long, whose appearance suggests the results of crossing an Earthly tarantula with a scorpion.

voor'skag   —a winged, evolutionary cousin of the *böll'skag*.

voor'flön   —a forty-legged, membrane-winged, pterydactyl-headed, flying Isi predator, growing to more than two hundred yards in length.

wWr'dts   —a dodecahedral protective enclosure of *mMj'q* by-products within which an adept works while summoning potentially treacherous extrauniversals for assistance in his practice of the *pwW'r*, or to protect his surroundings from potential side effects of their work; the first manifestation of the *pwW'r* to be discovered by the Isi.

wWn'dt   —precisely cut crystals of monolithic corundum: large, utterly flawless rubies through which *mMj'q* leaks into this universe.

wWyh'j   —a female Isi scientist, scholar, and teacher.

wWyhr läaq   —a male Isi scientist, scholar, and teacher.

CAST OF CHARACTERS

Peter Cory
—an Earthman; the penultimate development of a bloodline bred by the Isi for "affirmative" survival qualities.

Fafnir
—Gothyäl's *fmMl'hr*.

KjJnyrb'n
—a lesser Däa'mn.

Memphus
—Megonthalyä's *fmMl'hr*.

Megonthalyä
—a young *wWyh'j* of the Tenth Order; assigned to go to Earth and bring Peter Cory back to Isis.

T'fFelteshezr
—First among the Isi Council of Elders.

Rebecca Two-Knives
—Cory's security chief.

PROJECT *EXTREMIS* STAFF

G'lLhytl, Tenth Order; Sephiloyä, Fourth Order; H'tTirviq, Sixth Order; K'nNtïkï, Tenth Order; L'qQethonl, Fourth Order; Gothyäl, Tenth Order; T'dDalk, Seventh Order; Q'vVonykl, Fifth Order; Mrayäl, Fourth Order; H'tTosym, Fifth Order; Suvalyä, Eighth Order; K'dDempbato, Eighth Order; Metehiryä, Tenth Order; Kyärin, Seventh Order; Q'tTzekötl, Tenth Order; G'lLhaltn, Tenth Order.

ABOUT THE AUTHOR

DAVID R. PALMER was born in the Chicago area in 1941 and grew up there. He has worked at an amazing variety of jobs over the years (mail clerk, bookkeeper, junior accountant; VW mechanic, assistant service-manager, service manager, car salesman; appliance, furniture, and insurance salesman; school-bus driver; pet-store owner and manager; gravel-truck driver; intra- and intercity bus driver; typesetter, legal secretary, court-reporting transcriber—to mention only a few).

His pastimes have been equally varied, and have included (apart from *lots* of reading) flying, motorcycling, sailing, skindiving, photography—and racing (he was a Formula Vee champion in the sixties, in a car designed and built in collaboration with a friend).

Currently he is a certified shorthand court reporter (the term "stenographer" is held in very bad odor among practitioners of the profession) working in north central Florida with his wife, also a court reporter. Their family consists of (at latest count) four cats, two dogs, a parrot, and a horse.

Emergence was his first novel. Parts I and II appeared in the January, 1981, and February, 1983, issues of *Analog*, and were his first and second sales. *Threshold* is his second novel.

He is currently working on the sequel to *Threshold*, also to be published by Bantam.

BANTAM
SHOP·AT·HOME
C·A·T·A·L·O·G

Special Offer
Buy a Bantam Book
for only 50¢.

*Now you can have an up-to-date listing of Bantam's
hundreds of titles plus take advantage of our unique
and exciting bonus book offer. A special offer which
gives you the opportunity to purchase a Bantam
book for only 50¢. Here's how!*

*By ordering any five books at the regular price per
order, you can also choose any other single book
listed (up to a $4.95 value) for just 50¢. Some restric-
tions do apply, but for further details why not send
for Bantam's listing of titles today!*

*Just send us your name and address and we will
send you a catalog!*

FANTASY AND SCIENCE FICTION FAVORITES

Bantam Spectra brings you the recognized classics as well as the current favorites in fantasy and science fiction. Here you will find the most recent titles by the most respected authors in the genre.

R. A. MacAvoy

☐	23575-3	DAMIANO	$2.75
☐	24102-8	DAMIANO'S LUTE	$2.75
☐	24370-5	RAPHAEL	$2.75
☐	23205-3	TEA WITH THE BLACK DRAGON	$2.75
☐	25260-7	THE BOOK OF KELLS	$3.50

Robert Silverberg

☐	25097-3	LORD VALENTINE'S CASTLE	$3.95
☐	22928-1	MAJIPOOR CHRONICLES	$3.50
☐	24502-3	TO OPEN THE SKY	$2.75
☐	24494-9	VALENTINE PONTIFEX	$3.95

Harry Harrison

☐	22647-9	HOMEWORLD	$2.50
☐	20780-6	STARWORLD	$2.50
☐	20774-1	WHEELWORLD	$2.50
☐	22759-9	STAINLESS STEEL RAT FOR PRESIDENT	$2.75
☐	25395-6	STAINLESS STEEL RAT WANTS YOU!	$2.95

Prices and availability subject to change without notice.

Buy them at your local bookstore or use this handy coupon for ordering:

Bantam Books, Inc., Dept. SF2A, 414 East Golf Road, Des Plaines, Ill. 60016

Please send me the books I have checked above. I am enclosing $_____ (please add $1.25 to cover postage and handling. Send check or money order—no cash or C.O.D.'s please).

Mr/Ms _____

Address _____

City/State _____ Zip _____

SF2A—9/85

Please allow four to six weeks for delivery. This offer expires 3/86.

DON'T MISS ANY OF THE EXCITING NOVELS OF

MIKE McQUAY

☐ MY SCIENCE PROJECT (25376 • $2.95)

☐ JITTERBUG (24266 • $3.50)

☐ LIFEKEEPER (25075 • $2.95)

☐ PURE BLOOD (24668 • $2.95)

☐ ESCAPE FROM NEW YORK (25375 • $2.95)

Read all Mike McQuay's thrilling novels, available wherever Bantam Books are sold, or use this handy coupon for ordering:

READ THESE OTHER UNFORGETTABLE FANTASY NOVELS
BY AWARD-WINNING AUTHOR
R. A. MacAvoy

☐ **DAMIANO**   (23575 • $2.75)

☐ **DAMIANO'S LUTE**   (24102 • $2.75)

☐ **RAPHAEL**   (24370 • $2.75)

☐ **TEA WITH THE BLACK**   (23205 • $2.75)
   DRAGON